"Unger (*Nucleation*) makes hacking come alive in this ___. techno-thriller centered on the Swim, a virtual reality accessed by uploading a "persona," or a copy of the users mind, then downloading it again to retain the memories of the experience. Eliza McKay relies on her quick thinking and the computer system wired into her brain to make a living extracting people who've gotten stuck in the Swim. When the government hires McKay to extract agent Mike Miyamoto, it appears to be a normal job—except Mike's in the Swim on a criminal investigation, and what he's discovered has changed him so much that his persona refuses to reintegrate into the self he left behind. McKay must race the clock to extract him—but she's not the only one who wants what Mike knows, and her adversaries are willing to go to any lengths to stop McKay from reaching him first. VR programmer Unger mines her expertise to create all too believable scenarios and creative solutions, and the novel's at its best in the vivid, evocative descriptions of how hacking feels to a mind fully immersed in VR. The story dances between two worlds just as real as each other, pulling the reader along to an explosive conclusion. Cyberpunk fans won't want to miss this."
—*Publishers Weekly*

"Hooray for author Kimberly Unger's detailed vision of a cybernetic near-future in the technothriller, *The Extractionist*! We need more heroines like Eliza McKay, who are tough enough and smart enough to withstand the convergence of raw emotion and technology."
—Sande Chen, video game writer, *The Witcher*

"*The Extractionist* expertly harnesses the author's deep immersive knowledge of current and extrapolative technology to provide a comprehensive and realistic view of the future of the Internet, the Swim, and the future of nanotechnology. The novel is ably centered and grounded around a complex and well-drawn protagonist."
—Paul Weimer, SFF reviewer and critic

"Our heroine is a business consultant, but we live in her cyborg brain, we see every detail through her augmented eyes, and the future world she haunts is crammed with invention to the point of psychedelia. I quite enjoyed this."
—Bruce Sterling, author of *Schismatrix*

"Kimberly Unger reimagines cyberpunk from the ground up to deliver a smart, fully immersive thriller."
—Wil McCarthy, author of *Rich Man's Sky* and the Queendom of Sol series

"Kimberly Unger's *The Extractionist* is next-generation science fiction. It fuses cyberpunk attitude with diamond-hard science and alarming plausibility. Unger is one to watch."
—James L. Cambias, author of *The Godel Operation*

Praise for *Nucleation*

"VERDICT: Unger's (*The Gophers of High Charity*) video game credits are well matched to this space adventure. Dialog among rivals, teammates, and machine interfaces keeps the story moving quickly. Recommended for fans of technothrillers and those who appreciate a strong lead character navigating readers through the technical bits."
—*Library Journal*

"As a lifelong fan of science fiction, I've read it all. But it's always a surprise to be captivated by a new work and for her first novel, Unger's *Nucleation* delivers a rich world-building experience on top of a narrative that grabs at you and satisfies that urge for something fresh. I'm so looking forward to more from this author."
—Kate Edwards, Executive Director of The Global Game Jam

"Author Kimberly Unger has created an absolutely inspiring main character who demonstrates on how believing in one's conviction

and own intuition will always lead to truth. *Nucleation* is an immersive tale that has blockbuster scale and emotional story-telling you won't soon forget."
—Terry Matalas, showrunner, *Star Trek: Picard*

"A superb, smart debut! Love this woman who has to fight her way back to the top using her intelligence and expertise. The confident, sharp details made me feel I was there, in Helen's head, at each step of her remarkable journey. I can't wait to read more from Unger, a welcome new voice in science fiction."
—Lissa Price, author of the Starters series

"This smart, gripping debut weaves technology, embodiment, and corporate espionage into a tense vision of the future that readers won't be able to put down."
—Jacqueline Koyanagi, author of *Ascension*

"In technology we so often look to science fiction for inspiration. Kimberly Unger is the rare author with a foot in both worlds and it shows as she gives a thrilling glimpse into the future with *Nucleation*."
—Andrew Bosworth, Vice President of Augmented and Virtual Reality, Facebook

"*Nucleation* delivers top-notch suspense, deftly weaving together industrial espionage and first contact in a futuristic world that is all too plausible. Unger brings to her world a special sensibility for human psychology that gives realism to futuristic nanotech and corporate politics alike."
—Juliette Wade, author of *Mazes of Power*

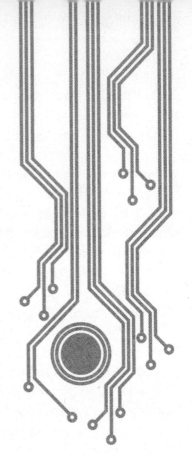

THE EXTRACTIONIST

KIMBERLY UNGER

TACHYON
SAN FRANCISCO

Interior and cover design by Elizabeth Story

Tachyon Publications LLC
1459 18th Street #139
San Francisco, CA 94107
415.285.5615
www.tachyonpublications.com
tachyon@tachyonpublications.com

Series Editor: Jacob Weisman
Editor: Jaymee Goh

Print ISBN: 978-1-61696-376-7
Digital ISBN: 978-1-61696-377-4

Printed in the United States by Versa Press, Inc.

First Edition: 2022
10 9 8 7 6 5 4 3 2 1

for Marc
00110100

ONE

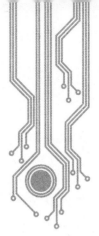

"Eliza McKay, I take it?"

Oh, perfect timing. . . .

Eliza Nurey Wynona McKay could have sworn that the red warning triangle on the side of the cup wasn't flashing a minute ago, but you never could tell with cheap paper circuits—they failed just as often as they worked.

McKay was in Singapore to meet with a potential client. A reference from an old friend, a message through a cheap "secure" service, and a meeting location delivered via self-destruct messenger—all suggested inexperience and overkill. In McKay's line of work, discretion was standard. Nobody ever wanted to admit a boss or a family member had gotten themselves trapped in a virtual world. Still, the reference had come from a colleague she respected, and it had been years since she'd spent some quality time in Lion City. So she'd made the trip.

Finally. McKay took a too-eager sip of coffee—and promptly drenched the table as she tried to spit the scalding mouthful back through the lid. She shoved her chair back just in time to avoid getting the coffee all over her lap.

The surge in movement kicked the Overlay into gear, clouding McKay's vision with data on everything—the temperature of the air, the coffee, the chair she was about to trip over, the distance from and mass of the table, as well as information on the coffee shop's history, advertisements, local alerts and police systems. The coup de grâce was a pop-up that obscured her last sliver of normal vision to inform her of the client's arrival. *So much for looking cool and collected.* McKay spun the computer in her head back down into sleep, restoring her normal line of sight. The Overlay, an emotive AI that ran the computer systems wired into her skull, was at her disposal on a moment's notice.

They sometimes disagreed on just what those moments should be.

It took McKay a moment to register the woman standing across the dripping bistro table with a helpful handful of napkins. The woman was probably taller than McKay even without the heels—a catastrophically red twist of hair and a teal blue overcoat meant she stood out in a crowd. Not what you'd expect from someone trying to stay under the radar. *But that might be the point.*

The Overlay slid one last reminder into McKay's field of view, telling her that the meeting was about to start.

"Erm . . . yes," McKay answered awkwardly. She took half the offered salvation and between the two of them the table was mopped and righted in a moment. "Sorry," she continued, "the coffee had a real kick."

One of the ever-present voomer robots bumped insistently against her shoe until she dropped the sodden napkins into its wide-open maw. The blue enamel paint on its leading edge was scarred from the overeager pursuit of dropped trash, and probably from the boots of a few local kids as well. McKay suppressed a flash of irritation at the idea of its casual mistreatment as it scooted away, burbling delightedly to itself in the satisfied tones coded into service robots everywhere.

"It must be a Monday," the woman opposite McKay said conversationally, and then took a seat without being asked. "I nearly took a caffeine shower on the MRT on my way here."

The smile she offered was more along the lines of *I know how you feel* than *my, what an idiot*, which suggested McKay had kept a touch of professionalism intact.

The Overlay did its job and told McKay the client wasn't carrying one of the encoded MRT passes on her person, suggesting she was lying. You could still buy a plastic pass at the train station. The Overlay might not see it, but her personal AI tended to deal in absolutes. It was McKay's job to interpret the results. *Lying to conceal how she got here? Making conversation? Setting up a backstory?*

The other woman displayed none of the nervousness that usually came with an inexperienced client. It suggested the roundabout connection hadn't been overkill at all. She was a professional of some sort—guns, information, or the silver needle of political intrigue—McKay wasn't sure just yet. She was reluctant to risk the distraction of a background check *during* a client meeting, despite the Overlay's eagerness to get on the job.

McKay asked the Overlay to stay in the background so she could focus on her assessment. Already this woman was throwing up contradictions that suggested this wasn't a run-of-the-mill assignment. No freckles. Eyes entirely human, and green to boot.

"Can I get you something, Miss . . ?" McKay paused for the other woman to fill in the name, but the woman's attention was elsewhere, rummaging around in a handbag that McKay hadn't noticed a few seconds ago. It was a risk of keeping the AI in the background, the human mind could get distracted, miss things. The Overlay could have provided the information in the space between eyeblinks, but the connection, the human connection, was critical. McKay sometimes had to remind herself of that.

"Unfortunately, Ms. McKay, I am already short on time this morning. I'm part of a group that specializes in the abuse of new technologies. . . ." She casually touched a spot on her neck as she rummaged, just below and behind the ear. *Tympanic speaker.* Her casual competence, the matter-of-factness, affected a good ten-foot radius around her.

"I need an extraction done, here in the city. . . ." Her eyes narrowed a fraction as something McKay couldn't hear got her attention. "Excuse me, I think we're going to have to reschedule."

McKay had just parted her lips to reply when she felt the all-over kiss of something very powerful charging up through the miteline that connected all the computers in her body. She recognized the feeling and had to stamp out the panic that threatened to follow. The woman's green eyes met hers, and everything about her expression told McKay to avoid what was coming next.

As if it had been rehearsed, they both got up from the table smoothly and headed in opposite directions. They each walked quickly, but not too quickly. McKay was already locking everything down in her head, making sure the Overlay was off, and not just spun down but OFF off. In a city like Singapore, it wasn't guns and bombs you had to worry about. Any attack would be digital, virtual, it would come from a place where Eliza McKay was uniquely exposed. An EM pulse could wreck every component in her head and nobody else in the room would be affected. She briefly weighed the risk of jail time for jaywalking against the cost of repairing her own internal computers, but the light was in her favor.

McKay hit the far side of the crosswalk just as the EMP went off in the coffee shop. No sound, no explosion, just the unearthly silence of electrical death.

TWO

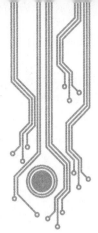

IT WAS INEVITABLE that the client would pop up again. There had been a *meeting* scheduled, after all, and she hadn't come across as easy to rattle. There were only a half dozen people in the world who could perform an *extraction*, who could pull a person's mind out of the virtual space of the Swim, even if they didn't want to go quietly. It meant this potential client's options were limited. If she'd gotten all the way down the list of experts to *Eliza's* name, it meant she was serious.

McKay's first action, once safely away, was to ask the Overlay to pull all the woman's salient details, and the AI had come up empty. *Contradictions.* No presence meant she was likely covered by one of the Big Three intelligence agencies. *Anything involving those guys means you're back under the microscope again.* Having US Info-Comm breathing down your neck was no fun, and they were the "good guys" of the lot. If they were involved, you could bet that Euro InTech and the Ministry were keeping tabs as well. It had taken her years of staying under the radar to even be able to leave the US without a check-in or a phone call. McKay wasn't interested in re-visiting that state of affairs if she could help it. Back when she still had all her programming licenses intact, she'd been able to afford the lawyers to save herself. That effort had burned through almost every asset she had saved up. Extractions didn't pay well enough for her to survive a second round of deep investigation.

Spread-eagled on the hotel bed, Overlay open wide to the Swim, soaking up the aircon and catching up with her billing, McKay felt the woman enter the lobby nearly thirty-five stories below.

Found me already? She reached out with just a corner of her mind to tap into and fiddle with the hotel's guest registry. She shifted the dates here and there to make it seem as if the woman had just missed her. She knew McKay was in town, and there was only one flight a day to San Francisco. It would be foolish simply to wipe herself from the registry entirely. She'd had a number of interesting clients in the past, a few missed connections, but it was rare that anyone pursued her outside normal channels. *Big Three,* she reminded herself. *A simple extraction isn't worth tangling with the Big Three again.* That allure was still there, though . . . working on something important, something game-changing. *They just never tell you that changing the game too much is as bad as not changing it at all. Critical success as failure point.*

But that reminder lost some of its power every time she said it. Her natural curiosity, her desire to find a way to *fix* things, to perfect the system, kept bubbling to the fore.

She closed her eyes and slipped a little further into the Swim of digital space. There were limits to what the computers built into her head could do, but she was going for subtlety. This was information gathering, not online warfare. *Yet.*

The Client stopped at the front desk, and McKay felt the computer systems giving way. Access probed, guided, caressed, and set free again by someone else's invisible hand. *Oh, interesting.* The numbers and connections paraded across her vision made the Client seem surrounded by a hard-edged halo of information. You could tell a lot about any given person by the nature and composition of that halo. In the Client's case, the halo wasn't hers; she was borrowing it from someone else. People moved through the world adding to and altering the flow of data, like fish in a river, sometimes moving with the current, sometimes against, but every languid flip of the tail or swipe of a credit card made changes. Someone like McKay, intimate with the flows and currents of information invisibly pervading every square inch of atmosphere, couldn't help but see that halo streak in from elsewhere, wrap her in a protective cocoon, and return to its source. *So who are you supposed to be today?*

She took a closer look at the client's borrowed digital plumage. Normally her business depended on discretion. Normally she limited the scope of her checks on potential clients. *Normally* she didn't need to know every detail of the whos, whens, and wherefores of the people involved to do the job. Normally, however, clients stuck more or less to the basic procedures that went with any contractual transaction. *But if we're dealing with something bigger than a teenage tech magnate stuck in a virtual porn site, maybe it's worth the extra effort.*

Extractions were often an awkward business. Seven out of ten times the person whose mind got stuck in the Swim was doing something that, while not necessarily illegal, was often socially embarrassing—either for the person directly involved or at least for the people around them. Even people who understood that an extraction was "optional" were still willing to pay up front for the process, just in case something important had been discovered that they wanted to remember. Since she'd set up shop, she had walked away from only two jobs. One paid far too well, and the family involved was in love with media attention. That type of scrutiny would simply bring her back up onto everybody's radar and there were still people in the Big Three who thought a bullet to the head was the best way to keep her retired.

The second had been because the client had been suckered into some place McKay really, truly, could not bear to tread. There were spaces in the Swim where the AIs swarmed, the information flowed so fast a human mind could only get a sense of gestalt, an overall concept. Trying to dig any deeper risked a mental break. In both cases she'd bowed out and referred the client to Ace. Ace didn't mind the limelight, the vidbit interviews, and he certainly never minded the fuzzy, crawly feeling left on his neurons after a trip into the AI spawning grounds.

McKay returned her attention to the woman in the elevator. *Freelance, stalker, or spy? Eenie, meenie, miney. . . .* The information halo fluttered and shifted, the data moving from something typical of a hausfrau on vacation to knife-edged business acumen. Thirty-five stories away, McKay whistled in appreciation. If she hadn't been watching in real-time she would never have seen the changes. She spun out a 'bot, a nearly mindless bit of code designed to execute a single simple instruction set, and sent it running down the ribbon to find the hacker.

Layers upon layers, like she's been changing identities for years. She's an agency player of some sort. The question is, is this trouble coming my way or a legitimate hire? Any misgivings she might have had about the extra scrutiny were rapidly crumbling under the weight of her own curiosity. She lay on the bed and inhaled the data, let it run through her mind as she looked for larger patterns, places the connections didn't yet match up, though she was sure the hacker controlling the flow would fill in that information soon enough. She was careful only to observe, not touch, the current of information. Whoever was keeping the Client camouflaged in the Swim would be on her like a rat on a French fry if McKay moved too hastily.

One by one she pegged three other people in the building with a link to the woman. Old habits died hard and keeping track of people by the eddies they left behind in the Swim was nearly second nature. McKay felt the bubble of momentary panic, the desire to retreat and pull the hole in after her, that had followed her for the past few years. *Not this time.*

McKay pushed past it, tucked it away in a corner of her mind. Two other people were hoofing it up the thirty-five flights of stairs that separated them; a third was in the lobby coffee shop picking up what looked like breakfast for the entire group. None were armed, one was wired up with a lot of miteline, but from here she couldn't get a bead on what kind.

They're the ones buying out all the palmiers, I bet. Bastards. The coffee shop had run out two mornings in a row, and they were her favorite.

When the Client entered the lift Eliza decided to head her off. It was some combination of ennui with the rest of her schedule and the curiosity the Client sparked by moving outside the box that prompted her. One by one she isolated the other three players, splitting their connections to the Client's halo and assigning them elsewhere, sending eddies and interruptions down the line. The fourth, the professional hacker, was probably offsite someplace. McKay's 'bot sent back an occasional ping to let her know it was still tracking, but it was halfway around the world already, and McKay doubted it would catch up with the mystery coder anytime soon.

Thirty-one. Thirty-two. She locked up the elevator and left the client stranded between floors. Whoever this lot of self-appointed suits were, they were running unencrypted, uncovered. It walked the line between sloppy and deliberate. The woman was protected in the Swim, but the rest of the team appeared just as they seemed to be. *Too loosey-goosey to be hard-core governmental, too clever to be corporate.*

"Excuse me." McKay suppressed a twinge of nervousness and spoke aloud to the empty hotel room. The Overlay in her head transmitted her voice into the Swim and carried it out over the speakers in the lift. The client startled—she could see her on the elevator's security camera—then paused as if listening to someone else. McKay felt the pulse of information reach out to her from her hacker, but this time something different danced on the edges of it. *New encryption, maybe?*

Better safe than sorry. She snapped that flow of information off and isolated the other woman completely.

"McKay?" the client asked aloud.

From a dozen floors away, McKay answered, "You're getting a little stalker-ish there. Mind telling me just what you want me for?" The data stream she'd interrupted leaked back, this time with a fresh dusting of encryption. She watched, fascinated, as it reintegrated into the woman's halo, trickling the encryption in bit by bit, layer by layer. *Clever.*

"I want to apologize for the EM pulse earlier. My sources suggest it's not directly related, but they've been wrong before. You come highly recommended. I'd like to continue our conversation."

McKay snorted. "You ought to speak with Ace Meander. He's in the book." Another data packet swept into her like a swallow on the wing, but McKay caught it and sent it spinning back downstream.

Persistent. Another and another tried to slip past. *Clearly, someone's upset she's been cut off.*

"I'm interested only in the best, Ms. McKay."

"Ace's advertisements offer a money-back guarantee in case of total personality death." That was a crap argument and she knew it. She was trying to bait her, see where the force of her opinions lay.

"I'd also like to point out that Mr. Meander advertises on the all-night shopping feed."

McKay caught the counter-stream of data the Client had quietly sent out, trying to make contact with her team, and closed it down. The swallow-like packets were coming more frequently, and she briefly lost herself in the duck and dart of intercepting them all. She was careful never to touch the packets of code directly, just manipulated the data around them to send them off in the wrong direction.

"Are you going to let me up, Ms. McKay?" The question's simplicity rattled her balance. She had, just for a moment, forgotten the other woman was waiting patiently in the elevator. A mind divided to the degree McKay's was—keeping the packets from reaching the Client, keeping the other teammates trapped in the stairwells, keeping the hotel from figuring out that the elevator had stopped—a mind in that state was easy to trip up. She had to choose what to let go of first. The lift won, coupled with a flash of conscience at keeping her trapped.

"Room 3516." Like reeling in a hundred clicking fishing lines,

McKay pulled herself painstakingly back out of the Swim and got up to put on some appropriate clothes. Some days it was easier to pull herself back to the real world than others. A fresh flash of panic, left over from her time working with USIC, was quickly stamped out. Ignoring it had become a rote reaction, a knee jerk. The Client was here to hire her honestly, and that meant an opportunity to reconnect that she didn't want to waste.

When the Client came through the door, she failed to knock. The Overlay picked up on the lack of protest from building security and gave McKay a quick heads-up that the halo had preceded her. The programmer on the other end moved one step ahead to open the way, then sealed it as she passed through. *Practiced, as if her team had kicked in doors before.* Whether that was simply a lapse in manners or a way to establish her authority, McKay couldn't tell. It was rude either way. The Overlay tickled her mind, reminding her there was still a 'bot out there looking for the other hacker. She acknowledged and spun the computers in her head down into sleep mode. It gave her room to focus on the woman she'd met just a couple of hours earlier.

They sized each other up again, this time with a little more bite.

There were subtle changes in the Client's appearance. A different jacket, the hair less red, more brown, suggesting some brand of miteware was tweaking the color. All subtle alterations that took a second to normalize, even after their face-to-face meeting hours before.

"Take a seat and tell me what you have in mind." McKay gestured to the room's only chair. She considered doing away with the pleasantries for the moment. *Courtesy costs you nothing,* she reminded herself. "And while you're at it, a name would be helpful as well."

The Client folded her arms across her chest and lifted an eyebrow. "Is my name really that important?"

McKay plunked herself down on the edge of the bed and sat on her hands to keep from fidgeting. "I have to know where to send the bill," she said mildly.

She saw the other woman's cheek jump, suppressing a smile.

McKay turned her back to the door. Like all hotels everywhere it had a single-entry door bracketed by the lavatory and the closet, both of which she checked visually before shooting the deadbolt on the door. It was a strangely physical action, after the tricks pulled on her behalf by her pet programmer. McKay realized abruptly that she was, in essence, deliberately cutting herself off. *It's a gesture.* As the bolt slid home, the room's *Do Not Disturb* protocols kicked in and her halo abruptly vanished, like a thread of smoke snipped off by a closing window. The change in Swim presence caused McKay's Overlay to jump and quiver, but it obeyed the silent command and stayed spun down.

"One sec." The Client pulled something from her jacket pocket and clipped it to her lapel, caressing it with a thumb before crossing the open space to the chair and sitting, all in one elegant, tightly controlled motion. Her attention flicked around the room analytically.

McKay knew she was being sized up when she saw it. *Small, single bed, standard business boring with the exception of the wall-length window looking out over the harbor.* It wasn't the first time she'd been judged by the spaces she could afford to inhabit.

"Nice view."

"On a clear day you can see Sentosa Island, Miss. . . ." McKay tried again. Now that they were face-to-face, it would be a simple enough matter to pull her fingerprints or some other solid characteristic and set one of the 'bots on the problem. But if they couldn't even get past her giving up a name, she wasn't about to take the job, curiosity or no.

"Brighton. Ina Brighton." She crossed her legs at the ankles and leaned back in the chair like somebody prepared to spend the day answering questions. McKay had a feeling it wasn't just an act, either.

"Relationship to the extractee?"

She cocked an eyebrow at that. "Extractee?"

McKay groaned inwardly. *Talking to spooks is like pulling teeth.*

Her quick smile apologized. "Sorry. It sounded like you were

talking about aliens for a moment there. It's been a very trying day."
The tension was broken by the utter silliness of the sentence.

"I can imagine. It's not every day someone wipes the spin out of an entire block of Chinatown."

"Less than a block, actually. It was a pretty small pulse." Brighton fished in her pocket again and pulled out a small leather case. "What I have here is standard NDA stuff with extra teeth. Plug your digital sig in, and I can tell you everything you need to know. You're on Mike's list."

List? I'm not on any of the good lists, just the blacklists. Out of everything so far, that one sentence bothered McKay the most. She had thought she'd finally managed to slip below the radar. The Overlay picked up on McKay's twinge of panic and started chasing the information down.

A snap of Brighton's thumb opened the case and she pulled out a plastic encased spin-wafer. McKay accepted it and shifted so she could reach the bedside table. She'd brought a scrubber with her, an air-gapped virus detector that could check the chip before she plugged it in to the computer in her head. She set the wafer on top and watched the LCD readout change as it digested the data. The whole process lasted less than a second.

"So does it pass?" The woman had leaned forward to watch.

"Hmph. Virus-free. The terms. . . ." McKay slipped the chip into the drive behind her left ear and closed her eyes. The Overlay flickered, scanned the contents, stamped her sig, and spat the wafer back out. She opened her eyes and handed it back. "The NDA is good. Can we get on with the details?"

Brighton folded the wafer back into the case. "Absolutely."

"Good." She leaned back on her hands and the bedsprings creaked slightly. "Why don't you start by explaining the situation to me?"

Brighton flipped the wafer case between her fingers for a moment, as if deciding where to begin.

"The beginning, please," McKay prompted.

She looked up, eyes narrowed.

"The beginning, such as we know it," she agreed. "Mike was plugged in nearly two weeks ago."

"Two weeks?" McKay's turn to be surprised. "You've already tried to extract him?" Two weeks was a very long time to leave a body plugged in. It meant proper medical support. On top of that fact, she would have to work with the mess someone else left during the initial attempts to extract the guy.

The case was getting more interesting by the minute.

"Rose, one of our programmers, has tried twice so far, but it shouldn't have been such a problem." Brighton chewed a thumbnail absently. "This should have been a cakewalk. Doing what we do, everyone's needed an extraction or two. It's par for the course."

McKay couldn't help noticing all of her nails were chewed down to the nub. More telling perhaps was the fact that she didn't make any attempt to conceal it.

"So what exactly do you do, and how many of you are involved?" *Porn? Some kind of government honeypot?* Had to be one or the other. Porn had the highest likelihood for persona revelation: pretty girl, multiple people involved.

"It's not porn. Grow up."

She hadn't said anything out loud. Brighton's expression changed her mind instantly. She'd heard that one before. Probably too often.

"It's investigative. I mentioned before that I'm part of a team of five specialists handling abuses of new technologies. Mike, our project lead, went undercover in the Swim to make contact with an informant named Miranda Bosch. After that meeting, we couldn't pull him back out. Whatever he learned, it was important enough that he wouldn't let us dump the information to wake him up. He insisted we bring in an outside specialist, which means you."

"Why does Rose think the extraction failed?"

"Rose thinks it's a technical glitch. Part of our undercover process is to build out the persona with specific skills and memories to match the cover we're using. She's of the opinion that something in all that extra code gummed up the works."

"You've talked to Bosch already? The informant?"

"No, we don't want to compromise her. If she's a viable line to our suspect, we want to keep her in place. A read-through of her Swim-logs says she also got stuck in the Swim after the same session and needed an extraction, just like Mike, but she elected to dump the experience and get out."

Figures. An average person got into the Swim through a persona, a programmatic copy of the mind that could think the same, act the same, experience the same. At the end of the session, all the new memories copied back and the person woke up with all those new experiences in place, as if they had experienced them literally. Something game-changing, life-changing, a shift in perspective, meant a persona couldn't be copied back, the changes were just too broad. So whatever it was, they had both experienced it, but it was important to Mike, less so to Bosch.

"Because she dumped out, she won't remember whatever went on between her and Mike." This was getting more complicated, *more interesting*, with every new detail Brighton let out. Lots of people tweaked their personas, their copy in the Swim, to fit with a role or add on skills, but that was usually built into the process, like wearing a uniform for work.

"Mike customized pretty heavily this time, lots of nonstandard traits added on." Brighton repeated the unspoken thought, like she was trying to convince herself of the point.

"So why don't you trust your own expert?" That was the big question. Why were they bringing in an outside programmer when they had a perfectly good one at home? Dealing with a pissy coder, someone insulted by management bringing in a contractor, meant hostility she was going to have to wrangle. In the worst case it meant someone actively trying to sabotage her to make a point. *Hell, if our positions were reversed,* I'd *be pissed.*

Brighton had to think about that one. *Or maybe she already knows the answer. Can't usually tell with Agents.*

"I don't think we can take the chance that she's wrong. This is a big investigation, one we can't afford to screw up. Look, Mike's a pro. The fact that he refused to give up that information to come back out means it's *got* to be something big. Case-blown-open big."

"The persona process doesn't work like that," McKay countered. "A persona is a copy of a person's unique qualities; all the *facts* can *always* be written out. What stops someone coming back out is a *revelation*, some piece of information or an experience that is game-changing for that person. Your guy didn't learn a new fact. Something in there changed his entire worldview."

That was the moment her 'bot chose to come screaming back like someone had lit its little byte-size tail with a blowtorch. Whomever it had found while following Brighton's trail had not been friendly. The Overlay sprang to life and began analyzing the data. The little bit of programming downloaded its findings frantically as it slowly came unraveled by whatever forces it had encountered out in the Swim.

McKay snapped her eyes closed and held up a remarkably re-strained finger, given the noise that the terrified 'bot was generating in her head. "Excuse me for just a moment." She turned her head away just a little too slowly, opened her eyes again just a little too soon.

For the first time, Brighton showed a touch of shock herself.

In full spin, in a dimly lit room, the effect of McKay's Overlay was startling. The sheer volumes of data swimming behind her eyes gave them a singular, unearthly glow. She excused herself and walked to the other side of the room, her back to Brighton, staring out the long glass window. In the reflection, Brighton sat back and steepled her fingertips, staring at her with concern. It was a trick of the way McKay's computers displayed information in the Overlay, some combination of direct stimulation of the cortex combined with projection mapping into the vitreous humor of the eye itself. She used to think it was a cool side effect, but other people's reactions had long since changed her mind.

At the moment, Brighton's staring bothered McKay less than the attempt to crash the Overlay. Someone had traced her 'bot back and had sent a handful of much larger, more aggressive programs after it. Brute-force hacks, all the sort of thing a script-kiddie could download off any mass consumer site, which made them harder to pin to just one person. They were guided with subtlety, and McKay recognized the handiwork of Brighton's little group in the sharp, swallow-shaped packets that delivered them. They were smarter this time. It took more of her attention to intercept and bat them down.

Once Brighton had engaged the room's privacy protocols, once she'd been cut off from outside communications, the room had vanished from the Swim in a whirlpool of data generated by the hotel's own security systems. Apparently, her hacker didn't like that idea and used the gap in the security McKay's 'bot provided to launch an assault on the only likely target.

Crap.

This was going to be one long fight from start to finish if they didn't reach an understanding in the next few seconds. *Best to turn the job down, kick this lady out of the room, and hop onto the next plane stateside.* She closed her eyes very briefly and spun off another few 'bots to handle the incoming assaults while she turned the rest of her attention back to the task at hand.

"Excuse me, but would you mind calling off your coder long enough for us to finish this conversation?" McKay turned back to find Brighton smiling. She knew exactly what was going on. *Oh, dirty pool is it?* She felt a flicker of irritation and followed it with her standard rejection.

"I'm afraid I may not be able to help you, Miss Brighton. Your best bet is to unplug the guy. You'll lose whatever experiences he had in the Swim, but it's the safest way to go." McKay shut her Overlay down abruptly, severed all linkages to all systems and closed everything out, spun every working processor in her head down into nothingness.

In the space of a breath, she was just your average hacker.

To an observer in the Swim she would have winked out of digital existence, like a fish plucked from the water by an eagle. More than a few processes had been interrupted, links left dangling, and raw data would rush to flood the hole where her presence had been. Messy. She'd have to spend an hour setting everything back up the way she liked it, but mucking with authority figures made for bad business, and whoever Brighton's hacker was, they had Authority written all over their code. *Too many games to be worth it. Not without a damn fine reason.*

"I don't test well," she said simply, "and I'm not interested in the kind of trouble that gets other agencies showing up on my doorstep."

Brighton's eyes narrowed, scanning her face, and McKay hit the switch on the side table that shut down the room's privacy barrier.

Brighton winced visibly as the several dozen contact attempts hit her comms all at once. She never took her eyes off McKay's as she tapped the spot on her neck to reply.

"Rose, lay off. Yes. That's an order. No. Tell Rice, too. Yes, I said tell Rice to stand down." She got to her feet. "Look, McKay." She paced the space between the room's only door and the chair. "We have Mike's persona trapped here, in Singapore, intact. We are willing to pay double your going rate, but we need to execute this within the next ten hours. There are no other agencies involved here, this is off the books. No muss, no fuss, in and out again."

Despite the voice in her head saying *No, no, no, no,* McKay couldn't help asking. "Why the time limit?" The client had reengaged that inner curiosity, the one she was trying to ignore. *The one that got you blacklisted and up on charges last time.*

Pulling a person out of the Swim, trying to preserve the experience exactly, that was as much art as code. It was different every time, it was an *experience* every time. The extra issues just made it all that much more enticing. She hadn't realized how much she'd missed it.

Brighton waited a long second, a debate clearly going on behind her eyes. "In ten hours the government of Singapore kicks us out, and Mike's persona gets away again." She blew out a long breath. "It took us weeks to track him down, and we need to get him out before he loses whatever he found in there."

"Kicks you out?"

"We're just the ANT office, Ms. McKay, our jurisdiction here is . . . limited."

Ah, finally, the truth. A group of spooks that would owe her a favor, operating outside their own purview, just might be worth getting into trouble for. *It's just an extraction, easy in, easy out, no higher-order agencies involved, well within the work you're allowed to do, right?*

McKay found herself answering even before she'd talked herself into it.

"All right. Where do we go next?"

THREE

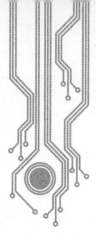

MᶜKᴀʏ sᴛᴀʀᴇᴅ ᴜᴘ at the fifteen stories of concrete and triggered the Overlay, painting her view of the world in light. This was the address Brighton had given, where her Vector7 team was holed up with their rogue persona. It had taken nearly six hours to write the custom code she needed for the extraction, even with Brighton's well-organized information. The other hacker's fingerprints had been all over that too. The notes suggested a mindset used to powering through their problems by brute force. She'd taken that into account when writing her own solutions. If power hadn't worked for the last hacker, then McKay's more subtle approach might be a better fit.

She now had less than four hours to get the persona back out. Plenty of time, as long as there were no new wrinkles.

Singapore's fabled Orchard Road had retained its capitalist supremacy for well over two hundred years and was not about to let go. Story upon story of glittering commercial retail expanded in fits and starts with the politics of the time, re-evolving into a series of shopping towns.

Solid on the outside, solid in the Swim, she mused and opened the connections wider. *Not a bad choice for a hideout.* The Brittle Moon building, converted and reconverted over time, began life as a hotel but had long since become one of those inverted storefront malls with all the former offices ripped open and fronted with glass.

The two-star hotel had been transformed into a rabbit warren of shops linked up, down, and sideways to the neighbors, the heavy duty city data-lines and even a good ten or fifteen privately owned links going out into the Swim. McKay prodded the Overlay, and it gave her the names. *Looks like Puredat and Bellicode are the main service providers.* Either of those could be a back door to the Swim, going in or going out. Brighton had assured her the operation was a secret, but someone trying to hack her through the Swim was something she always had to keep in mind. She couldn't rely on anyone else to double-check those routes; a hack would only inconvenience most people, but for McKay herself, and for Mike's persona, it could be fatal.

All the information flowing into and out of the building resolved into a three-dimensional pattern in her mind's eye—the imaginary concrete bunker space in her head she used for thinking. Nicely gridded, the older wires came with the building, snaking between the walls with as much precision as could be expected from a construction crew. The newer wires were more opportunistic, rather like a wayward fungus, intersecting, patching in, piggybacking and integrating wherever they could find a space. Here and there in the technology framework were knots, big tangles of digital security as dense as anything she'd seen before. She'd lay odds one of those knots was her destination, if there'd been anyone to take the bet.

"It's really that mess of connections that's the problem," a sprite's voice chimed sweetly in her head. In the corner of her field of view, Spike's icon flashed the customary three times before resolving into a relatively realistic human form, if death-punk hair and body piercings were still realistic. McKay grinned despite herself. Spike was a freeroaming AI who specialized in knowing things, rather like a freelance search engine. The term "sprite" was a misnomer, left over from when McKay and her older brother had programmed it a long time ago. They'd set it free in the Swim to see how it evolved over time and McKay was almost always delighted when it made an appearance.

The sprite turned its steely gaze on the building. "The security holes would be smaller if there weren't all the legacy wires there . . . there . . . there"—each *there* punctuated with a jab of a lean, steel-tipped forefinger at the Overlay, the various nodes flashing as it poked at them.

Legacy systems, old code hidden under newer code, were practically the bread and butter of her profession, knowing where those access points were would give McKay an advantage. She made a note of the nodes Spike pointed out. The sprite had a talent for information and data structure, and McKay didn't want to waste the time triple-guessing. She wanted to make sure that she was able to respond in kind if any attacks came in through the Swim.

"Well, this ought to be fun." Spike rubbed its hands greedily. "So who's the client this time? Teenage football hero trapped in the Tres Girls live feed?"

McKay rolled her eyes. "No, we've got something with teeth this time, a government agency called Vector7."

"Oh, yeah?" Spike looked as serious as possible. "And you were stupid enough to say yes?"

"One-day job, it's an extraction, so I'm well outside the restrictions that USIC slapped me with." McKay justified herself defensively. "I'm on Singapore soil, and *those* guys would rather hire me than shoot me. How could I say no? Besides, having at least one agency department who owes me a favor can't possibly be a bad thing." McKay lowered her voice as a passerby gave her an odd look. *Inside voice,* she reminded herself. Spike showed up in the real world to McKay through the Overlay, but it had no actual physical presence anywhere. McKay spun down the Overlay, and Spike winked out of existence before the sprite had a chance to answer.

Extractions were supposed to be handled onsite, where the victim's body was hooked up to the flavor-of-the-day virtual experience. Most people's virtual experiences were short-lived. They lacked the refinement and detail to cause the sort of revelation that might require an extraction. The equipment to get the kind of in-depth, full emotional experience that could trap you in the Swim was still on the expensive side, but like all technology, the price was rapidly dropping. Costs for parts came down, and the expensive and complex miteline that had been McKay's previous field of expertise had found its way into the consumer space. Ironic that if she'd just kept her head down and stayed a grad student for a few more years, she'd be an industry player instead of a bleeding-edge, exiled niche earner.

When McKay's license to program 'mites got pulled, she had started working IT for those same virtual parlors, improving the software, improving the emotional experience. USIC could chuck her back in jail, or worse, if she was caught programming miteline directly again, but her unique set of programming skills was still in demand. Soon she was getting a couple of calls a month, though most of them had her swimming through the sweaty bowels of some virtual, exotic dance hall. Parents and well-heeled spouses were usually happy to pay her a consulting fee to drag a daughter or a husband out of some pre-pubescent fantasy, even if it wasn't strictly necessary. The real jobs came along only once in a long while, yanking mathematicians out of carefully constructed simulations, CEOs out of economic constructs, people in places who really, truly, needed to have that change in consciousness written back out of the Swim into their own, living minds.

She bounced up the Brittle Moon's stairs two at a time. At least she could pick up a decent lunch at the hawkers' stalls in the basement if there was time afterward. She glanced at her watch. Still fifteen minutes until the meeting, but she hated to get anywhere on time. It made her feel rushed.

The retailers left in the building grouped together defensively, focusing their attention and their wares on the first few floors. McKay may as well have had TOURIST stenciled across her forehead. The quiescent Overlay barely twitched at the advertising content bombarding her. One of the very nice things about Singapore was the limit on adverts, one per customer in public spaces. Unfortunately, the farther from the beaten track you got, the more people tended to bend the rules, even in a state as well regulated as this. The Singaporean government didn't want to scare commerce off, but the farther from Orchard Road proper you got, the more ... insistent ... the entrepreneurs got. She kept a hand on her bag, shook her head *No* at yet another designer bag seller and nearly skipped the last two steps into the crowded elevator.

By the time she emerged on the eighth floor, the elevator was empty except for a Chinese man carrying a cooler that, judging from the heavenly smell emanating from it, came from the food stalls downstairs. A quick glance at the watch told her she was still running about five minutes early, which was just about right in her book. The guy with the food got off on the same floor. *Dammit.* Her stomach muttered something impatient. *Gotta learn to schedule appointments for after lunch.* The delivery guy vanished down one of the other office corridors. *Pity.* McKay refocused on the task at hand and found the door she was looking for.

Okay, go-time. She spun the Overlay back into life, and it showed her the large, ungainly snarl ahead of her in virtual space. The room she wanted was right in the middle of one of the thick, thorny places Spike had pointed out. *Tough, yes, but not inviolate.* She eased a connection out into the building's main trunk line and dropped a packet of information into the Swim. It contained a program that would spin up and call in a favor from Ace Meander if McKay didn't stop it before a ten-hour deadline. *Paranoid much?*

Spike's icon flashed twice and vanished from the Overlay, a part of that packet to Ace now, just in case McKay needed help from the outside. She knocked.

The door cracked open. "Yeah, you got a password?" The man inside was taller than she, but no more than an inch or so, just enough to ruin the eye-to-eye stare. McKay sent the Overlay a silent request to record and identify and got a single acknowledging blip.

Password? That caught her flat-footed for a second, but only a second. She'd forgot the kind of games that bored agents play. "There's no password. What are you on about?"

The door opened wider and she glimpsed a larger-than-necessary firearm being tucked out of sight. *So it's going to be a show, then? Biggest guns win? Grow up.*

McKay took a step back as the door opened up and the guy came out into the corridor light. One good eye was watery blue, the other cheaply regrown in the wrong color and not lined up quite the way it should be. Moonfaced, a shock of black hair and no overt scarring suggested he was classic, non-enhanced muscle, but one could never be sure. Expensive miteware enhancements, particularly the physical boosts called "jump," were hard to spot with the naked eye. *Could go either way, and with the Overlay quiet I can't pick anything up right now.*

"Spin it up. If you're her expert, I want to see your eyes light up like little flashlights." He waggled calloused fingers that looked about as lethal as the firearm. *Great, proper martial arts training to boot. Outgunned in every sense.*

In the back of McKay's mind, the clock continued ticking, chipping away at Brighton's deadline. It made her nervous. "Fine, but your boss is paying me by the minute." She spun up the Overlay and called out a half a dozen files at random, filling the edges of her vision with light. McKay used the opportunity as cover to pull in every signal from the room she could find, asking the Overlay to note who was there, who had miteline, what the Swim in the space looked like . . . she could run through all the information later. The man with the mismatched eyes stared without flinching, then nodded.

"She'll take it out of my paycheck, I'm sure. She said you were twitchy." A sneer tugged the corner of his lips, and he beckoned McKay through the door.

Twitchy? McKay stepped into the office space, noting an unsettling resemblance to the hotel room she was staying in. Bathroom just inside the door to the left, the foyer close, cramped, unnerving. McKay had to turn sideways to get past a second, much taller man just inside the door, giving her an uncomfortably close-up view of the guy's short, sharp chin. She left the Overlay spun up so the second guy could see the glow as well. *Yes, just me, the specialist you hired. Nothing to see here. Please move along.* She waited patiently to be scanned, frisked, rayed, frisked and scanned again. The Overlay continued to snap images, record faces and build out a framework of the team Ina Brighton had brought with her. Vector7 was a new branch, rolled under USIC's Abuses of New Technologies division, but McKay hadn't been able to dig out much more than that in the time she'd had available.

The disarray in the "office" was textbook stage dressing. Three old desks in need of some repair or at least a good makeover, all loaded with boxes of junk equipment, none applicable to any virtual application she was familiar with. Ratty couch, musty odor that seemed to leak out of the vintage air conditioner and creep along a floor crisscrossed with cables the Overlay registered as just for show—no power, no data. McKay had to watch where she put her feet. *Standard undercover front.* Lots of useless junk, assembled so anyone without some kind of Swim-access would get an eyeful of what looked like an illegal buy-and-sell operation.

The suite door to the left opened up and Brighton stepped through, surrounded by a puff of frigid air, definitely a cut above the lukewarm vapor being circulated by the older unit in the office. McKay caught a glimpse of walls papered over in white and a row of server boxes. Brighton's gaze went from her to the guy with the mismatched eyes.

"Is she clear, Rice?" Her voice belonged to someone already tired of being messed with. Rice put out an arm to stop McKay from moving forward.

"She's too clean, Ina. I mean, there's *nothing* on this one, no serials on her 'mite-sig, no live connections, nada, zip, zero." McKay felt thick fingers close in the fabric of her shirt. "I think your expert's a fake. Flashy eyes and consumer wires."

Looking for serials. Rice was looking for military-grade miteware, quickly installed, designed for brutal use and easy removal, but very powerful and very obvious. McKay's internal miteline was experimental, equally powerful but custom designed, custom built, and nearly invisible by comparison.

McKay turned to explain this, but a knock at the door made them all jump. Brighton glared at her as if she were the culprit.

"McKay, you get in here." She jabbed a finger at Rice and his partner. "You two, get the door. Clock's ticking and I don't want any screwups."

"It's just lunch," the tall guy whined. "Pei-meng gave me the address for that Ginger Dream Thai place on Market." The atmosphere lightened. McKay relaxed just a touch.

"As long as you two didn't put the order in under 'Spy Guys' like you did last time." Brighton snapped and yanked the door open. The breath of cold air tightened McKay's skin. The Overlay sensed the servers inside, got a glimpse of the information flow, and leapt to life, trying to connect to everything at once.

"She's all good, guys." Brighton touched her elbow briefly to guide her through the door. "Get the food, then seal that outer door. I want a mite-free closure all the way around. No one goes in, no one goes out until we're done here, even if they set the building on fire. Got it?"

"No problem." Rice elbowed his friend and went for the front door as Brighton shut herself and McKay into an office space turned refrigerator.

McKay stopped short about three steps in.

She felt the drag of the Faraday cage as she crossed the threshold. It constricted the connections the Overlay had been making, and the farther in she got, the more outside connections got cut. Like a slow, crushing squeeze, the connection to the rest of the Swim got thinner and tauter and then *pop!* Access to the outside was broken, like an earthworm pinched too hard between thumb and forefinger. Data-wise, nothing could get into or out of the room, not even Spike. She felt a brief flutter of anxiety, congratulated herself on dropping the fail-safe packet outside earlier. The room, and by extension McKay, would be safe from outside hacks as long as the shielding stayed intact.

The bank of servers lining the far wall was responsible for the cold in the room. Inch-thick ropes of shielded cable ran from matte black housings first into one set of boxes, then another. The processors in them could probably fit in the palm of McKay's hand, but the temperature control systems that supported them meant pounds of equipment and a drop in degrees so low she could see her breath in the air. Heat was death to quantum-spin processors.

"You can set up over there." Brighton pointed left as she sealed the edges of the door with a roll of the nasty, sticky stuff called "fly-paper," aimed at stopping spyware and other kinds of nanomites from infiltrating cracks and holes in the architecture. Get enough 'mites into a secure room and they could reconnect that room to the outside world, making it vulnerable to attacks from the Swim. Not as perfect as a proper clean-room, but the paper would be enough to keep out most attempts to gain access.

And where the hell is this guy's body?

The persona process meant there should be outside hardware, a sleeper pod, a fancy leatherette couch with wires all around, some place to keep the unconscious body of the person entering the Swim. There was nothing like that in the room.

McKay set her bag down on the only empty table and deliberately took her time laying out her kit, giving the Overlay time to integrate with all of the non-shielded computers it could find. It told her that none of this equipment had been online for more than a week and that all outside access had been cut off three days earlier, which fit with what Brighton had told her. It told her that there was, indeed, a persona roaming in the servers, but there was no body nearby to send it back to. McKay quickly played back their conversations, reviewed everything Brighton had given her. Brighton had neglected to tell her that part, and she'd gone ahead and made the presumption. *This is what happens when you get excited. You miss things.* The local AI that kept everything humming was pretty snooty, too. It just ignored the Overlay's login attempts rather than telling it to get lost. The Overlay asked McKay for permission to hack in, but she told it to wait.

"Soooooo. Where's your friend Mike?" Doing a long-distance extraction, with the living body somewhere else, was going to be a lot harder to pull off. Impossible, in fact, with the entire room locked down and shielded as it was.

Brighton turned rather quickly. "Ah, yes. Rosie?" She scanned the room, looking for someone.

"Yeah?" A pigtailed head popped up from behind a stack of boxes.

"Where's he at?"

"Umm." Rose couldn't have been more than thirty, tops, and the smooth motion in her fingertips as she slotted in wafers and closed up the server she'd been working on spoke of a lifetime of pulling hardware apart. Her thick black hair was shaved halfway up from the base of her skull, the top longer and severed into a half dozen pigtails that erupted at odd angles. McKay's Overlay pointed out the off-the-shelf 'mites that gave Rose's hair and the entirety of her eyes an inky, featureless black color. She had a skull full of miteline, but only to the highest level of consumer grade, S2. *A very tricked-out and modified S2.* Rather than a constellation of tiny pinpoints, three thumb-size contact points at the base of her skull showed where an outside computer could be plugged in to give her a boost. McKay had seen the setup before, a fairly standard interface with the advantages of simplicity and ease of repair. There were limits to what a consumer rig could do, which meant she was saddled with certain basic hard- and software restrictions. On top of all that, bare shoulders exposed by her tank top showed the unmistakable marks of an elaborate heat-sink tattoo system. They had been all the rage five years earlier, miteline tattoos that absorbed heat from the wearer's personal computing system and reflected it onto the skin. Some glowed red hot, others used the energy to power a luciferase reaction. Like all miteline they required a painful, expensive purge to shed them once the fun wore off. Hers glowed faintly, suggesting she had been processing something just before McKay came into the room.

Everything about Rose's presence matched the "big power" mindset she'd picked up on from Brighton's files and from the earlier attempts to crash her rig. But the resentment she'd expected was absent.

McKay relaxed just a little.

"Mike's in that one on the end!" She pointed at one of the nondescript matte black boxes along the wall, different from the others only by a barcode and a long strip of numbers and letters she presumed was some sort of identifier. The Overlay told McKay it was not a registered code and likely proprietary. She gritted her teeth and gave it permission to start guessing.

"Excellent, but where's the body? I'm here to perform an extraction, right?" McKay asked. She had extracted people from some of the oddest setups, but so far there was always a body, somewhere, to write the persona back to.

"You are. I apologize, Ms. McKay, but Mike's body isn't here. We were able to run him to ground, to trap his persona here in Singapore, but the body's still in San Francisco." Brighton finished taping up the doorframe and joined McKay at the table. "Rose, can you give her the breakdown?"

The opposing programmer cracked her knuckles. "Mike's being a bit of a slippery fish, so we had to get him cut off from all Swim-access. We need you to extract his persona from that array"—she indicated the flat, black boxes at the back of the room—"to a fresh persona in the restructuring unit there. Mike's been in the Swim for ten days total, but he was only supposed to be in for a few hours on an undercover job. The information he found might relate to our current investigation, and Boss Lady here"—she jerked a thumb at Brighton—"wants him extracted to a fresh persona so we can keep him together long enough to get back to his actual body."

McKay was floored by the request. An extraction required finesse, an artistic blend of psychology, neurobiology, and hard-core coding. Extracting someone from one persona to write it into another? That was just not done. She was going to have to take all the guy's personality quirks and hang them on a brand-new framework. If the change to Mike's mind was big enough, she might have to do a total rewrite, but she couldn't be sure. Brighton had provided her with a blueprint of Mike's mind so she could write the code she needed, but she hadn't seen what was left of the persona now.

"The persona process isn't that simple." The protest erupted from her lips before McKay could stop it. "A persona is a copy of a person's unique qualities. What stops an outwrite is a *revelation*, some piece of information or an experience that is life-altering for that person. Couple that with the fact that now you want me to re-persona his persona and I don't even know if he could be written back into his own body when we're all done."

The other two women exchanged looks: Rose triumphant, Brighton irritated. "He was close to proving something in our case," the redhead explained patiently, "we *need* that discovery. Mike wouldn't have refused to just dump it all unless it was critically important."

This is either going to be the outwrite of all time, or a total disaster. Again that thrill of anticipation, the one that always seemed to get her into trouble. So much of her job was bereft of discovery, devoid of new challenges. The idea of trying something new made it hard for her to stay cautious. She spent a few moments of focus considering just how much trouble she was in, then went back to laying out the components from her kit onto the table. If the work did turn out to be a major do-over, she didn't want to transpose digits in her haste. Emotion could be as big a contributor to error as alcohol or a lost night's sleep. It was something to be kept in check, especially once she put the headset in place. "Fine, I'll need a copy of the system specs for both systems and a fresh copy of Mike's persona code for the restructure."

"Rose?"

The tattooed girl wended her way through the clutter and fished a plastic case out of the bag slung across her hips. It contained well over twenty spin-wafers, each the size of her thumbnail, each holding a defining piece of the Mike persona. McKay held it to the light briefly, counting them out in her head, then laid the case in line on the table with the rest of the gear.

The first thing out of her bag had been the headset case. Roughly the width of a sheet of paper and as deep as a stack of pancakes, the headset was the big gun as far as McKay's hardware was concerned. She could do a lot with only her built-in computers, but adding the headset meant she could write information into and out of the Swim on the fly.

Everything she'd been doing was an advanced form of augmented reality, information being displayed in her line of sight, interaction with the Overlay's AI restricted to commands given and interpreted. With the headset in place, McKay could interact directly with the Swim in a fully immersive sense. She could bypass the persona process entirely with no risk of her needing an extraction herself. The headset was like adding a supercharger to an engine. There were trade-offs. It burned neurotransmitters at a hugely increased rate. It bypassed the mental filters that helped soften real-life experiences, could even go so far as to cause brain damage if she overused it. But it meant she was nearly unstoppable in the Swim.

By conventional programming, at any rate.

The Overlay had already established links with everything in the room it could find, but when McKay unzipped the padded, shielded case to reveal the headset, it positively thrummed with anticipation. She set the case on the tabletop and dug back into the bag. One by one she laid out a series of pre-mixed, off-the-shelf pop-top cans, each with a slightly differing concentration of neurotransmitter precursors, glucose, peptides, carbs, and caffeine. There was only so much time she could spend in the Swim before she started burning neurotransmitters faster than her body could make them. Taken in measured doses, the contents of the pop-top cans could extend the amount of time she could spend fully immersed in the Swim.

Brighton stared at McKay as the Overlay began spinning up to full speed, making its wireless connections to the headset in anticipation of a full-contact connection. With the headset now in play, her eyes would resume their unearthly glow. She knew the changes in eye color, her facial expressions, all tripped the "uncanny valley" vibe in anyone who wasn't used to working around experimental systems like hers. She'd had people leave the room entirely, poke her, been slapped once. Brighton made the extra effort to maintain eye contact, which she appreciated on some level, but it was less important to her now the deeper she sank into the experience. The connection was made, the negotiations concluded, and the Swim was calling. *At least she's staying in the room.*

"You call him Mike. What's his real name? Full name, if you have it."

There was a long, awkward pause from Brighton. "We can't tell you that. It's not covered in the disclosures."

Of course it's not. She started sliding the wafers they gave her into the scrubber she brought along. So far they were all just data. Introducing a virus or any kind of malware at this point could crash her system before she even got started. As they came out of the box she clicked them into her skull drive, counted to three as the Overlay stripped the data, and popped them out again.

"Everything you ought to need is on the wafers," Rose put in. "Full system specs for these servers and everything we have on the persona and all its modifications."

McKay's Overlay picked up the girl's own computers spinning up to speed.

"If I don't know anything about the person himself, it's going to make it that much harder to keep what you need. Was he charming, was he angry, did he have kids, did he like peanut butter, all that information will help me make sure I keep more of Mike and less of the modifications he made."

"You've got enough there, Rose made sure. Don't you want to sit down?" Brighton asked.

"Eventually. Not yet though, keeps me on my toes. But if you don't mind. . . ." She snapped the links her Overlay had slipped into Rose's personal systems. McKay's AI was built to be curious, bordering on rude. With the processing power of the headset it would hack anything and everything given the chance, even other people's miteware. "Rose, spin your computers down, so I don't get confused and extract the wrong personality." She grinned, but the joke was lost on the other programmer. Rose was less unsettled than Brighton, but also far more intense now that things were moving forward. She frowned.

"Boss...?"

Brighton held up a finger. "Do it, Rose. We need this to go smoothly."

Rose wasn't happy, but she complied. She removed her earpiece, slid the beltpack around her waist, and touched a few places inside it. McKay felt her presence vanish with a pop and a protest and the room was hers.

"Thank you." McKay picked the headset up again, pressed her thumbs to either side and triggered the system spin-up. More than a thousand threads of micro-optic fiber had been braided together to form the length of shielded hardline linking the headset to the hub still in the case, yet it weighed next to nothing in her hands. A series of blips skated across her vision as the Overlay and the headset met up and linked. Normally the data was the ghost overlaid onto the hard lines of reality, but the deeper she waded in, the more the situation turned on its head. The real world became the ghost, soft-edged myopic outlines visible through the Overlay's shells. She lifted the headset reverently and placed it on her own head, a faint clicking audible as the contact spikes extended and found the pinheads embedded in her scalp under the hair.

The real world vanished utterly. She stood in the headset's root construct, an open space that resembled a large concrete dome. No windows and only a single bathysphere-style hatch in the ceiling. Locked within her own head, as it were. It was always strangely freeing, retreating here. A shiver ran through her mind, settling everything more solidly into place and running out to her virtual fingertips before vanishing. She ran a series of code snippets, opened a large viewscreen on one quarter of the room, raised the lights to a reasonable level, and pulled a number of metaphoric filing cabinets up out of the floor. The high-concept was important. The idea behind the way everything was laid out would keep her mind from wandering off track, even after everything dissolved into light and impressions.

The viewscreen on the wall resolved and gave her a window back into the real world. Both women were staring at her now. Rose stiffened slightly when McKay turned in her direction, looking either uncomfortable or disdainfully fascinated, she wasn't sure which. *Don't much care, either.* She stepped forward and waved a hand in front of McKay's face, jumped back when she grinned.

"I *can* see you," she said slowly. Rose backed off and took Brighton's arm, leading her out of the field of view. McKay chuckled.

"What do you think?" Brighton whispered to Rose.

She doesn't really think I'm deaf too, does she? It was a common misconception, that the custom wires in her head overrode all the body's senses. It was a myth perpetuated by the deep-sleep state required by the persona process. It didn't apply to an experimental system like hers, where the data was written in and out of the Swim on the fly. Even as an S2, the highest non-military-grade system you could get, Rose should have known better. Her inexperience was showing.

"Well, she's got a pricey xWire setup. Dunno if that means she's got the chops or just the finances," Rose replied. McKay heard the programmer moving behind her. "Seriously, though, we're taking a risk here. You should have just let me bring in one of my guys."

"I can't trust any of your criminal hackers, Rose, even if you do. If I take Mike's situation up the food chain, our whole group gets in trouble. We're in a bind and this is our safest option. Besides, this one's on Mike's list. If half the reports on file are true, this should be a cakewalk for her."

"Then dump Mike out of the Swim and he can retrace his own damn steps," Rose observed.

"Whatever he found, Rose, it's got to be big. We can't risk it," Brighton countered.

"Either way, this chick probably can't do any worse than we did. C'mon, let me watch from the inside. I promise I'll stay out of the way."

"I don't want to have to hunt Mike down again, Rose." Brighton's voice was tight, stressed. "We can't keep tacking these side trips on. The case against Christopher and Bellicode is going nowhere without whatever evidence Mike found in the Swim. Christopher's lawyers are breathing down our neck to shut the whole investigation down and you're about to go offline to get your upgrades."

"Look, there's an opening, I've got to take it, you know that. Stuff like this is exactly why I need those upgrades. We can't keep bringing in contractors every time I slip up." There was an urgency to Rose's voice that didn't seem to fit the situation. McKay asked the Overlay to whitelist Rose's system, so that if she did spin back up, it would recognize her and stay out of her head.

McKay took one of the pop-top cans off the table. *Twenty minutes.* That's about how long the cocktail needed to work its way through the bloodstream and into the brain. That was also about how long she needed to get prepped.

"I'd still like to watch while she does it." Rose again.

"Maybe she'll take you on as an intern." Brighton, her voice low.

"She'd probably be a better listener. Bet you a dollar that this whole thing goes pear-shaped and I have to pull her out."

McKay started opening layers of data in the Overlay, finding the commonalities between the two systems. "Excuse me. Rose, is it?"

"Yeah." Grudgingly, Rose came back to the table, arms crossed defensively. *Great.* The cross-chatter made it clear that Rose had strong opinions about the whole process. Even if she wasn't openly hostile, McKay needed to keep her involved, if only so she could keep an eye on her. She selected a fingernail-size component from her kit on the table and waved it in Rose's direction.

"Could you please plug this into terminal five on the main array?" She handed over the plug automatically, trusting her body to follow the motions without too much direction. In her spun-up state, if she thought about it too hard she might have stuffed it up her nose, or dropped it entirely. The link between mind and body got a little cross-wired when the headset was up and running. *Stay professional,* she reminded herself. She took it and flipped it between her fingers.

"Terminal five is one way access, input only." A frown drew Rose's plucked eyebrows into a line.

"I know, but I need an encrypted point of access to begin." The world around McKay dissolved yet again as the headset sent feelers deeper into the two systems, comparing the information Rose had given them with the actual hardware in place.

"But it's not going to help you any," she began angrily, "you're going to have to open a dialogue. . . ."

"Rose. Do it." Brighton was still out of view, but her tone was clipped and commanding, as if she'd given that order time and time again.

"*Fine. . . .*" Rose shook her head. "If this isn't a dat20 relay, you're going to short something." She shook the chip under McKay's nose and stalked over to the servers, sliding one of the maintenance panels open with a touch more force than necessary.

She got it, Rose's frustration. Programmers had an inherent need to know how things worked, to understand rather than just execute. If she'd had more time, she might have spun the headset back down and explained more, but in this transitional state, just keeping tabs on both the real world and the Swim required a delicate touch.

The virtual space inside the boxes reminded McKay of luminescent stained glass, sheets and sheets of spinware, color coded for the benefit of the human element. She heard Rose fish around inside the box, the Overlay felt the connection come alive and leapt at it, burrowing into the system and dragging McKay along with it.

"Thank you," was all she got out. The server was a powerful draw, and she found herself dragged into the virtual space faster than she anticipated.

God, I hope I'm not drooling. She turned to check her surroundings. The headset had pulled her directly into the main array.

She saw eddies and whirlpools in the data caused by the loss of outside access. *Just a software lock . . . they didn't actually rip out the networking hardware.* A few properly placed lines of code and she could open the system back up to the Swim again. She turned in place, looking for the telltale patterns of a persona in the ether.

The system was practically empty, most of the data just filler, ups and downs placeholding until someone overwrote them, like chop on a lake waiting for a motorboat to come though. Even so, she could see the vaguest outline of a pattern. The array had been hastily repurposed, microwaved to reset the quantum spin rather than a proper reformatting. There were no games here inside the system. It was a trap, a prison for the Mike persona until it could be written back or wiped. McKay shuddered. *Cold, very cold.*

A persona was, essentially, an analog of a real, live human being. This one had been hunted down deliberately and locked away in solitary, the computerized equivalent of a five-by-five-by-five concrete box. Personas were temporary copies of a person, yes, but that didn't mean they didn't deserve the same consideration you might give them once back in their own body. Any illusions she had about the extraction being anything but asset protection evaporated and her estimation of Brighton dropped a notch.

She pinpointed the persona and slid across to get a closer look at it. It was close to its expiry, that was certain. Bits and pieces around the edges were already defunct, corrupted and commented out until they lost functionality. She reached out to make a connection with it, but found herself pushed away.

Interesting. Let me try this again, a little more manners, a little less code.

There was a brief pause, picoseconds, but in translation it took forever. The program opened up, and McKay found herself faced with a reasonable facsimile of the mind of Mike.

Busy was the word that came to mind. The mind she faced was chock full of information, packets of data neatly arranged, numbered, aligned. She saw the shifts and slides as it calculated and recalculated, finding patterns between the packets and reordering them according to what it found. McKay couldn't see into the packets. It was like looking into a library from too far away to see the titles on the spines.

First things first. She loaded two of her favorite persuasion programs and shifted her own appearance to a more open stance. "Hi, Mike. I'm here to get you offline."

"Bullshit." Quick, spiky thorns of frustration and aggression appeared all over the persona, forcing McKay back. "I told Rose to back off, I need more time."

Interesting that it mentioned Rose. Equally interesting the other programmer couldn't extract it, or even explain the situation to it, since it was communicative.

Brute-force tactics, maybe? She'd seen it in Rose's notes in Brighton's file, in the way she'd handled the attack on her in the hotel room. If she'd tried to just force Mike back into his own head, that might account for the persona's reticence. But it didn't solve the problem of why Mike had refused to come out of the Swim in the first place.

"More time is why I'm here. My name is Eliza McKay. I'm an extraction specialist. Brighton contracted me to rewrite your persona so she can get you back to your own body." *Sometimes bluntness is best.* The Mike persona calmed down fractionally, data shifting and clicking into place. It was defensive, really defensive, but responsive, which meant there was still something she could work with.

"Ah. You're on my list." The spikes went away entirely and it returned to the shifting, complex patterns that McKay had first expected to see.

"Yeah, after all this is done, can you give me a bit more information on this list you've put together? I'm not usually on any *good* lists anywhere these days."

"I keep a list of emergency experts, even if they've pissed off a few departments. We run into some really strange technology." Mike opened up a bit further. "If I'm going to let you to do this, I have a request."

"Hmmmm. What do you have in mind?" McKay asked carefully. Making promises to digital entities was tricky. Experiences in the Swim were often unfiltered, burned a bit brighter. Getting stood up on a date in the real world would be hurtful, but you could deal with it. Getting stood up on a date in the Swim could burn like someone had just killed your dog in front of you. The usual real-life filters weren't there. The process of writing a persona out to the Swim included versions of those filters: you could, in fact, tune them up and down as needed. Once a persona started to degrade, however, they started to lose effectiveness.

"Rose needs to be kept out of this extraction." The spikes reappeared, this time square and peg-like, reflecting Mike's inner turmoil. He didn't like having to make that request. Something in him fought against it.

"Doesn't she work for you?" McKay took a moment to examine the persona from the outside with a professional eye. It had been commenting out chunks of its own code, essentially amputating non-working pieces from the inside out. Brighton had said this was an undercover operation, extra code added to make changes to the persona, like a built-on disguise, but whomever Mike had been pretending to be, he was a bit more Quasimodo than secret agent now. Rose's fingerprints were all over it as well, code comments here and there, penned in her distinctive hammer-and-tongs personality. McKay couldn't tell at this distance whether she had helped construct the disguise or whether these marks were all from her extraction attempts, but they were causing more harm than help. *Jesus, what a hatchet job. No wonder she didn't want me in here trying to fix this.*

"Yes, but now there are other factors in play. Are we agreed?" Mike queried.

"I'll do what I can, but I'm just the contractor. I can't guarantee Brighton will listen to me over one of her own." *After a look at this rat's nest, I can see why you want her out of the process.*

"Good enough. Write me out."

It was that simple. The spikes withdrew, the access link extended.

The Overlay caught the thin, spiraling strand of connectivity and pulled it taut, giving McKay access to the code behind the persona.

Christ, what a mess. The programmer took a deep breath and waded in.

FOUR

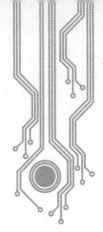

MCKAY COULD FEEL a pressure from the outside, like something was leaning on the locks that kept Mike's prison closed off from the Swim. It was silly: the box was only software-locked, the outer room was enclosed in a Faraday cage, cut off completely. The only egress was the finger-thick cable that now connected McKay's headset directly to Mike's server. The only way in or out was, quite literally, through McKay. Still, she could feel something out there, a presence in the Swim just outside the soft-locks and shielding that kept the whole of the room cut off. *Singapore police maybe? Third-party hackers?* She knew better than to ignore that creeping feeling that something was lying in wait.

"Hey, McKay! Wake up!" Brighton's voice filtered in from real-space. "Rose, get her out. I don't know how long that door will hold."

Door will hold? That didn't sound good at all.

"Didn't I tell you I was gonna have to pull her out?"

"You can gloat later. Get her out now."

McKay could spare a bit of focus, a small sliver of mind, to retreat from the server that imprisoned Mike to the concrete bunker in her head. She needed more time. Not much more. She'd extracted the lion's share of the persona. It would last a few more days, maybe a week, but she couldn't let go, not yet.

"Five minutes." She managed to say the words aloud, juggling the point of view of the copy of McKay talking to Mike and the core version of McKay handling the programming. She kept an eye on the viewscreen in her head as someone hit the door. She felt the vibration distantly, as if it were something outside, something twice removed. Rose passed quickly across her field of view.

"We don't have five minutes." Brighton appeared in the viewscreen, staring into her eyes. "McKay, finish it and get out. We have to microwave the drives and get out of here. Someone's coming in, and I've lost contact with Rice."

Shit. Microwaving the drives would reduce them to chunks of non-recyclable plastic. She changed tactics. Rather than repairing and rewriting, she started culling dead data, finding bits damaged beyond functionality and dumping them to her own storage while keeping the persona intact during the transfer. That was where extractions were more art than code—the decision-making, what to keep, what to alter, what could be saved and what must be lost to preserve the overall experience. She took a precious second to add an extra layer of security to the persona, something to let it pass unnoticed, at least for a little while.

The active sliver of McKay's mind turned her body to the table and picked up another pop-bottle, downing it without thought. From the corner of her eye she saw the door flex in its frame. The flypaper around the edges cracked. The headset picked up the pinprick signatures of 'mites flooding through the cracks and painted them into view, a billion ants on fire.

Of course this is going to suck. Why did you convince yourself it wasn't going to suck? The sliver of her mind split again and raced along one of the feelers the headset ran out. She touched the 'mites as they crept in through the cracks in the flypaper. She reached out with the Overlay and stroked them; they shifted programming under her guidance. She turned them back on their masters and set them loose. Destructive little buggers, cleanup 'mites, built to destroy other 'mites, chew up dust and crumbs and dump it all where it could be recovered to build something new. Someone had repurposed them, overriding their normally innocuous programming. *Illegal, that.* She found herself irrationally angry about the idea.

Her last big screwup had involved a method for re-engineering everyday maintenance 'mites back into "builders," capable of making more of themselves out of any available material. It was dangerous, stupidly dangerous. When McKay's government-sanctioned research finally succeeded, she'd been blacklisted, had her assets frozen, licenses pulled, and very narrowly escaped an extended stay in a military prison.

Whomever had reprogrammed these 'mites hadn't gone as far as McKay had: they couldn't make copies of themselves, they could just act under new instructions. It meant she could reprogram them in turn without having to worry about the consequences. McKay reeled in the sliver of her mind that went after the threat and reunited it with the whole. The pounding on the door stopped, which was something.

"Boss, they've stopped." Rose's voice.

McKay felt her presence appear in the Swim, like a tiger slipping into a river, severing incoming connections with aggressive swipes and stabs. McKay finished the persona rewrite while Rose stayed on defense, slipped one last line of code in, then fled back into her own head.

"Done." The real world reappeared with a *pop*, unlike the smooth transfer she was used to. There was an accompanying touch of nausea as her mind adjusted to the rawness of her own sensory input. The Overlay picked up the change in atmosphere—increased heart rate, 'mite threats—and adapted for speed, breaking off its contact with the headset and bringing up its own antiviral defenses. She thumbed the switches on the headset and felt the connectors release from her skull all at once. She'd have to forego letting the heat sinks cool off and rely on the aerogel in the case to absorb the excess. Heat was bad for spin. She didn't want to lose anything, but whomever was on their way in through the door would be far worse than a few flipped bits. Brighton pulled a serious-looking firearm from under her coat and leveled it at the twisting frame.

"Open the link, Rose. Let Mike out," she said grimly.

"But, Boss, you said. . . ."

"Do it, Rose. We can't carry the box out under fire, and I'm not microwaving Mike's persona after all this pain in the ass. We can find him again and write him back to his body later if we're not in jail." The door was under assault again, but it was stronger than whoever was on the other side. "Give me a hand here." She put the gun down and grabbed one end of a desk. Together they shoved it in front of the door.

"Is there another way out?" McKay asked. Rose tore open the housing on the secondary box and started flipping switches to turn the network chips back on.

"We bolted it shut when we put up the shielding."

"You know I'm going to have to charge you for medical if they get in here." McKay started shuffling her gear back into her bag, taking precious time making sure the pieces were slotted into their proper places. It was rote, an old, ingrained habit that even impending gunfire couldn't shake.

"As long as it's not overtime. Your rates for that are criminal." Brighton retrieved her firearm and kept it trained on the door as the assault changed shape.

"Watch for 'mites," Rose said, and yanked up a panel in the floor.

Brighton pulled a pair of heavy sunglasses out of her pocket and slid them on. McKay felt the agent's S1 miteware fire up. The Overlay gave her a ghost of what Brighton was seeing as she started targeting the outlines of figures on the other side of the door.

As soon as Rose had the floor up, McKay's Overlay leapt at the unshielded presence of the city hub. In a moment, it had a connection to the city's main information hub, unreeling data on the potential weapons in the room and options for action. *Why is the floor shielded? Who the hell shields a FLOOR?*

"Get down!" Brighton barked.

McKay locked up, some combination of neurotransmitter crash

and the very real possibility of getting shot. Memories from the last time she'd been in combat flickered, suppressed, at the back of her mind, adding to the mounting panic. She clamped down on them and continued methodically arranging the components in the bag like it was the most important task of the day.

"McKay, you finished writing Mike over?" Brighton elbowed her to get her attention, snapping her out of an anxiety-fueled reverie.

"Yes. Done."

"Rose?"

"One sec." The female coder unreeled a good six feet of hardline and clipped it to the exposed hub under the floor. McKay felt the Mike persona go by through the Swim like hot water from the tap. "Okay, Mike's out."

"Good, now everyone *get down*." Brighton caught the back of her shirt and dragged McKay toward the floor. Another loud bang at the door; smoke began seeping in around the edges.

We might really get killed in here. McKay dug into the Swim and started a search for the blueprints to the Brittle Moon. If they had just papered over the other door with shielding, they could probably get out that way.

"Boss, they're using an autoram to get in. That door's got maybe two hits left."

Shit, that means Singapore police. McKay's overlay linked up with Rose's, and she got a shot of double vision before she reminded her AI to knock it the hell off.

"I'm getting more 'mites." Brighton took a small spray can from her jacket pocket and crawled toward the door, spraying as she went. McKay saw the new wave of 'mites coming in like white-hot sand, but when Brighton misted them, they vanished.

"Did you guys check out the crawl space when you took this room over?" McKay asked Rose, who was a mere two feet away, monitoring the trunk line. Commercial buildings in particular held space, often significant space, between the floors for vents, cable lines, electrical—all the elements that needed regular access for repairs, but that still needed to stay out of sight. The blueprints showed that the Brittle Moon was no exception.

"Crawl space?" Brighton asked.

Rose looked shocked. "No, we didn't think the building had it. This is retail."

"It started out as a hotel thirty years before that." McKay pulled the blueprints out of the Swim and sent them to Rose's own Overlay. "There and there. Rose, can you hack that autoram to slow them down?"

"Can? Yes. Should? No. If they're Singapore police, it's going to be trouble. Same reason the Boss doesn't put a few rounds into the door. We're not officially here, and if we kill anyone or make a mess, we're fair game." Rose ripped up another two squares of institutional tile and stuck her head under the floor.

"I thought you had a ten-hour deadline."

"It looks like someone changed their mind, but an email warning would have been nice," Brighton said sourly.

"Looks clear, Boss. We can get under the floor and come up in the secret hallway behind the room."

"The door's armored, McKay," Brighton added. "It's the frame that's going. Send me the spec, Rose, so I can see what you're looking at." The redhead's glasses flickered as they tried to keep up with Rose's S2 and McKay's more advanced xWire systems. "Go. Rose, you first. McKay, you follow. Meet outside if you can. If not, drop her at her place and meet me at the theater."

"I do love Kabuki," Rose said cryptically, and slid her feet into the crawl space. "C'mon, McKay, let's go." She vanished under the floor. McKay looped her bag over her shoulder and followed suit.

"Are you coming?" Looking up from the crawl space, McKay could see Brighton silhouetted against the fluorescent ceiling lights. She backed toward the hole in the floor, weapon still trained on a door that looked less and less like a barrier to entry. "Eventually. Get a move on, or I can't pull any really dirty tricks."

She shook the spray canister violently with her off hand and unleashed another barrage of repellent at the 'mites riding in on the smoke. The Overlay did not like the new batch of 'mites at all, warnings going off everywhere and obscuring her vision. Brighton looked over her shoulder with a grin. "Get out of here. This is what *we* do. You don't need to get involved any more than you have to."

McKay had no clever response, so she just nodded and dropped after Rose into the sticky, dark crawl space.

The aircon that kept the offices at a livable temperature meant the air in the hallway stayed hellishly hot, so small wonder an enterprising soul offered them a couple bottles of ice water at ten Sing each when they slipped out through the emergency exit of a luggage exporter down the hall. McKay was so overheated she didn't even try to bring the price down and bought two for Rose to boot. *No sense being rude.* The Overlay had been forced to shut itself down as her body temperature rose outside the computer's tolerances. Rose didn't seem to be having the same trouble, one of the benefits of consumer-grade hardware.

They headed down the stairs at the other end of the hall as the building's fire system kicked in, thrown into gear, no doubt, by the 'mite incursion upstairs. The fine snow of fire retardant coated everything, blanketing the inside of the building with white. *And it tastes like ass.*

Rather than leave the building, Rose led her down to the lowest level, and they headed toward Orchard Road by way of one of the underground tunnels crisscrossing the area. Since the entirety of the Brittle Moon had to be evacuated after Brighton's bolt hole got raided, two more people covered in white dust were unremarkable in the crowd. Rose and McKay simply swept along on the ever-present tide of humanity.

After twenty minutes of ducking and darting, Rose brought her to a courtyard centered around a large, Hellenistic-style water fountain. The people striding purposefully about on business ignored them studiously. Four different corridors lined with food stalls led out, each to the basement of another building.

"We wait here." Rose leaned close and steered her to one of the benches that surrounded the fountain.

"For what?" McKay asked irritably. The crash was upon her, the inevitable drain after an intense session in the Swim. She'd had no chance to take the rest of her boosters and was slowly sliding into mental exhaustion and depression. She needed to get back to the hotel and mix up something to counter the heavy use of the headset, and all the sneaking around irritated her. The lock she normally kept on her emotions was starting to crack.

"Boss'll be along in just a minute." Rose plunked down next to her and stretched her legs out.

"So she got out then?"

Rose snorted. "Yeah, she's good at that." She tapped her temple briefly, the trigger for her own scaled down version of the Overlay. The bottles of water had helped get her own computer back up to par, but she didn't have the neurotransmitters to burn. McKay kept her own Overlay spun down and as a result, she almost missed the shift in Rose's tone.

"So, tell me," she went on blithely, "why'd you go X?"

McKay frowned. "What kind of question is that?"

She held up a hand. "I didn't mean to be rude. I'm just curious. I mean I got my wiring put in five years ago, and I keep thinking about upgrading, so I thought I'd ask." The words came in a rush, as if she were trying to take them back even as they left her lips.

McKay sighed. She'd heard the question more than once, and very few people ever listened to the honest answer.

"Because it's what I do." It was a truth, of sorts. The real reasons were much more complicated, not the sort of details she wanted to put out there, where anyone could get at them. It had taken her a better part of a year to even design the miteline, back when installing such a system was as experimental as you could get. Months of adjustments to guide the 'mites to make just the right connections, training the Overlay, oh, *that* part had sucked. It had been worth it, though. It had given her a savant-level ability to understand and program 'mites. All of which had been made irrelevant when the government had seized her licenses.

The idea only made the depression move in faster.

Rose stared at her, blinking. *Not the answer she expected.*

"That fits, I guess." She lifted a hand to finger the contact points on the back of her skull. "I need to find a way to jump my gear to the next level. This job . . . well, you saw what was up back there with Mike. I need more processing power, I need a better edge. There's an opening here in Singapore. One of the docs can fit me in for a hardware boost, something special, something custom."

McKay fished around for a diplomatic way to say it and came up empty. "That. . . ." She waved a hand vaguely back in the direction of the Brittle Moon. "That wasn't a processing power problem back there. That was a personal problem. Mike didn't want you writing him out, for whatever reason. He was fairly clear about it and you couldn't have forced him out without destroying the persona." She shook her head. *Again and again and again*, people insisted on regarding persona as programs, when they were really people. People took time and consideration. She tried again.

"Look, if you're thinking about upgrading again, give me a call when I get back to the States, and I'll run through it with you. I get it. It's not easy to keep up sometimes. But if you rush it, or the custom hardware is not a good fit, you're asking for a psychotic break or something even worse. I'm just out of brain-wattage to talk you through it all right now." She scrubbed her hands through her dusty hair, sending a fine shower of retardant powder into the air. "Crap. Does that count as littering? I'm not really in the mood to get arrested today."

"I'll think about it," Rose said sourly.

She got to her feet as Brighton approached. Even without the Overlay, McKay could read the redhead's disappointment, even anger, in the sharpness of her movements, her refusal to make eye contact. The 'mites had shifted Brighton's hair to a straight jet-black that blended with the look of passersby. Unremarkable in the crowd but her purposeful tread and the way she spoke into a handheld comm-unit, actually barking orders into it, ruined the effect. She stalked past the two of them and down the leftmost corridor without a backward glance.

"Well, she's going to be pissy the rest of the day," Rose noted, as if her earlier annoyance at McKay's suggestion to wait had vanished. "You're clear to head back to your hotel. Better get a move on." She waltzed after Brighton at a distance, the two of them lost in the sea of people before McKay got to her feet.

Well, that's just choice. She stared at the sea of black-haired heads flowing from one corridor to the other, slowing only to eddy around the vendor carts before changing direction and moving again. There was always a letdown after a job, of course. Being part of a team, even just for one gig, made going back to being a solo act feel just a little empty. Coupling that emptiness with the realization that someone had been actively coming in the door after them made her shudder. McKay wanted a really, really hot shower, maybe a long soak in the hotel bath. She got to her feet more steadily than she expected and turned in place, deciding which corridor led back to the metro. After the events of the past hour, having to read the signs without the Overlay's help seemed completely unreasonable.

Damn signs.

FIVE

THE CONCIERGE didn't look twice as McKay passed through the hotel lobby, probably because he'd seen weirder things than a tourist doing a very poor impression of a ghost. McKay would have been right at home in the well-worn *True Singapore Ghost Stories* pulp collection someone had left in her nightstand.

The hotel had a water feature, a wall of trickling liquid to produce a sort of natural white noise that kept the lobby serene and quiet, hushing the squeak of rubber and the tap of leather as people wandered through. The entire building, from lobby to toilets, was done up in varying colors of cultured stone and bamboo, adding to the feeling of enforced calm the same way a straightjacket might. Even an auctioneer might feel compelled to whisper. McKay swiped two of the complimentary water bottles off the counter on her way to the bank of elevators and downed one in the foyer waiting for the doors to open, washing down the handful of neurotabs she picked up in a mini-mart that catered to Western tourists. She hated the emergency tabs. The premixed shots were smoother, but unless she wanted to spend the rest of the day in a state of unproductive black depression, she needed a neurotransmitter boost now and she couldn't be picky. She'd just have to put up with the side effects later.

A half hour later she was singing the praises of whoever invented institutional-scale water heaters. Off-key, mind you, but singing.

Hot showers were a vice McKay never even tried to get past. Sonic showers were recommended for people with external contact points, but they just weren't the same. They lacked the hedonistic appeal of hot water sheeting over the entire body.

"So, how'd it go?" The voice in her head was Spike's. The distinctive nasal twang always came through, no matter the layers of encryption or compression. The spike-and-skull icon on the Overlay flashed, and McKay gave it access while she toweled her head and left the shower's warmth for the shock of the air conditioning.

"Not as well as I'd have liked," she answered. "The extraction turned out to be a total persona rewrite. It would have been fun, except for the almost getting killed part." She steered her brain away from the tight, tense memory of the escape.

The sprite didn't bother to materialize fully. Instead, the skull icon merely flapped its jaw in time to the words sounding in McKay's head. *Tacky.*

"Anyone famous?"

McKay spread-eagled on the bed and stared at the patterned ceiling tiles. "I told you it was a black-hat thing. They were looking to extend the lifespan of a runaway persona."

Spike materialized at the foot of the bed, mostly, though its lower legs and feet intersected the coverlet. McKay frowned. She would have to recalibrate the Overlay's perception filters. *All the running and hiding earlier must have knocked something out of whack.*

"Lifespan? How far gone was it when you started?" The sprite's lanky avatar didn't seem to mind being out of sync with the environment. McKay opened the maintenance settings in the Overlay and started fiddling with the sliders.

"Not too bad, all in all. There was some degradation, but I think I carried the core elements over. I lost a few bits here and there, but mostly ancillary memories, smells, stuff more appropriate to the person than the persona." McKay reminded herself to blink. The air conditioning dried out her eyeballs, but she hated working with her eyes closed. Her lab at home had much more precise atmosphere control, but she didn't do paying work from there very often. There was miteware for that, of course, the sort of thing you installed to control rate of tear flow and deliver moisture to the cornea, but there was a limit to how many body systems you could enhance before things got confusing and the 'mites started to disagree. Even "jump," the 'mite systems the military designed to enhance muscles, endurance, and reflexes, had their limits. One could go bionic, of course, replace entire limbs or more, but that was extreme and expensive.

The rough, cheap neurochemical tabs had set her on edge, and she blew out a long, silent breath to settle down. The tea on the dinette in the hallway would require getting up again, which she meant to put off as long as possible. The Overlay's limited intelligence picked up on her restlessness and began running diagnostics on the 'mites that populated her neural pathways, checking and rechecking how quickly she was burning through neurotransmitters and how long it would take for her to recover from the extended session with the headset.

"Did you make a copy for your library? Can I see it?" Spike rubbed its hands together.

"No, not this time. There were other factors." McKay fiddled with the filters and watched Spike slide around erratically while she adjusted the Overlay's ability to track physical objects in the environment. She jerked one adjustment all the way to eleven and stood the sprite on its head. "I did save the corrupted bits, so I can take them apart later, but most of it looks like garbage." A few more mental flips of the switch readjusted Spike to a more normal orientation. It didn't help much. Spike never bothered to render out shoes, but at least McKay was sure the Overlay was reading real-space properly. The sprite had begun its existence as a search program, barely able to render out an image of itself. The garish choice in attire was a testament to how much it had evolved over time. *Or not.*

"Mind if I take a look anyway?" Spike's current incarnation resembled nothing so much as an experiana beach bum, down to the

Hawaiian print board shorts and two-day stubble. It tried a smile for McKay's benefit. "Pretty please?"

"I signed a pretty nasty nondisclosure, Spike." She rolled over and reached for the clean shirt draped over the back of the chair. "I'm sure they could have me arrested or defrocked or something."

"Like you need another government agency after your head. At least this group almost got you killed on accident. After that, arrested is just an inconvenience," Spike said brightly. "C'mon, ple-e-eeeeeeeeeeeze." As the last word formed in McKay's head, the voice modulated into something that made her grind her teeth. *Inside voice* meant she could not plug her ears, and Spike had a way of getting around the Overlay's controls.

"All right already. But I'm invoking total privacy on this, no distribution whatsoever, not to humans, AI, search databases, zip, zero, nada. It can come back to me, but otherwise should not see the light of digital, got it?" As she spoke aloud, the Overlay popped up the encryption algorithms and bound the file before the copy left her virtual hands. Spike could decrypt it, but only while in the concrete illusion of McKay's headspace. A single reading would degrade it. It wouldn't survive another copy.

McKay fumbled the buttons and tugged her shirt into place. *Break time is over.* Something had settled out in her mind, and she had the urge to get moving, to get out and into the crush of people before someone else tracked her down. *A shame, really.* Singapore was one of her favorite places to do business, and she didn't like feeling uncomfortable when she had to do business. Ideally the job was done, *she* was done, but she knew from experience that different agencies had different definitions of "done." McKay ignored the familiar flutter of panic. The Overlay obligingly brought up her skybus ticket home. Another twenty-four hours before departure. She called up the booking site and bumped up to an earlier flight. Sixteen hours pressed shoulder to shoulder in cattle class with an absolute stranger was not at all appealing, and she waffled a moment, debating the wisdom of staying in town the extra day just so she wouldn't have to downgrade her ticket. Common sense and general nervousness won out, and she swapped. It gave her three hours to stop in at Saiid's. The two engineers had done the lion's share of their graduate work together—McKay never missed a change to meet up.

"I thought you said you were dealing with a runaway persona. What's up with this data?" Spike derailed her train of thought.

"What?"

"The data. These elements aren't part of the original. They're add-ons, tacked in after the persona was recorded." Spike did a little street-magician thing with its hands and pulled up a window of code, framing it between its long fingers. "Look here. And here. See the discrepancies in the strings?" Spike sprouted a third arm and pointed out the elements worth talking about.

Despite lots of caveats, the process for copying a living personality into a digital persona was simple and straightforward. The core process was standardized, nearly the same in every available system. The code bits Spike showed her didn't fit that process. McKay dropped back onto the bed and opened her own copies of the files to compare to Spike's. "Brighton described this as part of their process, a way to modify the persona to fit an undercover operation."

"On the surface, it looks like a persona. Look here and here. These are the standardized calls for a Bellicode 2041 base."

"Christopher's line of machines?" Brighton had mentioned that Christopher David was the focus of Mike's investigation. His tech company, Bellicode, was the maker of the current generation of persona creation software. Top of the line, so the persona process should have gone smoothly, end to end.

"But the other elements don't fit. They'd suppress some of the personality elements, cause a conflict. And you've got some other coder's comments all over this thing; those weren't helping at all." Spike highlighted another few lines for her benefit.

"How serious a conflict?" McKay began running comparisons,

searching her collection of interesting code snippets and calls looking for anything similar.

"Serious enough to change the actions of the persona significantly. I've met more than a few personas in this kind of disguise. Vector7's work went a lot deeper. They didn't just change your guy on the outside, they changed him on the inside too." Spike's usual snarky commentary was absent, indicating it was onto something serious.

"What, an actual different thought process?"

"Maybe. You might get a different expression of the same processes, or you might get an entirely different person."

"Damn." *This is what I get for taking their intel at face value. Should've grilled Rose while I had the chance.* McKay had known the Mike persona had been heavily adapted to resemble someone else for whatever undercover purpose he needed. Rose had gone through and commented out large swaths of the "disguise" code when she'd tried to extract Mike herself, but she'd accidentally caught chunks of Mike's original persona code at the same time. Mike's disguised persona had actually been "thinking" differently, so the experiences of *that* version might be too different to fit back to Mike's living mind. It would be like trying to stuff a size eight foot into a size six shoe. McKay had cleaned it all up, gotten Mike back to something approaching his original self so he could be extracted later, but she had missed how the difference between the disguised Mike and the real Mike might experience things. That game-changing experience might have been specific to one version or the other, and whoever did the final extraction needed to have that information in hand.

"It's not like you to miss something like this, Eliza."

"I was in a hurry," McKay snapped. "They were breaking the door down."

The sprite spread its hands wide in a gesture of appeasement. "I'm just saying there's some serious weirdness going on here. You're going to have to take another look at this situation."

"No kidding." McKay cringed at the idea of getting involved further, of not being able to extricate herself before the shooting started up again, but more responsible thought processes soon took over. She already had to get back in touch with Brighton, to let her know what Mike had said about not allowing Rose to conduct the extraction; now she'd have to let her know that the rewrite she'd performed might not have been enough. Brighton still might not be able to extract Mike when they caught him again. The whole damn effort might have been wasted. She replayed the day's events in her mind, focusing on the last few minutes before they ducked into the crawl space. The panic she'd felt at the time varnished the memory, made it sharper, harder to look at.

"She told Rose to turn the persona loose again. The last thing they did was open up the link to the Swim. Then they microwaved the whole rig, or they said they were going to," she said, half to herself. "So Mike's free in the Swim again, we just have to figure out where." She thought a moment more. "Spike, I'm heading to Saiid's until it's time to catch the flight. Little India's a bit Swim-lite, so it will be easier to stay off everyone's radar for the time being. I'm going to give you an identifier. I'd like you to find the persona with it."

"What? You didn't have time to put the thing back together prop-erly, but you had time to tag it?"

"Just go. Do I need to make it a special request?" A special request meant she'd owe Spike a favor in return. She tried to save those for the really troublesome asks.

"No, no." The sprite spun itself back into the jaw-flapping icon. "I'm going. What flight will you be on?"

"Twenty-one-forty-two, with a stopover in Seattle, but I'm going to hit Saiid's on the way to the airport." McKay got up and started canvassing the room. She was compulsive in her organization, espe-cially when out of town. On a good day, she could lay a hand on every possession with her eyes closed and not trip over her shoes.

Spike's icon vanished into the Swim, taking with it McKay's false sense of security. *Just because you're paranoid. . . .* The adage echoed in her head, taking on Rose's sardonic tone. As if someone flipped a switch and sucked all the carefully reconstituted calm from her mind, her ability to pack coherently came unglued along with it. She stuffed the last few belongings into the duffel, folding be damned, and sicced the Overlay on finding the access code for the staff elevators down the hall. A few seconds later she was headed downward, sandwiched between the laundry carts of two disapproving housekeepers. If all went well, the 'bot she'd left in the system would make it look like she was still in the room until her scheduled checkout the next day, meaning that a live person had to go see if she was really there—and all that would have to happen in real-time. *Real-time is good, real-time is slow.* She would have plenty of time to get to the airport and back to home ground before the sticky hit the fan.

Don't look back.

SIX

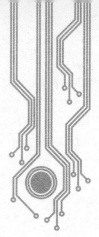

SAIID AND MEERA'S SHOP was right in the heart of Little India, settled among markets selling farm-grown produce brought over from neighboring countries, amid small shops selling carved and inlaid wooden artifacts and the overpowering smell of spice. Saiid and McKay had both specialized in 'mite design on different sides of the ocean for different design studios—the pair thrown together in the last years of graduate school. Saiid had turned his not inconsiderable design skills to creating new types of material for industrial and commercial use while McKay had gone into designing miteline systems to interface with the brain. When McKay's design license had been pulled by USIC, Saiid had been one of the few who hadn't regarded their friendship as toxic to his career.

"Feh." Meera's first word was a sound of amused disgust. "You look exhausted. Drink that, sit there, and I will get my husband for you. He's upstairs playing that game with the boys."

McKay obediently dropped her rear into the seat and took a sip from the teacup Meera handed over. Her glare pinned her there until McKay took another, less-tentative sip.

"Better," Meera said briskly.

McKay tipped the cup for a better look at the custard-colored beverage. Saffron milk, Meera's go-to for stress relief. The fact that she had it ready to hand meant that Saiid was working on something new, and it wasn't going as planned.

McKay's gaze wandered upward and the Overlay picked out the tight knot of information in the room upstairs where Saiid's house network fed into the city hub. Packets fairly flew from it, slicing invisibly through the air on their way to a dedicated server somewhere.

"From the look of it, he might be winning," she said dryly. Meera snorted.

"They let him think so, Eliza, but sooner or later they get bored fluffing his ego and mop the floor with him." Quick steps took her past the standing bolts of fabric at the rear of the shop, and she vanished behind a curtain that tinkled faintly when it moved.

McKay kept her seat, her posture ramrod straight. For security reasons, the shop was not connected to the city hub, an isolation she usually found refreshing, in small doses. Industrial espionage ran rampant in places like Singapore and Saiid had responded by cutting off as much unnecessary access to the Swim as possible. The game console and the basic house communications were set apart, physically separated from any of Saiid's research equipment. Contrasted to the rest of McKay's day, the hours spent in and out of virtual spaces, it was a little unnerving, like being trapped in a box. She fought the impulse to pace impatiently, instead turned her attention on the Overlay and opened it back up so she could work. On the bus ride over she had given it instructions to pull the faces of Brighton and her team and run down anything it could find in the social spaces in the Swim.

After all that shooting and running, the gloves are off. As the contractor on the job, it should be a one-time incident. Whoever came after Brighton and her team would be focused on them, not the hired computer hacker. She didn't want to ping Brighton again until she was in the air, well on her way back home, but the need to reconnect still hanging over her head made her nervous, jumpy. The milk helped counter the jitters, and a stiff application of logic finally shut up the little voice in the back of her mind that had been chanting *Run! Run! Run!* By the time Saiid and his kids had finished their game, she had a solid lead on one of Vector7's people through an old video chat that someone had posted online, and was working on a second.

"Miss McKay, I am delighted to see you were able to find the time to stop by!" Saiid's voice filled the room before the man himself was visible.

McKay turned her head away from the voice out of habit until the Overlay had been spun back into stillness. They had been friends since grad school, but still the tailor insisted on calling her 'Miss.' McKay found it baffling but never managed to get him to change, even with the careful application of alcohol. Saiid called everyone outside his family mister or missus, regardless of the proper social niceties.

"I'm on the next flight out, Saiid, but I wanted to stop in and say hello at least." She got to her feet.

"Of course, of course, but your timing is impeccable. Come and see what I've been up to!" He ushered McKay up the familiar, impossibly narrow stairs.

They had spent a year in Singapore together finishing up their fellowships. Saiid's grandfather still owned the shop, and McKay had rented the space under the second floor stairs as a bedroom. The stairs were exactly the same as she remembered. Number five creaked alarmingly if you set your foot in the center, and she slid her foot to the far right edge out of habit. Steps twelve and seventeen had short risers, so you tripped if you didn't pay attention. Saiid paused on the landing and shouted down the hall to his sons.

"Cutter, Rafferty, mind the shop, please!" Without waiting to see if the boys responded, he pressed on up the next flight, McKay in his wake.

"Oh, don't tell me."

Her friend's excitement was contagious. Despite the madness of the rest of the day, McKay found herself being drawn in.

"Yes, exactly." Saiid fairly danced up the last stairs. "I got the new designs finished just this morning."

"Have you tested them yet?" Saiid's custom-assembled filaments were in demand with the kinds of companies who made bullet-resistant underwear, but that wasn't why McKay had stopped by. *Saiid's been working on a new fabrication 'mite for three years. Maybe he's finally cracked the silk problem.* The unique physical properties of spider silk had spawned a dozen man-made clones, but each fell short in one aspect or another. It had become Saiid's passion project, creating a perfect replica of the material for use at a broad commercial level. From a 'mite-design standpoint, it was complicated and fascinating. McKay quickened her pace and took the stairs two at a time.

She emerged into the vat room. A generation or more ago, according to Saiid's grandfather, the room held a dozen sewing machines and cutting tables, but the engineer had given it a new purpose. The wall plaster was clean, the floor tiles shiny and waxed by hand, not by 'mites. A couple of the sewing machines were still there, tucked into the corners as a reminder. Spin boxes replaced the cutting tables, a scene eerily like the one laid out in the office McKay had been chased out of earlier. Against the wall were five large 'mite vats, each roughly the size of a person, all bolted to the building's reinforced frame.

The first vat was a generic unit, retrofitted and slapped all over with official Government of Singapore General stickers. Sing Gen kept a very tight rein on anyone who used nanomites for development, with key-encoded burn boxes. Any time Sing Gen wanted to come in and destroy everything they could do so, just by punching in the right keycode. Getting a license as a private business was expensive and meant the disruption of weekly check-ins (and the attendant niceties that went with them). However, Sing Gen was also nothing if not practical, and Saiid had a talent for bringing business into the country. *If the entire neighborhood ever gets eaten by runaway 'mites and turned into silk thread, at least they'll have a record of who was at ground zero, I suppose.* Two other vats held the specialized 'mites Saiid used to create the materials for his business. She'd helped Saiid develop and code that first generation of "knitters" back in grad school, 'mites they'd designed to extrude and bind custom threads to order. Unlike the large-scale manufacturing used for artificial fabrics, Saiid's 'mite-driven process meant small-batch exotic fabrics were within easy reach, whether for fashion or industry. *The big money's still in industry, of course.* The fourth vat was Meera's and bore her mark in complex patterns drawn in marker paint, crisscrossing and spiraling around its plain metallic housing. The fifth vat was a new, sixth-generation prototype enclosure, complete with Sing Gen burn units, designed to let the General Purpose 'mites build new 'mites to specification. These were the dangerous ones. Most 'mites were disposable. They had a limited lifespan; they were designed for a single purpose. GPs could endlessly replicate, they could build new 'mites to spec, they could even modify existing 'mites. Small wonder Sing Gen and every other government on the planet kept them under tight control.

McKay had to admit to a certain twinge of jealously that Saiid still had access, could still build something new.

The tailor led McKay to the fifth vat and tapped the glass with a finger. "Here they are. If this works, my fortune is made, my friend!"

McKay folded her arms across her chest and grinned. "Your fortune's already made, Saiid. This one's for your soul."

"No, no, no, don't jinx it." Saiid gestured wildly in denial. He handed McKay a spin-wafer, and the hacker plugged it into her skull drive without hesitation. The Overlay sucked up the encryption algorithms and connected with Saiid's own internal computer. An S2 setup like Saiid's still required goggles or glasses so he could "see" the Swim but the rest of the system was so finely tuned it practically sang. McKay dropped into the Swim-space between them and waited for Saiid to catch up.

Saiid dropped into the Swim and gently shoved McKay aside. *Right, sorry about that.* She was there to observe, not to help, not to intervene. The 'mites swarming in the vats were Saiid's pride and joy, and Saiid had a tendency to get short-tempered when it came to his pride. McKay stepped back as the designer approached the fifth tank with a long pipette tapered down to a nearly invisible tip. A flip of his thumb revealed an access port, and Saiid slid the delicate pipette in up to the crosspiece and sucked an angel's breath of 'mites from inside the vat. At the equipment table, he deposited the bright blue liquid into a clear, teardrop-shaped container. Saiid sealed it shut and suspended it point down over a small glass dish on the table. Through the Overlay, McKay saw fine patterns of miteline tracing the table's surface, linking the container on its stand, the glass dish, and the boxy, refrigerated spin units.

"Are you ready?" Saiid cracked his knuckles, and McKay watched the links to the GPs open up, delivering the activation codes for the prototype 'mites and bringing them online. The whole process took place in the space between thoughts, and the new 'mites got to work. Within moments, a thin strand of golden fiber visible only at just the right angle trickled out and puddled in the dish. McKay held her breath.

"I'm starting with just a single thread generation on this one," Saiid explained. "I've been having trouble getting the assemblage right."

"So why the special container? Why not have the 'mites create the entire strand?"

"The narrow end has a draw array to refine the thread as the 'mites create it. I tried to let the 'mites do all the work, but the chemical mix isn't there yet. The tensile strength is still too low."

McKay watched the commands flit past, the 'mites on the table communicating with Saiid's system and the remote simulation of what they were supposed to be doing. Much like extractions, nano-mite design was as much art as science. People who needed something done above and beyond the current 'mite standard sought out people like Meera or Saiid, or McKay, for that extra kick to the design process. The instructions for any individual 'mite had to be built into it, written into the structure of its body, if something so small could be said to have a body, every molecule encoded with data set into the electrons' spin. A truly efficient 'mite had but one purpose and nary a spare atom in its being.

The thread streamed out and piled up on the glass. Saiid muttered something, and the commands to the 'mites shifted abruptly. He was showing off a bit. Sensors in the table beneath the glass dish fed information back onto the strand and Saiid threw that information up onto the Overlay for McKay to see. A series of cryptic comments with a code McKay was not familiar with made Saiid grunt.

"No. Didn't work." He shut the process down.

"No, wait . . ." McKay began, but Saiid's kill order filled the nearly empty containment sphere with a puff of smoke. "Aw, man!"

A straight, black frown replaced Saiid's smile so fast McKay would have missed it had she not already noted Saiid's bitter frustration rippling out in the feedback through the Swim.

"Saiid . . ." McKay had just breathed the name, but the smile was back. Saiid took a deep breath, popped his goggles off, and dropped them on the worktable.

"Serves me right for showing off!" He turned to vat number five and threw the kill switch to burn the latest batch of 'mites.

"I could take a look," McKay offered, but Saiid shook his head.

"No, not yet. I'm not ready to have someone else solve it for me just yet, and I'm not ready for you to be imprisoned if your government catches you trying." He picked up the smoke-filled container and shook it by his ear. "But you'll be the first one I call when I am that desperate." McKay's connections to Saiid's system abruptly snapped as time ran out on the decryption codes. "Let's go. Meera's making tea, and I'm sure there's something with sugar on it left in the kitchen somewhere."

Behind them the countdown on vat five ended, and the GPs began their careful deconstruction of the failure. McKay stared at the fist-size glass teardrop a long moment, resisting the urge to pick it up and take a closer look. The Overlay locked on, following her thoughts, and began feeding her data, but she closed her eyes, shutting the process down. *It's Saiid's project, hands off.* Still, it took an effort to leave the puzzle behind, and follow her friend down to the kitchen.

After they all shared the five very small cups of tea and a tower of day-old besan burfi between them, Saiid volunteered to give McKay a ride to the airport. His oldest son was the only one in the family with a vehicle, slick and sporty with all the music stations tuned to something high-pitched and squealy. Manual drive only, no AI controls, something McKay found deeply unnerving, especially with Saiid's tendency to slide between lanes without checking the opposing traffic.

"Meera and I will be in San Francisco over the summer for the conference. I know you can't get within 100 meters of the event, but we could drive down and meet up?"

"Sounds like a plan. Send me your itinerary when you book the tickets." McKay took the reminder of her persona non grata status with good grace, and popped the door. The government here might not care if she hung around with a guy who had a whole vat of builders in his basement, but back home the scrutiny was much tighter and treason was a word not taken lightly.

"Safe journey."

"Me? You're the one in a car without an AI."

McKay waved as Saiid swept the car back into the flow of traffic, then turned and headed through the gate to customs. She'd been red-flagged again, as the security personnel found the possibility of contraband 'mites far more interesting than explosives.

Once settled in the ass-end of the skybus, she sealed her sunglasses on and closed her eyes. The Overlay helpfully slid Brighton's contract into her line of sight, hazard terms and rates picked out in red. She hadn't taken on a project with questionable components for quite a while, the figures looked a little low compared with the feeling of panic she'd been trying to avoid for the past several hours.

She started her search with the original contact point three days earlier. There was an intermediary, Lee Wei Hau, an associate professor at Stanford who'd worked with McKay designing basic user interfaces, and he had forwarded the message from a party needing an extraction. It didn't seem odd at the time. Universities were the first places people looked for an extraction, and Lee Wei had sent her clients before.

In her mind's eye, a single blinking dot appeared with Lee Wei's name underneath it, hung there for a moment, then populated outward in a series of possible contacts, all linked by pale blue lines. McKay examined each in turn, points of commonality, people and events she shared with Lee Wei. A hunch said the contact wasn't random, that someone had chosen to contact her through Lee Wei and knew he would pass the job on to her. There were maybe half a dozen Extractionists in the world that operated on her level; they all knew each other, so the close contacts crossed and recrossed. Ace, Turlow, Annie, Misha, they were all on speaking terms. Someone should have given her a heads-up. Nothing jumped out right away, so she began to expand the search. The Overlay finally picked up on one name: Renier Wayze. She slid the first data spiderweb aside and started another with this second name. The data was thinner, fewer links to follow, and the Overlay bogged down trying to pull data from the limited Swim access in the cheap seats, but she found one point of commonality. Renier attended a lecture series Lee Wei had given on adaptive customization just over a year earlier. Not a rock-solid link. She wished she had Brighton's name on that guest list, but Renier was a start. McKay's search revealed Renier had been jump-wired, had his muscles and nervous system 'mite-enhanced in the military, five years before professional athletes made that particular upgrade trendy. *And just which of Brighton's merry band of agents might have been wired for jump?* Renier, it seemed, had also had several biologic replacements. There was no photo available, but having an eye regrown was just too much of a coincidence. It had to be Rice under another name. *Or maybe Rice is the fake name and this one's real. Either way, this is my first lead-in to more information on Vector7.*

"Excuse me, ma'am." The soft voice broke her concentration. It shouldn't have, but she deliberately pitched it to get her attention.

The Overlay faded into the background, and the flight attendant's face came into focus. "There's a call for you in the forward lounge, Miss McKay."

"What?"

She smiled tolerantly. "A call, for you, Miss McKay. In the forward lounge."

McKay extricated herself from the seat and followed as the Overlay expanded, sidelining the investigation to connect with the jet's communications system. Anyone looking to contact her could have done so straight through the Overlay, even in the air. There was no reason to use the plane's array.

"Booth number three, Miss McKay." She smiled the serene smile you saw in all the adverts. "Please push the call button if you need assistance."

"Yes, of course. Thank you." She slid sideways into the three-by-three sound-resistant booth, one of four in the forward lounge, and flipped the switch that brought the monitor to life. The airline communications array routed the call to her; the Overlay automatically focused on intercepting the data swimming to the monitor while McKay focused her attention on the caller.

"Hi, Eliza." The monitor's aqua blue background framed Rose's face and made her look washed out, like she hadn't slept.

"Um." The use of her first name threw her a bit. "Rose?" She was the last person—well, maybe next to last—she expected a call from. *Over an open comm array to boot? Something's way off base.*

"Yeah. Boss asked me to contact you, make sure there were no aftershocks. I didn't think you'd get gone so fast." She flashed those even, white teeth.

"Guns and destruction really aren't my thing," McKay replied. "There didn't seem to be any advantage to sticking around, especially since your deadline expired." *And why are you calling me like this?* So far all of her dealings had been with Brighton directly. It felt like Rose was making an end run around her superior, which didn't seem right.

Rose looked distressed. "We're on our way out now. They weren't happy about how everything turned out. Look, our 'friend' jumped to the mainland. Boss is going to bring you back in." McKay could practically hear the finger quotes as she avoided saying Mike's name on an open line. She spoke in a rush, voice lowered, maybe afraid of being overheard.

"You do realize this is an open array," McKay said coldly.

She paused and the Overlay pinged a warning. The line was corrupted, feeding information back along the Swim as they talked. Could be Government of Singapore listening in, could be any number of bad actors trolling the airline's communications for sensitive information. Old-school identity thieves never went out of style. *Better cut this short.*

"Your boss knows where to find me."

"Yes, but I wanted to talk to you more about going xWire. You said I should give you a call, and I have to make a decision right now, today." The words came out in a rush. "The opportunity here in Singapore is for real, I won't need to stay on a wait list and I can get wired up before I head back home." She obviously wanted to keep McKay on the line, keep her talking. McKay recognized the urgency, the tone of a salesperson desperate to make a sale. Rose wasn't calling to ask questions, to walk through the decision. She was calling for reassurances. She wanted to hear it was a good plan, that she should take the shot.

But based on what she'd seen in Singapore, it wasn't a reassurance she could give. She didn't know the other programmer well enough, she didn't know if the brute-force tactics Rose employed were from inexperience or preference.

McKay suddenly had a very bad feeling.

"Turn it down. If you're still asking questions, then you haven't done enough work on the front end." If it was a ploy, Rose'd picked the right topic. *If she's really looking at going X in such a hurry though. . . .* She didn't want to think about the end result of a rush-job on xWire. Her conscience wouldn't allow her to cut the conversation short, just in case. McKay had known at least two people who had suffered the consequences of a bad upgrade, and they'd both known what they were doing. She didn't want Rose to be the third.

McKay asked the Overlay to keep an eye on any incoming trouble and settled into the seat. "Look, pass it up. When you're stateside, come to my office and I'll go through the specifics with you."

"I can't pass it up," Rose said, urgency still in her voice. "I'm on the near-edge of obsolete as it is. I can't keep up. I couldn't get our friend written out, they brought you in to fix it. Do you know what that means for me? I need to get to the next level or I'm going to be off the team." Overtones of panic crept in.

Oh boy. That's a warning sign right there. There was an ever-growing demand for people with fully invasive systems like her xWire, or more commonly the military-grade S3's, but the risk of psychological breaks was high enough that an employer couldn't fire you for refusing an upgrade. If she was getting pressure from Brighton, from her team, that was another part of the problem. The snippets of conversation she'd heard suggested that Brighton, at least, might be an ally to Rose, but that might not be enough.

"Okay." She paused to think carefully about what she said next. "Look, first of all, why would they give you trouble over one failed extraction? That's a specialty task and whatever your guy did to his persona pretty much made hash of the whole thing from the get-go." She had to tread carefully. If Rose had deliberately botched the extraction, there was some kind of internal politicking going on. If she really had just made a mistake, or gotten in deeper than she could handle, grabbing more powerful hardware wouldn't be the quick fix she thought it would be. What she needed was more and better training, not faster hardware. But teaching was harder to assign a dollar value to, harder to track as a "win."

"It's just standard work stuff. We disguise the persona so it's harder to track the live person down if someone gets upset. I've done probably half a dozen of those already so this was. . . . Well, it looks like a pretty big screwup. It was weird, though, he wouldn't *let* me write him out. That makes it look even worse, like he doesn't trust me to do my job anymore."

"He's normally your team lead, I take it?" Still no names. The Overlay was starting to get twitchy as something started plucking around the edges of their conversation. Everything Rose related lined up with what she'd gotten from Brighton already, but that didn't prove she hadn't botched the outwrite on purpose.

"Most of the time. We've had to step up the past couple of weeks to cover for him. Things are a little uneven if he's not around to keep everyone on target."

"Can I ask why you didn't just dump the persona when the second try failed? It's not going to kill him, you're only losing the copy, it happens all the time." *Tread carefully. Nobody wants to talk about their mistakes, missy, not even you.*

"It's a big antitrust investigation. We've been on it for months, and our friend thought he was finally getting somewhere. We think, well, Boss thinks our friend's got the answer that will close the case."

Okay, so it's important, the chew-on-your-soul kind of important. Rose's motivations were a little more clear, a little less suspicious now. *Big important case, chain of command coming unraveled, job possibly on the line, all valid reasons to think about an upgrade.* xWire was "experimental," highly tailored to the individual, and dangerous. It could trigger any number of mental illnesses if it wasn't done with care and forethought. Engineers who had failed to make the transition ended up spending months, and in one case years, at St. Dyna's while they underwent therapy to recover.

"So why are you looking to jump to X instead of something like an S3? You're part of a government group. They can get you access to the military-grade hardware and the design work there is rock solid. You could be back up and running in a matter of days. Most programmers top out at S3. You'd have top-of-the-line hardware and be in good company. There's a community there you could tap into that might help you out."

She continued carefully. The Overlay snarled for her attention. Whatever had been pecking at their communications had gotten aggressive. McKay gave the Overlay another set of antiviral codes to work with, something to keep the attack at bay for a few minutes. It was big, whatever it was, she could feel it now, trying to thrash its way into the trickle of communication, causing the feed to stutter.

"I've done the math. X is where I have to be, it's where I *need* to be."

Ooooooh. She recognized that flat, belligerent tone. She didn't need the Overlay to tell her what Rose was thinking. She still wasn't taking the advice, still was simply seeking validation.

McKay's conscience wouldn't let her give it to Rose, not with all the potential downsides.

"All right, well, if you still want some advice, can you at least send me your specs? I can give them the once-over. Did you get your psych checks handled already? If you've got any precursors, *any at all*, you've got to design around them or you might not come out the other side. We're talking psychotic breaks, catatonia, any number of—" McKay spoke quickly, trying to convince her before the Overlay needed to cut the communication. *You're going too fast to make a good argument. This needs a face-to-face.*

"I'm good, really I am. I hired an expert to handle all the design work. I'm ready to go." Rose's gaze shifted at the end of the sentence, breaking eye contact.

"Why don't I take a look. . . ."

"I don't want the information getting out there. Boss doesn't need to know. You understand, right?" She clenched and unclenched her fists, then reestablished eye contact. Nervous wasn't the right word to describe her body language. "Driven" fit better.

The Overlay warned her again: whatever was trying to hack in through the comm array was tied directly to Rose's communication. She was holding the path open. McKay had to get off or risk the hack getting through.

"Rose, I have to go. Turn it down. Trust me on this, okay?" McKay snapped the switch and had the Overlay scramble the signal for good measure. It obliged, then gave her the source of the call.

It had come from her abandoned room at the hotel.

SEVEN

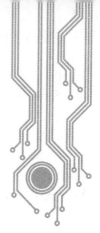

WHEN THE CAB pulled up outside the postage stamp–size house, Eliza McKay was torn between being glad to be home and sorry to be back to the normalcy of her everyday existence. Business might take her to the far side of the planet, but she always felt rooted here, to a very small patch of engineered grass and concrete and the family and friends connected to it.

She tipped the driver well enough to be sure the karma clerks would smile and the cab pulled silently away, leaving her gazing at the house, breath hanging in the morning air. The place had been her grandmother's for nearly a century. Technically, it still belonged to the family trust, but McKay had been living there for the past few years. It needed a caretaker and she'd needed a place to live that didn't require a background check. The paint was robin's-egg blue today, white trim, the perpetually neat artificial nanograss that had been the product of her first miteware patent, and beds of genuine native plants that seemed to thrive on chronic neglect. The roof sat at a somewhat jaunty angle due to a decades-old renovation gone awry. From the outside, it looked just as it did the day her grandmother passed away in the front bedroom.

But that was on the outside. She spun up the Overlay, and the house lights flickered on. It was a dense presence in the Swim, like a gravity well in the sparsely populated fabric of the neighborhood.

This part of the peninsula had always been light on connectivity, no major hubs, nodes, places of business, nothing to cross-connect or interfere.

The house itself was smarter than some of the people she knew. She had done all the work herself, cutting into the drywall and crawling under the building with the spiders and the feral cat Grandma'd named Schrödinger due to its seeming ability to walk through walls whenever someone tried to corner it. The spiders succumbed to a deadly mix of shoe-mashing and insecticide, and she was pretty sure the next generation hadn't forgiven her. She'd found a half-inch long wolf spider in her sock drawer when she'd packed for the flight to Singapore, just waiting for her to make a mistake.

When she slipped into the Overlay to look at the house, much like she had for the Brittle Moon nearly two days earlier, the view was orderly, patterned, nodes neatly arranged, a design she'd had in her head since she'd first started dreaming about miteware.

The doors unlocked as she approached. The house recognized her from the Overlay's caress. *Don't open the door. I'm not so damn lazy I can't open my own front door.* The central heat kicked on, keeping the living room at a reasonable temperature despite the cold and fog of a Peninsula morning. Once inside, she should have felt that unoccupied quiet that comes after a few days away. She stopped just inside the front door and propped it open with her bag.

A sort of sixth sense comes with living in a space for a while. The mind memorizes the little things and notices when they are out of place, even if you can't remember if the couch pillows were on the right or the left side when you left, or if it was possible the heater blew the magazine on the table open when it came on. It triggered that *look and see* impulse in the back of the brain.

Spike's icon appeared in the Overlay and unfolded into its projected human form. "Aah." It stretched its arms wider than any real-live human could. "Home sweet home! Nothing like it, really."

McKay's attention was still on the wrongness in the room. "You don't actually live here, you know."

The simulacrum was offended. "True, but neither does the dude hiding in your bedroom."

"Dude? Is it Dash?" McKay held her breath a long second, fearing it might be someone else. The Overlay connected to the house sensors and fed her information on the past few days. *There it is.* The signature string she was looking for. She breathed a sigh of relief. Her baby brother must have forgotten the key again.

"Ayup." Spike affected a drawl of unknown origin and leaned nonchalantly against the wall. "When you're done rousting the riff-raff, I've got some new data for you on that persona and his merry band of chasers."

There were no cameras inside the house, so she'd have to check on Dash in person. "Can you give me a data-flash? Faster that way." McKay slipped the bag inside the door and closed it. Six very soft steps should have been seven, but she had to sidestep the creaky floorboard. The bedroom door was open just more than the width of her head, so she peered in without touching it.

He sprawled face down, asleep or unconscious, on the bed. Blond hair tousled the way that came only from an expensive salon or a night of booze, drugs, and loud music. Since he'd chosen to crash at her place, instead of the designer couches of any of his friends, McKay put her money on the salon.

She skated the six steps away from the door and swung around the corner to the house's minuscule kitchen. She couldn't help indulging in a little sibling payback. She rifled through the cabinets and found her ancient, noisy blender. She cracked both trays of ice into it as loudly as possible.

McKay gave it a five-count, but not a sound from the bedroom. She dropped in a cup of water, popped on the lid and hit the highest speed.

"SHIT!"

Aaaaaah, that's what I was looking for. Judging by the noise, he'd caromed off the doorframe, then the wall, trying to escape the inevitable. Spike doubled over in a paroxysm of laughter, taking its cue from McKay's frame of mind, then spun itself back into its icon, which wiggled and hiccupped and vanished.

"Eliza, you JERK!" Dash stomped into the kitchen with a force that made the creaky floorboard squeal in protest.

"MORNING!" she shouted above the blender's grinding roar and ducked back into the fridge for a half-empty carton of orange juice. When she emerged, she found herself pinned by the sort of gaze that was probably the reason Dash stayed single.

It's far less funny if he decides to actually *kill you.* Even McKay, who'd been the target of that gaze since elementary school, questioned the wisdom of threatening a slushy wake up call. Only briefly.

"Orange or cranberry?"

"Slushies on a morning this cold?" His voice, acid. "You're not fooling anyone, you know." He swiped the carton from her hand, shook it to gauge how full it was, and upended it over the blender. Since he had to reach across McKay and over the open fridge door, his aim was less than perfect.

"Nice." She slid her feet out of the way just in time to avoid the splash, then ducked to fish the eggs and bacon from the fridge. A quick jab in the abs got him out of the way so she could close the door. "Mop that up, willya? The ants invade if I leave anything out."

"Whatever. Welcome back, by the way." He slid around her to the pantry. "Got any protein powder that hasn't congealed yet? Might as well use up the ice."

"Eye level, far left. The label fell off, so it's just the canister." McKay chucked the bacon into the microwave and punched up enough time to make it nice and crispy. "Dare I ask what you're doing here?"

Dash Merryweather McKay was the youngest of the McKay kids. As a result, he grew up surrounded by technology of the sort most MIT grad students dreamed of getting the grant money for. Combine that with the "fashion icon gene," and the violent clash of an engineering degree and deep-seated love of design landed him a job with Robester and Ping, makers of the most stylish tech out there. Their 'mites even came in designer colors.

"Are you going to burn the eggs too, or are they just an offering for the ants?" he asked.

"Burn 'em. There's only enough room in the kitchen for one. I'll come back and chuck them in the wave-thingy when you're done." McKay headed back down the hall to reclaim the bedroom.

"Nah, I'll get the eggs. The least I can do after freaking you out." The gas stove, a relic like the rest of the house, lit under the ignitor's clicking protest.

"You did not freak me out," McKay called back firmly.

"Well, I didn't think you'd mind my crashing here. There's the big RnP event in the City this week, and I had to get out of tech-central for a day."

"Hey, I resemble that remark," she called back. The Overlay meshed with the house systems, and she felt it flowing around her, each wire, each pool of data.

"No, you don't," he quipped. "Your shirts have buttons." More noises from the kitchen. "And I've picked up a new admirer. Since you've pretty much wiped this place off the map, it seemed simpler to hop the BART and spend some quality time with my favorite sibling."

McKay shook her head. She and Dash got along great for forty-eight hours at a shot, but longer than that and trouble started.

"So where'd you just get back from?"

McKay rummaged in her drawers for fresh clothes and picked a shirt *without* buttons and with the logo of one of Dash's competitors to boot.

"Singapore. Thing with a client."

"Sweet! Good client, bad client? Bring me anything?"

"Interesting client. In the worst sense of the word. And no, you can buy tourist crap on your own time." She walked back down the hallway to the living room. There once was a dining room, but the living room swallowed it up, much the same way her lab had swallowed the garage downstairs. She didn't eat-in much.

"Hah!" He waltzed out, smoothie in hand. "Well, at least they weren't shooting at you this time." Dash held up the glass. "I left you some." What was once the unnatural orange of processed juice had turned the muddy color of street gutters after a summer storm. *Not at all appetizing.* McKay was pretty sure that nothing in her cupboards was that precise shade of brown.

"Pass, thanks." The Overlay pinged softly. A car had pulled up out front. The house informed her it was a rental, but the corporation's name was under was a shell—no assets, no business, no names.

"Shit," she muttered. Outside, the house probably still looked deserted, shutters closed, lights out, not even footprints on the grass. She set the plate down and opened up the links. To the casual observer, the house's pattern resembled one of those knotty places where the new and legacy communication systems came together, fought for supremacy, and moved on. All around the neighborhood, houses tapped into the city lines, and knots appeared where the city had consolidated or replaced its own trunk lines with service from lowest-bidder contractors. The house showed her a window zipping down and a flash going off inside the car. *Pictures. That won't do at all.*

The Overlay spun a thought out along the city line, a snippet of code that found the camera's connection to the Swim and chewed its way back up, consuming any image that resembled the cottage until the window zipped back up and the car moved on. The little bit of code returned, disgorged the images, and expired without a whimper.

"Hey, doofus!"

She blinked. Dash was watching her through the kitchen doorway.

"Try not to do that in the kitchen. You're going to set yourself on fire."

McKay tried to engage the Overlay only when alone or on business, but with family it was easy to forget. Dash, in particular, was merciless.

"Oh, and you're drooling there." Dash plunged a straw into the blender cup and took it with him into the living room.

"Thanks for that." She scooped her breakfast into a stale tortilla and added Diablo sauce. After fifteen hours in coach, she needed the extra kick, especially since a nap was not at all likely with Dash in her space.

"There was a photographer outside taking pictures of the house." She stuck her head around the door to find Dash already on his cell phone to the office. "I don't think he's looking to catch *me* in my skivvies, so I'm going to assume he's one of yours." There was no evidence that the guy was tied to Brighton and her group, and Dash would kill her if he even suspected she had taken a government gig. The fallout when InfoComm, her old bosses, had burned her and pulled her licenses affected the whole family to some degree or another, from loss of assets to out-and-out search and seizure.

"Like anyone would want a picture of *you* in your skivvies. Do you know what rag they work for?"

"No clue. I just wiped the data. I have to log some stuff in downstairs. I'll be right back." Dash waved and turned away.

From the bedroom she retrieved the headset case and Spike took that opportunity to flash her. A five-second data whiteout straight into her visual cortex, flickering images her mind would absorb unconsciously. *Oh, brilliant timing, Spike.* She took a deep breath and rode it out.

After twenty minutes or so, she could access the information from her own memory, but she'd be blind for the count of ten to both the Overlay and her normal vision since the optic nerve rebelled at the intrusion. She put her hand against the wall and counted the seven steps to the top of the stairs. When she'd first put her miteware in, glitches were not uncommon as the 'mites got used to interfacing parts of her brain with the Overlay. She took such things in stride, for the most part, but navigating the stairs while blind was still not easy.

"One flash, just like you said," Spike said innocuously. McKay counted out the last few seconds of the whiteout, and when her vision reasserted itself, she faced Spike's digital visage less than a foot away. She jumped.

"Jesus, Spike, could you lay off?"

"Sorry. Would you like the highlights?"

"Yes. Please."

"Um, yes, right." Spike hemmed and hawed a second, then spun itself back into its icon. "Your little super-secret spy group is called Vector7, led by Michael Hieronymus Miyamoto, but I'll bet you that's an alias because who the hell would use 'Hieronymus' as an actual name. Currently has five additional task members with really cool alias names like Ianto and Bluebird, subset of the Abuses of New Technologies office, charged with 'new technology violations'— ooh, I like the sound of that!"

"Yeah, maybe we can skip the rest of the highlights." McKay snagged the headset case off the dresser and turned to go back downstairs. "Why Vector7?"

"ANT is broken up into seven different groups, each focusing on a different vector of tech vulnerability, hence vectors one, two, three, and on up to Brighton's Vector7. You've got your good old standbys like blockchain, crypto, and antiviral but some of the groups get pretty sophisticated. Vector7 is tasked with looking into Swim-slash-human interaction and persona technologies."

The fact that Brighton and company were legit couldn't mean anything good, not for McKay, anyway. *God, I'm getting more paranoid than usual today. Like they'd need to set me up if they really wanted something. Back up the system, then a nap, in that order, before I start prying up the floorboards looking for bugs.*

"Eliza, these guys are too close to USIC for this to be a coincidence, don't you think?" Spike's usually flippant tone was colored with concern.

"I'm hoping that's going to work to our benefit. Maybe I can convince Brighton to help me get my licenses back, if Vector7 is in a position to do that. I can't exactly pass that up." McKay stepped lightly: the stairs to the lower level of the house were tall and steep, one wrong step and she'd end up sliding bumpily to the bottom.

"And if she can't?" Spike's image resolved on the lower stairs, looking up. McKay passed through it without slowing down.

"All I need is a piece to get the ball rolling. If I can make this go for Brighton's group, get their boss Miyamoto to put in a good word with the right guy, we can get the reinstatement process started."

"Are you sure you want to go there?"

McKay turned the corner at the foot of the stairs and nudged the door to the lab open with a foot. "Abso-fucking-lutely."

EIGHT

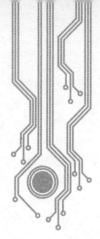

McKay woke up when the clouds in her dream winked out. Not the bolt-upright, heart-in-your-throat standard horrific dream wake up: she simply opened her eyes and was instantly aware, as if she had been awake for hours. The Overlay was not spun up, but she felt it, a tiny trickle of signal that evaporated as soon as she turned her attention to it, so faint that she figured it must have been left over from the dream. Falling asleep while linked up to the Swim was something she tried to avoid. At best it made for strange dreams and uneasy sleep, at worst she could accidentally crash the whole house.

She sat up in the chair and ran her hands through her hair, fingering the tiny metal connectors embedded in the scalp. Her mouth was dry, probably more from the central heat than from the dream, and something was blocking her vision. She blinked at the yellow haze dancing in front of her eyes, then brushed it away with a crumpling sound. Dash had found her napping in the lab and stuck a yellow sticky note to her forehead with one word in his blocky script: "DROOLING!"

He must have gone back to his conference. She hadn't *meant* to nap in the lab, but the comfortable chair needed a warning label, and she didn't think to set an alarm when she sat down to sync the Overlay with the house computer.

The stairwell was by far the coldest area of the house. Without heat, it stayed ten degrees below the outside temperature on a good day, so McKay attributed the hackles rising on the back of her neck to the chill rather than anything out of place. The Overlay said there was a message from Dash, but she put that off for the moment.

Maybe the dream and the chaos in her mind explained why she was taken completely by surprise.

The man who came out of the hallway pinned her up against the refrigerator with a shove, and McKay found herself jammed face-first against her own appliance, one arm twisted up behind her back. The assailant hadn't brushed his teeth either.

"Ow," was all she managed to get out. The Overlay, shocked into action, began to record and analyze the situation. None of the solutions looked promising as long as the other guy had all the leverage.

"Got her, Rey!" the man holding her ground out from between clenched teeth.

Rey? That meant there was at least one more in her house. *IN. MY. HOUSE.*

Surprise attacks relied on those few seconds of shock that locked up an average person's response. Under those circumstances, McKay was no different than the man in the street, and she knew it. Her internal computers didn't extend to sped-up reflexes; she had never gone in for the quasi-mythical double-cortex that let you load previously unknown martial arts in a flash. The pressure on her arm tightened, and she spun the Overlay back into quiet, keeping only the tiniest link open to the house and asking it to notify police services about the break-in. The guy shifted his weight. McKay's knee buckled as her right shoulder joint protested and threatened to pop.

"Ow! What the hell do you want?"

"Eliza Nurey Wynona McKay . . . ? Yeh poor thing! Hell of a set of names your ma stuck ya with."

With her head crammed up against the fridge, McKay couldn't see who was talking. Rey, whomever she was, stood in the doorway between the living room and the kitchen just behind the man holding her pinned.

"McKay's good enough for you." Her mind raced, searching for something, anything to explain why she was held hostage in her own kitchen. The Overlay was designed to guess what she wanted, and it got it right this time, opening the thin connection to the house just a little bit wider, allowing her to connect with the security system. There were no cameras or sensors inside the house, but the outside was supposed to be covered in all directions. How had they gotten in without the system picking up on it?

"Good enough for you," this time the guy holding her added his two cents. "Damn, you're fulla yourself, ain'tcha? Unimaginative too, I bet." The voice was unremarkable except for the kind of accent that came from learning English through some virtual university's self help program. The house told her police were on the way and that her Overlay's internal dictation recorder was activated.

"Everybody's a critic," McKay responded tightly. "I'm much more imaginative when not jammed up against an appliance." Pain wasn't something she appreciated under any circumstances, and the thug with a grip on her seemed uninterested in her comfort level. She closed her eyes briefly and let out a breath, feeling the pain and pressure surge and recede. *Just breathe and wait for an opening.* The little, panicked voice in her head faded into the background.

"Too bad for you, then." Her assailant chuckled.

"Imagination is not required, Ms. McKay, only compliance." McKay heard footfalls as the voice explored the house. A warning rippled up through the house connection. Rey, or one of her accomplices, was trying to link into her systems. *Someone with a lot of horsepower and not much finesse.* Multiple attempts from within the Swim, over and over, had tied up the house security systems while the live bodies walked in through the front door. It was almost a real-life version of a denial of service attack. *The house was so busy protecting against a hack from the Swim, it didn't notice these guys walking in the front door.*

"Mind telling me what I did to piss you off?"

"We are looking to acquire some information from you, Ms.

McKay, and we have a very short amount of time to do it." Rey's voice returned from the end of the hallway and drew closer. "Your house system notified the police, so we are down to ten minutes before they arrive."

"I think you've got the wrong person." The guy holding her relaxed the pressure somewhat, and her right arm tingled as the blood returned.

"I think not, Ms. McKay." The footfalls came into the kitchen and paused on her off side, where she couldn't see the speaker. The voice was so near her ear, she could feel the woman's breath. She repressed a shudder.

"Ina Brighton is coming here to have you find Mike Miyamoto's rogue persona. We are very interested in finding it first."

A cold touch—a very light, very cold touch—on her ear made McKay jump, and the thug leaned into her tighter.

"What're you . . . ?" More cold on the back of her scalp and the *tic tic tic* rain-stick sound of contact pins sliding home. "What! *Hey!* NO!" McKay bucked and twisted, but she was pinned. The thug threw an elbow against the side of her head to keep her still. The Overlay spun up in response to the unexpected input, leaping at the chance to reconnect with the headset, then recoiling as it made contact with an unexpected system. *NO. NO. NO.* Never had McKay imagined something *like this*. The Overlay was firewalled and secured against all manner of virtual threats, but direct input was something else entirely. She felt a sick twisting in her gut. *They can access everything.*

Not if I can help it. McKay closed her eyes and retreated into her own head to block everything else out and write code on the fly, adapting the existing security protocols to the new situation. When something came in too fast she blocked it manually, recording the commands and setting them up on a loop to block attacks at the same nodes again and again. The pain in her shoulder scrabbled at the edges of her mind, and she dove in deeper, abandoning the physical to try and save the virtual. She didn't dare open up a link to the House to try and give herself a boost. If she failed, they could waltz right through her head and into her main computer. She stemmed the tide of panic that threatened to swamp her concentration. *None of that.*

"Ms. McKay, there is no point in resisting." But the voice was slower, slurred. Rey's attention was divided between hacking McKay and keeping tabs on the real world. McKay felt the pauses and stuttering as she spoke. *All power, no finesse.* Whoever this gal was, she was outgunned, and she didn't even know it yet. McKay's confidence rushed back. If "Rey" was having trouble even speaking, then there was a good chance she was having trouble focusing on her own security. McKay might be able to incapacitate the hacker—but she wasn't sure what to do about the muscle. *Let the cops worry about that bit when they get here.*

She stripped away the metaphor and worked directly with the underlying code. McKay split her attention again and again, little slivers of her mind each running their own sequences of denial and counterattack.

One small piece of her attention changed the connection parameters on the fly, something like changing the combination on a gym locker while someone else is trying to open it. *Awkward.* Rey opened up a grid and launched an all-out, old-school, brute-force attack. McKay fought the urge to laugh.

Her own counterassault was not doing so hot either, but then it was just a diversion. She opened the tiniest link to the main hub for the neighborhood instead. Rey was using far too much horsepower to be self-contained. She had to be pulling from an outside system, much the same way McKay used her headset for a boost. She located the connection, a broad, venomous rope of code streaking along the bottom of the Swim, tied into the waste management maintenance communications, of all things. She integrated her own code string, first into the maintenance string, then from there into the toxic code.

In her mind the data resolved, showing a breakdown of Rey's

hardware like a giant engine spinning its wheels. Whoever wired the gal's head had done it cheap and dirty. Tons of processor power, that was certain, but not properly interfaced with the gray matter. There must be little more than a thumb-size processor embedded in the back of the woman's skull. They likely even excised some of the brain to make the processor fit. It had just enough memory to keep it from crashing but the rest was all someplace else. Rey was just a tool, a remote terminal for someone smarter.

Christ, she's one step up from a dumb terminal. Someone's running all this by remote.

McKay conscripted one of the few unused memory chips in Rey's system and packed it tight with her own code, nothing fancy, nothing that would draw too much attention, something that might give her a few more clues to work with.

The hot shock of her shoulder popping out of joint caused her to slip and drop to her knees. She snapped back to herself abruptly, her own lines of code stuttering and failing. For an instant she scrambled to keep the Overlay online, killing every stray process she could find. Rey's system crashed hard in response. *Whoops! Didn't mean to take you down with me, but I'll take what I can get.*

"Rey, cops!"

The painful snapping as Rey yanked the contacts out of the back of McKay's skull was nothing beside the grinding ache in her shoulder. The foot in the ribs that followed caused her to lose her concentration completely.

"We want to know where Miyamoto's persona is hiding, Ms. McKay," Rey hissed in her ear, "and we will be back to ask again."

McKay stayed curled up on the floor as they left, running panicked fingertips over the damaged nodes on the back of her head. The Overlay spun code across her vision, reassurances that the shoulder was reparable, recommendations for treatment, information on her heart rate, brain wave patterns. McKay wasn't listening. She wanted nothing more than to scrub her brain with a wire brush, to go through and delete every little bit of programming her assailant had brushed up against. It was a nonsensical idea, a product of the adrenaline and the fear and the pain trying to convince her brain she needed to crawl into a hole and hide.

The little snippet of code she planted would kick in as soon as Rey rebooted. It wasn't terribly complex, more like a keystroke recorder to keep track of every command from outside into Rey's system. It wasn't big enough to transmit information. What it would do was wait until McKay sent Spike to make contact. There was room to store perhaps the last twelve commands. With any luck she'd be able to get a bead on who Rey was talking to, where she was making her connections. If McKay was lucky, it might give her a direct lead on just who had hired her. The police wouldn't be able to act on it, but in her current state, McKay wasn't about to let Rey, whoever she was, walk away from a hacking attempt. Rey was going to have to pay.

NINE

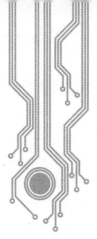

It took McKay just over two hours to deal with the police. Two hours and nine minutes she sat and ground her teeth at the pain of a separated shoulder while they insisted on testing her for substance abuse, and the shock of the assault played over and over in her head. She shouldn't have been surprised. Her reflection in the mirror over the fireplace looked out at her, pale faced, glassy-eyed. S1 Overlay technology was becoming commonplace, like cell phones and wearables had before, but most people considered anyone S2 or higher some special kind of wacko. As an xWire, law enforcement outside the center of Silicon Valley regarded her as one step shy of a total psychotic breakdown and took a certain amount of care to be sure she wasn't going to turn into a murderer on their watch. At the moment, she certainly looked the part. Things might have gone more smoothly if Dash had still been there, but he had left well before Rey and her thug had made their appearance. McKay was very careful not to mention Dash by name. The last thing she wanted to do was get him directly involved.

She got back to her feet and saw them out, then leaned heavily against the door once the bolts were shot. When she regained her breath, she made her way gingerly back down to the lab. Like most spec houses in the area, hers came with a sort of half basement. Her grandfather used it for decades as a workshop, a place to store wine, beer-brewing equipment, water skis, unused treadmills, fish tanks, whatever the detritus of discontinued hobbies and movement through life left behind.

As a grad student, McKay had rented the space from her grandmother, hauled all the memories out for the mother of all yard sales, and laid in hundreds of feet of fiber-optic cable. The cable eventually gave way to the more delicate threads of miteline that she had programmed to crisscross the yard under the nanograss and climb through the walls of the House. The process had been very similar to the way she'd had to program 'mites to climb through her own skull in order to install the Overlay. She doubted Grandma would recognize the space now, drywalled, whitewashed, tiled, and polished. Unlike the upstairs, the space was always seventy-two degrees and that night it seemed a tiny bolt hole, secure against a world that was getting a lot weirder. She wanted to lock the door and stay hidden away until the damage had been undone.

"Spike!" she said aloud. She felt just comfortable enough to spin the Overlay back up to relink to the House systems. The sprite unlimbered itself from its icon and stretched for effect.

"Finally woke up, did we?" Spike began, then paused, wide-eyed, as the House system updated it on recent events. "Eliza, what the hell is going on?"

McKay rummaged through the vacuum cupboard until she found her stash of painkillers and washed some down, with a shot of neurotransmitter precursor mix from the minifridge under the counter.

"We're going to find that out." McKay dropped into the armchair. Now that she was safe, closeted away, she needed to do something, focus on anything other than the ache of the shoulder and the empty gaps where the broken contact points in her skull had gone offline. Spike wandered around in her field of view, checking stats here and there.

"Don't you think you ought to see a doctor about that shoulder first? Maybe give Ibarra a call to talk about the fact that you've been assaulted, what, twice now in the space of two days? Or at least run that diagnostic program that came with your wiring?"

"Wiring's custom, Spike. Nothing came with it other than what I put in." McKay closed her eyes to focus on the Overlay. "Besides, the joint popped back in, there's not much else to do for it." She raised the arm a couple of inches, then changed her mind as the joint protested with a sharp spiderweb of pain. "As long as I don't get slammed into another refrigerator or something, it just needs rest and a lot of muscle relaxants. The 'mites can have it back up to snuff in a couple of days."

"And you got your medical degree by mail, or did you actually attend an online class?" McKay was pretty sure she hadn't programmed in Spike's acid tone.

"Fine, I'll call my brother tomorrow so HE can wag his finger at me and tell me it just needs rest and pills. Can we get moving on this? I need to get back in contact with Brighton to figure out what the hell is going on."

"That pack of special-ops kids from Singapore? You're actually going to follow up with them?"

"The same." She slid the headset case onto her lap with her good arm and popped the catches.

"So you have anything I can start with, or am I just supposed to read your mind?" Spike snapped. "Oh, wait, someone already tried that one."

"Yeah, and look what happened to her."

"And you. She came close to compromising your security here . . . here . . . and here. You're going to have to make some changes, and I'm serious about talking to Ibarra." Spike pulled a pen from its pocket and scribbled a few lines of code in the air. "Here, I found a pre-release patch for that antivirus software you're so fond of. It's unlikely a script-kiddie like your new 'friend' Rey will know to get around it."

McKay made a face. "Rey's not the problem. I got a look at her system specs. Someone else is running the programming by remote.

She's just a dumb-term with legs, a way to make a direct connection with my hardware, rather than trying to hack me through the House computer or the Swim."

"And you think this is tied to what you went to Singapore for?" Spike slid back into its icon as McKay settled the headset and winced as the contacts clicked into place. She would have to look into that later. The headset interface was designed to go on functioning even with ten percent of the hundred or so little pinprick contacts damaged. The 'mites that crawled around the inside of her skull would begin repairs, if they hadn't already. She made a note to add the upgrades to the firewall as soon as possible and the Overlay pinged acknowledgment. The real world faded into the background as she settled into the chair and the combination of painkillers and endorphins did their job.

"Something like this, using a human mind as proxy, it *would* be right up Christopher's alley, from what I understand. He's one of the first xWires out there." So far, Christopher was the only other serious player McKay was aware of. It made sense that he would try to get to Miyamoto first, if that agent had actually found a critical piece of evidence.

Spike, meanwhile, sorted through the rest of the data. "She was running a MAU 500, looks like, all off-the-shelf stuff with a warranty-voiding custom twist." Spike's specialty was information, ferreting it out, finding where it came from, where it lived, and what it did in its spare time. If he said so, it was so. "I got voice recordings, but no visuals. Maybe there's a print match we can do?"

McKay opened her eyes again. Someone else was pushing data through Rey, but no one would install a rig like that for just a single shakedown, that was just stupid. Maybe this chick tried to hack people for a living? Also just plain stupid. Most of the time you could get around a fortified computer system by drugging someone at a party and stealing their keycard. "Spike, are there any professions who use something like Rey's setup?" It made much more sense that she was doing double duty, she had a day job somewhere that required her particular hardware design.

"What, you think this gal's moonlighting?"

"Could be. There's not much call for a skull-size quad processor, so it's got to be a specialty item."

"Right. I'm on it." Spike's icon flashed and it jumped back into the ether. "Anything else you want me to pick up while I'm out? Vicodin? Quart of milk?"

"Funny."

"Someone's at your door." With that cryptic comment, Spike's icon faded out in a giggle of bubbles.

Door? McKay didn't have time to wonder. The House system said someone was waiting on the steps. She got to her feet reluctantly and padded upstairs. *Probably the cops again with another couple hundred questions.* She stopped at the coat closet and found a length of steel pipe left over from some improvement project. A friend had taught her how to use it, and the drills were still a part of her exercise regimen, when she followed it. She'd never used it outside the gym, never landed a blow other than accidentally, but the heft of the pipe made her feel marginally more confident, a little less of an easy target.

A peek at the outside image feed showed her the porch light was out again and at least one shadowy form waited patiently outside. She sighed. *At least they're not trying to break in the door.*

She turned the handle and let the night air in. "Well, come on in."

Ina Brighton stepped past her into the foyer, smelling refreshingly like she'd just stepped out of a shower rather than off an international flight. Rice was close behind her, smelling equally fresh, and outwardly none the worse for wear after Singapore. He didn't look nearly as perky as Brighton, though. He paused a moment, toe to toe with McKay, then dropped his mismatched gaze to the steel pipe in the programmer's hands. McKay was in no mood for mind games and banged the front door shut, ignoring the bulky man's smirk.

"Come have a seat." She guided them into the living room and gestured toward the couch, social norms taking over as if on autopilot. "I'll be with you in just a sec." Without waiting to see if they sat down, she padded the seven steps to the bedroom to change her shirt. The House brought up the lights.

The absence of pain and the aftereffects of stress made McKay want to sleep. She didn't want to stim up and negate the effects of the painkillers, but a quick change of clothes and a couple of very tentative one-armed stretches got the blood flowing and her brain back on some sort of track. She could hide in a hole later. Something was off about the timing here. Rose's call on the plane meant she'd still been in Singapore, so either they had left her there and hopped a flight around the same time she had, or they'd winged it back on a private flight. Either way, government only moved that fast when opportunity was afoot.

She did up the last button and left the shirttail hanging out of the pants. "Can I get you two something? Coffee or tea maybe? You must have come straight from the airport, am I right?" The House was so small she barely had to raise her voice to be heard in the living room. She instructed the House computer to start the coffee maker, heard the creaks in the floor as they moved about the living room in her absence.

"We're just fine, Ms. McKay. We're here to talk about a bit of a problem." Brighton's voice floated down the hallway.

Oh, crap. Did they know about the persona already? Had Rose already tracked it down in the meantime? She would have preferred to tell them about the potential problems herself. *Professionalism.* She hoped they weren't going to be pointing guns at her when she came back to the living room.

"Did you say something?" Brighton asked. She leaned a hip against the leather sofa and craned her neck to raise an eyebrow at McKay down the hallway.

"Nope. Just one sec while I grab some coffee. Are you sure I can't get either of you anything?" She kept the conversation as nonchalant as possible while the kitchen steamer spat black death into a mug.

"We're still on Singapore time, Ms. McKay."

"Cocktails, then?"

"Can we get on with this? Like you said, we just got off the plane."
An irritated edge sharpened Brighton's tone.

Time to see what a little pushback will do. "You know, I was thinking
about that. The last flight from Singapore landed at 11:25 p.m. yesterday, and the next won't arrive until a quarter to nine this morning,
presuming SFO lifts the fog warning by then." She was feeling reckless. She was prepared to wait until they showed their hand before
bringing up the persona. She took a big sip of the coffee. Horrible, it
always tasted horrible, but the heat and burn kicked her brain into
high gear.

Brighton perched on the edge of the couch, sizing up McKay
again. The Overlay picked up increased tension in her form; a constant chatter of signal was streaming into the redhead's S1 from
someone offsite. *Something's shifted. The urgency is different. She's
on her home turf, maybe?* Now she was being more critical in her
assessment, more careful in how she sized up the other woman.
Because of that, the Overlay was being a little more critical in the
information it showed her.

"You're right, we caught a C4 back after everything went to shit.
If you remember, Ms. McKay, you were hired to perform an extraction. That situation remains unchanged."

McKay winced inwardly at her arch tone. Technically, she was
right. She hadn't yet done an extraction per the terms of the contract,
but after the switch-out they'd pulled, she was sure a decent lawyer
could shoot that down. *If there were a decent lawyer who would give
you the time of day.* She sat down in the armchair across from them
and drummed her fingers on the armrest.

"I think the legal definition of an extraction includes a body, Ms.
Brighton." That got another glare from Rice. *Fine. Let him glare.*

"As I told you before, Ms. McKay, we have a body. What we need
now is to get the persona back. We'd like to expand your contract to
help with that as well. Rose seems to think you have a way to track
him down faster than we can." Brighton waggled a bright blue wafer

between her fingertips. Her appearance had changed in the time they'd been sitting in her living room. The hair was still red, though off toward strawberry blond, but the eyes were still that clear, natural green. There were 'mites for that. She'd clearly installed them in her hair. *Why not the eyes as well, or the fingernails?*

McKay took the wafer and turned it slowly in her fingers, considering. They were a match, really, Brighton and Rice. They didn't sit together like colleagues; they were more like partners, two pieces of the same puzzle. The Overlay noted how they worked in concert. While Brighton focused on him, Rice carefully monitored the rest of the room. Since both were wired, the stream of information that ran back and forth between the two of them was easy for McKay's computer to pick up and tuck away for future analysis. Encrypted connections could be broken, given enough time, but the constant stream of chatter was telling. They were on alert, keeping secrets on top of secrets. Brighton had worn HUD glasses in Singapore; McKay knew she was S1. Rice was something else. Boosted by the House computer, the Overlay could now pick up on the military-grade miteline in the man's body. Wired for "jump", Rice's natural reflexes had been artificially enhanced at some point in his career. There must have been a signal jammer of some kind in place when they'd first met in Singapore, because now the signature was unmistakable.

Jump was a class unto itself. It enhanced: sped up nerve signal strength, enabled the musculature to exceed its usual tolerances, steadied the hand for truer aim, any number of tricks that took advantage of the body's natural functions. Beyond that, you were looking at bionics, total replacement of limbs, but Rice did not seem to have gone down that road just yet.

Just give them the go-away price and be done with it.

"There's a problem with the persona," McKay said flatly. She made her decision even as she opened her mouth to say the words. Brighton frowned, and she briefly wished she could take them back.

"Mike was undercover, right? You said you all add changes to your personas for undercover work, high-level stuff. This was some-thing more involved. The changes I was seeing went all the way down." McKay held up her hands as Rice stood up, menacingly. "Now, wait a minute. Am I right or not?"

Rice looked from McKay to Brighton, then back again. "Boss, that's not in the brief you gave her."

Brighton nodded slowly and kept her eyes on McKay. "Yes, but we didn't hire her because she's an idiot. Sit down, Rice, or go keep an eye on the front door if you must, but don't interrupt."

Rice swallowed so hard his Adam's apple bobbled. Any sort of jump made people edgy. It was a well-known problem. McKay made a note to finish researching the guy in depth. If Rice was Brighton's second, she would have to deal with him, probably regularly. McKay was fine with that, but she'd have to be careful. The big man shivered, a classic gesture to burn off the effects of a jump reaction and took up a position between the couch and the foyer, leaning against the wall with his arms across his chest.

"Right." McKay looked from one to the other. Brighton looked vaguely amused, probably waiting for McKay to tell her something else she already knew. "You know this already, don't you? You knew I'd have to strip the false elements to make the transfer."

"I would be surprised if you hadn't." She uncrossed her legs and stood up in one smooth motion, hands behind her back. "Rose also suggested you might have tagged the persona when you did the re-write, some way to track it down and identify it, no?"

Dammit. "I'm starting to feel superfluous."

Brighton smiled, a genuine smile, and McKay had the impres-sion it was entirely for her benefit. "It's my job to stay on top of such things, Ms. McKay."

"Even with the tag, we're talking a needle in a haystack here. We're so far outside standard territory they haven't even put a dragon on the map as a warning."

Brighton held up another wafer, an orange one. "Look, McKay, we need this done. If money alone isn't the issue, then I'm sure we can come up with something to make it worth your time and trouble. Everything you need should be here. Mike's investigation centered around one of the big law offices in the City. Christopher is one of their biggest clients, not just through Bellicode, but they handle his personal affairs as well. They even hold an office space for him to work out of when he's in the City." She pointed to the blue wafer between McKay's fingertips. "But that's all you get until you sign up officially. New terms, new contract."

McKay held the blue wafer up and eyed it doubtfully. *Wonder if they're color coded.* McKay found herself wishing she could hack Brighton's brain. *What is she up to?*

"Who else is involved?" she asked finally. Brighton started and looked meaningfully at Rice.

"How do you mean?"

"An EM pulse in the center of Chinatown, someone sends the cops to bust in the door on the first extraction. This evening a couple of strongarm types broke into my House and tried to hack into my head." McKay tapped the side of her skull for emphasis.

Brighton iced over. "What did you tell them?"

"Nothing relevant. What I want to know is, can I expect more of that kind of thing? Because if I have to stare down my own mortality, then the price is going to have to be quite a bit higher." She recklessly jammed the blue wafer into her skull drive and affixed her digital signature. "I want all my 'mite licenses reinstated." The wafer ejected into her hand, and she held it out to the redheaded Agent.

It was Brighton's turn to hesitate. She cast a glance over her shoulder at Rice, who was quite deliberately looking the other way.

"I don't know if we can do that. That's out of our jurisdiction."

"That's crap. I know what Vector7 is allowed to do and not do. You didn't even have to bend the rules to bring me in on this job in the first place: working in the grey areas is right in your damn charter. If you want me to risk getting myself killed for this, it's going to have to be a fair exchange." That brief chance to see Saiid's engineering, the infectious delight at getting to design something new on a nanotechnological scale, had reminded her of what she'd lost. It stung.

"Do you *remember* why you were banned in the first place, Ms. McKay? I have read your file. I know exactly why they threw you under the bus." There was an edge of contempt there.

It might be deserved: McKay had seen the reports that had been filed after the Ulatek lab got eaten, but she wasn't about to stop pushing. She could do better.

"Then you know *less* than half the story. I want my license reinstated. Put me on probation, move a minder into my guest bedroom, whatever you need to do to make yourselves feel better about it, but find a way to get my rights back." McKay pushed back. There was a good risk Brighton'd simply tell her to go to hell and go find someone else to do the job. A quick glance told her that Rice was watching intently, but the man's face remained impassive. The encrypted chatter between Brighton and Rice intensified: they were having some kind of argument that she wasn't privy to. This was Brighton's call. The big, silent guy wasn't about to step in overtly, but he was certainly going to add his two cents to the debate, out of earshot. McKay counted a good twenty seconds before Brighton gave up the orange wafer in exchange.

"Okay. *After* Mike's been safely extracted. What you're asking for isn't as simple as signing a few forms. It's going to take some time."

Liar. With the least flicker, her eyes avoided McKay's at the essential instant, and the Overlay warned her in big red letters. Whether or not she knew it consciously, some part of Brighton knew she might not be able fulfill that end of the bargain. Still, if she could get McKay even one step closer to that goal, it would be worth the risk she'd be taking.

"Fine, I'll get your rogue persona back. Next question, is the body local? In Singapore, I was able to patch him back together, strip off all the junk you added on. I'm going to have to write him back into his own body on this go-round." McKay sat back and asked the

Overlay to start sorting the information Brighton had handed over, flashy eyeballs be damned.

A number of things became immediately clear. Bellicode might be the center of the antitrust investigation, but Vector7 had identified Christopher David, the former CEO, as the focus. *That's not going to go well.* Christopher was well known in the tech circles as a lazy genius, more Edison than Tesla. He had parlayed the work of other engineers and designers into an empire that still remained the go-to for top-of-the-line technology. McKay's own patent for the nanograss outside her House had already been ground through that particular mill. Her only saving grace had been that the university held the actual patent, as it did the patents for any technology developed within its walls. Institutions like that had long memories and bore expensive grudges. Christopher had finally caved in and licensed the tech; the royalties kept McKay in ramen and neurotransmitter precursors. The court case had made a big enough splash that USIC had sought her out and offered her a job, doubling down on the patent protection to sweeten the deal. She wasn't sure Christopher would even remember her name, but McKay was sure going to enjoy helping Brighton take him down a peg.

Miranda Bosch, Mike's would-be informant, had been new to the Swim. She'd been hired by Bellicode six months ago and she'd hired Mike outside the firm as a tutor to get her up to speed on the new hardware. Nothing unusual there, especially if she'd wanted to ramp up quickly, but that kind of training usually lasted a few weeks on the outside. She and Mike had been meeting in the Swim for a good three months.

"Mike's already on the move to St. Dymphna's."

Ouch. That was a name that made any tech-head wince. St. Dymphna, nicknamed Dyna, the patron saint of the troubled and mentally ill, was also the guiding light of the hospital that specialized in dealing with tech-related psychosis. Their guests ranged from military personnel with S3 wiring in their heads who had trouble re-adapting to xWires like herself who had snapped on install, or experienced some kind of trauma in the Swim. It wasn't a place any-one wanted to become too familiar with, but it was equally likely she'd pass through its doors sooner or later.

"And what about Rose? Can we keep her out of the extraction? Mike was pretty clear that he doesn't want her involved, but he wouldn't say why."

Brighton closed her eyes for a long second. The conversation be-tween her and Rice fell suddenly, eerily silent.

"Rose won't be a problem. She's still in Singapore cleaning up some of the mess we left." Again, Brighton's eyes avoided contact.

McKay missed it this time, but the Overlay didn't. It reeled off medical information and recovery times. *Oh no.* She didn't pursue the line of questioning, in part because she didn't want to see where it ended, but the Overlay helpfully laid it all out in her line of sight. Rose had gone under the knife without any further discussion, and hadn't begun recovery yet. The Overlay highlighted words like "med-ical coma" and "mite-induced pathology." McKay had to work to keep the horror from reaching her facial expressions. It was too soon for a full prognosis, but Rose was teetering on the edge of her own worst nightmare. She wondered if Brighton and Rice had known what the other programmer had in mind. *I wonder if they would have stopped her if they did.*

TEN

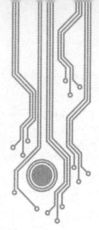

"You know, you really ought to let a doctor take a look at that shoulder."

Another coffee shop, this time off Union Square, somewhat down-scale from her usual haunts, yet more comfortable, with its ragged assortment of cast-off furnishings and a floor that approximated the color of coffee grounds. *Not by design, of course.* The linoleum had been yellow once, but the place never bothered to invest in scrubbers or any sort of miteware, for that matter. The guy across from McKay sat with his feet up on a spare chair, stockinged toes waggling through his sandals. Trevor Baldwin was idly tapping an index finger through news articles on a page of e-paper, never looking up as he spoke to his friend. McKay's sneakered feet were up on the same chair, but she was paying more attention to the foot traffic outside than to the guy across the table from her. The Overlay's linkages were extended, keeping track of other wired systems, touching security cameras, dipping into the pools and eddies surrounding the local businesses. The hyper-awareness that followed the assault in her home was starting to give her a headache.

"It'll be fine. Ibarra came over last night and took a look." Reflexively, she tried to raise the shoulder; she did every time she thought about it. It twinged when she moved it, but she couldn't help it, like poking at a blister.

"EMT brother? I thought you weren't talking to him." Trevor didn't look up. He came across about as average as McKay did, a bit shorter, a bit heavier, and a lot more unkempt. The design engineer managed to stand out anyway, from sheer force of personality.

"No, no, that's the other one." Ignoring the madly flashing icon on the side of the cup, McKay took a long sip of something that probably woke up as coffee, but had been pounced upon by the barista who beat it into something more like a confection. She made a face and put it down. "Ugh. That's the last time I let you order the drinks."

Trevor located his own beverage without looking up from the news feed. "That'll teach you to be on time next time. I ordered the special, just for you. So, tell me more about this system you're looking for."

McKay handed a wafer over, and the other engineer sandwiched it between thumb and sheet. The text and images changed, flooding outward and changing into the schematics McKay spent part of the evening sketching out.

"You got all this from less than two minutes in her head?"

"I grabbed her system logs on the way out," McKay explained. "I'm not sure she even knew the OS would keep track of all the upgrades and changes to her hardware."

Trevor snorted. "Most people don't, which is why warranty repairs are way down." He pored over the page, shifting the images this way and that while McKay debated dumping the coffee fluff and getting something with a bit more burn to it.

"It just doesn't make a lot of sense," Trevor said finally. He jabbed at the image. "That's a very specific type of rig, good for only one or two things, and neither of them jibes with strong-arming some geek in an alleyway."

McKay's thumbnail gouged the flashing red light on her cup. It ignored her and went on pulsing, despite the fact that the beverage had been drinkable for quite a while. She hadn't given Trev all the details. *Because nearly getting hacked in my own House is too fucking embarrassing.*

"Well, not all my clients are off the high-society roster."

"Yeah, but this is encryption stuff. See this here, here and here? This chick's main job is to crunch a lot, and I mean a *lot,* of numbers, as fast as the spin allows. Finance, maybe telemetry analysis."

McKay leaned forward to examine the sheet, called up her own copy of the diagram in the Overlay and made notes. "Codebreaking, maybe?"

"Sure. All the really heavy hardware would be elsewhere. She would just have to go onsite to plug in and Swim the crunched stuff out, like a remote interface made of meat."

"How about compression algorithms? Software or entertainment piracy?"

"Heh heh. Sure, she could be dribbling the latest and greatest blockbusters with something like this, but, really, trying to hack your rig with this was a joke."

"So why even try it?" McKay wondered aloud. She gave up on the coffee extravaganza and waved the waiter over. He skated across the five feet of shop space and took her mug with a smile. "Can I get an extra-large coffee, just black?" He frowned like she'd asked for a rat in a cup. "Please? Just black, no cream, no sugar. Just coffee?" He rolled his eyes and skated back to the counter.

"Best guess? Someone who doesn't know any better figured this would be the best setup to tackle an xWire with."

"Someone who knows nothing about it, then?"

"Or she took the job and figured she could make it work. People use their hardware for edge cases all the time, right?"

The waiter returned with McKay's fresh drink. She paid and added a tip for the extra trouble, which he took with a smile. McKay raised the cup to salute the barista as well. She got a three-fingered salute in return. *Jerk.*

"Even so, they almost cracked the base-pair firewall in sectors 249 and 116." Trev continued on, ignoring the exchange.

McKay was still uneasy about it. Even with the fixes Spike had recommended, she'd spent a couple of hours tightening up security in her head.

Trevor eyed her and dug around in his back pocket. "Here, try this one." She handed McKay a grimy yellow wafer. "The sectors you're talking about rely heavily on single-point encryption, like a lot of standard stuff. That there will bring those sectors up to six-point, a whole different species of nut to crack."

McKay accepted it gratefully. "Thanks, that will help."

"You think that chick's going to try again?"

"No fucking clue, but I'd like to be on guard against her friends, if she has any." She slipped the wafer into her breast pocket. "How about finding who installed this gal's rig? I'm not up on who the specialists are anymore."

"Well, the heat management would have to be elaborate." Trevor chewed a thumbnail. "You'd need a battery of those tattoo sinks or maybe something new and nifty. I hear Bellicode has a new saline coolant system. Christopher's company has all the cool new toys. Your best bet, though, is gonna be Clive."

McKay was in the middle of a cautious sip when Trevor said the name, and came perilously close to burning herself again. "Clive? You mean Jive Clive? With the robot hair plugs?"

"Miteline, not robot, and didn't your first set of patents involve something along the same lines?" Trevor extracted the wafer from the sheet and handed it back.

"Yeah, I'm just holding a grudge because he installed a competitor's design." McKay grinned. "Last I heard he'd added some upgrades to it so you can barely tell where the 'mites begin and his real hair ends."

"Don't be a total dick. He's down in Sunnyvale, I think, working at one of those places that does the outpatient stuff—the lightweight SIs, cortical UIs, stuff like that." Trevor called the news feeds back up and started through them again.

"What, a mass-product place? Like getting your lips injected or your eyes lasered? That's a bit of a downer for someone with his degrees. He was an ass, but a pretty brilliant ass."

Encryption, decompression, number crunching. There has to be some sort of sense here.

McKay stared out at the ambling fits and starts of humanity as they passed the coffee shop on their way to the square and wondered again at how normal everything seemed. The Overlay began searching for Clive, popping up recent journal articles and theses published here and there. She remembered Clive. Who could forget Clive? He was the guy in the lab who might tell you how long his penis was an hour after he met you, whether you were a girl or a guy. He was an oversharer on a great many topics and his built-in inability to filter meant you always knew exactly what he was thinking, even if you didn't want to. It pushed him into behind-the-scenes work where he didn't have to interact with other people often, and pushed him to the fringes of any friend groups. He was good at his specialty, designing heat systems to keep computer processors cool, in people or in wallboard or in desk models. Not super innovative, but rock solid. If you brought him a high-risk design he could give you back a solution that would last a lifetime, or at least a few tech-cycles.

Spike's icon was notably absent. The sprite didn't care for people as a species, and vacillated between avoiding contact with McKay entirely when she was out in the real world and popping in and out at inopportune times as noisily as possible.

Trevor glanced sideways at her. "Dude, clip your shades on."

"What?" The Overlay dimmed. She hadn't realized she'd spun it up so far.

"The eyes, man. You really need to put your shades on or something when you dip into the Swim like that. It's way too creepy." Trev shuddered and returned to his paper. "Total uncanny valley territory." Trevor, notably, was completely unwired, shunned the stuff, preferred to do all his design work on papersheet with a stylus or fingertips.

"Yeah, Dash says I start drooling."

"Oh yeah? Dash is your really hot brother, right?"

"Yes," McKay said stiffly. "My *little brother.* The one that's off-limits, dick."

"Yeah, but he's still hot."

McKay did not answer, just scaled the Overlay back, suddenly a little self-conscious. She refocused her attention on the world, and suddenly a bright *bip bip bip* light pattern in the corner of her vision galvanized her. *What the hell?* Her heart rattled in her chest and she caught herself before the impulse to duck took hold. *That's going to be a problem.*

The guy holding the camera saw he'd been spotted as the Overlay focused in and brought up a magnified image. He turned and bolted before McKay got to her feet, but the Overlay had his image and scanned the databases for a match. McKay watched the guy sprint out of sight.

"So what, you've got a fan now?" Trevor had looked up long enough to register what McKay had seen.

"Probably just a tourist taking pictures of the shop."

"What? This dive?" The engineer looked around incredulously. "We're sitting in a national icon, and I never even knew about it?" They both burst out laughing.

"All right, yeah, I got no clue. There was a guy following Dash the other night and I ate all his pics. Maybe this one's the follow-up." McKay dug for the sunglasses in her pocket and settled them over her eyes. "I'm going to go find out." The *bip bip bip* told the Overlay it was a high-end digital camera. It had not picked up a feed, so the photographer wasn't transmitting the images, just storing them in the camera's drive.

"Good luck with that. Just don't let him start shooting at you." The other engineer grinned at his own pun, already immersed in the newest feeds on the page beside him.

"Thanks for the upgrades, Trev." McKay took the coffee with her and rejoined the trickle of humanity on the sidewalk, the first of the coffee-break crowd venturing from the sky-rises into the thin, spring sunshine.

She began walking in the direction the photographer took. The foot traffic on the streets was moving smoothly, and the transits were on time. She could run the Overlay at full spin without bumping into people too often. Her comm filter had culled nearly a thousand messages, which was light for a Tuesday. Two were potential clients, along with a couple of jokes and off-color tech-humor articles from Dash, and an editorial on finding a date from her mother.

"Eliza." Spike's icon flashed expectantly in the Overlay. She granted it access, and the sprite appeared alongside McKay, walking through the trickle of humanity.

Inside voice, McKay reminded herself.

"Quite right," Spike rejoined. "After all, you wouldn't want to be mistaken for one of the homeless fellows who carry on half a conversation, would you?"

"An internal dialogue can be trickier than you think," McKay responded aloud. A guy standing to her left gave her a puzzled look and moved off before the light changed.

"See what I mean?" McKay shifted to her inside voice, speaking directly to the construct without the words passing her lips.

Spike folded its arms and gazed regally at the passersby. "You're just ahead of your time. In twenty years, all these poor office drones will be so wired up they'll make what you have look like someone superglued a pocket-calculator inside your skull."

McKay winced. "Thanks for the visual. Got anything for me?"

"My, aren't you in a hurry. While you're here, can you wander through the Digistyle shop? They have this really nice new music player I've been dying to check out."

McKay snorted. "I don't think so. The last time I took you in there, security escorted me out."

"Yeah, they really go top of the line on everything, don't they?" Spike's obsession with high-end consumer AIs got out of hand occasionally. McKay had installed an interface block in the sprite that prevented too much fooling around, but she was never a hundred percent sure it was effective. She took a left on Geary, deliberately going a few blocks out of her way to the BART station.

"So do you have anything for me?" she prompted.

"Oh, *fine*." Spike cupped its virtual palms together and flashed her. A painfully bright torrent of data erupted from its hands and cascaded into McKay's optic nerve. Blinded and afraid she'd lose her equilibrium, she stopped walking.

"Ow! *Spike!*" Migraine pain raged in her forehead, then vanished as her system absorbed, assimilated, and redirected the data into her gray matter. *Goddamn pissy prima-donna. . . .* When the Overlay reasserted itself, the sprite was gone. "What the hell?" She opened her eyes to find herself staring into the face of a vagrant. "I was talking out loud again," she said, half to herself, half to the gap-toothed grin in front of her.

"Wotcherself, mate." The vagrant looked vaguely familiar and jabbed a long, dirty finger at McKay's forehead. After a second, she realized she was looking at Rice. The mismatched eyes were a dead giveaway. "Yer gonna walk right inta trouble, you are." *Good god, what is that smell?* Rice slapped her roughly on the injured shoulder and wandered off, shaking his head and muttering.

McKay ground her teeth and stared after the departing figure. On one hand, it was interesting to know they were keeping an eye on her. On the other. . . . *Fucking OW.* Well, the other hand, or shoulder, still hurt like hell, and it reminded her that some people didn't like her very much. Rice might just be waiting to catch the show when Rey and her friends showed up again. *Surely Brighton has a better handle on her people than that.*

The Overlay pinged and informed her she'd been infested with 'mites. *Rice! That rat-bastard.* That wasn't going to help at all. She clicked through a couple of different optic filters until the 'mites showed up, a palm-shaped pattern on her jacket. They weren't doing much, and she was torn about what to do. She could dump the jacket and the 'mites, but Rice was supposed to be on her side. She hesitated to shrug off something that could prove to be a help. *So what, crack one of the little suckers and see what it's got? Unless Brighton's little crew is TRYING to get you to toe over the line back into trouble. A little time, a little quiet, maybe a little nonflavored coffee. Just taking a look shouldn't be out of bounds.* Without the headset to hand, McKay was at a disadvantage. The extra hardware was what allowed her to interact directly with the Swim, what allowed her to manipulate data on the level needed to perform an extraction, or to program 'mites, for that matter. To pull this little guy apart, she needed access to a more powerful computing system, and here in San Francisco, there was only one place that kept an open tab for her.

Katie's, open 'round the clock, was the quiet sort of space where a programmer, even a possibly drooling programmer, could spend a few hours dipping into the Swim without anyone giving her trouble. Since McKay was already on the square's upper levels, she needed only take the spiral walk to the rooftop of the Uter Building and duck through the back door of MiWong's Kitchen and through the side gate to the rooftop lawn space. Going in through her front door with an open infestation would trigger Katie's 'mite-dusters, and the fine mist would short out the little machines before she could get a good look. The outside lawn was open to the air and so had a lot more tolerance. If the 'mites turned out to be something inconvenient, then she'd take a quick turn through the dusters on her way out to clear them off.

Katie's rooftop garden overlooked the fifteen vertical stories of Union Square. At the very bottom, the park was still there, live grass lovingly encouraged by natural sunlight reflected downward through several levels of walkways, open-air shops, and balconies. The roofs of the surrounding buildings had all been conscripted for gardens and open-air spaces, but Katie's had by far the nicest setup. McKay had programmed the nanograss herself, a favor that earned her unlimited access to the massive array of spin-servers that made Katie's so attractive to the tech crowd. On any given day, it afforded access to a metric ton of spin-power to a host of day traders, navigation coders, AI evolutionists, and the like. *And the outdoor bar service doesn't hurt, either.*

While the Overlay happily linked up to Katie's array of servers, McKay found a bleached-out teak lounge at the rear of the garden and claimed it.

"You coming in to say hi?" Katie's voice sounded in her head. One of the requirements for using the spin was two-way access. No secrets. You wanted to use the spin, you had to leave your system open to Katie and her AIs. It helped to keep the less savory elements out of the data pool. If you had a secret to hide, you left it at home in an encrypted drive.

"Hi, Katie! Not today. I just need a few minutes on the server to check out a 'mite I picked up. I'll be out of your hair in five." McKay settled herself on the lounge and folded her hands on her chest, staring at the tendrils of gray fog swimming in the blue sky overhead.

"Two questions. What the HELL do you think you're doing playing with someone else's 'mites, and do I need to check for infestation after you go?"

Always practical. "I don't think so. The grass ought to eat anything I drop." The lawn was hostile to competition and tore wandering 'mites down to their components, a special perk that both the nanograss colonies at her House and Katie's patio had in common.

"You're not bringing any trouble with you, right?" Katie was one of the few people still speaking to her after McKay's fall from grace a few years earlier. She never appeared as an avatar in the Swim, voice only. She was a purist, preferred to keep human interactions real-time, face-to-face without the virtual buffer.

"Not at all, and don't worry. I'm not doing anything I'm not allowed to." She engaged the Overlay's analysis protocols to examine and analyze the 'mites, determine their structure—and from that, their purpose. "This little guy's a tracking class I think. Guy I bumped into must have a jealous girlfriend. I want to strip it down and see who made it."

"You know better, and I do too. If somebody's following you, then somebody thinks you're messing around again. So. Are you in trouble, or are you just LOOKING to get into trouble?" Katie's symbol resolved itself on the Overlay, plain and unadorned, more a blip with an attitude than a proper icon.

"That's what I want to check out. I think it's just a transfer, seriously, some guy just bumped into me on the street. I'm not doing anything noteworthy this week." *Liar.* She wasn't sure if Katie would buy it: she had a nose for that sort of thing, but there was a certain amount of social deniability she extended to all her friends. If McKay were caught, really caught, modding 'mites again, the fallout might strike anyone who could be proven an accomplice—friends and family included. Robert, the oldest of the McKay kids, had suffered a heart attack during the chaos that had struck the family following the court case. The medical review team had ruled it natural causes, but more than a few family members felt that Eliza was responsible. Family was the biggest thing that kept her from just jumping ship and moving to someplace like Singapore, where the governments would be happy to put her in golden handcuffs designing 'mites for their industry. She didn't want her penchant for living on the edge to affect them any more than it had already, but on some level she just couldn't help herself.

"Check it and kill it. You know what an infestation does for business." She cut the link. Simple, efficient, and not even a little bit stupid . . . that was Katie. McKay could count on her keeping an eye on her while she pulled this little guy apart to see what made it tick. She was counting on that . . . it could keep her out of trouble as long as she worked within the rules that had been imposed by USIC as a part of her plea bargain. She relaxed and spun the Overlay up to full speed. The whole process would be simpler back at the House, but working on the fly gave her a rush, just a taste of what she'd been capable of before she'd been stripped of her licenses.

The Overlay found the nanomite and tickled it, bringing up a set of physical attributes that matched the feedback. 'Mites were a highly specialized breed. Since the programming was built directly into the physical architecture, a look at that architecture revealed what the 'mite was supposed to do. The makers used several common body types as a base, mostly off-the-shelf, cookie-cutter stuff. *But you, my little friend, you look like a custom piece of work. Someone built you for this from the ground up, didn't they?* Strictly communications: this one didn't have the signature sharp edges or destructive grinders like the nastier bugs out there. It was fast, streamlined, elegant. It had a single purpose, to drop off the target at an appointed time, when a signal was received, when a certain set of conditions were met, then find the closest communications array and transmit a location. *Simple enough, no muss no fuss, no extra data, just a time and a GPS location.* She breathed a long sigh of relief. At least they were relatively harmless. *Odd, though,* she thought. Vector7 came across in her research as underfunded and unloved by the parent agency. *Strange they should have something so . . . custom.* She shut the file. Maybe it wasn't so odd, just disappointing.

The Overlay pinged. Finding Clive should have been a straightforward task, but the data was convoluted, following employment records, transcripts, research papers, and other sorts of bits and bytes generated by daily life. It reminded McKay of watching stones skip on a pond. Every so often, Clive appeared in the Swim, but just as quickly he vanished again, not a mean feat. A cloud of data followed almost everybody. *Is he switching identities, working as Clive only when the work was noteworthy but running his life as someone else the rest of the time?*

McKay knew roughly where Clive worked, but the in-and-out interface installation industry had come into its own within the last year, with two or three franchises to a town. She didn't want to simply drive all over Silicon Valley and knock on doors. In another three years they would all eat each other and resolve into something more regulated, much like any other franchise war in history. Until then, they cropped up in mini-malls and repurposed office buildings and kept each branch at an inconvenient distance from the next.

Despite the metaphor, the Swim was a vast place. In terms of informational real estate it was virtually endless. Even as old information was dredged up and consigned to the archive files, new data was created and set free to fill the space. There was no way she, or even the Overlay, could search it thoroughly. That was where the 'bots came in, slivers of program copied over and given a single task—automated and mindless. They took the instructions she delivered and were off like minnows in the Swim, finding traces and bringing them back again and again.

McKay sprawled comfortably on the teak lounger until Katie's communications array signaled a message for her. "McKay here."

"This is Rose." In her mind's eye, the voice resolved into the edgier programmer as she'd first seen her in Singapore, though the communication was voice only, no avatar, no image.

"Rose! How can I help you? Did you make it back to the States?" She popped the sunglasses off and rubbed her eyes to get them tearing up again. There was a quick flash of relief . . . *she must have made it through okay, but why is she back at work already?* . . . followed by an equally quick stab of guilt at her own unconscious willingness to jump to the guilt-free answer. McKay knew why she was back. Tech never slept, and tech espionage slept even less.

"Any luck tracking down Mike so far?"

"I'm getting closer, but I'm not sure you need to be worried about that. Your boss has it covered. How'd the upgrades go, are they settling in yet?"

The Overlay queried her about an anomaly it found in the comm feed. Katie's system agreed and started to track down where the call was coming from. *More strangeness.* The relief vanished, replaced by an uncharacteristic pang of guilt. Maybe everything wasn't all right after all.

The caller paused . . . a very long pause. McKay fought the urge to fill the space with words. Something was wrong. The conversation should not have been as strained as it was: the direct questions, the focus on information wasn't right. The caller might not even *be* Rose, not with the warnings she was getting from both Katie and the Overlay. Or it might be Rose, but if something had gone wrong with her implant surgery, she might be talking to a new version, a postbreakdown version.

The longer it took the conversation to wind down, the longer the trace had to run, so she was going to have to say something. If it wasn't Rose on the line, she needed to get a bead on who it was.

"Look, McKay, you've got to convince Brighton to drop the persona and just unplug Mike. They've got him at St. Dymphna's or I'd do it myself. Please, they're not listening to me on this." Rose pushed forward first, words in the kind of rush specific to people, not AIs or 'bots.

That set off alarm bells. The idea of simply unplugging Mike, going against his express wishes, made McKay uncomfortable. More to the point, it should have made *Rose* uncomfortable. She'd tried to extract her former boss twice already. The idea that she'd just unplug him on the sly didn't fit.

"Rose, what do you mean you'd do it yourself?"

There. At the tag end of the phrase, a blip, transmitted just as the signal vanished abruptly, cutting off contact. The Overlay picked it up and beat Katie's system to the punch, isolating and crushing the virus as it came in. The call had been severed with prejudice, and the two AIs squabbled briefly over who got to deliver the coup de grâce to the malware that had come down the connection.

McKay was starting to feel besieged.

It wasn't so much that her usual caution was being teased into paranoia, but that it kept getting justified. *And now something's up with Rose. Why does someone keep pushing to wake this guy up?* Whatever the copy of Mike Miyamoto had found in the Swim, someone or *someones* wanted it lost, buried. That fact alone legitimized Brighton's case for trying to save the persona, to write Mike back out.

And you're going to be caught in the middle again. The thought made her mouth go dry, sent a shiver down her spine before she pushed it back out of her mind. *But if you quit now, none of this is going to get resolved. The only way out is through.*

She flushed the remains of the virus out of the system and started pulling back the 'bots she'd sent after the data on Clive. The urge to move, to change locations to escape whoever that had been on the line was almost overwhelming.

"Got him!" Spike's disembodied voice sounded right in her ear.

"Got who? Clive or Mike?" McKay got to her feet, distracted by the possibility of new information.

"Clive, of course. It's not like he's hiding or anything. It's more like he's pretending to be a hedge."

McKay shook her head with a smile at the classic comic book reference. "So where do I find him?"

"Interlink."

"Interlink? The 'UI While U Wait' guys down in Sunnyvale?"

"The same."

Oh, this ought to be choice.

ELEVEN

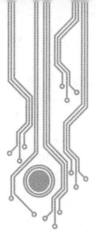

McKAY SHOOK HER HEAD at the cartoon infographic on the office wall. Its goal was to explain the procedure to nervous patients, but the illustrator had missed the mark. Interlink catered to a solid middle-range of working professional, installing for them basic consumer-grade versions of the Overlay inside her own head. The technology had come a long way since she'd begged and borrowed as a grad student to buy the five ounces of builder 'mites that now lived inside her skull.

At that time, a cohort of 'mites had to be individually programmed to crawl through the brain and link up in the proper order in the proper locations. McKay used the better part of a year on the initial design and went through half a dozen vat-grown practice brains from PenTech's medical college getting it right. The Interlink process was different, faster and corporate clean. What had once been an intimate meshing of custom components had become as soulless as the AutoPods that schooled on the freeways.

Thinking about it sometimes made her queasy.

The nice thing about Interlink was the total lack of human contact on the front end of things. The hands-off check-in process, supposedly programmed to keep people from gaining direct access to their techs, gave the Overlay Clive's current location in a matter of moments and wished them a good day as well. McKay had to resort to some computerized cleverness to physically get back into the medical suite, but security was simplistic and Clive was happy to have the company. Through the room's rectangular window McKay and Clive watched the computer-controlled trolley slide the patient into the MRI.

"Relax, Mrs. Applewhite," Clive said into the speaker.

The woman, a heavyset suburbanite in slacks and a red sweater with a large grey cat on it, raised one hand to acknowledge the instruction. Clive smiled at her reassuringly and turned to the array of controls beside him. Long, abnormally thin fingers played out a series of instructions across the input membrane, and the screens lit up.

When the countdown began, Clive retrieved the spec sheet McKay had drawn up and turned it over in his hands, frowning. "You know I can't tell you anything about this gal. I have to follow the same patient protocols for everyone who comes through here."

"But you did design the rig, right?" On the other side of the window the MRI array began to spin and pause, spin and pause as the magnetic fields focused and crossed inside Mrs. Applewhite's skull. Installing basic, consumer-grade miteline was a simple procedure: a half an hour or so under the MRI's twisting arms, flush the excess 'mites out of the system, and you could have someone fully rigged within a day. A far cry from the extensive code-and-test process her own rig had required. Unconsciously, McKay rubbed the scars at the hairline on the nape of her neck.

"Yeah, I did the original design, but she's had some additional work done here, here, and here. Voids the warranty." Clive handed the paper back and turned his attention to the console to initiate another MRI run. On the dozen or so viewscreens, multicolored scans of Mrs. Applewhite's brain pulsed gently, the lines and branches of miteline slowly coalescing along the paths traced by the rotating magnets.

"You warranty your work?"

"Depending on what's been done, yeah," Clive said. "This rig was done through Interlink on a formal basis. I did the design, though, and Interlink handled the install with all the caveats applied."

"So it was all aboveboard stuff, nothing X." It wasn't really a question. McKay folded the sheet and tucked it into her back pocket.

"When it left our shop it was. The new stuff she added, well, the original system wasn't set up for that. I'd say it was custom, probably *discount* custom." The sneer practically dripped from his lips. Clive pressed the large green button on the console and spoke into the intercom. "You're doing great, Mrs. Applewhite. Just a few more minutes." Mrs. Applewhite wiggled her fingers. She couldn't have done much more than that with her head locked into a plasti-fit restraint.

"Any idea who handles that kind of custom work?"

Clive steepled his fingers and stared through them, then came to a decision. He rattled his fingers across the desktop membrane, cuing in the next sequence of pulses. The MRI spun into position and the images on the screens followed the 'mites' progress as they migrated to the visual cortex.

"There was a group of them, all getting similar rigs," Clive said finally. "I can't give you any details. That violates our agreements"— he turned one eye on McKay to emphasize his seriousness—"and I have no desire to jeopardize my setup here. You have to understand that." McKay nodded assent and stifled her questions. "This group all needed heavy-duty heat-sink systems put in as well. I don't handle that kind of work, so I referred them to a guy I know up on Market Street, in the City."

"Skin work?"

"If they used Tommy, then yeah, that's his specialty. He does a lot of lower-end business, quick 'n' dirty stuff." Again the one-sided stare. "His business is a bit riskier in general, and he might be able to tell you what you're looking for."

"You said it was a group of people? Any theories as to what kind of work those rigs would have been good for?" McKay rubbed a hand over the contact points on the back of her skull. She'd been hoping everything would go smoothly, that Clive would be a little more willing to talk about his work. She needed to find a lever, something to convince him the client wasn't worth the protection.

"I dunno, a group of rich punks with an idea about secure data transport. They pay me to run the equipment, not talk people out of poor life choices." Clive avoided McKay's gaze. Not just turned to check the patient's progress, but deliberately turned away, as if he were afraid McKay could tell he was lying.

"Look, Clive." McKay paused and allowed the Overlay a single blip to show her Clive's readings, heart rate, rate of spin usage, muscle feedback. The other programmer's left hand was trembling very slightly; he was nervous about something. *Maybe honesty's the best policy.* "This gal tried to hack my rig. She and a friend broke into my place, busted up my shoulder, and did a pretty good impression of one of those horror-movie head crabs. I'd like to find her."

The Overlay registered a spike in Clive's heart rate. The MRI pinged its completion cycle, and Mrs. Applewhite slid silently out of the rings, still strapped to the table.

"Very good, Mrs. Applewhite. One of our technicians will be in to escort you out in just a moment." Clive released the intercom button but didn't turn to look at McKay. "So you're trying to find this chick yourself then? Why not get the police involved?"

"You know why." McKay said quietly. xWire was highly experimental, highly dangerous, and to the cops, just a little past insane. McKay's conversations with the police about the incident had already proved fruitless. One nice bluecoat gave her her psychologist's number, just in case she needed to "talk to someone."

"Can you prove she did it?" Two green-coated technicians freed Mrs. Applewhite and raised her from the table, checked vital statistics, ran a scanner over her skull to see if the 'mites were locked in properly.

McKay shrugged. "I don't know yet, but someone with this rig did it. I yanked the specs off her before she pulled out. If you can just point me to the field she works in, that will help."

"She tried to hack you? YOU? With this rig?" Clive stabbed a finger at the pocket where McKay had tucked the spec sheet.

"Yep."

That seemed to clinch it for Clive. "What a fucking moron. Her name's Rey Arkady. That whole little group of them works for NWaS. One sec and I'll give you the contact number."

"NWaS? The big law firm up in the City?" *The one that handles Bellicode and Christopher both.*

"The same. You'd think they could afford a more custom install job, right? Or at least smarter interns."

NWaS's name was in the information Brighton had given her, a private law firm that handled a range of big-name clients, the biggest of whom was Christopher David, owner of Bellicode, the largest and most deeply embedded of the wearable engineering corporations. The guy Mike Miyamoto had been investigating.

The math seemed pretty damn clear.

The techs led another patient into the room, a man who looked too young to be going bald, in a low-end jacket-and-tie combo. He was jumpy, and they had trouble getting him in position. He kept raising an arm or sitting up or rolling his head this way and that.

The console beeped a rapid warning, and the screens lit up with information. Clive turned back to the console immediately. "Crap, this one's a phobie." He touched the intercom. "Protocol Three, guys." The two techs paused, and one bent to speak to the patient.

"No notification," came back through the speaker.

"Protocol Three," Clive repeated. The tech spoke with the patient again, or appeared to, placing a hand on his shoulder. When he straightened up again, the man on the table lay much quieter.

"You knock them out?"

"Yeah, insurance reasons." Clive signaled the techs he was ready, and they slid the table into position. "Half the time they don't disclose phobias for fear of not getting the procedure, so we do a brain-scan first."

"And you're picking up the brain activity? What if he's just freaked out?" McKay moved up to the window to get a better look.

Clive shrugged. "Better to knock them out either way. The system can't always see the difference between phobic and non-phobic fear, but if we injure somebody, or if the procedure gets fouled up because they're jumping around, there's a lot of trouble all around. We need to move them through efficiently and give the machine a chance to do its work."

"What about psychotic breaks? Do you see those often?" McKay failed to stifle the question. Her last contact with Rose, if it had truly been Rose, was still bothering her, chipping away at a corner of her mind.

"Almost never at this level anymore. You can put an S1 or S2 in with a letter from the family doctor. I presume the military S3's have a process, and well, you know how tricky the custom xWires can be, but we don't handle those here. Why, are you starting to hear voices?"

"I always hear voices," McKay quipped, "it's when they start giving you instructions that they get troublesome."

Clive eyed McKay thoughtfully. "You think this is all kind of creepy, don't you?"

"It's a lot different from when we started. A lot more. . . ." McKay paused, looking for a word better than *impersonal*.

"Sterile," Clive filled in. "Sure, but this is the safe end, the plug-and-play. These people here"—he indicated the people in the waiting room and procedure queue with a broad gesture that probably included Interlink's entire customer base—"they're looking for the next step up from a handheld mobile or a pair of VR goggles. They want some way to watch the game while they're in church or to check their mail on the road, or an easy entry into running a persona in the Swim. They don't want to *literally* rinse their brain in data like you do. Hell, even I don't want to get *that* deep into it and this is my job."

The Overlay whispered that Clive had sent the contact information for Rey Arkady and requested a return receipt. She waited a long second before giving the Overlay permission to accept. It would leave a data trail, which she wasn't comfortable with, and she couldn't imagine Clive would want hanging around either. *A test, maybe?* She asked the Overlay to release a 'bot to find the receipt and consume it along with the record of the original message.

"Thank you for the help, Clive."

"Yeah, well just don't tell her I sent you. I don't think this chick would have the brainpower to find out I told you about her, but I'd rather not find my box full of hate mail in the morning." Clive keyed in the MRI's next sequence, and the invisible fingers slipped into the man's skull and guided the 'mites to their places. If McKay had looked away, she would have missed the change in his expression as Clive's own computer system reported that her 'bot had torn up the receipt. The Overlay read it as satisfaction, she'd proven her trustworthiness on that count at least.

"No problem." McKay left through the loading dock, just in case the reception AI figured out she wasn't supposed to be back in the tech area. She had a concrete place to start, which was exhilarating in and of itself. She could run a parallel search and try to figure out who the other players were—and if she should worry about any more midnight visits.

The Overlay spun up when she hit the parking lot. A contract offer had come in through her business contacts. *Oh, great timing.* It was a rush order, preprinted with the terms of employ and a clearly dictated timetable that meant she would have to hustle if she wanted to accept. An extraction, business-oriented. *That would be refreshing,* she thought. Corporate systems tended to be nice and clean, virus-free, no knots or legacy systems, more like drifting in a lake than swirling in the chaotic swims and eddies she was used to dealing with. She asked the Overlay to negotiate a slightly higher rate due to the time constraints, and it came back with a number just a bit higher than her usual fee, but not desperately so. And she could use some quick cash since Brighton's job had not paid her yet. *That settles it.*

She grabbed the first unreserved AutoPod out of the lot and settled into the "driver's" seat, allowing the Overlay to link up to talk to the communications system and the hive-style AI that controlled the car. Like all of the self-driven vehicles, it was accustomed to being ignored by the passengers, so it leapt at the chance to chatter at a program outside its own collective. McKay resisted the urge to eavesdrop, which wasn't easy given that the conversation was at least partly going on in her own head, and opened up a link to Dash.

"Oh god, it's you again." Dash's icon rolled into her view as the AutoPod cruised northward, seeking access to the highways. It was his private identity, the blue-and-ice icon reflecting his personal tastes, rather than the front-facing red and grey he projected for the company. "You want something, I can tell, because you're calling from the road somewhere."

"That's because I get my best ideas when driving."

"Lounging, you mean. When was the last time you even touched a steering wheel?"

"I think I was ten. Can I run a company name by you? New client stuff."

"If you must."

She sent him the name and logo from the new contract. The Overlay had been able to verify the client's existence, their business reputation: that part was easy. Dash had a better sense of what was really going on in the tech world, behind the PR spin and public interviews.

"That's weird. I didn't think Holbrook, Esq. was doing any deep-Swim stuff," he replied after a long moment.

Another day, another time, McKay might have been a little less careful about who she sold her services to. *But a little extra caution is a good thing, right?*

"Weird?" she repeated.

"Nah, it's just a little unexpected. These small lawyers tend to work with the Joe-average clients, you know? They specialize in finance work, taxes, that kind of thing. No big enemies, no big secrets, basic startup stuff, you know?"

McKay felt the tension ease out of her shoulders and she settled herself more deeply—*lounge-ly? lounge-i-ly?*—into the AutoPod's "driver's" seat.

"Any ties to Bellicode that you know about?"

"Bellicode? Not directly that I'm aware of. But they're up in the City so they probably show up at the same coffee shops, maybe share a patent lawyer or two. You know how cozy it gets. Oh wait. . . ."

"Wait what?"

"So you know how expensive the rentals up here in the City are, right?"

"Holbrook's subletting?"

"Yeah, from one of the big law firms. Borrowed prestige and all that."

"Which one?" McKay tried to ignore the feeling in the pit of her stomach.

"Nebuchadnezzar, Warloc and Schmidt. Christ, how do you even get a name like that? They must have gone and found some poor kid with the name Warloc and sent him to law school just to get that level of badassery in the partner name." Dash's casual snark was comforting.

Nothing was tripping her alarms. These guys were just another member of the tech scene. . . . *Except.* . . .

"Wait, NWaS's is Bellicode's law firm?"

"Yeah, one of several. NWaS handles a lot of different tech clients and they subcontract the legal grunt work. While Holbrook's probably not 'officially' part of NWaS, they would still do research and serve warrants for them. Probably best to just treat them like they are part of the bigger dog, and connected to Bellicode, just to be safe."

"Okay, perfect, just what I wanted to know."

"Hey, Ibarra pinged last night, said you wrecked your shoulder. What was that about?"

Uuuuuuuuuuuuuugh. Family talks.

"Someone slammed into me the other afternoon at the gym, nothing big, but it popped my shoulder. Just bad physics," she lied offhandedly.

"Okay, well, let me know if you need anything, okay? I don't think he told Mom, but just in case, make sure you answer all her phone calls for the next couple days, okay?"

"Of course. Don't want her to freak out or anything."

"Take care."

TWELVE

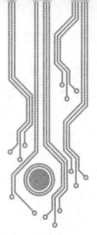

"Cozy" may be the understatement of the year. The AutoPod disgorged her at the address on the contract. Dash had been spot-on. The building itself was owned by NWaS and, while there remained a slim chance the new contract was legitimate, it was looking less and less likely by the minute. *Still, this might be what you need to get out ahead of this mess.*

The entire frontispiece of the corporate offices of Nebuchadnezzar, Warloc and Schmidt, LLP was of lucycrete, the semi-translucent concrete popular in the previous decade. Even in full daylight the interior lights gave the surface an unearthly glow, and the workers' shadows inside wandered around the surface, fading in and out. Under the Overlay's digital gaze, the data flow reflected the surface's eerie, crawling nature. Layer upon layer of systems, a lot more legacy than she would figure for a legal firm as fast and as mean as NWaS. The older, slower conduits were still in use, eddying around, piling data on top of itself while through the newer cables the Swim slid past like quicksilver. Here and there she saw hints, fits, and starts of a pattern, but she couldn't be sure. The whole thing was a virtually impenetrable block of data. *The only way you're going to get anything out of that is from the inside.* She spun the Overlay down and locked it tight. No input, no output. She wasn't about to give Rey or anybody else an opening they could exploit and the proximity to Christopher,

Brighton's person of interest, made her nervous. *Hell, everything makes you nervous right now.*

She could have avoided the gig altogether, but she couldn't ignore the chance that it was, in fact, a trap laid by Rey. The security upgrades to the Overlay's software were in place; she had the headset ready to hand this time. She was looking forward to turning the tables on the guys who had broken into her House and tried to hack into her head.

Walking into the main lobby from streetside interrupted her reckless train of thought. Where the building's exterior felt crawly, organic, the interior space was precisely organized. The patterned red-on-almost-red marble had been cut and laid out to draw the eye to the reception area, a neat visual trick, very low-tech. Security personnel stationed in the corners were dressed in muted colors to match the tile so the eye passed right over them. *There's more stuff in here not to look at than to look at.*

"Excuse me, Ms. McKay." The secretary at the main desk was entirely human, hired for the job rather than an AI construct. Chiseled, blond, his smile was real if not entirely genuine. A well-balanced stance and casual command pegged him as ex-military, rigged for S3, invisible except when he turned and the pinkie-thick umbilical cable running down his back swayed into view. Former military, not what she'd expected in a receptionist.

"May I see your credentials, please."

"Yes, of course." McKay grinned and set the knapsack on the counter, fishing in the front pocket for her ID card. He returned her smile with enthusiasm. His own version of the Overlay likely caused the twinkle in his eye, but the effect was winning. "If I might ask," she continued, "why are you working in reception? You can't tell me you went S3 just to incorporate a speed-filing protocol." The Overlay muttered in the background and countered connection attempts from his S3 system, but stayed spun down.

"The job has its perks." He took her ID and laid it face down on the scanning plate. It would pick up her fingerprints and traces of

McKay's DNA, then compare them to the data encoded in the thin plastic.

"Oh, yeah?" The read on the ID should have been instantaneous, but he did not return it to her right away. *So what am I missing here?*

"Free legal representation if I have to run any of my combat protocols." He swept the card up and flipped it over in his fingers—fast, very fast, almost certainly jump-wired without the stutter, probably in tandem with the S3. *Stunning control. I wish I could get a closer look at his programming.*

"Have to or want to?" she countered as he handed the card back to her with a flourish. She slid it into her back pocket without a glance. On a less hectic day she might have asked for his contact point, just on the off chance he might say yes. *Sure, just what you need. Street-ninja wannabes jumping you in the middle of a date.*

"Your appointment is with Pearson and Whit on floor twelve." He indicated the elevator bay with a flick of his slim, manicured fingertips. "Lift three has already been encoded to accept your presence. Please don't try to get off on any floor other than the one encoded. I'd hate to have to use my free perks on you."

"If only I were so lucky, Mr. . . ."

"Teddy. Teddy Hall." The sparkle was definitely not data-induced.

"Thank you, Mr. Hall." She scooted to the elevator before she ruined the rapport. *Maybe I can get his number on the way back down.*

Unlike the wooden *tap-tap* of wingtips, the sneakers of the guy who came across the lobby behind her squeaked infuriatingly on the polished floor. The sound muted when the floor transitioned to carpet and the man passed her by. The reflection in the elevator doors' polished surface gave McKay the impression of a heavyset man dressed in corporate standard, which made the sneakers all the more incongruous. *Goddammit. Brighton's case is making everyone look like a bad guy.* The staff member vanished through a door labeled *Staff Only*.

She fingered the strap on the knapsack as the elevator slid into motion. The air there was perfumed, a soulless floral that somehow teamed with the wordless music to make the ride seem less dull. A calm voice, perfectly in line with the music, informed her she was on her way to the twenty-third floor, would arrive presently, and that NWaS wished her a pleasant day.

With the air and the music's somnambulant effects working their way into her brain, she almost missed it. *Twenty-third floor?* Her appointment was on the twelfth. She clamped down on the urge to spin up the Overlay, and punched the button for twelve. *Elevators don't glitch.* She felt contact attempts on the Overlay, but nothing beyond the ordinary. The soothing voice assured her that manual floor selection was unnecessary. She punched the button twice more. The voice adopted a decidedly irritated edge. She learned that an escort would take her to her appointment and that she should *have a pleasant day.*

Escort. Lovely. Problems in scheduling were common enough, but she was disinclined to be taken by surprise again. *Too many people trying to strong-arm me this week.* Her hand hovered over the emergency stop button, but she couldn't bring herself to press it. She had to play this out and see what happened next.

The elevator sounded the arrival tone, and the doors slid open. McKay stepped to the side and punched the door-close button. Nothing happened. The arrival tone chimed again. Still nothing, and the soothing voice returned to tell her that her escort was waiting.

She stepped out and got a bit of a shock. Mirrors cut into squares and rectangles, anywhere from one by one to one by three littered the wall across from the lift, and the McKay in the mirrors was not someone she recognized. The stresses of the past week showed in a tightness in the face and circles under the eyes that were not there before. *Christ, you're starting to look like a grad student again.* She glared at the image until the hunted look vanished, replaced by something a little more defiant. *You're here to get a bead on the situation. Confidence is key,* she chastised the woman staring back at her from the mirrored square. At least she wasn't climbing into a darkened limo outside a seedy roach motel. McKay chuckled at herself. The situation was getting to her. If she wasn't careful she'd be scared out of the Swim altogether. She stepped out into the foyer, and the lift doors slid shut behind her.

"Ms. Eliza McKay, I presume?" The man who appeared around the corner was petite in a bantam rooster kind of way. Slightly but strongly built, tricked out in the corporate dark blue pinstripe, he slid forward, beaming broadly. "Welcome to Nebuchadnezzar, Warloc and Schmidt, Ms. McKay. My name is Aaron, Aaron Tanh."

McKay shook his hand, her nervousness evaporating in the face of the obvious corporate entity. "Sorry, I'm a little confused. I thought I was meeting with someone from Pearson and Whit?"

"Pearson and Whit sublet floors eleven and twelve. They let us use their name when we are trying to stay under the radar. I'm sure you understand that having one of our junior members stuck in Swim-space is not the kind of thing we want to have noised about. It makes the firm look . . . less than professional."

"The gentleman at reception. . . ."

"Ah, yes, Teddy? I'm sure he suggested all manner of dire things should you get off on the wrong floor?" This last was phrased as a question but felt more like a statement. "I was supposed to brief you on twelve, then bring you up, but management needed the twelfth floor conference room. Come with me?" Before McKay could get a word in edgewise, the small man led her deeper into the offices. "You will meet with Mr. Kevin Holbrook. I presume you brought the signed NDA with you?"

"Yes, of course. If I can ask, who referred you to me? It's always nice to be able to send a thank you to a former client." McKay thumbed the smallest pocket on the knapsack open and drew out a wafer stamped with her business logo but didn't hand it over right away, kept it between thumb and forefinger, waiting for the conversational break that would let her pass it over smoothly.

Tanh brought her to a locked door, which seemed odd. Offices often had a high degree of security, but usually all on the outside.

She couldn't remember when she'd last seen an interior office door locked. *Unless it's the supply cabinet. Those usually need a keycard, retinal scan, and the blood of a first-born to get into.* She wondered if Teddy downstairs was in charge of hunting down overusers of sticky notes and Liquipens. Tanh passed a hand over the doorknob twice before resting his palm on it. *Palmchip or some kind of higher-end biometrics, maybe?*

McKay was feeling less confident that this was some sort of trap. If it was a legitimate gig, she couldn't afford to foul it up. A bad word from a firm like NWaS could cause her some trouble. If it was another in the long string of jabs between Brighton and Christopher, this time she'd be forearmed.

"Ah, here we are, Ms. McKay." Tanh palmed another door open, a far more serious-looking barrier. "We cleared the floor to give Kevin some privacy and to reduce drag on the server." Detection panels gridded the fist-size windows and some enterprising soul had taped a manila folder over them, blocking any chance of a peek inside by normal means. Tanh stepped through first, and McKay followed, passing him the data wafer with the NDA. *A proper gig then? They've got me here . . . if it's a setup, why keep carrying on?* The temperature dropped abruptly as she crossed the threshold, and her eyes adjusted to the dim of the server room in no time at all.

There were a hundred or so servers inside, thin, black, with cooling units twice the size of the sleek matte boxes. *Bellicode manufacture, top of the line. Makes sense that Christopher would want anyone who works for him using the company hardware.* The Overlay in her skull fluttered in anticipation. *Not yet.* The heat coming off the servers fended off the aircon nicely, and she felt the temperature climb back up as she got closer. There was a joke among the IT guys back at school, "Dressing for distance." The people who worked on the far side of the room from the spin-servers invariably wore sweaters; those who worked close up ended up in shorts.

Rows of shelving littered with empty component boxes, hard-copy manuals for version upon version of software upgrades, toolkits, electron spin manipulators, the usual array of server-room mysteriana, all there. Two interface stations as well, the blue leatherette version of her comfy chair at home. *Well, they have the right equipment at least.*

A man in the same corporate costume as Tanh occupied one of the chairs, semi-reclined. Unlike the walking, chatting, highly polished Tanh, the guy was a bit on the scruffy side. The armrests cradled forearms sheathed in input sleeves, the better to monitor blood gases and deliver the necessary drugs to keep the body unconscious longer-term. The persona machine, the hard- and software package that actually did the work of writing a copy of a mind into the Swim, covered the entire back of his skull, thumb-thick ropes of miteline continued over the side of the headrest and down to the computers at the base of the lounger. Half-lidded eyes could have belonged to someone taking an opportune nap, or locked up in Swim-space.

"So how long has he been in the Swim?" McKay narrowed her focus with an effort and began laying out her kit components, one by one. A closer look at the guy on the table told her, *Not a normal gig at all.* Unlike someone asleep or in a coma, the nervous system of a person written into the Swim was held in a sort of stasis, locked up and prevented from any new experience that might cause an error in the outwrite. The result was an odd rigidity, a lack of flex in the limbs this guy just didn't have. *So if this guy's not stuck in the Swim, just what the hell is going on?* She pulled on a pair of blue nitrile gloves to protect herself from any 'mites trying to make the jump to a new host.

"We're looking at ten hours now." Tanh peered down his nose at the figure strapped to the table. "He pulled two all-nighters getting a client brief finalized. Regulations limit us to six hours in the Swim with a mandatory two-hour recovery period. Mr. Holbrook here overrode the regulatory protocols to complete his assessments on time."

McKay selected the smallest flashlight and turned her full attention to the guy on the lounge. Whatever else might be going on, he was down for the count. She couldn't take the risk that there might genuinely be something she could do to help.

"What do you know about his rig?" She examined the connection points, fairly basic S2 gear on the outside. Single connection point at the base of the skull. Deltawave "Featherlite" X20 plug, three prongs, double-safety rated. *Expensive, all manufactured by Bellicode, but solid. It's real Swim-gear, and he's actively linked in, but not actually trapped? So they want me to link in voluntarily, to see what's going on?*

"Rig?" Tanh took up a spot on the other side of the door and watched with fascination, the way people do for a smashup on the freeway.

"Yeah, the computer in his head. Do you guys have a copy of the spec sheet? It would help to know what's in there before I start rummaging around." *Let's see how long I can keep this rolling.* McKay gave the Overlay permission to open the tiniest secure connection and started layering encryption on top. The Overlay understood her caution and found a secondary path into the NWaS computers via the cooling system rather than the regular communications line. It would come at the problem through a side channel and give her an idea of what they had planned if she linked in. McKay slid a palm-size piece of e-paper under the unconscious man's right hand on the armrest beside him. The surface shimmered, reading the pulse, respiration, blood toxin levels, basic health stuff.

"Nothing on file. Can't you just go in and have a look?"

Light flashed into Holbrook's eyes elicited no response; the pupils were tightened down almost to pinpricks. Classic sign of a cortical overload. The Overlay reported back with the same. Someone had crashed the man's rig from the inside, and there were additional presences in the Swim. Familiar presences. The Overlay recognized Rey, the asshole who'd tried to hack her skull, but also. . . .

Rose? That can't be right. What the hell is Rose doing here?

McKay hesitated, unsure of what to do next. She'd come ready for a confrontation, but the presence of Rose changed the game. Was she there undercover as part of Brighton's crew? Or was there something else going on? Maybe Mike had another reason for keeping her out of his head.

Shit.

A cortical overload tripped over the line into medical emergency, and a week ago, McKay would have jumped in without hesitation. They were setting the stage for her to fully drop into the Swim through the headset, a move that, unlike their previous attempt, could give them access to anything in her head if they could get through her security. And if Rose was there, coupled with the resources NWaS had at their disposal, McKay wasn't sure she could beat them in virtual space, not here in their own house.

Jesus, are they just taking advantage of this poor bastard, or did he do this voluntarily just to get me in here? She asked the Overlay to call emergency services, just in case. She wouldn't be able to offer anything but basic support, but she felt guilty not doing anything.

"You need to get the medics in here now. This guy's not suspended, he doesn't need an extraction. There's something else wrong."

Tanh got angry, the neatly plucked brows knotted and a very noncorporate flush darkening his already brown face. McKay was putting the kit away and caught the expression out of the corner of her eye. The change in the voice was unmistakable.

"Are you sure? Perhaps you should plug in and take a look, just to be sure. . . ." The voice—hard, flat—made the back of McKay's neck prickle as if she were at ground zero for a lightning strike.

"Look, I'm sorry . . ." she began, but the words died off as she turned and faced the dark, snub barrel of the pistol pointed at her from across the room. *Not paranoid enough, apparently,* the voice in her head chided her. They wanted to hack her from the inside and Tanh wasn't above forcing the issue. The Overlay retreated, shutting off all outside contact again, but now mapping the interior of the room, keeping track of objects and spaces and letting McKay know the fastest route to the door.

The barrel of the gun was the only thing McKay could see, the only thing that mattered. The tremors started in her fingertips. Mind stuck in a loop. *Not again. No. No.* The Overlay intruded with deliberate flashing patterns and moving lines, giving her something else to focus on, readouts skimmed across her line of sight showing her options, something she could DO. *Action matters.* Her heart rate stuttered, then slowed, calmed. McKay found her voice again after a long moment staring into the black eye of the barrel.

"So what's the deal here?" She slowly laid the penlight back on the table with the rest of her kit and swapped it for a similar-looking item. Tanh's aim seemed a touch shaky, and McKay's inner voice screamed at her to move. *Slowly! Don't give the guy any reason to twitch.*

"Rose said you were a careful one. I think you need to make a proper assessment of Mr. Holbrook's condition, just to be sure you can't help him. It does seem to be an emergency, after all," Tanh said with effort. Clearly getting more comfortable with the weapon, his body language suggested he would have no qualms about pulling the trigger. The gun jerked in the direction of the second persona machine. "Why don't you take a seat there and plug in so you can get a better idea of what's going on?"

The pistol's little black maw exerted an irresistible pull on McKay's attention. She looked away with conscious effort and refocused on the knapsack—though she could feel the weapon there, gaping at her, even with her eyes turned away. *Not panicking. Not panicking. Not panicking.* Somehow, McKay was far less afraid of getting shot than she was of letting them hack into her head. Most of her gear, including the headset, was still packed, so if she had an opening she could grab it and go, but Tanh still blocked the door. On the whispered advice of the Overlay, McKay shifted her stance to put her body between the knapsack and Tanh's direct line of sight.

"Okay, okay. I'll go in and double-check. Don't get excited." The knapsack would pack a pretty good wallop, but she needed to get closer for that. The item she'd swapped the penlight for was heavy in her fingers, and she maneuvered it to rest in the palm of her hand. It was hardly larger than her thumb, but decidedly less pacifistic. It was outdated by at least ten years, too, so the building's security AI shouldn't be looking for it. *This is just going to suck, one way or the other.* After the last few days of mind-twitching paranoia, McKay found herself very calm. The Overlay wiggled for attention and fed her situational data only, no links out, no connections to anything, but it showed her an escape. The pistol, it told her, had a very limited range and broad plasma scatter. *Probably so it doesn't punch through the cubicle next door.*

"Hang on, I have to get the rest of the gear out." McKay tapped the side of her head nonchalantly. "Custom rig. I need the adapter or I can't plug in." Not entirely fiction, but she made a point of pulling a handful of repair parts and plugs out of the kit and examining the ports on the lounge. She was betting on the fact that Tanh was unfamiliar with the hardware side of things. His job was just to make sure McKay plugged herself in; the guys waiting in the Swim were the real muscle.

When McKay turned from the lounge a little too quickly, the gunman's eyes flickered to follow. The Overlay picked up the jitter as they tracked a little too fast and overshot McKay's position. *Ah. Jump-wired.* The Overlay took that little piece of information and ran with it, outlining everything in her vision with relevant information. Unlike Brighton's friend, Rice, or Teddy downstairs, Tanh had the discount hardware, prone to overshoots and the jitters. Tanh came closer, more confident now that McKay seemed compliant, and took up a position on the other side of Holbrook's unconscious body.

"You know, you really ought to have the paramedics standing by, just in case I'm right," McKay said mildly. The Overlay calculated and gave her a plan of action with a fifty-fifty chance of success. McKay moved components around on the table, comparing them to one another while the Overlay computed situational data, displayed trajectories and impact points over McKay's own vision, showing her exactly what she needed to do and in what order. McKay flicked her left wrist, shooting the drive she was fingering off to the left. She would have winced at the clatter it made as it skittered across the desk, doubtless scrambling the data within, except the movement sequence had to continue, and she couldn't afford to lose momentum. As long as she followed the steps and timing the Overlay had laid out, she should be fine.

As the Overlay predicted, Tanh's eyes shot after the movement, shoulders shifted, the jumpwire taking over and tracking the drive in flight. The gun barrel followed automatically. Military jumpwire was designed to prevent glitches like that; Tanh's was cut-rate "civ-tech." McKay relaxed and let her own motion carry through, following the path drawn out for her by the Overlay. The flat of her off hand, and the palm-stunner concealed within, connected with Tanh's gun hand, delivering an electric shock to Tanh and his weapon simultaneously. The roar of his weapon deafened and blinded McKay as her stunner shorted and discharged the firearm. Tanh was locked stiff as a board before he hit the ground.

McKay didn't wait. She snagged her kit and headed for the door, relying on the Overlay's map until the afterimages faded and she could see again. The exhaust fumes from Tanh's gun filled the confined space, and the environmental systems ground into action to suck up the foreign particles. Once the building's HVAC picked up on the residue, all hell would break loose. Her ears rang with a persistent whine. *Lovely. Now I get to add eardrum repair to my billing.* The Overlay begged for linkages, to touch and connect with the building systems to map a way out, but she kept it under control. Tanh was trying to get her into the building's server, where her hackers would have the advantage. If Rose was working with Tanh, waiting for McKay to drop into the Swim, that was a can of worms she couldn't afford to open.

"Hold up!"

She heard a voice dimly through the ringing, presumably Tanh's. *Fat chance!* She kept going, half-blind, following the route the Overlay painted for her. The blast had shattered the calm in her head, and she stayed as low as possible.

"Dammit, cover the elevator!" Tanh's voice barked the order.

The Overlay pinpointed the second voice on the local map. She'd presumed the cubicle maze was empty, but her clearing vision showed her three, four, five heads prairie-dogging to get a bead on her location. McKay dropped to her knees and scooted sideways into an empty cubicle. Without allowing the Overlay to link to the building's security system, there was no way to track them.

"Enough!" a new voice rang through the empty space.

Now what. . . .

"What the hell are you playing at!"

"Sir. . . ." Tanh's voice, pleading somewhere behind McKay.

"I said *enough*. Unless you want your contract terminated with prejudice, Mr. Tanh, I suggest you explain this."

Tanh made a choking noise. McKay wasn't sure if it was from the acrid fallout or the reprimand, but he didn't sound comfortable either way.

Serves you right, asshole. McKay had been on the receiving end of that scornful tone before, albeit shielded by a cadre of university lawyers at the time. Christopher David. Innovator, entrepreneur, warlord of informational systems technology, CEO of Bellicode, on the board of directors for Gransdata, McAmber, and Genolink. The term *mobster* was not appropriate, despite what the media implied about the man's business practices. Like all warlords (tech and otherwise) he did some good stuff, maybe more bad, and some would require the hindsight of history to sort out. McKay's only personal experience with the man to date had been the court case over the nanograss patents and that had been an experience she'd rather not have again.

McKay's vision recovered, and she found herself focused on a well-worn patch of bluish-grey carpet and a lone red paper clip the cleaning 'bots had missed. She picked it up and fingered it, then slipped it into her breast pocket and checked out the rest of the space she was hiding in. The three and a half walls were filled with the sort of detritus unoccupied space accumulates. Coffee mug with a heart and a picture of some unidentifiable genetically engineered pet in a mustache, stacks of files slipping off square, an empty stylus box. The Overlay let McKay know that if she wanted to throw the mug she might brain one of them before the rest gunned her down, but otherwise the cube was bare of friendly options.

"Eliza McKay—if I may call you Eliza—I assure you this . . . incident . . . is concluded."

Shit. Well, maybe you'll get that monologue you were looking for after all. The Overlay warned her about three new people, too few to cover all the escape routes, and it was fielding connection attempts from at least five different sources. Unless she connected through the headset, Tanh's teammates couldn't pressure-crack her security, but that didn't mean they couldn't cause her a world of trouble. They were still waiting for her, just via the invisible medium of the Swim rather than whipping out guns in Christopher's line of sight. *They didn't expect the boss to be here.* McKay stood up with as much attitude as she could muster and leaned on the cubicle's frame.

"I would prefer just McKay, if that's all the same to you."

Christopher stood between her and the lifts, which was unfortunate and probably on purpose. The Overlay pointed out that the coffee mug from the cubicle might just be useful if she hit Christopher in the head at just the right angle. McKay hated the idea of scrambling the man's truly exquisite rig in an escape attempt. Of course, one move on their boss, and the guys with guns would light her up like a moth in a bug-zapper.

Slightly in front and to the right of Christopher stood an unexpected surprise: Miranda Bosch, Vector7 informant and arguably the root cause of this whose mess. And she was upset. Not the fearful, *why are guys with guns in my office* upset, but the more deeply offended *who the actual hell hired these idiots.*

McKay suddenly had an inkling of why Mike had picked her to try to get at Christopher. She shouldn't have been imposing. If they'd been standing face-to-face, Bosch would have just come up to her chin, a height achieved via platform shoes and perfect posture. Hair the same color gold as Teddy downstairs, but slicked back into a braid to stay out of the way. While Christopher was clearly in charge, the impression was that she was simply conceding the role, that if her boss hadn't been present, then Tanh and his underlings would have gotten something harsher than a raised voice.

Christopher smiled when McKay spoke, not the sharklike grin one saw in the news feeds but a quick, genuine thing, flashed once, then reined in again.

"Fair enough, Ms. McKay." Christopher was just slightly taller than McKay. Pale with unnaturally salt-and-peppered hair, he looked even more washed out in the office lighting. His face bore visible scars, left over from when miteline was still a DIY project. He could have had them repaired, erased, but rather wore them like badges of honor. Most first-generation xWires did. Like McKay's, his contact points were nearly invisible, hidden under the shock of graying hair, but unlike McKay, his eyes were permanently enhanced. Their original blue had been subsumed by the miteline that riddled his entire body, if the newscasts were right. The iris and pupil were nearly the same dark shade, an effect that tripped a familiar, uncomfortable response.

"Now that those in my employ have seen fit to bring me into this project a bit more . . . abruptly than I would have liked"—Christopher shot a look at Tanh, and McKay could have sworn his eyes flashed red for an instant—"I find I must make you a proposition."

The attempts to connect into the Overlay stopped abruptly and the presences lying in wait in the Swim all vanished. McKay couldn't tell if Christopher had taken some kind of direct action or if Tanh's cohorts had simply quit the field. Either way it meant she could focus on the real world a little more closely.

Bosch and Christopher exchanged a look, the Overlay picking up a quick flash of connection between them, an encrypted communication she had no hope of hacking into. Their body language conveyed the handoff. Bosch had brought the incident to Christopher's attention; it was up to him to deal with the rest.

Now that's interesting.

"I'm listening." McKay felt her calm returning. Christopher was an asshole, but not the kind of asshole who had people gunned down for giggles. *As far as I know, at any rate.*

"It is simple enough, Ms. McKay. I know that certain agencies have contracted you to track down a rogue persona. I want to know what progress you have made."

McKay laughed, a short, sharp sound that rang hollow in her own ears. "You've got to be kidding me. All this drama just to get a line on a wild goose chase?"

Christopher frowned, as quick and fleeting as his smiles had been. "Yes, I see. All right, then, come with me, please." He directed that impassive gaze at the three guys with guns. "You three, get back to your stations, and let the EMTs up to take care of Mr. Holbrook. Tanh, you come with me."

Christopher turned and headed for the elevator without further discussion. Bosch faded back, clearly staying behind, but the long, considering gaze she gave McKay left little doubt.

She knows who I am.

McKay didn't move. She had come expecting (and had found) a trap. She hadn't expected yet another interested party to reveal itself. It was becoming clear that she had underestimated just how important Mike's undercover discovery was to more people than just Brighton's team of spies. Bosch was more than just an inside connection. She was Christopher's right hand. She had intercepted Tanh's ambush and still, as far as McKay knew, kept the secret of her and Mike's meetings in the Swim.

This is getting very *complicated* very *fast.*

Tanh showed up next to her cubicle. "Get a move on," he snarled from between clenched teeth.

The coder stopped and locked eyes with her assailant before moving to follow Christopher. Curiosity had the upper hand over indignation, as usual. *And Tanh might just kick my ass for fun once we're out of Christopher's sight.*

The entrepreneur waited for them by the elevator. "Good, I was afraid you were going to be difficult."

"There's still time. It can take me up to an hour or two to really piss someone off," McKay replied offhandedly.

Another tight smile. McKay had the impression these were the genuine article, little slips in an otherwise indifferent mask. Christopher passed a hand over the call button and the doors slid open. *I would have expected someone like Christopher to be more hands off, rig connected directly to the building operations rather than messing with things like palm encoders.*

"After you, gentlemen. I have to set the security code behind us." Christopher gestured McKay and Tanh to board first. Tanh obeyed without hesitation. McKay took a second longer, but followed suit. The saturnine computer voice was curiously absent. McKay allowed the Overlay a little more leeway and the computer in her head connected with the elevator's AI.

Christopher hadn't *needed* to make a sound since they exchanged niceties nearly three minutes earlier. Through the Overlay, McKay could see how the systems within the building were almost part and parcel of the man's own internal computers. The "palm encoder" Christopher had used on the elevator wasn't real, it was the kind of visual habit McKay was very familiar with. It kept people from scooting away from you when you sat down next to them. It eerily echoed the way McKay managed her own interactions, niceties like making sure the Overlay was spun down before making eye contact.

"So exactly what is this all about?" McKay posed the question. Someone had to ask first, and she didn't really care about losing points to Christopher. In the wobbly reflection on the elevator doors, Tanh glowered at her from the back of the elevator. McKay decided to go the annoying route and gave him a big smile, teeth and all. *Unappreciated, of course.* She sidled an inch closer to Christopher's henchman, well into the man's personal space. The next youngest of seven siblings, she'd had decades to practice irritating people, and Tanh was the easiest target she'd had in a long time. *Let's see how tightly wound you really are.*

"Not yet, Ms. McKay." Christopher held up his hand. "I am a figure of interest, and while the government is required by law to respect my personal space, my competitors are not."

"Even in your own building," McKay commented, as the doors bumped closed. She wondered about allowing the Overlay to attempt an external connection, but that would leave her a little more exposed than she was comfortable with.

"Indeed. I have read a bit of your work on fractal configurations in neural system design, Ms. McKay. An interesting idea there. Have you had any luck expanding it to the 'mite-scale design stream? That was your specialty, if I recall."

McKay was briefly at a loss. The fractal paper was one of the more obscure things she'd written. Christopher was letting her know she'd been researched. The Overlay flashed her the abstract, refreshing her memory. "It's been used, but designers still prefer the more standard Aldus-Meyers patterning systems."

"Yes, well. The math is simpler." Another fleeting smile. "Still, there is a certain elegance of design attractive to those working above the mass-manufactured tech, isn't there?"

"Among Xs maybe, but it's lost on consumer-grade implants, I think." Before McKay could say more, the elevator doors opened soundlessly, not even a ping to warn them. The space beyond was cold and dark, but when Christopher stepped out the lighting came up slowly, warming the room from the floor on upward.

"My office. NWaS permits me to borrow this space unofficially while in the City." The lights revealed a large, rectangular sub-basement space divided and subdivided by glass-panel displays. Some showed sheeting lines of code, some flickered between images, others had been written on in black marker, equations and brainstorming all in a precise, linear hand that looked uncomfortably like McKay's own. Another unnerving parallel.

Cozy.

Somehow "permits" wasn't the word McKay would have chosen. Plenty of startups saved an office for a key investor or an adviser, but a firm like NWaS took that to a whole different level. Close-cropped carpet and glass walls made the space feel crystalline, mazelike. The air, server-room cold and unusually still, radiated up from the floor. McKay stopped and stared at the space between her sneakers for a moment, trying to decide whether or not to be outraged. The Overlay registered the carpet's mottled 'mite-controlled threads and fed back information on their structure and programming. They were based on McKay's own patent, the license code hidden way, way down in the information string.

"Do you like it?" Christopher returned to McKay's side, beaming at the flooring like a beneficent parent. "The 'mites provide climate control as well as maintain and adjust the surface depending on the foot traffic. My own design."

"Impressive." The Overlay responded to her roiling emotions and snapped the recorder in her skull on. *There's no way he doesn't know that's my patent. I know when I'm being poked at.* "Did you mod it off that grass over at Katie's?" McKay needled back, just in case Christopher needed the reminder.

Christopher's look turned decidedly black.

"Well, it's an order of magnitude above that cheap trick." He flipped a hand idly to dismiss the comparison. The mask of civility slipped a little, revealing an unpleasant touch underneath. The look he shot McKay was calculating, a little less benevolent CEO, a little more business-class elite.

Cheap trick, my ass. They had only met face-to-face once before, and even then, McKay had been a minor player, shielded by the university's patent department. Having Christopher taunt her with her own technology was irritating, but McKay refused to rise to the bait. The nanograss patent was the most public of McKay's creations from her years as a 'mite designer, but hardly the most interesting, or dangerous. Tanh shouldered his way past McKay and followed his employer.

In sharp contrast to the light and glass, the desk in a corner of the room was like the center of a black hole. Some sort of dark wood, it reflected no light. Christopher seemed drawn to it, his feet hardly touching the carpeting. Tanh followed. His boss seated himself behind the structure and pulled a drawer open.

"My proposal is simple, Ms. McKay. I want to know what you know about Mike Miyamoto, and I want to be kept abreast of what you find out as you continue to work for Vector7."

McKay had not expected that. Actually, McKay wasn't exactly sure what she expected, but having Christopher turn around and hire her to do something the man's far vaster resources could have handled without even an extra purchase order seemed a bit mundane. *Unless he's trying to piss off Brighton somehow. Now that's an interesting idea. He's definitely got that petty undertone.*

"I'm under NDA with my client, Mr. David. I'm not about—"

The older man cut her off with a casual gesture. "Your current contract says nothing about the information's final ownership, I've seen it. I'm not even asking you keep me updated in real-time. It's all legal and aboveboard. Someone has been trying to point Vector7 in my direction, and I would rather not be caught off guard if I can help it." He extracted a small palm-size tablet and poked at the surface with a stylus. "You are already doing the research, Ms. McKay. I'm simply offering to pay you to save me a copy, after the fact, if you will." He held out a hand to Tanh, who passed over a thumb-size data wafer. Christopher plugged the wafer into the tablet and tossed it to McKay. "The amount there effectively doubles your take-home on the project, am I right?" he asked mildly. "A reasonable offer, I'm sure you'll agree."

So Brighton's got him pegged as the Big Bad, but this is too low-key a response. He should be ranting and calling down legal recourse. McKay looked at the tablet. *Enough to pay off my lingering legal debts, possibly get a lawyer to help get all my 'mite licenses back if Brighton doesn't follow through.* It was tempting, and it would allow her to hedge her bets, but if Brighton got wind of it, she'd probably fire her on the spot. *So which is the better option? Faith that Brighton can make good on her promises, or faith in the kind of cold, hard cash that can buy better lawyers?*

"Contract terms?" she asked automatically. It was the freelancer's response, keep digging until you find something you can't live with. The discovery that Miranda Bosch was highly placed, and that McKay had no real insight into her motives, meant that Christopher's offer was the riskier bet.

"There as well." Christopher indicated the tablet with another vague, theatrical gesture. "So far I'm up to one assault a week. That's starting to become a problem. Can you keep your people from bothering me?"

Oh, you didn't know? The furrowed eleven that appeared between the older programmer's eyebrows was gone almost before McKay registered it. Christopher's gaze narrowed to a thin line, followed by an equally thin smile. "Of course. I don't tolerate disagreements between people *in my employ.*" The gaze shifted to Tanh to the left of the desk, who was doing his best to bore a hole in McKay's skull with the sheer force of his dislike.

That's going to suck for you, buddy.

"Delivery by data wafer only, strictly arm's length," McKay countered. "I don't want to link up with your systems, and I don't want you linking up with mine."

A long pause followed that one, but Christopher acquiesced. "Of course. Any form you prefer."

An even longer pause while McKay read through the rest of the terms. The Overlay recorded everything, but she would have to attach her digital sig to the original. Standard stuff, seemingly boilerplate, but she didn't dare miss a word—and she dared not plug it directly into her skull drive in hostile territory. She ground her teeth against the confinement but resisted the urge to do things the quick way, focusing instead on the right way, with her own grey matter. Line by line she read through the document, aware the system hoped she would run out of patience and link up to finish it. *I am a rock.* The Overlay stopped pushing, and grumbled at her.

After what seemed like an interminable slog to McKay, probably twice as long to her observers, she ejected the contract wafer from the tablet and tucked it into her breast pocket next to the paperclip. She tossed the tablet back to Christopher, resisting the urge to bean Tanh with it. *Because that would be childish.*

"Done, then?" Christopher arched an eyebrow and slipped the tablet back into the desk without so much as a glance.

"More or less. I'll sign it back at my place and send you the original by courier in the morning."

Christopher leaned back and steepled his fingers, as if they'd suddenly touched on a topic that interested him. "Why in the morning?"

McKay shrugged the knapsack into a more comfortable position on her shoulder. "I don't trust you."

"Fair enough."

THIRTEEN

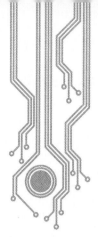

FOR MCKAY, hitting the outside of the NWaS building was like suddenly taking a big gulp of air after holding her breath for far too long. She stood a few seconds, letting the Overlay connect to the City systems, bring in news feeds and weather data, feed her data on every little thing within link's reach, including the urine content trickling down the city gutter next to her. *That last bit of data could have been left off.* She could have done without the smell too. McKay dropped a note asking one of the courier services to pick the contract up at her place in the morning for delivery to NWaS. There was little doubt in her mind that Tanh or someone like him would try to monitor her communications, so she slipped that one out with a little less encryption to convince them she had bought in.

McKay jammed the contract wafer into the lockbox as soon as she got back to the House, setting the scrubber to work on it. She instructed it to strip the text and burn anything else on the wafer, then dropped heavily into the comfy chair.

"Jesus, Spike, this is getting too damn complicated." She rested her head in her hands and rubbed her eyes, setting off sparks in her vision when the pressure reacted with the 'mites. The sprite was nowhere to be seen or heard. In fact, McKay hadn't seen him since the day before at Katie's. Spike was rarely absent for that long at a stretch. *It's a program, not a puppy. Spike can take care of himself. Itself,* she corrected.

She stared moodily at the lockbox. The lights in the faceplate fluttered merrily as it ground through the data spun into the chip's crystallized plastic surface. *Nothing yet.* It was a stupid old trick, burying a virus in a contract. After she was baited with her own patent, cheap, petty tricks seemed right in line with Christopher's mindset. Tanh was another story, especially since he'd invoked Rose's name back at the ambush. She kept popping up, but never with the major players. It felt like she was maneuvering around the sidelines, pushing buttons to get reactions. Christopher was aware that Brighton was after him, but surprisingly unconcerned. Bosch had moved to rescue McKay; was it possible that she was still playing both sides? McKay had expected something different, some kind of revelation on meeting Christopher face-to-face, but she'd come away with the feeling that the senior programmer was not the driving force here. This investigation was more of an annoyance than any real trouble.

Feeling kind of full of yourself, eh? You're not big enough to be a problem for a guy like Christopher.

McKay and Saiid had designed the scrubber, cut off from any system, both Swim and hardline. She had to plug the wafer in manually, and the operating instructions were 'mite-encoded into the hardware, inflexible, unchangeable. Its function was simple enough: read the files, execute anything executable therein, and trigger any encoded viral activity. Sure, there were antiviral agents, quite good ones you could install, but after having her own head crashed more than once, and that time Saiid lost an entire shipment of bamboo simfiber because one of the vats got infected, she'd decided to be a lot more careful before plugging stuff into her skull. Within a matter of moments, the box began spitting out a long tongue of thermal paper with the whole code from the card printed out. She ignored it for the moment and leaned back in the comfy chair, diving into the reams of information the 'bots were bringing back on Mike and the rest of Brighton's team.

When the box exploded, she just about jumped out of her skin, scrambling, too late, to put the bulk of the comfy chair between her and the source.

"Shit!" She began frantically searching for the fire extinguisher while plastic hissed and puddled on the desktop. Small bits of hot RTV and crystal ate pinholes into the comfy chair and stuck to the walls and ceiling. The Overlay screamed at her, flooding her vision with information. The power surge tripped a series of breakers, and the House cut the power to protect itself, abruptly dropping the room into darkness. The Overlay helpfully threw up a wireframe outline of the room and everything in it. The sputtering puddle of slag on the table oozed toward the edge of the cold, stone surface. McKay found the fire extinguisher under the legs of the comfy chair. A quick twist and a yank and it expelled a fine, sticky mist at the puddle, leaving McKay in a room choked with fire retardant and burnt plastic. She hit the button for the wall exhaust, swore when it refused to turn on because of the power outage, and shut the door behind her to keep the fumes from flowing up the stairs into the rest of the House.

"Well, that was a new twist," she remarked to no one in particular. She leaned against the door and waited for her heart to stop racing. The brief, sickening image of what might have happened if she'd plugged the wafer into her skull drive flickered at the forefront of her mind, and her knees went watery for a moment. The Overlay brought up the House systems map, showed the surge's path through the lines, tripping protective circuits in half a dozen locations. Different nodes showed red, others were nonfunctional, grayed out. *Dammit dammit dammit. Not my House again.*

And, of course, someone started pounding on the front door.

Rattled, McKay took the steps two at a time, trying to connect the Overlay to the outside camera to see who was putting a dent in the paint, but the cameras were gone, the link to the nanograss was gone, maybe not *gone* gone, but out of commission until she could undo the damage from the power surge. She was so focused she nearly missed a step when Spike materialized square in her line of sight.

"What the hell?!"

The sprite seemed not to notice her discomfiture. "There you are! Look, there's something you need to. . . . What's that smell? And what the hell happened to the main server? It looks like a tornado went through the secondary drives." The sprite suddenly seemed to parse that something was wrong and spun back into its icon.

"Spike! I'm busy. Later, please."

"But. . . ."

"*Later.*" McKay tripped on the landing and stuck out the wrong hand to stop herself from hitting the wall. The injured shoulder made a crackling that was more feel than sound. McKay's yell of pain and frustration was audible through the front door and possibly three houses down.

Spike wisely vanished during the interchange between the programmer and the laws of physics. The pounding on the door resumed, but re-injuring her shoulder cleared McKay's head, pushed everything else out of the way. She hooked her thumb into her belt loop to support the injured arm and opened the door.

Rice, out of his homeless suit and dressed more in keeping with the neighborhood, was poised to pound again. McKay stared at the upraised fist, then shifted her gaze to Brighton, who stood a few steps back. Neither agent looked happy. In fact, the look in the woman's clear green eyes bordered on murderous. Still, manners were manners.

"Ms. Brighton! To what do I owe the pleasure?"

"*Pleasure?*" The blast from the lockbox paled beside her outburst. "I wouldn't say it's a pleasure to find out you're sidelining for Christopher!" She advanced through the front door and backed McKay into the living room under the weight of her fury. "Pleasure is going to be firing your sorry ass because. . . . What the hell is that smell?"

The odor of burned plastic and god knew what else had followed McKay's rush up the stairs and pervaded the upper floor.

"Christopher's idea of a binding contract." Gallows humor was the best she could do. "Can you shut the door behind you, or do you want to do this on the front step?"

Rice wordlessly shut the door behind them, none too gently.

"What the hell is going on this time, McKay?" Brighton's tone was a fraction less harsh.

McKay braced herself for argument, then realized there was no benefit and let the moment go with a long breath. "Brighton, your timing, again, is impeccable. Come on downstairs. You can yell at me while I finish cleaning up."

"Cleaning up what?"

"What's left of my equipment." A quick glance over her shoulder showed her that, while somewhat mollified, Brighton would likely start in on her again as soon she gave her an opening.

"I was scrubbing a contract wafer for malware, and it blew up, literally. They must have impregnated the plastic with something." McKay opened the door. The exhaust fan had worked, yet a trickle of haze erupted from the lab when she opened the door.

"Smells like SireniaV," Rice told his boss. "You can soak just about anything in it, and when it gets enough of a static charge, kaboom."

"Lovely. I wonder if that's his standard business practice," Brighton returned acidly. The edge seemed off her ire, which in McKay's opinion was a good thing. She'd managed to dodge the knockdown drag out that seemed inevitable when she'd opened the front door.

"Would you guys mind staying out here?" McKay pointed them at the postage stamp of a backyard and retrieved a galvanized steel bucket languishing by the back door, leaving it open so the agents stairs, but Brighton remained standing, distracted again by a communication coming into her ear. McKay repurposed the bucket as a trash can and shoveled the remnants of the lockbox into it.

"Don't worry, McKay, we're not here to pirate any of your tech toys," Rice drawled.

"No, you're here to fire my ass because you think I sold you out to Christopher." McKay held the smoking bucket up to Rice's face as she passed.

She walked the bucket across to the corner of the yard outside so the contents could finish outgassing as far away from the House as possible. Things were moving way into hardball territory, and her usual state of denial wasn't cutting it anymore. McKay returned to the lab and surveyed the damage, the Overlay tallying repair times and costs as her gaze lit on one burned patch after another. It was mostly surface, but at least she could get to work without choking to death on the fumes. And she desperately wanted to get to work, to lose herself again in figuring out the players and purpose of this whole mess to keep her mind off the bullet she'd just dodged.

The blast splattered the walls and cabinets with soot and blackened plastic—but the 'mites were already at work cleaning up there. The granite tabletops, cribbed from a chem lab that went under, were unhurt, of course. She opened the server cabinet. All the little green lights save one were dimmed. The lockbox was isolated from any network, but it still had to draw power and had been plugged in right alongside everything else with minimal surge protection. McKay hadn't considered the effects a power surge from the lockbox might have. *Going to have to report this one to Saiid so he can tweak the design.*

"We've been keeping an eye on you, Ms. McKay," Brighton began, somewhat more mildly than before.

"Good job there."

"Hmmmm. Well, SOMEBODY destroyed the tracking 'mites we left on her." Brighton's look made clear what a stupid move she felt that had been. "Arm's length seemed a good idea back when we didn't consider brute-force tactics to be part of Christopher's pattern."

"You didn't consider? They're a part of somebody's pattern, that's for damn sure."

Rice glanced at Brighton, who nodded. McKay caught a snippet of data as it passed between them.

"This kind of thing," McKay railed on, gestured at the smoking bucket, "is the wrong fingerprint for Christopher. He buys companies, crushes stock values. Something like this is way too lowbrow."

Rice got to his feet and stepped across the yard to the still-smoking bucket. He retrieved a chunk of plastic and vanished upstairs into the house with it. McKay heard the front door snick open and close again with surprising speed.

"Christopher handed me the damn contract himself. Maybe he's downgraded his tactics, or maybe someone else is in the middle of all this." Words nearly failed McKay and she gestured tightly at the ruin in the lab space. "I don't usually have to worry about lethal overspill into the rest of my contract work."

"Tell me what Christopher wanted. How did that meeting go?" Brighton had followed Rice back into the House and now leaned against the wall at the base of the stairs, arms crossed, effectively blocking McKay's exit. The action was not lost on McKay. She decided to give up the abbreviated version.

"In a nutshell, one of Christopher's employees tried to set me up for something, probably another system-hack, guy named Aaron Tanh. Christopher called him off, seemed pretty pissed about the whole thing. He said he wanted to be copied on anything I found out about your missing persona." She beckoned for Brighton to precede her up the stairs. After a long hesitation, the agent complied. McKay pulled the glass door to the back yard closed behind them and set the lock.

"I didn't trust Christopher enough to drop a sig there in the offices, and now I'm not sure I would have come out at all if I hadn't agreed," McKay said.

"We know Tanh," Brighton admitted. "He's a known associate of Christopher's, tends to be impulsive in the punchy-stabby kind of way. He probably figured he could get whatever Christopher wanted out of your head without the boss getting involved."

"That doesn't quite match up with what I saw. He brought up Rose's name while he had me under the barrel of a gun. So if he is working for Christopher, that means your programmer is in on it too. And why the hell does everyone seem to think that STICKING A PLUG INTO MY SKULL is going to give them unrestricted access to my thoughts?" It was a rhetorical question, but after a second failed attempt to hack her head, she felt like it had to be shouted. Brighton ignored the outburst. "On top of that, I got to meet your contact, Miranda Bosch. I don't think she's the mid-grade UX designer you guys think she is."

"Tanh's not to be trifled with, McKay," Brighton said over her shoulder as she topped the stairs and passed into the living room. "And stay well the hell away from Bosch. We don't want Christopher to have even an inkling that she's been working with us." She turned and waited for McKay without taking a seat.

"Yeah, I kind of figured that out when the box exploded. So what the hell am I supposed to be doing here? I can't even conduct regular business without having to check and see if it's some sort of trap first."

Another communication made its way to Brighton's ear, McKay could feel it through the Swim. She called the Overlay and asked it to crack the encryption on the communication link. No more secrets, no more guesswork. Whatever information she was getting or giving, McKay needed to know.

The swallows were back, the signature impression of Brighton's offsite hacker. McKay had figured it was Rice she was talking to, but it was the same programmer that had been keeping her undercover when they'd first met back in Singapore. *It feels wrong for Rose though, someone else.* Brighton paced the room, turned to look at her.

"The faster you help us get Mike back, the faster all this is out of your hair."

"Really? You think these guys are going to leave me alone as soon as I perform the extraction? I didn't sign on for the paranoia train here. I need to know everything that's going on so I don't get blindsided again."

"I'm putting a team member on your house. I didn't expect you would be targeted directly. No one outside Vector7 is supposed to know you've been hired for this, not even the rest of ANT. I don't like it, but I'm not giving you anything that's going to compromise the rest of the team. You work with what you have." Her mouth set in a firm line, like she expected McKay to argue.

"Fine. They can use the spare bedroom." She was past arguing, just hoping for twelve hours without someone trying to hack, crack, blow up, or otherwise cripple her.

"Ha ha," Brighton said mirthlessly. "I'm talking to Lyman now, he'll set up something remote for starters."

So your ghost coder has a name. Good to know. McKay asked the Overlay to see what it could dig up.

"I'll get a warm body outside your place tomorrow." Brighton paused, one hand on the doorknob. "Let me know when you find something on Mike, and don't fucking give it to Christopher until I get a look at it first."

"Are you kidding?" McKay faked a shrug with her one good shoulder. "I don't work for guys who wreck my gear. The overhead's too high."

"Just so we're all on the same page with this." The eyes took on the appearance of green chips of ice. "I'll be in touch, Ms. McKay."

"I'm sure you will." McKay shut the front door behind her and shot the bolt. Then she fetched a dining chair and jammed it under the doorknob. The action made her feel marginally safer.

FOURTEEN

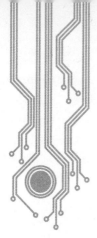

THE REPAIR TIME was going to slow her down. It was a welcome inconvenience, forcing her to re-task, to fix something that she actually had a chance of fixing. It allowed McKay to regain some semblance of control. The breakers between all the House electronics had been tripped, minute miteware circuit breakers connected to a much larger magnetic switch. She needed a few minutes of shoving furniture and a double-dose of painkillers for the shoulder to get into the various secret alcoves to get all the computers in the House reset properly, but soon the Overlay's soft green lines and dots confirmed she'd done it right.

McKay went downstairs long enough to retrieve the headset in its diamond-patterned case, deliberately avoiding *looking* at anything in the wrecked room, just grabbing the case and shutting the door again. The 'mites were taking care of the damage to the cabinets, but the rest would require scrubbing and some paint as well.

The master bedroom wasn't as conducive to drifting in the Swim as the office and its comfy chair, but it would have to do. Now that the hardware in the House was all up and running, she had to run maintenance on the software to match. She chucked herself onto the bed and descended into the Swim as soon as the last of the pin connectors clicked into place. The data flow within the House was slow, sluggish after the disruption and damage downstairs. McKay felt sluggish too. She wallowed in the data, pushing through rather than slipping and diving. Eddies caught at her and pulled her this way and that as she tried to visit each spin-server in turn. *Spike was right.* The primary computer was hammered: the data it passed to the rest was jumbled and garbled, passing down the line, flowing through each server, bouncing from one to another, making the drives thrash to no good effect. She changed the connections, re-braiding them one by one and stripping all the garbage out. It seemed like forever in the Swim but probably took only an hour in real-time.

As she sank deeper, the master bedroom around her vanished into the large, cavernous concrete space that represented her own mind.

Spike's icon flashed in the corner of her vision once, twice, three times before turning sideways, and the sprite emerged, shimmering and vaguely serpentine in the full flow of virtual space. In the Swim, the sprite could assume any form it chose, unconstrained by the rules of McKay's Overlay.

"Are you done with the meat-puppets yet? Because this is kind of important."

"Let's hear it." McKay closed her eyes and the felt the flow pick up around her. The refreshed House computer took up its duties with a will. The grass outside came back online with a vengeance, screaming belated alerts that Brighton and her surly sidekick had left. McKay calmed it, acknowledging the alarms and resetting the sensors. The miteline in the grass was still her old, clunky prototype, still able to accept new commands and parameters, unlike the modern hard-coded commercial grass at Katie's or the patent violations at Christopher's office. Leaving it in place had been an "oversight" when her license had been stripped, so she treasured the chance to reprogram it.

"Remember the tracking code you added to the Mike persona? The 'bots picked it up at the Uokohaiden Credit Union two days ago, but we've had an attrition rate of sixty-five percent since then."

"Attrition?" Had McKay spoken aloud, the word would have been a bleat of surprise. Attrition meant something was destroying her 'bots, not just evading them. An echo in her perception suggested she had said the word aloud, but in her own House, she could be as weird as she liked.

"Inside voice, please." Spike confirmed her suspicions with a snarky grin. "Yes, it looks like a hostile program, or programs, are hunting them down and unraveling them."

"They're 'bots. What's the point?"

Spike shook its silvered, bony head. "Something's trying to keep them from reporting back to you. None of the bunch that came in direct contact made it back to your systems. We've known where he is for hours, but no one made it back to tell you."

"Goddammit, this is going to take a long session, isn't it?"

It wasn't a question. McKay was already clawing her way back out to real-space to mix the neurotransmitter cocktails she was going to need. She was already feeling the effects of stress and time in the Swim and decided not to risk a crash, not if she was going to face down Mike. Spike followed, dropping in resolution and detail as the program transferred itself onto McKay's Overlay and resumed its human form.

"All right, guide me on these. I need something for focus as well as the usual run of boosters." McKay sat up, pulled the headset case over and fished around inside for the smaller case of glass vials and plastic canisters she used to concoct her boosters. Back in Singapore she'd had time to pre-mix them, have them ready to hand. Today was going to be a little more off the cuff, since she didn't know just what was waiting for her, or how long she'd be under.

"All right, start off with ten ccs of dioxepine red. The one on the far left with the green cap." The sprite squared its thumbs and forefingers up like a picture frame. When it drew its hands apart the space between them became a sheet of data, an elaborate page of light with instructions written out.

"Got it." Cross-legged on the bed, McKay grabbed an empty plastic bottle. "How many are in the sequence?"

"For this run, with your hyped-up nervous system and the drugs you took for the shoulder, I'd say four. Here." Spike passed the page to McKay. "You know, this would be much simpler if you just used a timed-drip IV line. It would save you the trouble of choking the stuff down."

McKay grabbed a pipette from the kit and roughly measured another ten ccs of what looked like black cherry syrup into the bottom of a shot-size plastic squeeze bottle, then added the next three liquids in sequence, capped the bottle, and gave it a vigorous shake.

"That's a step too far, even for me. I spend enough time in the Swim as it is, I don't need to start installing stents to stay in longer."

"Wuss." Again Spike showed a snarky grin.

McKay couldn't remember if facial expressions were part of Spike's original code or if it picked them up during the decade or so it'd been free-roaming. She mixed up three more doses, following Spike's instructions.

"That's Latin for 'not-insane,' right?" McKay drank off one of the neurotransmitter shots and grimaced. There were few flavors that could make any mix that involved caffeine and l-lysine taste better than awful. She got comfortable, kept one of the shots in one hand, set the other two on the bed in easy reach so she didn't have to break concentration to take them later if needed. The Overlay seemed to shiver in response, and the concrete amphitheater took shape around her once again.

"I thought you were going to redecorate this place." Spike gained resolution again as it transferred back to the House servers. "And why do you keep it so cold in here?"

"I did redecorate. The floor's different."

Spike looked down as if the floor of the virtual space had become covered in virtual snakes. "Oh yes. Ferroconcrete is such an aesthetic upgrade from plain old concrete."

"It was cheap. Are you going to show me where we're going, or what?"

"And you wonder why no dude will date you after you bring him in here. Bachelorette city."

"How the hell would you know?"

Spike spun itself into an icon, not the rattle-jawed spike and skull McKay knew so well, but something simpler, a fifth grade geography homework assignment, not worthy of hacking, cracking, disbanding, or mucking with at all. McKay did something similar to her own appearance, no sense in going out without cover. She looked up at the circular hatch in the ceiling of the concrete dome and cycled it open with a thought, giving herself direct access to the Swim beyond.

The metaphor of the space was important. It reminded her to set and reset the software firewalls that protected the House systems from an outside attack, an attack she was starting to feel was inevitable. The stress inhibitors in the mix she drank whisked that thought away, took with it the chattering fear that she'd been keeping crammed into the corner of her mind. She had more immediate problems, *actionable* problems, like who was tearing up her 'bots and what she was going to do to them in return.

Spike slipped out into the Swim and McKay stepped aside to avoid the data trickling in—half notes, prefixes, bits and semicolons dripped from larger, less efficient programs as they traveled, leaving a snail trail of data in their wake. McKay leapt up and caught the lip, then pulled herself into the digital current. A quick look back into the bunker showed a copy of herself left behind, the core version of McKay, the original, as it were, cross-legged on the concrete floor in a puddle of data, eyes closed and drifting as she followed the action, relaxed for the first time in days. The extra power the headset afforded gave McKay room to split her attention into multiple copies, an advanced form of the persona process that Mike had used. The danger was that McKay's experiences in the Swim were sent right to the brain. No buffer, no chance to soften the blow if something went wrong. A livemind experienced everything in the Swim at full volume and a careless engineer could wind up, *had wound up*, with a brutal case of PTSD, or worse, without proper precautions. Multiply that by every copy McKay created and the risk kept climbing.

Spike shifted gears and found an eddy in the currents around the House firewalls. McKay executed a quick flip and followed him. Around her, a cluster of smaller programs skimmed and darted into the eddy like minnows, around and down until it flushed them all out into the City trunk line's broader currents. Spike fed them information in quickly fired packets that looped out in the Swim like homing missiles and came back.

In an instant, the host of smaller 'bots surrounded McKay, swarming like pigeons, picking and pecking, shoving each other aside to intercept Spike's data packets. They could be malware, search 'bots, viruses, crawlers, scavengers, inhabitants of the Swim's sticky underside, some coded and forgotten, some released or dumped like a bag of unwanted kittens; some were set free like little digital panthers to stalk and do harm, others designed by some kid who didn't understand how to write in the unravel to finish them off when their tasks were done.

Spike fired another dozen or so packets, probably dummies, then dove into the main current. McKay stayed a moment, watching the lost 'bots squabble. Some got the packets and destroyed them or turned them into tiny, malformed copies of themselves. One broody search program cached a couple of packets and guarded them with an alley cat's jealous eye. Three lost 'bots—taken over, rewritten, and repurposed by Spike's data packets—displayed their new master's spike-and-skull icon. They too flung themselves into the Swim, flitting away on whatever errand the more sophisticated program gave them.

McKay tethered herself to Spike and let the sprite tow her along while she reviewed the situation. One of the 'bots McKay sent looking for Mike Miyamoto's persona had located its quarry in the City Swim, where the ten square blocks of corporate sector hubs dumped their information into the pool. Its report placed Mike at Ban National Insurance, from where she could integrate with the system and then use the company's internal network to drop back out in any one of a dozen locations worldwide.

Curiously, while the little 'bot had recorded the persona going into and coming out of a half dozen corporate systems, it always came back into the City Swim somewhere, circling the same spaces. *Looking for something, or someone?*

McKay shifted her attention back to the original version of herself, waiting in the bunker of her own mind, and opened her eyes. Around her the dome came to life, bringing up the Ban National system's schematics. Like any bit-island in the Swim, an edifice like that affected the flow of data around it profoundly. Once inside you got a direct route to a handful of much faster privately owned servers, but also to a host of seedier, undoubtedly virus-laden and kludged-together legacy systems as well. *Why Ban National, and why all the hopping in and out?*

What exactly do you want, Mike? McKay asked the data silently. Clearly something game-changing had overcome the persona, something that altered the concept of perception so completely that the system couldn't parse how to write it back. Not likely information, as Brighton expected, not a fact, but an experience, a revelation—but what? What could a guy in a special operations unit discover to cause such a turnaround? That sort of thing was usually the purview of porn seekers and genius-level mathematicians.

But maybe that was the point. Maybe whatever had happened to Mike in the Swim hadn't been work related. Brighton was fixated on the idea, sure, so was Rose. She had no clue what Rice was thinking: the man never said more than three words at a stretch.

In the five years since she set up shop as a freelancer she'd seen a wide variety of reasons to perform an extraction. Occasionally, committing one's mind to the copy process afforded an unusual level of self-examination and clarity. Sometimes you just figured something out about yourself or your worldview that didn't fit any longer. A few upscale therapists had her on speed dial for patients of theirs who finally made a breakthrough. Maybe whatever had happened to Mike had been the same.

Not that Brighton would listen to her on the subject. Or maybe she'd already figured that out and wanted the change in Mike's mindset written out anyway. She was using work reasons to help her boss hang on to that growth. *Now that's an interesting thought.*

In the back of her mind, McKay mulled over the problem of what to do with the rogue persona, provided she could corner it. *Dismissing the persona-version of Mike as a rogue is the wrong way to think about it,* she reminded herself. Whatever its proper nature, the persona had at least the perception of free will, which meant that it had a goal, an end to attain, and it was McKay's job to sort that out.

The modified, undercover Mike would have one set of motivations and the new, stripped-clean Mike would have another. That's got to be the focus of this next conversation. What does he want now?

McKay refocused and jumped herself back to the copy of herself being pulled by Spike through the Ban National internal network's knotty system. Like many companies, they just kept adding systems, new on top of old, so the access point was there, somewhere. McKay just had to figure out where they put it. She dove down to the Swim's slowest bottom levels.

Spike found it first. There, in a thousand sticky lines of code, the sprite found the access point, folded itself flat, then flat again, and slid in sideways with McKay close behind. The access point dithered a moment, opening and closing like a spiky anemone, then went about its business as McKay and Spike slid into the system's slower, thicker Swim stream.

Piece of cake. McKay reconfigured herself into something more powerful, something that could shove through the morass of data. Ban National had a direct link into the Peninsula Technological University systems, a thin pipe Spike led her through next. McKay was beginning to feel a little stretched.

The university system was far more chaotic than the City or even the multiple layers of Ban National. It was more like diving into the crazed technobubble under Berkeley. Communications packets, long looping strings of data, some non-optimized software oozing slowly along the floor, uploading and downloading massive copyright violations. Inexpertly written student projects, trailing long brittle spires and tails of unnecessary code, puttered along on their way to the different course servers. It was like wandering through a natural jungle experiment gone wild—until Spike side-slipped into one of the puddles of data housed by PenTech's swimLab.

The creepily pristine space inside was very quiet and very well organized. McKay moved very carefully. Unlike the messier public institute servers, the swimLab was dedicated to research and development projects that affected the Swim. It meant any security she was likely to encounter was experimental, something she would have to code for on the fly. Spike's icon shimmered and faded, and McKay followed suit, matching her outward appearance to the orderly semi-translucent bits of information parading through the space. The Mike persona, if there at all, must have done something similar, disguising itself as something that belonged.

Spike's icon hovered nearby, pinging McKay occasionally with little packets of information as she discovered traces of Mike's passage. Tripping the system alarm to flush the persona out would be quick but costly, and McKay'd likely risk getting Spike and herself flushed as well. She was about to call off this segment of the search when Spike pinged a warning and something shot past.

Dammit, there he goes!

The shimmering form of Mike's persona flashed as it erupted from hiding. Three more blips shot by in close pursuit, the recognition codes identifying them as the remnants of her cloud of little 'bots. Spike's warning stopped McKay as she turned to follow.

A long, opaque tentacle of malware streaked past and struck one of McKay's 'bots, unraveling it into flashing lines of code that faded into nothing as they errored out and failed. McKay's glance followed the darkness back to the main body squeezing itself through the narrow pipe into the swimLab. It roiled along the floor, a mass of tentacles that reached out constantly, touching, retrieving, collecting, assembling. It resembled nothing so much as an octopus made out of the space between keystrokes.

McKay's tiny construct babbled as it came undone, firing data packets in all directions in a virtual death scream. Its remaining two colleagues swooped through like minnows, picking the packets up and scattering. What was worse, the 'bot's remnants stuck to the tentacle as it drew back, clips and phrases of code McKay recognized dangling limply like cut seaweed.

"Follow Mike, make sure he gets out." She pinged Spike with the instruction and slipped into a form more apt for pursuing the few remaining 'bots. The tentacle came again, but they were all well out of range, and it retracted this time without a prize.

McKay was careful not to antagonize it but watched and analyzed the code as the swimLab's security noticed its presence and started to sling attacks at it. As a piece of programming, it was messy—a solid, tightly coded inner core under layers and layers of junk, useless numbers, defunct functions. Unlike the garbage code in the inexperienced student work she'd seen in the Peninsula Tech main servers, this was calculated, written to confuse and disguise. This beast of a program could lie in the bowels of some legacy system for weeks like a malformed crocodile, waiting for an event to trigger it again. As she watched, the opaque tentacles whipped out repeatedly, stilling the whirring security protocols and silencing the half-empty server. There was something oddly familiar about it.

Just where the hell did you come from?

Her first thought was that it belonged in the swimLab, a pet project maybe, or a rough draft of something yet to be polished. She could see the familiar lines of a basic AI program in there, but parts were missing: it seemed incomplete. If it belonged, lab security should have ignored it. *That's what's been destroying my 'bots. That's what Spike brought me here to see.*

That Beast was hunting Mike, keeping him on the run, which meant that McKay needed to keep track of its movements as well. McKay wrote a silver string of code and flung it. Like a remora, it would fasten on the underbelly of the Beast, invisible among the sheets of misdirection. McKay would need to be better prepared to tackle a program this complex. The remora would tell her just where to come looking when she was ready.

McKay changed her focus, prepared to make the jump back to her own head. She didn't wait to watch the remora strike, and she didn't see the Beast cast an attack back in return. The slip of bad code the Beast sent out, dark and oily as her own had been bright, caught her unawares, getting a hook into her as she made the jump. *What the hell was THAT?!?* McKay jerked, felt herself coming apart around the edges as she frantically triggered the code that would dump her out of the Swim and back into her own head. The Swim copy of herself screamed as it came undone, rattled her as she opened her eyes back in the vault of her own headspace again.

Too goddamn close. She shuddered and stared around the concrete vault, reassuring herself that she was, in fact, back in her own skull. She'd never been caught like that before. Disassembling a program or persona was one thing, but she wasn't even sure what would happen to a livemind caught that way. She'd had nightmares about it—every xWire she knew had secret fears about what it might do if you tried to take a living mind apart as if were a program. She didn't know anyone who'd tried it.

In theory, you could snap back to yourself like a ball on a rubber band, or the unravel might work just like it did on a persona, leaving you to wake up back in your own skull with no recollection of the event. It was also possible that the shock of having your living personality unraveled would leave you brain dead, or even dead-dead.

She eyed the door in the concrete ceiling of her own mind, debating shutting the link off entirely, but Spike hadn't returned, and she wasn't comfortable shutting the sprite out just yet. It was probably foolish; the program lived and breathed the Swim, but McKay couldn't help feeling like she'd abandoned a friend.

But maybe she could do something about that.

McKay brought the filing systems up, racks of carefully organized tabs holding his library of programming gems, sketched in light against the metaphor of the space behind her eyelids. She pulled open a large workspace with her hands and began to write in the air. Every so often she rifled the cabinets, pulling out saved snippets of code and plugging them into the imaginary space. The algorithms and phrases glowed faintly, changing colors as parameters changed and checks failed. At one point she tore a whole segment out with her fingers, crumpled it into a ball, and chucked it on the floor. The hexagonal concrete tiles shifted aside, exposing a long, bright tongue snaking from a toothed maw to grab the discarded snippet and draw it in for disposal.

Finally McKay was satisfied, or at least mostly so. She tore the code down in one long movement, like ripping off a sheet of paper, and carried it between her hands to the chamber wall and attached it, smoothing it against the cold concrete until it sank in, glowing numbers and letters etching themselves into the surface, then skittering away like little shining crabs, vanishing. They were patches; add enough of them and over time they'd create new vulnerabilities. For now they'd offer additional protection, just in case the Beast followed her home.

McKay repeated the ritual twice, then a third time, but rather than fuse the final round of code with the defensive concrete structure in her mind, she folded it over and over until the packet was the size of her thumb. In a moment, she wrote out another 'bot and sent it into the Swim with instructions to deliver the packet to Spike. She felt a twinge of guilt at what had happened to the previous batch of 'bots, but they were created to be disposable. The 'bots weren't people, or even full-blown AIs, but that didn't make her feel any better when they were shredded while following her instructions.

McKay made more adjustments, tightened security here and there. The link between herself and the now-destroyed Swim copy of her mind had been cut. The Beast shouldn't be able to follow her back.

Unless the Beast can pull something out of the 'bot it took. Shit. And I thought I was already getting paranoid. The 'bots always knew where home was, where to come back to. She hadn't coded them to specifically wipe that information because she hadn't anticipated something was actively going to attack them.

Spike, as "search engine with issues," had been running around in the Swim for a decade. McKay had always just assumed it could take care of itself.

So what's got you so nervous now?

The code she sent to Spike was defensive, extra protection against the kind of brute-force malware the Beast seemed to be based on.

Something about the Beast code was familiar, something she'd recognize if she just had enough time to focus on it. Something that made her very uncomfortable. McKay sat back in the chair and had the Overlay call up all the information she'd managed to collect so far.

One. It was hunting the same persona as she was. *Two.* Whoever sent it knew she was involved, and was actively looking for her programs specifically as they scoured the Swim for Mike. That, at least, gave her a very narrow field to work with. *Three.* Despite its outward amateur appearance, the Beast was a program written by a very skilled somebody. That helped keep Christopher at the top of her list, but still wasn't a smoking gun. Brighton had skilled coders on her team, but it seemed counterproductive for any of them to have written it: they had a proper inside line on Mike. *Unless they need to get to him before I do? That makes even less sense.* That idea put Rose back on the list, but the code she'd grabbed didn't match her style. Lyman, Brighton's offsite coder, hadn't stepped into the ring at all. McKay hadn't even had direct contact with him.

The Overlay scrolled through the layers of Beast code she managed to come away with, text changing color to show where fragments started and stopped, what functioned and what didn't. Most of it was junk, a few telltale pieces hinting here and there at what lay underneath. The trick was going to be in figuring out what pieces mattered and what had just been added as layers of obfuscation. The hand was familiar; the way the code was commented, the choices the programmer made, all suggestive, but she couldn't put a face to the program. She would have to collect a copy of the complete Beast program if she hoped to get a good look at what all those layers concealed and who put together such a nasty brute-force bit of software.

McKay spun down the Overlay and emerged from the Swim. The walls of her bedroom resolved around her and she flopped onto her back on the bed. The comforter softened the impact and she left the headset in place, wrapped around the back of her skull. She wasn't ready to take it off yet, wasn't quite ready to disconnect completely while Spike was still out there with the Beast.

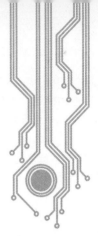

FIFTEEN

In the dream, the shower was no help at all. McKay turned the scrubber on her knuckles, trying to get the remnants of the Beast off her hands, her face. She felt sticky all over, as if she had literally walked through the thing on her way out. *Jesus, Spike. . . .* The latest upgrades had snapped a tooth all right, but the cost! She shuddered, though the water was as scalding as the wretched old heater could get it. Digits and values sluiced out of the showerhead and over her body but did not wash away the marks of the brawl-fest she'd been through. She scrubbed anyway, calling configuration after configuration out of the air. Purges, cluster scrubs, nothing seemed to help. As she worked over her hands, her arms, her chest, she became aware of a second pair of hands touching her, following her movements. Well-used, delicate, they touched her skin and the marks faded, running off into the code swirling down the drain. The hands' touch was firm, not much subtlety but plenty of confidence. Up her chest to her shoulders, the nape of her neck, everywhere, they touched and the marks faded along with the memory. Someone blew breath on the back of her skull. Warm lips brushed her ear.

"So convenient to find you in the shower." The voice was female, contralto. Familiar, though she couldn't place it. Truth be told, she didn't try to place it. The hands moved downward, tickling her stomach, her hips, data cascading over the backs of the firm hands as they moved. The unknown woman pulled in closer. She closed her eyes and felt the heat of her breasts against her back, her lips on her shoulder. She turned, feeling her skin slide against someone else's. Eyes once a glorious brown sheeted over with light. Her pigtails were undone; dark wet hair piled around her shoulders and clung to her skin like the tattoos that covered her back and arms. She stepped in and trapped her, one hand behind her head, fingers in her close-cropped hair. When she kissed, her lips were dangerously hot, hotter than McKay expected, and when they came up for air her tattoos glowed, venting the excess heat to protect the spin. The liquid pouring from the shower struck them and hissed, vaporizing on contact. She responded to her own need, fingers tracing the patterns in her skin. They felt like hot wire, molten and flexible. *Too hot.* A part of her mind warned her, a part soon shoved into a corner by more primal forces. A need driven by too many close calls, by the sense of mortality invading her tightly controlled universe.

She moved her hands again, stood on tiptoe to press her hips in tighter. The steam filled the tiny shower, equations and calculations fragmenting under the heat and dissipating into the air, gently caressing her skin. *Too Hot! TOO HOT!* The damned voice wouldn't shut up, distracting her, unwelcome, like a mosquito in her ear. McKay pulled away to search for the source, but the other woman's grip was firm, and she pulled her back down, one hand on the nape of her neck, fingering the unbroken skin of her scalp, the other hand fingering far more important parts below. She heard the *tick-tick* of the barbell in her tongue darting between her teeth.

TOO HOT TOO HOT! The Overlay finally broke through the dream, viral incursion warnings overriding everything.

"Shit!" Rose shoved her away, hard. Her head should have hit the cold tile shower wall, but the illusion was shattered, and McKay convulsed on the bed, senses awash in conflicting data.

"Next time."

Rose's voice was fading, and McKay lashed out in some combination of fear and frustration, bringing the headset to bear on the source of the attack and unleashing antiviral software with a shout that made it out of the space in her head and into the real world. Her counterattack hit something in the Swim, McKay felt it give, come unraveled, but she was still confused, trapped in the space between waking and the concrete bunker in her mind. The headset reacted defensively, slamming everything shut, pulling up the firewalls, cutting her off and spinning the Overlay down so she could recover.

In a heartbeat she was alone again, curled on her side, gasping as if she'd been kicked in the gut. *What the hell was that?!* The Overlay was silent, awaiting her command to unlock and spin up, to reestablish the blend of mind and machine that were a part of almost every waking moment.

She'd fallen asleep waiting for Spike with the link still open. Stupid, yes, but the dream, the contact, that hadn't happened before, that *should not have been possible.* She released the headset and counted to ten while the hundred or so tiny spikes retracted from the contact points in her skull. She dropped it unceremoniously on the pillow and scrubbed her hands through her hair. The headache emerged slowly from behind her eyes, through the temples and into her neck. Maybe, just possibly, someone had cracked her defenses and established the link to keep her occupied, to keep her from what? To do what, exactly? *And why the image of Rose?* It couldn't have *been* her, not with the middle-of-the road, off-the-shelf rig she was sporting the only time they'd met.

Unless it was. Actual mind-to-mind contact required xWire at the very least and a set of very specific specs at that. Rose had gone under the knife in Singapore. Maybe she'd come out with a rig to waltz right into McKay's systems.

The viral defenses are reactive. The Overlay ought to automatically block anything trying to get in without permission.

She reached for the headset case. *Shit.* Her hands, the front of her shirt were sticky. She had crushed the plastic squeeze bottle, the neurotransmitter cocktail left over from her recent dip into the Swim with Spike. The rest of the pieces came together. She hadn't removed the headset; she must have fallen asleep while trying to put the puzzle pieces together. That explained the headache, the jitters in her vision, probably even explained the dream. The brain could only generate neurotransmitters so fast before resources ran low *and a full-blown serotonin crash is exactly why you don't do some dumb-ass thing like sleeping with the headset running.*

The neurotransmitter cocktails would get her brain back up to speed in time, but there'd still be a wait before she could get into the Swim in any meaningful fashion. She could spin up the Overlay. Even in her reduced capacity it could tell her what had happened. She just couldn't bring herself to do it just yet. McKay swallowed the painkillers and scrabbled about on the comforter until she found the remaining squeeze bottles. The programmer downed them both and levered herself up onto her feet. A shower helped, and she stayed under the spray until the House's rickety old heater coughed up the last of the hot water and the sunset turned the light in the living room to a darker shade of orange.

A sound filtered into the steamy bathroom, something not-digital, a *ping-ping* that tickled a memory somewhere. The cloud of steam that followed her from the bathroom dissipated in the colder air, and the noise grew louder. *Jesus, what now?* She couldn't place it. None of the ambient electronics would make such a sound. It was tinny, out of date. Mildly alarming.

If someone's going to blow up the House, they're hardly going to put a ticker on it, she chided herself and retreated to the bedroom for a pair of pants. *With today's luck I'd end up on the street with nothing but the damn towel to my name.*

A quick pad through the House revealed the source, a very un-bomb-like box mounted on the kitchen wall, half forgotten. It was the hands-free telephone speaker for the House, old fiber-optic technology that the state required in every home in case of an emergency. It had been years since she'd heard the alert with her own ears. Once she recognized it, the sound was strange, a sharp ping more mechanical than digital. Vaguely nostalgic, comforting, like nothing harmful could ever come through the phone line. She punched the button on the speaker.

"McKay residence." Again that tingle of nostalgia. The older form of address was automatic, drilled in by her strict old grandmother over the course of a dozen summers.

"Dude, *you're* on the landline? What the hell?" Trevor was possibly the only person outside a surfer experiana who still said "dude." *And he's the only one who would have thought to contact me using the old, City-mandated landline.*

"Yeah. Yeah, there was a thing."

"A thing? Dude, Ron just pinged me, said your computer system's been quarantined, nothing in or out."

"Shit." It felt as lame as it sounded. "I haven't been back in yet to check what happened."

"This is a City Quarantine, dude! We wanted to make sure you weren't in the Swim when it went up."

I . . . I have no words for this.

City Quarantine was bad, expensive and—more to the point—crippling. She wouldn't be able to access the Swim from the House for days, or longer. Whatever else the bizarre dream might have been, it had been part of an attack on her system that had tripped the City's antivirus software. That was the other problem with neurotransmitter depletion. It was depressive. She hadn't considered, *wasn't able to consider,* all the ramifications of her sleeping sojourn into the Swim, hadn't had the willpower to open up the Overlay and check. She was shut out until the City sent in a specialist to verify the servers were clean. She'd need new permits, and all her careful work to make the House nearly invisible in the Swim was now a do-over.

"Jesus-H-Fucking-Christ," she said quietly. *Inside voice, moron!* She closed her eyes and leaned against the fridge. During a long pause on the other end, McKay heard other voices in the background, too indistinct to make out.

"You okay, dude?"

"Yes and no. Someone's coming after me, and I'm not sure who just yet."

"Need any help?"

McKay opened her eyes and stared. Set into the backsplash above the stove was a round 'mite-engraved tile, a complex circuit board pattern her oldest brother made for their grandmother in high school. Old. Familiar. Something she saw every day without actually seeing it. A puzzle piece fell into place, followed by another as her mind, free of the Swim's constant babble, searched for input.

"Yes. You remember the lockbox?"

"The one you and Saiid built in, like, twenty-four hours? Should've patented that fucker."

"I think I need to do something just like that again. A twenty-four-hour engineering hack, start to finish. Think splatware. Meet me at Katie's?" A plan was forming, the pieces locking together. There were other programmers in play. The Beast code and whomever was controlling it, whomever had attacked her home system, they felt like different people, different techniques. McKay kept getting caught out; she was too far behind the problem to get a handle on it. *If the problem is too big for just me to handle within the Swim, maybe I can take the problem out of the Swim entirely. Specialized hardware and a place to drive the program to, a system with access points to pull the persona out of the Swim long enough to get it back to the original body and write back without any more degeneration.*

"Meet after work?" Trevor asked again, and McKay realized she'd missed the last few seconds of the conversation.

"Yeah, bring your gear. I want to knock as much of this thing together as possible."

"Can you send me a spec?"

Trevor would be good for an all-nighter for the design, though McKay's running tab at Katie's might take a serious hit. Getting the miteline baked in properly might take an extra day, maybe two. She would make a couple of stops on the way to get components but doubted she'd need anything custom for what she had in mind.

"Not yet. Quarantine, remember."

"Dammit, now you're just teasing me. Okay, send me what you have in mind when you can." The landline clicked, but McKay barely heard it.

Down in her office, a night with the fans running had left only a slight tang in the air, like the aftermath of a nicotine kiss. Two attacks so close together had done a number on the House systems. Blowing up the lockbox had been all physical, but the recent "dream hack" had effectively cut everything off from the Swim.

White fire retardant dust powdered every flat surface in the space. Even the comfy chair looked ghostly in the light through the door. Worst of all, there was utterly no sound. Every blinking light in the room was frosted over and dimmed, every server silent. No hum to stir the air and ear. It was like walking into a tomb. *Or a library.* She was reluctant to disturb the dust, but it was everywhere. Every touch left streaks and smudges and fingerprints.

She searched through the cabinets above and below the granite-topped worktable and fished out a neoprene cooler, one of the semi–hard-sided units with a shoulder strap and some defunct tech startup's corporate logo emblazoned on the side. Into the kit went a half dozen palm-size sealed boxes, a large tin of off-the-shelf miteline, not that she could program it. Snips, twists, nudgers, a handful of pinhead LEDs, three different sizes of blank wafer-sets, and a handful of other useful items like painter's tape and heat-transfer gel. She raided the minifridge and threw in four one-ounce squeeze bottles, as well as five vials of neurotransmitter precursors and an eight ounce bottle of caffeine in suspension. *Katie's stuff is good, but I'm going to need something a little stronger.*

Last, she stood just left of the sliding glass door to the backyard and counted the floor tiles. Had the Overlay been up, she could have called up a map to simply show her the loose tile. As it was, she counted eight up, six over, and took away two to find the one with a hinge. She tap-tap-tapped the center point, and the 'mites holding it together unzipped. The tile divided into two, and McKay flipped the halves back to reveal the space beneath.

Underneath was a 'mite vat, a portable miniature of the ones in Saiid's lab. Long since defunct, it was the perfect size to store her computer backup drives. It was one of the many tokens she kept around from her former life. At some point she'd had some hope that she'd get her licenses reinstated quickly, but over time each of those tokens had fallen into disuse or been repurposed.

A slender, braided rope of miteline penetrated the side and connected it to the long-silent server array. She removed the entire thing, vat and all. A quick pinch and a twist separated the wire, and the unit went whole into the cooler with everything else.

McKay's damaged shoulder protested the weight, and she shifted the cooler to the other side. The 'mites had been doing a reasonable repair job over the past week, but wrenching it again didn't help matters. The headache from earlier, beaten into submission by the precursor cocktails plus painkillers plus shower, was starting to re-emerge.

She closed the door behind her. The room would keep, the servers were offline, safe from whatever or whomever had broken in while she'd been dreaming in the Swim. For the moment, she had bigger fish to fry.

But first she had to build a net.

SIXTEEN

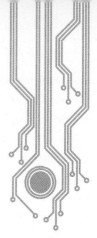

FOR MCKAY, a trip to Parts was akin to taking a four-year-old to the toy mall. Little more than a warehouse-size lucycrete box and half a square mile of parking lot, it housed endless racks of wafer boards, stamps, cooling units, paper water, power supplies, clamps, cutters, designer color quantum dots, thumb-size jars of 'mite-powder sealed in shatterproof Lexite, and more.

Some enterprising soul had jammed a lunch counter against the rear wall, which gave the place an oddly diner-ish smell, even in the kit-digital section where McKay was debating the risks of the Janski unit (had to be bolted down to a table) versus a smaller, sexier 2500-gauss unit. She decided on neither and wandered down the aisle. She always spent twice as much time as planned and usually allocated a solid hour even for the simplest errand.

It would have been nice, cathartic possibly, to lose herself there, to ignore every other mad thing going on in her life, but she needed to meet with Duck before heading on to Katie's. The pieces of code she'd managed to pull from the Beast weren't enough to reconstruct all of its programming and purpose, but Duck worked for the Smithsonian's digital forensics lab. She had the single largest library of code samples on the West Coast. If she could match up anything from the code McKay had grabbed to something in her library, she'd be able to get a better handle on what she was dealing with.

McKay had an uncomfortable feeling that the Beast wasn't something she could avoid dealing with.

Less than an hour before, she had walked the half mile from her House to the transit station and spun up the Overlay in one of the semi-private comm booths there. Eddies and ripples from the quarantine on her neighborhood hub filled the Swim. It was a City quarantine all right, judging by the layers of encryption, the software they had patrolling, sort of like a broad-spectrum closure. Shut everything down and bring in the scrubbers. *Messy. Clumsy.* But letting whomever had come after her think the crash had taken her out of the picture entirely might be an advantage. Some breathing space would be refreshing.

The schematic she had begun work on spun slowly in the corner of her vision. Spin computing was what made the Swim go round, but it was massive and it had to be kept running. Turn off a quantum-spin computer and the q-bits that held the information would become disorganized:, you couldn't save anything the way you did on a hard drive, it wouldn't stick. That meant you couldn't "air-gap" a persona, couldn't put it on a pocket drive and tuck it away in a drawer the way you might protect company secrets or military strategies. A persona was just too big and too volatile for traditional media. But there was a method that suggested that you could freeze or crystallize q-bits, put them into a stable and portable system. It had been done successfully before, but as personas were created to be disposable, there was little market for it. But if Eliza McKay's biggest threats were stalking her within the Swim, then taking Mike *out* of the Swim might give her an advantage. But that wasn't the kind of hardware even a place like Parts' extensive back catalog covered. It was going to have to be built from scratch.

McKay stopped at the 'mite showcase and peered through the glass at the small, Lexite cylinders. Looking only, no touching. If she tried to check out and pay for one of the little tubes of pre-programmed 'mites, as single-task as they might be, she'd spend the next two weeks in jail while the police and intelligence services and her lawyer argued over whether or not that specific style of 'mite-tech was covered in her ban or not.

She didn't have that kind of time right now.

The heat rolled off the acres of parking lot and sweat prickled on her skin. McKay headed to the closest unreserved trike with the AutoPod logo on the back, punched in her access code, and got *Engaged* on the panel, which meant that whomever used it last hadn't logged out.

Two tries later a slim, three-wheeled vehicle granted her entry. She set cooler and kit on the seat before she slid in. The blast from the 'pod's aircon welcomed her as the car adjusted its settings to match her preference file. The engine hummed on, and the Overlay linked up with the vehicle's limited AI servers.

After a moment's hesitation, she asked the Overlay to find Brighton and link her up. McKay had run the thing off the cuff so far, but she would need Brighton's help once she had the persona literally in hand. The Beast chasing Mike would be a problem, but she could deal with it later, once she finished with the extraction end of things. *Get the persona out first, then go gunning for the thing, loaded for bear.*

She rescanned the box specs and gave the 'pod the coordinates for Katie's. The flywheel spun into motion, backing her out of the parking space with smooth precision. She kept one hand on the steering wheel more out of habit than necessity. The 'pod acknowledged the change in destination and left the parking lot to merge with the flow of traffic.

Spike's icon flashed into view, turned a putrid shade of green.

"You know how I hate these things." The sprite's voice in her head was fuzzy.

"Spike! You okay?"

"Except for the motion sickness, fine. Did you know your whole neighborhood got quarantined?" The rolling icon righted itself and regained its color.

"Yeah, there was a thing."

"A thing? You got *cracked*, my girl!" Spike was a little too gleeful for McKay's personal comfort, even with the crummy sound quality. "So, who was it? Was it Boris? Tell me it wasn't Boris!"

McKay winced at the name. Boris Takashi was a reasonably well-known cracker with a penchant for messing with any xWire he found in the Swim. He hadn't targeted McKay yet. The programmer did not look forward to that inevitable encounter.

"No, not Boris. I don't know who it was. The headset fired off Protocol O-Nine, and I haven't had a chance to get back in yet."

"Ouch! Hey, I have a data download for you, but this connection won't hold it. Where are you headed?"

"Katie's, but I can stop over at Ishitomi's public access before I hit the City, if it's important." McKay called up the route map and pegged several public access ports on the way.

"Ugh. How about AXY? The imports always mess up my translation matrices. All my colloquial terms get overwritten."

"Whiner." McKay sent the 'pod AI the AXY coordinates and got a flat error tone that told her no course adjustment was available just then.

"Eliza, what was that?"

"Shut up now, Spike." McKay put the plans away and opened the 'pod control panel. The destination had been changed, circling her back toward her own home instead of taking her to Katie's. She was pretty sure she hadn't been responsible. She inputted the change request again, and again got back the flat note and a polite refusal.

"Great, just great." She tried to disengage the AI and switch to manual control, and was again told politely that such an action was against company regulations except in the case of AI failure.

"Spike, when was the last time a 'pod AI failed?"

"Um, never. Not off the test track at least. It's a hive-AI, distributed network cellular communications, the usual walled garden stuff." The icon turned green again. "I'd also like to point out, however, that there have only been twenty-five recorded crashes since the self-driving lanes were instituted."

"Mmhm." McKay stopped listening and settled deeper into the seat.

"If you crash the car while I'm uplinked with you, I may never speak to you again."

"If the car crashes, you may not be able to speak to me again." McKay accessed the 'pod's array directly. She started by asking nicely. *It never hurts to ask nicely.*

The little vehicle abruptly jinked right, rapping her injured shoulder against the door. It began to accelerate, the flywheel beginning to whine.

"Ow." She would have to make it quick. The AIs used in 'pods were notoriously resistant to outside hacking. If the steering functions were starting to glitch—she involuntarily grabbed the seat as it jinked again—then it had already been pounded on more than was good for it.

The impact was short and sharp, as if someone hit the outside of the 'pod with a baseball bat. The AI started bleeding code into the Overlay, random strings and loops of data shattering as the control program came unraveled. McKay caught an impression of the hacker, stripes and claws and heat, and sicced the Overlay on identification while she swiveled to see what had hit the AutoPod. The vehicle emitted an ominous *klunk*, and sparks shot out behind like a comet's tail.

"Holy sh—" The vehicle slewed sideways. Grabbing the steering wheel with both hands did nothing to stop the slide as the engine ground alarmingly. McKay shut the link to the 'pod AI down with a thought and changed the Overlay to predicting trajectories and impact. Bad news was they were in a middle lane. *Good news is the two cars in front of me are gonna miss by—*

The impact from the car behind her, the one she hadn't yet factored in, spun the 'pod and flipped McKay's world end over end. The Overlay's warning came just in time for her to fling herself sideways and head down as the roof crumpled like a soda can in a clenched fist. *We're gonna die gonna die gonna die. . . .* The voices in her head chanted a protective mantra that cut through the jumble of sensation, the squalling of metal as the 'pod slid on its roof. In the Overlay's space behind her tightly closed eyes she saw the traffic patterns change as the other AIs picked up on her distress and shifted, pulling away and around and to the side of the roadway. The influx of data matched the cadence of the panicked voice in her head. *We're gonna die gonna die gonna die....*

In that odd, pre-impact mind frame, she found the plural somewhat disturbing. When the 'pod hit the guardrail and went over, the final impact shook loose her hold on consciousness, and the data exploded into black.

SEVENTEEN

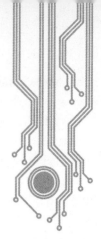

THE EMT SHINED the light into her left eye, the barely perceptible flicker in the bulb canceling out the reflex to close it. Had the Overlay been up and functioning, it would have simply shut the iris to protect the structures within. The fact that it didn't tightened the knot of worry in the pit of McKay's stomach. The tumbling 'pod had cracked her skull against the doorframe when the side airbags deployed a fraction of a second too late and a fraction of an instant before the lights in her head went out. She'd come to propped up into a sitting position against the concrete divider behind the ambulance, shoulders draped in an emergency blanket.

A frown flickered across the medic's face as he checked the readings on the penlight. "I'm showing some pretty extensive 'mite tracing in your skull. What category system are you wired up with?" He plugged the tool into the kit beside him. Like all medical equipment, it sported the same red lacquer as the Singapore buses and the medical trinity in white—crescent, cross, and star.

McKay frowned with the effort of keeping her mind focused on the question. "X," she muttered.

"Crap. Well, you've got a concussion for sure, but I can't give you anything but traditional medicine because of the risk factors."

Par for the course. The insurance companies covered only the most basic forms of internal system architecture, and they never covered the computers themselves, just the deeply integrated wires that connected them. As xWire, McKay had no medical insurance beyond basic 'mite support, but EMTs weren't supposed to care about that.

"How about repair systems? Any Lolli25s or Glasspaks?" The EMT listed off a few of the more popular first-aid 'mite packs as he selected an instrument designed to pick up damage in different densities of flesh and bone. The more sophisticated medical scanners could even analyze McKay's internal miteline and offer treatment options. McKay recalled when Ibarra had first brought his medical kit home from school one weekend. They'd gone through all the instrumentation together, theorizing ways to make it more efficient, more accurate.

"Acers version thirty-eight." McKay offered up the brand name in a half-hearted mumble.

"Aces and Eights? You Silicon Valley kids always have the exotic stuff, don't you?" The EMT looked through the kit. "I have a generic nutrient and component mix here I can give you if you'll sign the waiver."

McKay nodded her assent and barely twitched when the ring of tiny needles punctured the skin on her forearm. The injection site started to itch as the medical 'mites in her system woke up and congregated under the skin, collecting the nutrients and carting them off to repair her body and wiring. They were getting dangerously close to overworked.

"I presume you'll want them to target the systems in your head first? There's not much else other than bruises and abrasions. That shoulder injury is a few days old, but it looks to be healing well. You came through this mess without screwing it up again." His tone was light, conversational. When McKay didn't respond, he snapped fingers under her nose. "Hey! Don't go into shock on me, buddy."

The whole left side of her head ached, and McKay closed her eyes against the sudden brightness in the air.

"Shit." Another sharp jab to the arm, higher up, closer to the vein.

As the drug entered her bloodstream, her focus snapped back. The EMT sprayed something that smelled of menthol on the left side of McKay's head and probed it with a coated fingertip. "That shot should help take care of the shock. The scans show your skull isn't fractured, no signs of bleeding in there, but some of your wiring took a hit, probably broke some connections. You're going to look like the losing end of a boxing match until the 'mites are done with your head."

"Ow." McKay touched her cheekbone, the skin sticky from the topical. "You sent the localization instructions already?"

"Yeah, the 'mites will start with everything in your head first, bio and wire, so expect for the rest of you to feel like ass for a couple days. Take it slow, but don't just crawl in bed and check out for the weekend or you'll risk a blood clot somewhere before the 'mites are done." The pinlights over the EMT's ear flashed in multicolored sequence, and McKay thought she heard a faint hum. "Sorry, gotta go log this in. You stay right here, okay? I'll see where your insurance company wants me to take you."

"Thanks."

The collective 'pod AI slowed and shunted traffic so no one outside the initial crash was affected, but the grind and roll of her little vehicle's death had attracted half a dozen police cars like sharks to a seal carcass. McKay shuddered. There had been a death, no doubt about it. She'd still been linked with the 'pod AI, trying to assess the damage when something speared it and tore it apart from the inside. The cops didn't count AI deaths: much like personas, AIs were disposable.

She watched as a seventh car slid up and disgorged a tall, slender figure. *More official rubberneckers.*

She closed her eyes and rested her head on her forearms. Whatever the EMT had given her for the shock was a powerful boost, but the Overlay remained stubbornly offline. She needed to get someplace where she could reboot and run a proper diagnostic. A few deep breaths and she began to trace the pattern of loops and whorls outlining the neural network in the Overlay in her mind's eye. She had gone over them a thousand times getting the 'mites injected in the first place, picturing every connection, every crisscross and dip. At the moment, however, her thought processes were not up to the task. The pain in her head intruded, and the images stuttered and faded in the empty space behind her eyelids. She hoped Spike had gotten back out okay. Footsteps crunched on the roadside as the EMT returned, probably with the bad news that she would have to cover the painkillers out of pocket.

She raised her head to find Brighton staring at her with an unreadable expression.

"I was just about to call you." McKay waved a hand at the Auto-Pod corporate van. "They were right. You really shouldn't text and drive." She suppressed the irrational urge to laugh. *Bad form to laugh at your own jokes.*

Brighton snorted. "You realize you're the only person on record to crash an AI car?"

"Technically, the AutoPod was a trike, the Econotrike 247 to be exact. Most certainly not a car." McKay swayed to her feet, tired out from the explaining. "How about off the record? I hear they're up to twenty-five." Her head protested, then quieted as the 'mites effected repairs.

"That's classified." Brighton took her elbow and guided her toward the police vehicles. "Try to look upset. You're being taken in for a statement."

"What?" She stopped short. "Someone hacks my car, and *I'm* under arrest?" She yanked her elbow from the agent's grasp.

"Not THAT upset. We'll get the statement to make the local PD happy, and I'll get our guy to take a look at the damage in your head." She spoke in an undertone, her attention on the cop cars rather than McKay, and renewed her grip.

"Can I postpone the statement? I have to get to Katie's for an appointment."

"Just get in the car." Brighton's tone was less friendly. She held a hand up to the gaggle of officers around the battered trike by way of goodbye. In a continuing fit of goofiness, McKay saluted the fallen vehicle before getting into the car's back seat. The interior of Brighton's car was much cooler than the edge of the embankment, and the sound of the road dimmed as Brighton shut the door. McKay leaned back and closed her eyes for a second as Brighton slid into the front seat.

"Please tell me you're gonna be driving manual." She fought the urge to giggle. Whatever the EMT had given her was making her decidedly loopy as it peaked. The green eyes in the mirror warned her, but she really, truly did not care.

"Not. Now." Sharply. The car's console lit up at Brighton's touch and the windows polarized and faded to black.

"Fine. Wake me when you get to the City." She closed her eyes again.

"*Hey!*" A sharp jab in the knee popped her eyes open again. "Don't fall asleep on me. You're in enough trouble as it is."

"I didn't *do* anything." The car pulled away from the accident site. Outside the window she saw the trike's crumpled bumper vanish into the official AutoPod company van. Somewhere deep in her brain a 'mite repaired a connection, and she remembered what she had been working on.

"Crap."

The green eyes in the mirror narrowed. "What's wrong?"

"I left all my stuff in the car."

"Jesus, someone just tried to kill you, and you're worried about a few hundred dollars worth of junked electronics?" Brighton shook her head. "The EMT said you took a hit to the head."

"No, no, the headset's in there, somewhere. I have to go back for it." The sick feeling in the pit of her stomach had nothing to do with the blow to her head. Without the headset she was seriously crippled. The airgel and ballistic housing should have protected it from the impact; the case itself required specialized hardware to open without her DNA sig, so as long as no one ran over it with a truck, it should be okay. She felt exposed, vulnerable.

Brighton's slender, scarred fingers played across the vehicle consoles, and the front windshield faded to black. Windows displaying police records and accident data began opening up. Brighton reduced the view outside to an eighth-scale image and casually threw it into the corner of the display with a flick of her wrist. The movements all well practiced and clean, as if she'd spent years digging through data even before S1s became commonplace.

"The paperwork hasn't gone through yet," she mused, and plugged in another query.

McKay rolled her head against the seat and drank in the data with her eyes, trying to fill the empty space in her head that the Overlay usually occupied. She felt her neural reflexes trying to open links, reaching out futilely to touch the Swim. Whorls and eddies of data saturated the vehicle's interior, she could almost feel them, and she traced the half-imagined patterns with her mind like unseen currents in the air.

"It looks like SMPD is impounding the 'pod." Brighton paused. "This can't be right. Suspected attempted suicide by AI?" McKay heard the seatbelt pop as the agent leaned around to face her. "Is there something not in your profile, Ms. McKay?"

"You have got to be kidding me." McKay just stared at her. "Where the hell did that come from?" Suicide by AI was something off the media feeds, when some tragic soul decided to end its existence by mucking an AI system up so bad the program had no choice but to end a person's life to prevent additional casualties.

"Says here a boyfriend called in a tip, worried you were going to do something stupid." She turned back to the console. "Here it comes. The vehicle's gone to central impound. Personal effects are being brought to the main station for us. Oh, lucky you! They're planning a psych eval in your honor."

McKay stifled a groan. It was like having her brain swaddled in plastic wrap, not being able to reach out, to touch anything, and now THIS, this farce over her sanity.

"Our records say you're relatively stable. Any idea where this came from?" Brighton wormed through the police records as the vehicle weaved through traffic. McKay closed her eyes and focused her attention inward. The 'mites worked faster than the body's own repair systems, but they only set up a framework, stopped bleeding, stitched torn tissues together until the body caught up. She ran her fingers over her scalp, touching the contact points, checking. One or two shifted under her touch, and she ground her teeth at the feeling of wrongness that trickled into her skull. The 'mites would reset them, scaffolding the bone, but she would have to be very careful with the headset for a few days.

If you ever get it back.

"Tell me about Mike Miyamoto, Brighton." *A change of subject might be nice.*

"His full name wasn't in the disclosures."

"You didn't hire me because I'm stupid. I was on my way to contact you. I found the persona."

"You found him and you didn't call me?"

Maybe it's a good thing she's not driving.

"McKay—"

"I was on my way to contact you, remember?" she snapped, irritated. "Look, someone crashed my House system. I found your persona, but someone else is after it as well. A really nasty piece of software is pursuing it and someone tripped the City Quarantine; my entire fucking neighborhood is offline. Until the City clears my access, I have to head offsite to finish this up."

"Where is he now?" She heard Brighton's fingers playing with the strings of light crisscrossing the console.

"Peninsula Tech's swimLab system, last time I saw him."

"Of course." The cars communicator chirped as she pressed a button. "Lyman. He's in PenTech. Or was, before that lockdown we recorded. No, no, get on it now, and watch out. She says there's something big and nasty in pursuit." She shut the link with more than necessary force.

"How's Rose doing?" McKay asked into the silence that followed Brighton's conversation with the elusive Lyman.

"She's still unavailable. Lyman's the lead on this now. So, who's this new player?"

"Not sure yet. I have to get a look at the code behind the thing before I can trace it back to the owner." She was hoping Duck's pattern library, with the quirks and foibles of thousands of coders on record, would be able to help her out on that score.

"Shit." Her fingers drummed the console nervously. "We've been focusing on Christopher, but if there's someone else involved. . . ."

"What was Mike working on, specifically? What was that particular dip into the Swim for? The docs you handed over are pretty broad." Another connection got made inside her head, and something flickered in her vision, a ghost in the empty space behind her eyes.

"I told you, he was working a contact inside Bellicode, level-three UX designer by the name of Miranda Bosch. The two of them had met in the Swim maybe ten times. She was a wealth of inside information."

"Christopher doesn't handle day-to-day operations at Bellicode any longer, it's all top-level stuff. And there's no way in hell Bosch is just a production designer."

"Christopher's got a few private projects going on that Bellicode's providing cover for. Bosch is on one of those teams. He's building something big, something we need to get out ahead of before it goes live."

"What?"

"Can't say. I mean, I *won't* say, but it's as much because we don't really have the whole picture yet. The pieces we do have are complete enough to give us an idea, but not complete enough to bring charges."

"So you think Mike's learned something about one of those special projects?"

"I know he did. What I don't know is what *else* happened in there." Brighton's turn to be irritated. "I know he experienced some sort of revelation in there; I suspect he got a look at the bigger picture, something outside the scope of the privacy abuses we were originally looking into. If it's about Christopher's private projects, we've got to know everything."

McKay let the silence hang between them.

"The investigation is under massive pressure from the outside. We're being told to put up or shut up in no uncertain terms." She let out a long sigh. "Mike's evidence, whatever it is, is our only chance to keep it open and possibly cut off whatever Christopher has planned."

"And if you can't?"

"We'll have to start over, but by then we're going to be playing catch-up. The damage is going to be done."

McKay finished fingering her skull and scrubbed her hands through her hair as her addled brain slotted this new information into what she already knew. She turned to stare out the window at the sound barrier running alongside the freeway, protecting the houses with a glassine wall of lucycrete and colored plexiforms. She realized abruptly that she wasn't looking at a single problem: there wasn't just one thing to be solved here. Christopher, Rose, and Mike all had to be treated as separate pieces, not locked together side by side in a puzzle, but overlaid on top of each other and intersecting here, at the point of Mike's extraction. Now that she could see the differences, see around the edges of each problem, she could tackle them one at a time.

"We're here." The SMPD sign slid past her view and dragged McKay out of her reverie to the more immediate problem at hand. "Statement, psych eval, then you'll be released back into my custody."

"Custody?"

"You crashed a 'pod, Ms. McKay. You're going to have to spend a little time sorting that out." There was a smile in her voice, even if it didn't make it to her eyes in the mirror.

"Can your guy Lyman backtrack the caller and at least find out who called me in for psych? I'm offline, and I don't think they're going to let me access anything but the public terminal." She spoke a little more meekly than she might have otherwise. Had the Overlay been up and running, she would need only minutes to sort out who was messing with her. Having to ask for help grated on her pride, to say the least. She tried not to let it show.

"I'll sic Lyman on it and we'll see what he comes up with."

"Thank you." The car slid to a stop outside the station entrance, and the front window cleared to show the afternoon sky outside.

"Straight through those doors and tell the lady at the front desk you want to speak to Lieutenant Yun. He's an old friend of Rice's, and he's going to help us out on this one. He'll take your statement, set you up with the psych guy, and get you out as fast as can be expected."

"Yun, right. Don't you need to escort me in or something?"

She rolled her eyes. "Grow up, McKay. It's not like they found you standing over a body."

The dying AI's stuttering shriek sounded in McKay's imagination as she spoke. "I'm not so sure about that." She shuddered against the guilt and slid across the seat to pop the door open. She hadn't been able to do anything to save the AI. "If you can, I need whatever information you have on this big idea of Christopher's. Knowing what Mike might be trying to save will make it easier to get him to come quietly."

"Got it." She heard the distance in Brighton's voice as someone comm'd in, and the car's front window went dark again.

She slammed the door and crossed the lot quickly, the summer heat prickling the back of her neck. The station was fifteen miles north of her place, a good ten degrees cooler normally, but this week it meant only that her sneakers wouldn't melt to the asphalt if she stood still for a moment. She paused outside the range of the door sensors and checked her reflection in the glass. The entire left side of her head was already purpling up and contrasted sharply to the white T-shaped bandages holding the worst cuts closed until the 'mites got ahead of the game. The cosmetic stuff would come last: getting the wires in her head repaired and the Overlay back online was of primary importance. She straightened her shirt self-consciously and stepped through the doors. With luck, the psychiatrist would be someone she knew, and she could get out before the sun went down.

EIGHTEEN

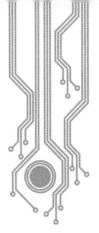

"*Where the hell did you learn to drive?*" McKay was still in the depths of the SMPD police station when Spike's indignation rang through her still-traumatized systems. She resisted grabbing the doorjamb for balance as the Overlay winced and stuttered offline again. McKay took an extra second to get a handle on the wave of nausea before straightening up. Had the sprite found her ten minutes earlier she would have been slogging through the last of the psychiatrist's questions. The man had very grudgingly agreed that McKay was not, in fact, a candidate for suicide by AI, but still put her through nearly three hours of questions and evals, all of which could be invalidated if the head scans showed more damage than the 'mites could reasonably handle. It was the usual fine line she had to walk. Some psychiatrists still felt that the experimental wiring in her head was a clear sign of any number of psychological illnesses: there was always one more test that had to be run, one more signature needed.

The Overlay came stuttering back online again while she dictated her statement to Lieutenant Yun, and she began running diagnostics on each subsystem. Spike's little outburst suggested the Overlay might be ready to link up to the data flow from the Swim, so McKay kept herself disconnected. The moments of clarity among stretches of grey, nonresponsive fog were getting longer, not at all unusual for a concussion. The monitor the EMT had injected along with the nutrient mix whispered in her ear that the Aces and Eights were making excellent progress. She should expect the fuzziness to pass in a few hours provided she suffer no additional trauma.

The AutoPod corporation had not yet filed charges, but Yun suggested she retain a lawyer just the same. *Something in there about sharks and minnows, too, but a gray moment sucked the detail out of that bit of wisdom.*

There was a public access port in the station lobby. McKay slid into the booth and engaged the privacy screen. She selected a jack, wiped it down with one of the disinfectant wipes provided, and plugged it into the receptor behind her other ear. The landline would keep the information flow to a trickle, would help her avoid overloading the Overlay. She needed to make contact with Trevor. She couldn't trust the components she'd picked up earlier, not after the shock of the 'pod crash.

Pulling Mike out of the Swim entirely would solve one piece of this puzzle; it would give McKay breathing room to solve the others, or so she hoped. Trev could probably get the parts in the City, but McKay had to send the component list through the Swim, which meant it would be vulnerable. *Not many choices if I want to get the work done tonight.*

She closed her eyes and assembled the packet in her mind, cupping it in her hands and layering the encryption on before releasing it into the trickle of the Swim flowing through her head. It floundered, splashed, then waddled off half-submerged like a chubby zoo platypus. At the output node it stretched itself thin, elongating and twisting to fit the pathway out until it flicked its flattened tail, and was gone.

McKay sighed. The "platypus" encryption was slow, but it was strongest she could manage with her crippled systems. She opened her eyes and regarded the reflection in the booth's terminal screen. The cuts were already sealing up as the skin was pulled together and stitched. The bruises were fading to yellow around the edges as the Aces and Eights biorepair 'mites cannibalized the damaged cells and recycled them. Using the body's own materials meant close to zero chance of rejection. She'd reabsorb anything the 'mites used as part of the natural, long-term healing process. None of that knowledge helped the ache battering down the analgesics the EMT gave her.

Half an hour later, Brighton found her scrunched down in the seat farthest from the door, eyes closed, forehead resting on her knees. McKay only looked up because of the angry weight to her footsteps. It took a few moments for her to register the agent's identity amid the fog.

"Got anything?" she finally asked.

"In the car, but it might not help much at this point. You okay?"

"Getting better by the moment. They decided I wasn't trying to go out with a bang, at any rate."

The agent led her out, barely slowing as the glass doors shot open at her approach. McKay stretched to keep up. She didn't need the Overlay to pick up on body action and micro-expressions; everything about Brighton in that moment rolled off as angry. Her car waited by the curb, engine still spinning.

"Get in."

McKay complied silently. At least Brighton opened the front door for her, so she probably wasn't under arrest any longer. Whatever was pissing her off, she hoped she wouldn't catch any of the splash damage.

"What . . ." she started as she clipped the seatbelt in place, but Brighton slammed the door ferociously and cut her off, striding purposefully around to the other side of the car

"The transcripts are gone," the agent snapped as she slid into the driver's seat.

"What?"

"The transcripts are gone," she repeated slowly, knuckles whitening on the steering wheel. "The transcripts are gone. Mike's session data has been screwed with. It's all fucking gone."

"Um. . . ." Now back online, the Overlay stretched and shook itself like a cat, smoothly linking into the car's systems and feeding the data into her vision. McKay winced in anticipation, then relaxed as the information flow moved smoothly. The lurking ache in her skull subsided. Whatever the repair 'mites had been working on, they'd fixed something critical.

"That's not good."

"Thank you, Captain Obvious," she snarled and punched the car into gear. Her hands stabbed through the symbols in the air above the console. McKay decided to keep her mouth shut and let Brighton get into the details.

"Lyman, our loaner from Homeland, says the system was hacked from outside, very quietly, very carefully. He would never have noticed if we hadn't sent him back in to look for the transcripts."

"So it was an outside job?"

"At first glance, yes, but only to get into the system. Once inside, whoever it was accessed the information using our internal passcodes. Add to that the fact that those two guys you asked us to track down, the ones who broke in to your place? Our investigation tied them to Christopher. On top of that, one of them received a payment from our department about two years ago." She glanced into the mirror, and the lines around the green eyes reflected the worry in her voice. "He's one of Rose's contacts."

"Coincidence." McKay spoke the lie to deflect the worry in Brighton's voice. As the word fell from her lips she knew it sounded as stupid aloud as it did in her head. *She knows damn well that coincidences like that don't just happen.* McKay considered, just for a second, confirming Brighton's theory, but decided against it.

"I can't afford to think that way." Brighton's voice evened out, as if the admission had focused her anger. The Overlay backed up that assumption. "Whatever revelation Mike had in there, it's got something to do with Rose. She's been running a string of outside contractors for a while now, and the deeper we dig into them, the more of them we find are tied to Christopher as well. I don't know if she was playing both sides or if she was just taking advantage of the black-market talent pool." She glanced back over her shoulder at McKay. "I'm sorry. This is a deeper mess than you signed on for, but this new information means we have to get Mike out more than ever. I've been giving Rose the benefit of the doubt because of our history, but if she deliberately interfered, there could be bigger problems. Our whole investigation might be compromised." She held a wafer up between thumb and forefinger. "Here are the contacts Mike was working on, including Bosch. Every name, every record."

McKay took the wafer tiredly and tucked it into her shirt pocket. The repairs she'd engineered for Mike's persona back in Singapore would soon unravel, if they hadn't already. Mike's time was running out and suddenly having Brighton in her corner where Rose was concerned lifted a huge weight. Relief flooded McKay's already stressed out system for a moment, followed by a fresh fear that she still might not be able to pull all this off.

"If I take Mike out of the Swim entirely, then we can keep the persona safe until we can get it back to Mike's body. I just need to get a few things in order first." The Overlay pulled up her design spaces for the splat drive and spun them in the corner of her vision. The knock on the head must have shaken a few stray ideas loose, because she could see flaws in it, places it could be streamlined, elements she could discard.

"Speaking of which." Brighton lifted something off the seat next to her and handed it back. It was the headset case. McKay took the case in trembling hands and rested it on her lap. Suddenly, briefly, everything was going to work out.

"I got it out of impound for you," she explained. "The case hasn't been opened, as far as I can tell. I hope your gear is still intact."

"Thank you." She fingered the diamond-patterned surface, feeling nicks and scores in the steel where it had slammed around the interior of the trike when it rolled. She felt a particularly large scar and jagged asphalt pebbles embedded in the surface. The Overlay trembled, encouraging her to open it and spin up the drives, to make sure everything was okay. She told it to shut up. She didn't want to waste Brighton's moment of openness; she needed to figure out what her next steps were going to be.

"So Christopher's out as a suspect?" she ventured.

"Feh," Brighton made a disgusted sound. "He's been cleaning house. One by one, our windows into his org are getting boarded up. Couple guys showed up dead; Bosch hasn't been seen in the Swim for weeks. Right now, trying to get Mike back is paramount. Once we have him back we can reassess."

McKay turned her head to watch the passing traffic. She hadn't noticed they'd reached the freeway and were heading north toward the City. She called up the details of her plan of action and sicced the Overly on rechecking the information.

"I have a plan," McKay started again.

The green eyes in the mirror were nonplussed.

"A plan for what?"

"I may have a way to pull Mike out of the Swim completely, long enough to get him to someplace where we can safely write him out."

"Bullshit."

She winced. "Now wait. . . ."

"Bullshit, McKay. We don't have the equipment, or the funds, to pull an *entire* persona out of the Swim. It can't be done."

"But. . . ." The Overlay tried to get her attention, flashing orange and red warnings into the corners of her vision.

"For a gal with a fully wired-up brainpan, you're pretty damn slow." Brighton's hands flickered across the consoles, calling up files, deleting some, corrupting others. With the Overlay in play, McKay watched her wipe the last ten seconds out of the vehicle's memory. *Neat, surgical. Shoulda picked up on that sooner.* She got the hint. Splat was bleeding-edge technology with all the glitches, risks, technical hurdles, and major badass issues. It wasn't illegal, just . . . experimental. It wasn't far enough along yet for anyone to *declare* it illegal. Brighton didn't want anything about it on the record.

Dammit, this whole thing is going to be hard enough to explain to her without having to talk in circles.

"So don't talk, moron." Spike's icon flashed in cadence with its voice, no longer so tiny.

"So what then, sign language?" Brighton's quick glance at the mirror told her she'd complained aloud. *Inside voice, dammit!*

The skull rolled its eye sockets meaningfully. "It's not like your degree is in home economics, dolt. Just encrypt the information, and let her guy crack them on the other end."

"Brighton just confirmed that Rose is involved," McKay spoke into her head, careful not to let the phrase reach her lips. "So if I send Brighton the plan, there's a chance Rose is going to lay hands on it."

"Rose? The freaky xWire wannabe?" Spike whistled in appreciation. "You sure know how to pick 'em."

"What do you mean?" Something in Spike's manner screamed *secret.* "What do you have, Spike?" McKay brought the full weight of her concentration down on the itinerant program.

"Nothing. I mean, nothing your redhead there doesn't already know." Its pixelated thumb jerked at Brighton. "Rose is offline. She went under the knife back in Singapore, had a full set of Xs plugged in. Nice stuff too."

"And?"

"And. . . ."—Spike shifted uncomfortably—"and she cracked. Total personality fracture."

"What?" McKay felt like someone had filled her chest with ice water. *Jesus, she cracked.* It was like hearing someone you knew died, but worse somehow. She already knew two people who had gone X and failed to make the transition. Rose made it three. All of a sudden Brighton's reluctance to lay blame with Rose became clear. Standard procedure following a break involved a chemical coma. Rose should have been offline for days at this point.

To the layperson she would have been unconscious, unresponsive, but McKay had a more intimate knowledge of the medical process. Whatever team was caring for Rose would have been bringing her back out of her coma at regular intervals, checking connections, trying to assess the damage. Unless they had deliberately limited her ability to connect, which was only likely if she was being cared for by specialists, she'd have been able to access the Swim during those sessions.

The on-again, off-again pattern of the attacks on McKay certainly fit that scenario.

"Sure, there were precursors. Classic stay-away stuff, but she went to Anselmo's in Singapore, paid up for the privilege, anyway." Spike shrugged. "If you can't stand the heat. . . ." The ice in McKay's soul vanished, replaced by something far blacker. Nobody deserved what had happened to Rose. She wouldn't wish that even on an asshole like Christopher.

"Get out of my head," McKay said quietly, not bothering with the inside voice. She raised the pressure on Spike, excising it from the Overlay as ungently as she knew how. The sprite squeaked and fled back into the Swim.

"What was that about?" Brighton's eyes in the mirror showed concern. The vehicle's AI was feeding reports back to her on the links McKay opened to contact Spike. Now she cut the connections. McKay didn't feel like continuing the conversation, ANY conversation, just then, but made the effort. There was still work to be done.

"Why didn't you tell me about Rose?" McKay stared out the window as they rolled off the freeway and into the spiderweb of roads and elevations that made up the City. Her thoughts roiled in her head, impotently scrubbing data, rearranging connections and information, trying to DO something to fix it, even though she knew full well there was nothing to be done.

Brighton measured her words carefully: the Overlay counted the milliseconds between each one. "What about Rose?"

"Total personality fracture? She's not *just* unavailable, she's in an induced coma over at Singapore General."

"It wasn't relevant, not to you."

"Not relevant?"

"No, it's not." Brighton turned in her seat. "Look, McKay, I know Rose came to you with questions before she went in. That doesn't mean you're responsible for what happened after."

"And you're okay with this?"

The Overlay warned her off again; again she ignored it.

"No. No, I'm not okay with this. Rose was a part of my team, I've known her a hell of a lot longer than you have." The look Brighton pinned her with was bleak, warning her not to dig any deeper. This was hard enough already. "So I've got to support her on the medical, while looking into having her arrested and brought up on charges if she makes it out of the coma. *Okay* is not a word that even belongs in the same paragraph with all the rest of this mess." Brighton's voice stayed steady, measured. The Overlay told McKay a different story: sky-high stress levels and a series of bruises on her hands and forearms that suggested Brighton had been spending some serious time with a punching bag at the gym.

"Sing Gen doesn't have the kinds of experts she needs. You need to get her over here." McKay had the Overlay call up her contact points, the half dozen friends and neuro-experts who specialized in experimental miteline systems. Brighton might have the government list, but McKay had the geniuses, and better yet, she had their personal contact information.

McKay wasn't a first-generation xWire, not like Christopher, but what happened to Rose could happen to her on the next upgrade, the next time she adjusted the Overlay. It was a constant, quiet specter that she spent a lot of time ignoring and an equal amount of time preparing for.

"She's being transferred. We've got access to some of the best."

"I'll share my list if you share yours." McKay packaged up the contacts and had the Overlay pass them to Brighton. "Any of these guys should be willing to take a look. Use my name. Don't go all special-ops bossy on them, I might need to use them myself someday."

"But your miteline system's already in place."

"It's not quite that simple. You miss a beat, get a bad bit of code, and what happened to Rose can, and sooner or later probably will, happen to any of us."

"That's rather fucked up."

"And that's why we rarely tell anyone about it. Can you let me off at the Embarcadero?" McKay didn't want to answer that unspoken question, didn't want to start a conversation about the impending risks involved with xWire, about why and how someone might jump to that decision. "I need to walk something out." The Overlay touched the vehicle's AI again to apologize, then took over the controls and allowed McKay to steer the vehicle to the curb.

"That's an awful long way to walk unprotected," Brighton began, but they were already on Bryant Street's third level, skimming down to the water's edge following McKay's instruction. "Hey!"

She made an effort to regain control of the car's AI, but the Overlay had made a convincing case and it ignored her, sliding up to the sidewalk, popping the door locks so she could exit into the cold, waterside air. "McKay!"

"I'll be fine." She ducked out of the vehicle and slammed the door. The AI rolled down the front window as she passed. "I'll contact you again as soon as I'm done. I'm just heading up to Katie's."

Brighton leaned across the passenger seat to look her in the eyes. "You're not going to tell me any more, are you?"

"It's personal. Not relevant to what we're doing here."

Brighton paused, a long pause with a studied look that said she didn't believe her.

"Like knowing about Rose wasn't relevant? You going to be okay?" she asked.

"Yeah." McKay straightened and stared up the hill toward the heart of the City. "Fine. I just have a few details to work out. Then we should be good to go."

"This master plan you have?"

"Yeah."

"It's a good plan." She must have read the file already, skimmed it while they were talking.

"Of course it is."

"Call me when you're ready to go. I'll ask the medical team to keep Rose under sedation until we're done, just in case." She rolled the window up, and the car pulled away from the curb. McKay watched it move through the patterns of light filtering down through the layers of City strata until a building blocked her view. She shivered. Someone once claimed the coldest winter he'd ever spent was summer in San Francisco. On the Embarcadero, where the layers of the City were thinnest, the wind slipped in off the water and crept through the seams like a cold, damp house cat.

McKay jammed her hands into her pockets and started up the hill.

NINETEEN

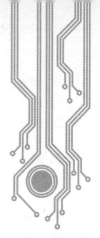

IN A FORMER LIFE, the City had the reputation for hills that ripped the brakes from any substandard vehicle and left them smoking on the sidewalk. Over the decades, the scaffolding of streets and airways had moderated the hills at the highest level, but they were still there, underneath, where the patches of sunlight filtered between strips of engineered concrete and cascaded into the artificially lit underside of the Old City before vanishing in the shadowless space.

Coming to see Duck was a side trip, a little bit off her primary purpose. Getting Mike out of the Swim was paramount, but as long as the Beast code was coming after Mike, and by extension McKay, then she needed to know more about it without the added risk of actually trying to face it down again while unprepared.

Her angry stride modulated to something less purposeful as the Overlay sang, not a literal song but rather the sound of links opening and closing, reaching, touching, probing connections and the varying timed responses, all with a rhythm and a meter that overrode thought like the sound of waves when standing by the seaside.

Slower steps took her uphill toward Market as she focused on the data. She probably looked like a ghost or a lost soul to passersby, head down, eyes alight, as the Overlay remade the walkways, glowing with information on composition, traffic patterns, establishment logos. Only the impact of her soles on the sidewalk connected her to the real world.

When McKay felt safe enough to clear her vision, she passed the foundations of the historical wreck that housed Katie's and wandered roughly clockwise until she was standing outside a wrought iron gate. Whereas Katie's occupied the highest reaches of the New City, Duck had chosen to establish herself in the basement. The venerable "painted lady" house still sported the defiant blues and yellows of its historically accurate paint job, even as the City had grown upward to block out the sun. McKay raised a hand and placed one fingertip, the middle one—because she'd been just that kinda person once upon a time—on the scanner. Without any outward sign of recognition the gate slid silently back and swung inward just an inch or so.

"*Mizz* Eliza Nurey Wynona McKay!" The joyful voice rang out the instant the door across the marble courtyard slammed open. "You look like you came out of the losing end of an audit," the older engineer said as she closed the distance across the courtyard.

"Something like that," McKay said ruefully.

For a librarian, or a "signature analyst," as she styled herself, Morgan deKuyper was loud. Loud of voice, loud of manner, loud of mind. Working hard on a problem, the woman could generate a Swim-eddy three servers wide, and that was without writing herself into a persona-state. She topped McKay by nearly a foot and sported eyebrows that had been shot through with silver the last time they met, but were now a rich black. Vanity was perhaps Duck's most obvious failing. Like McKay's, her skull was riddled with wiring, but only as far as S2, and unlike McKay, she took pains to keep her head clean-shaven. In a fit of subversive self-indulgence she'd got her velvet pate tattooed with pale blue lines to mark the mite-line tracery under the skull. Mucking with the periphery, add-ons, wearables, and 'mite-driven interfaces was fine in Duck's oft-voiced opinion, but actually subverting the grey matter itself was a bit over the top, so while she could operate computing systems at a fairly high level, it was still all one step back.

"I hear you were in Singapore. Why the hell would you ever come back here?" Duck ribbed her good-naturedly as they led the way into the house.

"Oh, you know better, Ducky. Home is where my stuff is. I see your shampoo-free lifestyle is still going strong."

What Duck never talked about was that one lost summer when she tried to upgrade to xWire and failed. She'd been well-prepared, and the university had provided the support she'd needed to recover, but it had taken time and it had taken a toll. When they'd first met, in fact, she had written McKay off as one step shy of a straitjacket for even trying, and her success had rankled for a while. They had, over time, found common ground somewhere in the middle.

"I tell you, the reprogramming job you did on the 'mites saves me an hour of waxing every Monday." She patted the top of her head proudly.

McKay grinned. "Just your head, I hope. I didn't code them to colonize any other body parts."

Duck laughed out loud at that. "Now that you mention it. . . ."

McKay held up her hands to forestall the rest of the sentence. "No, no, that's more than I need to know, thanks!" She stuck her fingers in her ears, and Duck's laugh was audible even through the make-shift blockage.

They crossed into the main foyer, and Duck led her through a little blue wooden door to the "office."

"So, how are Theresa and the kids?" McKay asked by way of conversation.

"You got here just in time! They're off to the grandmother's for the week." Duck's gangly frame dropped into an abandoned rolling chair and kicked it across to a wall that had once been concrete but was now packed nearly solid with flat-panel displays.

"Oh, god. You're going to have to eat your own cooking for a week?" McKay commandeered another chair, shoving it over in a far more stylish fashion. She fell back into the cadences of college life without a second thought. *All you need is cheap beer and some pirated music.*

"Screw that! Felicity's delivers now." A negligent hand indicated a pile of empty takeout containers on the side table. "Oh, hey! Are you doing anything tonight? There's a robot rally in the basement of Denali's at nine."

"Not tonight. I'm meeting up with Trevor for a design session."

Duck looked at her mournfully. "I was hoping you could bring your Alice AI along, see what she can do with Carson's new body." She turned back to the panels, and McKay felt Duck's computer system come online. The Overlay linked in without a by-your-leave. The librarian hadn't changed her security passcodes since the last time McKay was around.

"You should have called ahead. Original Alice got retired, but she has three or four new iterations we might try. I just need a longer heads-up next time."

Duck shrugged. "I pinged you, dearie, but they all bounced back."

"Yeah." McKay felt suddenly sheepish. "I got jacked. Whole system shut down, quarantined, the works."

The wheelie chair turned to reveal Duck's expression, jaw agape.

"Oh, you've got to be *kidding* me! You? Missy techno-weenie from hell? Was it Boris? Tell me it wasn't Boris!"

"No, it wasn't Boris, thanks for that."

"Sorry, man!" The grin belied the apology. "So, to what do I owe the pleasure, then? Need to use the spin?" Duck turned back to her screens and started clearing them, shoving clips of code, windows with recursive images, to the sides. Mini spin-servers with live copies of her collected references, close to a hundred of them, filled Duck's basement, each smaller than a shoebox, all accessible with a well-placed thought.

"I ran across something unpleasant in the Swim. I'm wondering if you can help find who coded it." McKay popped the wafer out of her skull drive and held it out to her friend.

"Ugh. You could just link in and drop the code. Wafers are so half-a-centon ago." She slid the wafer into one of a dozen slots on the desk. The door-size rectangle of polished wood held ports and drives for every dominant media type for the past thirty years. She'd even dug up an old serial connection once and used it to pull data from a handful of laptops she'd found in the basement of a priory school years earlier, mostly vintage music and bad essays, nothing historically valuable.

"Is this what crashed your house?" Duck asked. The heat-sink tattoos that crisscrossed Duck's skull glowed faintly with the heat the miteline transferred from her own processors and dispersed it into the air. McKay frowned. They shouldn't be running hot, not on initial spin-up. She had the Overlay run a diagnostic, picking up the minute 'mite-sigs and comparing them to the baseline she'd recorded when Duck first installed them.

"Let's see now. . . ."

McKay abandoned the wheelie chair for one of the thickly patchworked leather wingbacks Duck "restored" in her spare time. Bits and pieces, that was Duck's passion, either piecing together the complex patterns she used on the furnishings or pulling the signatory bits out of a thousand lines of code.

Over time, every programmer develops a library, snippets of program that work particularly well for one task or another. One alone might not be significant, but combinations of usage could be mapped the same way painters' signature brush strokes could be used to sort out uncredited works. Duck had the largest sample library McKay had ever seen, and that was on top of access to the Smithsonian code records.

"Shit, this is messy. What'd you do, rip this bit out with a chainsaw?" The code showed up on the largest monitor bracketed by bits of red text where the phraseology terminated without the usual tags and closures.

McKay hadn't had time to look closely at the whole bit of the Beast she'd involuntarily brought back into the headset's bunker. The Overlay picked up the lines of text and assembled them into a dimensional metaphor in her mind, tracing the Beast's outlines in the space behind her eyes.

"Heh, check this out." Copies of the code spread over the entire wall as Duck compared them to her samples. "This bit here, here, and here is designed to attach garbage code without affecting the way the core program runs. It's like taking the program and bloating it up to a hundred times its size without affecting the speed at which it executes." Long, skinny fingers stabbed at one section highlighted in green. "That there, that's the actual executable bit of code. The rest is just junk."

"So it's a new program then, not something that got ditched or degraded?" McKay relinquished her comfy seat and stepped up to the desk.

"Maybe. The decay rate on these things really depends on the coder and the environment they're hanging out in. I'd lay odds that this is a lurker of some kind, hangs out in the Swim until someone gives it an instruction. All this extraneous junk is camouflage."

"Could be to protect the source code," McKay put in. "You'd have to grab the entire thing, if you could get close enough. Otherwise, you just get a fistful of useless numbers and a couple out-of-context lines of programming."

"Ee-e-eh." Duck drew the syllable out into an expression of disgust. "Yeah, you've only got two lines of usable code here, probably from the source, and it's all new to me. I gotta thank you for bringing it in, though. I can add it to the collection."

Shit. McKay's fists tightened. Duck pulled the lines of code into view and highlighted them. She recognized them from somewhere, somewhere very close, she just couldn't place her finger on it yet. Something Christopher coded, maybe? Something he stole? McKay hoped learning who programmed the Beast would be a step in the right direction. "Is it enough to work with?"

The monitors' colored light blended to white by the time it illuminated the far wall, throwing ominous copies of Duck's gestures around the room. She cracked her knuckles and the table surface lit up with the projected keys and toggles of an old-school lightboard.

"Heh, heh, heh. Watch and see, my young apprentice. I can trace almost all of the junk code back to where and when it first showed up in the Swim, then use that to figure out where your mystery code came from." The screens flickered and danced as Duck ran comparisons, her fingers tattooing a rhythm on the tabletop. "Mind some music?" Without an answer, something fast-paced, mostly full of horns and maybe a bagpipe, started up.

"As long as you don't engage the disco ball," McKay joked, straight-faced.

Duck snorted. "I never play anything under sixteen hertz." The codes on the screens shuffled and reshuffled as she searched. McKay knew the visuals were just for her benefit, like a dummy-up presentation for a client. The Overlay gave her a swimming play-by-play of the algorithms on Duck's servers, but she boxed it up and slid it into a corner. For once she wanted to enjoy the illusion that someone else was running the show.

"Here we go, look. This dummy code here was slewed off Randal and Ellis' failed commute predictor, that big piece of software that ended up shutting down half the traffic lanes? Those there are off an advertisement for Biggies NY Pizza." A 3D view of the local Swim took over the center monitor, shunting the code samples to smaller monitors on the sides. "Now, the Feds scrubbed Randal and Ellis' big screwup from the Swim over five years ago, so we know this code you brought me musta been around before then."

McKay watched as the junk code was stripped, each piece identified and assigned a locus on the map. As the pattern evolved, the Overlay began matching patterns in her own head. The most recent snippets were right on top of her recent travels; the older ones were all over the map.

"Hmm, that's strange," Duck mused aloud.

"Stranger than the rest of this?"

"You never bring me anything boring. Look here." Duck shoved back from the table, and the lightboard vanished. "This bit of software entered the Swim here in the City, probably six or seven years ago. It traveled all over, picking up bits of camouflage, but always returned here, probably reporting back to whomever programmed it. Since we programmers tend to be a lazy lot, I'd be willing to bet it was coded in the same building." One of the loci grew and turned into a tiny star. "It picked up most of its camouflage straightaway, but it probably keeps adding on. I've got recent snippets from Beijing and Singapore."

"Singapore?"

"Yeah, I've got one string from a local advert for Ginger Dream Thai to-go, but that's not the most interesting bit. Look at these locations." Duck's fingers danced and a second star appeared on the map. "About two years ago, this program's home base changed. It stopped coming back here and started reporting back to someone on the other side of the country."

Ginger Dream. Brighton's team had ordered from the restaurant in Singapore just before everything came under attack. The Overlay reminded her that it had been just a couple of weeks prior. For a moment, McKay's sense of time and space slipped and she felt as if she'd been working on solving this problem for months. The Beast code had been there, too, lying in wait.

"What do you mean?"

"I mean this program's been sold or traded or hijacked or something. You're not looking for the original coder, you're looking for whoever took it over later. Someone clever enough to repurpose it, but not quite clever enough to actually fully reprogram it."

McKay felt a click—a physical, audible *click*—in her head. Perhaps one of the 'mites made a final cross-connection while making repairs. Perhaps she was just tired and beat-up enough to start thinking outside the box. The Overlay picked up on her new train of thought and rummaged around in her personal files, coming up with a match to the two lines of code that Duck had isolated.

She'd been right: the code was from someplace close to home. Someone had swiped the code she'd used to build Spike and co-opted it to build this programmatic monstrosity. *Holy shit.* McKay sank back into the chair and just stared at the lines of code the Overlay had pulled for her, trying to wrap her head around the connection.

Spike was unique, an emotive-driven search program whose logic had been based on a living persona. Catching it, and copying it, should have been no simple task. The idea that someone would have used that copy, had turned its seek-and-find capabilities to seek-and-assassinate, made her vaguely ill.

"Do me a favor, Duck," she finally said. "Wipe it all."

"Oh, hey! At least let me keep the core strings for the library!" Duck protested.

McKay chewed a thumbnail. Odds were, a snippet of code buried in someone's personal library would never attract any notice.

"If you do, encrypt the hell out of it," she said finally. *Duck gets high-clearance stuff all the time. She should know the drill.* The screens shifted subjects one by one as the wafer shot out of the slot in the desk. The analyst waggled the wafer over her shoulder. McKay took it and slotted it back into her skull drive.

"Gotcha. Nasty players on this one, right? I thought you were still a persona non grata. Are people still throwing you work?" The Overlay picked up the layers of encryption Duck was using, giving McKay a probability countdown that approached, but never quite made it to, zero. As close to unhackable as you could get as long as humans still needed to get access. "Oh, and one other thing to keep in mind," she added nonchalantly.

McKay pulled herself out of her uncomfortable reverie. "Something else?"

"This bad boy's not autonomous. I mean, someone's got to direct it, point it at a target, or ask it to find something. It's not going to go flailing about."

"You got all that out of two lines of code?"

"This isn't about the code, this is about the behavior patterns based on where it's been. It's being sent, it's being directed. It could deliver information without ever returning to home base. Something is calling it back, over and over."

So it's not a perfect copy, more like a reboot.

Spike was about as autonomous as a piece of software could get. Knowing that the Beast wasn't independent was helpful, but it didn't allay the guilty feeling that her code was out there in the Swim, hunting down Mike's persona. Someone might be co-opting it, but it was still her code.

"I can burn it to hard copy with the other toxics," Ducky continued, oblivious to her silence. "You got a name I can tag this with?"

McKay was silent for a moment. "Yeah, I think I do." She got to her feet. "Thanks for the help, Duck."

Duck took the hint with good grace and keyed the burn sequence. "You doing your session with Trevor up at Katie's tonight?"

"Yeah, Trev's going to help me out. EE stuff mostly."

"Sweet. I might drop by if the rally's a bust. Drinks are on you." Her grin hinted she might bring a few friends as well. Duck rarely missed a chance to spend the night out.

My tab is so *going to get cut off tonight.* McKay tapped the side of her skull. "If this job doesn't get my drives wiped, I'll give you all the details."

"Shit. If I'd known you had a client I'd make *him* buy the drinks." Duck shook her head. "Trev's looking for you. He just pinged to see if you were done here."

The Overlay confirmed Trev's query. McKay replied and got a confirmation faster than she anticipated. *He must have left work early to get to Katie's.*

"Got it. See you later?"

"If Carson forgot to put a reverse gear into the robot like he did last time, you will!"

"Fat chance of that." McKay grinned at the memory. The crash had been spectacular. It had taken Carson months to live that down, but the robots he'd turned out since were twice as wicked. "We're angling for the private room in the back, server seven."

"Gotcha."

When McKay hit the sidewalk again the day had turned gloomy, the bright splashes of sunlight eradicated by the fog rolling in off the ocean. The greenish photophoric lighting enhanced the ground-level walkways and parks in response to the dimming natural light. The Overlay completed its diagnostic runs, finally telling her that over eighty-five percent of the available hardware in her head was repaired, the rest mostly nonessential systems. A disturbingly high percent of those were integral to the heat sinks, but she planned nothing heavy duty that night. She would keep her eye on the heat levels and hope nothing else got weird.

TWENTY

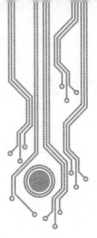

When McKay hit the front doors at Katie's Tea Emporium and Server Farm, rather than sneaking onto the lawn out back, the vibe was entirely different. The building felt more alive, especially now that the sun had gone down.

The elevators dumped passengers into the foyer-lounge, the main bar less than ten feet away, monolithic and mirror-backed. Patrons broke and flowed around it into the rest of the open space arranged with sitting areas, conveniently positioned lounges, tables, viewscreens and behind them, the doors to the conference rooms. The space was open, warehouse-like but the clever groupings of tables and couches broke it into smaller, intimate areas that made it feel more like a cozy neighborhood coffee shop than the high-tech haven it had become. Traces of its former lives riddled the place. An oxygen station stood in one corner, mostly disused, a karaoke machine doubled as an end table by a vintage couch, not one but two disco balls hung from the ceiling, and a set of overlarge French doors gave access to the rooftop.

The crowd was just changing over from the itinerant coders and entrepreneurs, freelancers and day-traders who rented legitimate server space by day. After work, the showboats and night owls came out. At least three different guildhalls took over the screens to conduct in-game raids, and VR enthusiasts projected all sorts of imaginary things into the Swim. By 1:00 a.m. they occupied all the public viewscreens in the place, and the late-night crowd of observers gathered to drink and watch as racks of spin-servers on the floor below churned out virtual worlds and detailed, home-grown experiana.

"Well, well, if it isn't my favorite gardener!" Lolly was the AI running the bar that evening, his flat viewscreen "face" showing a cleft chin, a perky smile, and large white teeth that were a better fit for a horse. The metal framework and hydraulics of the robot body were concealed beneath a threadbare three-piece suit.

"Lolly," McKay responded carefully. The AI had started referring to her as "the gardener" after she'd programmed the nanograss a couple of years ago. "Is Katie around tonight?"

"Isn't she always?" The AI rolled his "eyes" and jerked a plastic thumb toward the back office. Of the AIs Katie had on staff, Lolly was by far the chattiest. Another night, McKay might have allowed herself to be caught up in conversation, but she had too many things to do.

The Overlay talked to Katie's servers and let McKay know that Trev was in the "Den," the most cramped and least desirable private room. *Smart move.* No one would get pushy about how long they had it, and assembling the splat drive would take hours at least. The Overlay stepped in, passing Lolly a drink order, adding nutrient shots for the 'mites that were still rebuilding McKay's face. With luck she might look mostly human by the time they were done.

Lolly shot something purple and syrupy from a polished plastic fingertip into a highball and topped it off with a twist of orange peel. McKay contemplated ditching the fruit, but her stomach reminded her she'd missed the chimichangas at the parts store. Unfortunately, the menu at Katie's focused on the drinks, and most of the snacks available were either the high-salt kind that went great with a beer or sticky, decadent treats that required coffee to break up and wash down.

"Thanks, Lolly!" She took the drink with her and rounded the massive bar, weaving through the groups the elevators disgorged every few minutes. The Overlay kicked in and outlined everything in the space in a soft glow, collecting data on everything within sight and picking out the outlines of the doors in the dim of the club lighting.

A quick twist of the door handle gave her access to the Den. Trev had been busy setting up, with the couches all shoved against one wall, another left clear and covered in e-paper for Trevor to work on. Tables covered in an array of components and tools lined another wall.

"Dude, you made it!" Trev levered himself out of a chair. His grin turned to alarm as he caught a good look at the damage to his friend's head. "Jesus *shit*, dude! I heard about the 'pod crash, but I didn't think you got, like, HURT hurt." He shuddered. Trev's avoidance of pain under any circumstances was notorious.

"No worries. The 'mites took care of most of it." McKay tried to sound reassuring; Trev tried to look like he'd been convinced. "This is just cosmetic." *I hope.*

Trev seemed willing to buy into the fiction. "Dude, cool. I got your message earlier. Took me half an hour to decrypt the damn thing, but I got all the components."

"Excellent." McKay took another longish sip and set the drink on an empty tabletop. The Overlay fed her data on each component Trev had laid out on the table, all pretty good stuff, though she wished a few brand choices had been different. *But, hey, everything on the list is here.* She felt the grey lifting as the neurotransmitters and caffeine hit her bloodstream and trickled into the brain. The painkillers had long since worn off, but her 'mites had been hard at work and the dull throb was little worse than a headache.

Trev grinned. "So, what's the project?"

"Hang on a sec." McKay closed her eyes and extended the Overlay to check the ambient space for, well, anything odd. In her mind's eye, the air was thick with data slipping back and forth, but nothing out of the ordinary, no strange whorls or eddies where an outgoing link could hide.

Getting paranoid?

"C'mon, spill it, dude!" The engineer rapped his knuckles on the paper-covered wall.

McKay couldn't keep the grin off her face. "We're going for splat."

Trevor's normally pale complexion dropped a shade paler, and his watery blue eyes widened a fraction. The Overlay picked up the response and unnecessarily fed McKay details on heart rate and pupillary response. She knew from the start that trying something like this would psych Trev up, whether it worked or not. Splat was a sexy idea from an engineering standpoint. Building a portable drive that could compress and hold the massive amounts of quantum-spin information needed to create a persona was right up Trevor's alley.

"In one night?"

"Let me finish."

"You'll still be insane when you're done."

"Well, we know that already." McKay allowed the Overlay to send the information, and the plans she had worked out in her head appeared on the wall of e-paper, spreading across the pages like spilled ink. "I'm being dramatic. We're not quite going for locking down the quantum spin. We're looking at something simpler, sort of an end run around the problem. It's more like going for smoosh."

Trev stopped listening and stared at the layout, ran a finger over the lines of code, tapped it now and again to pull the images apart into an exploded view, then pull them back again. "So the end goal here is to pull something really big out of the Swim and move it from point A to point B?"

"Yep."

"It's not Spike, is it?"

"Nope."

"It's not theory, though. You actually need this to work?"

"Yep."

"Okay, let me get my head around this."

McKay snapped her sunglasses into place, sealing the edges.

Trevor would need about half an hour to work through the plans, familiarize himself with the details during which she wouldn't get another word out of the engineer. McKay conscripted one of the threadbare chairs and made herself comfortable. She retrieved the headset from the depths of its case and settled it into place, allowing the Overlay to unlimber itself, to fully take advantage of Katie's servers. Spike was sending packets of data back that pinged her consciousness with increasing urgency, which meant the sprite was doing a proper job of researching those names Brighton had given them in the car. McKay shifted her attention fully to the Swim, and the room faded into the concrete bunker in her head.

The files on Miranda Bosch's recent trips into the Swim were waiting for her. She had been a digital virgin when she'd picked up a job at Bellicode, no miteline in her head, not even the kinds of medical 'mites that were currently finishing up the repairs to McKay's skull. Getting S2 miteline was one of the very first things she did, all covered by Bellicode's frighteningly comprehensive insurance. With that, she'd been able to write out into the Swim as part of her day-to-day employment, and that was where she intersected with Mike. Ms. Bosch first dropped into the Swim on the office equipment once or twice a week, but over the past two months she was going in every day. TThen, about a week before Mike's refusal to write-out, she acquired an account at a private persona parlor and started dropping into the Swim after work.

So what drew you in deeper, Ms. Bosch? Or is this just all lies from the bottom up? The pattern fit. People new to the Swim always had such a period, when the newness and fascination of immersing oneself in the data flowing through the world became their most favorite thing for a while. The newness usually wore off in a few weeks and people returned to their usual pattern of existence. *But not for Bosch. Once she connected with Mike those Swim sessions got longer, more frequent. Too long and too frequent for them to just be passing information: they're spending time together. Actual quality time.*

It wasn't beyond the pale that she'd known what she was doing.

The Miranda Bosch she'd met at NWaS certainly seemed capable enough. She could have been getting as much information off Mike as Vector7 had been getting from her.

"Dude!" It took McKay a moment to realize Trevor was trying to get her attention. She backed carefully out of the Swim just enough to make eye contact.

"Hey, Eliza. You're still insane, but it's looking like a good kind of insane."

McKay blinked rapidly and refocused in a hurry. "I'll tell my therapist." She peeled herself out of the armchair.

"But your design is all messed up. No way you can do what you want to do with it." Trevor began making notes on the tablet in his hand. The Overlay kept track of Trevor's notes, throwing them up in the corner of McKay's vision with the changes outlined in red.

Well, shit. The whole plan revolved around getting Mike out of the Swim. If she couldn't do that, she wasn't sure she had time to come up with a plan B.

Trev rummaged through the components until he found what he was looking for. "But lucky for you, I have a better idea." The engineer picked up one of the boxes and checked it against his notes. Trevor joined McKay at the wall. "Here, look." Quick taps brought the schematics back to page one. "This whole section here, this is good."

"Okay."

"The rest is crap."

"Ooookay."

"You're trying to pull a persona out of the Swim, right? Maybe not Spike, but a client or one of your friends over at the university?" With a furrowed brow, Trevor regarded the wall of designs. "Yeah, we can do that," he said finally. "I'll need access to your Spike program, and it would help if you could stay in the Swim. We can run the test simulations faster if you can manage them from the inside."

McKay exhaled, unaware until then she was holding her breath.

"You got it." She sent a packet after Spike, a little 'bot with instructions to have the sprite put its Bosch research on hold and get back as soon as it could. She asked Katie for access to the big server, something dedicated they could run without worrying about fighting for space with the Emporium's gamer clientele.

Watching Trevor when he was being brilliant was akin to watching a really good stage magician work his tricks. Trev was totally unwired, not even stage one, so he did everything through the tablet and his own gray matter. He stood in front of the wall and, more than just create, he directed, hands moving counter to one another. Equations, line speeds, tensile strengths, 'mite compositions, all sketched by stylus onto the pages and joined, line by line, digit by digit. The limited processor within his tablet accessed the servers through McKay's Overlay while the engineer built the simulations, slotted pieces together, updated, removed, as Trevor scrapped one idea and substituted another without pause.

The session was eerily silent. Unlike Duck, Trevor hated music while he worked, and McKay cared little about the silence either way. Neither one made a sound. McKay posted her questions directly to the paper, and Trevor answered there. Spike showed up on the wall, disturbingly two-dimensional, at some point, and Trevor sent it off chasing some obscure research on quantum-spin technologies out of the Zhangzhou province.

"Dude!" Trevor's voice cut through the silence.

McKay had been focusing on trying to decrypt Miranda Bosch's Swim-logs to see what she and Mike had been up to. The simulation was finished, she noted with some surprise. She'd lost track of time.

"Dude, run it up on the wall."

McKay wordlessly shifted the simulation from the headset to the wall for Trevor to review, and checked the clock in her head. The session had eaten most of the nighttime hours. The Overlay flashed warning symbols, fatigue poisons high, precursors were having trouble crossing the blood-brain barrier as her limits neared. She ran the risk of dropping into microsleeps if her brain rebelled at the lack of proper downtime.

Just another day or so, then I can drop offline and nap for a week.

McKay shoved herself to her feet and downed the drink Trev handed her, brain freeze notwithstanding. Her system registered the influx of fatigue scrubbers in the slight tingling in her fingertips and shoulders. McKay knew she could run on a chemical mix for only so long. She'd have to find a way to wedge in a few hours of actual sleep if she was going to keep running the Overlay and headset at full efficiency.

"Right. Haul your ass over here and check this out. This is going to be a pain in the ass for you, but it ought to do the trick."

McKay pulled herself to her feet, ignoring the momentary wobbly feeling in her knees, and inspected the plans Trevor had sketched up on the wall. The end result was larger than she'd expected and Trevor had gone for liquid nitrogen as the solution to keep the drives cold. That meant an extra tank, depending on how long it took her to get the persona back to wherever they were keeping Mike's body. *So you're looking at lugging around, what, twenty pounds of extra weight in the form of that nitrogen canister? That's going to be fun.*

"The colder you can keep it, the better the compression on the spin, and you're going to need it all to fit a persona in there," Trevor pointed out.

"What kind of linkup?" Writing out a persona took a high-speed cable, it wasn't the kind of thing McKay could do wirelessly. She could have done it from her House system, but with everything offline and quarantined, she was going to have to find another location.

"That's the pain-in-the-ass part," Trevor restated his earlier assessment. "Pulling out something the size of a persona is going to be a multi-hour proposition over a regular line. If you can get to a high-speed cable, I mean really high-speed, the kind used for a fully immersive virtual experience, you can cut that down to an hour, which is important."

McKay felt a chill in the pit of her stomach. "I can't just hand this thing to someone else, I'm going to have to be onsite to make it work, aren't I?"

"You're going to have to literally run it through your headset to make the compression work." The other engineer held up a hand to forestall McKay's question. "You're going to have to write the persona out, so all the editing you normally do, all the unnecessary bits you have to chop off when you do an extraction, you're going to have to do that to get it to fit, then you're going to have to write out again from the drive back to your living person, whomever the hell that is."

So there's a pause in the middle. I do the first part of a regular extraction, trimming and reducing the persona down to just the parts I need to save and store all that in the drive. That's going to tie me and the headset, literally, to that drive until we get back to Mike.

"You're right, this is going to suck."

"Well, when you pull this off, be sure you document it all, okay? We ought to be able to pull at least a paper or two off it." Trev threw himself onto a couch and put his sandaled feet up. "Going for splat— you're a friggin' lunatic, you know that? Still, this is probably as close as we're gonna get."

It would hamper her ability to deal with the Beast if it caught up with them during the transfer. *I'm going to be relying only on the headset to make the transfer: it means that almost everything is going to be tied up when I start the extraction.* If she'd been able to handle it remotely, here from Katie's for example, it would have been perfect, with the power of a dozen spin-servers to back her up. Still, she had a way to pull the persona out of the Swim and that was a big something to have.

"So when do we start building?"

"Now?"

"Yeah, now's good. I'll order a pizza."

TWENTY-ONE

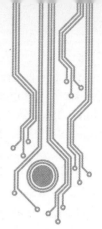

WELL, AT LEAST HE'S STILL all in one piece. Deep in the Swim, Mc-Kay stared down at Mike's persona. She'd left Trevor in charge of finishing the drive and followed Spike out to make contact. She needed to explain the plan, to outline exactly what she was going to be doing.

Mike floated across from her, never quite still, always moving, shifting, clicking. The degradation was starting to show in the snapped-off teeth on the gears, the grinding behind the constant clack-clack-clack of the puzzle pieces sliding together.

"You wanted to meet." The persona stayed well out of reach. It remained paranoid, careful. McKay moved carefully as well, trying not to spook it. She needed time to explain the plan and she needed Mike's willing participation. McKay knew she wouldn't be able to pull this off if she had to drag the persona out of the Swim, kicking and screaming.

A 'bot winged past, piping a shrill warning as it lit out, the last surviving remnant of the original group she'd sent to find the Beast. Mike flinched, feeling the virtual pressure wave pass as the Beast neared their position. This time, McKay came prepared, not to fight, but to hide. Mike moved; the persona balled up and tried to get away. McKay twisted in the surge of data, creating an eddy that cloaked them both. Mike tried to continue his escape, but McKay blocked him, keeping him from leaving the protection of the eddy as the Beast crawled into view.

It moved through the Swim with that otherworldly grace reserved for octopi and eels. It surged forward, feeling its way, tentacles dipping into the muck at the bottom of the Swim and bringing up random strings, bits of advertising and programming. It layered them, tried them on for fit, discarding some and adding others to the camouflage. McKay's few remaining 'bots orbited it like sparrows on a hawk, never getting in too close. The Beast moved slowly, slower than she remembered, as if the hand directing it had been lifted. *Another mark in Rose's column. If she's been put under again, that would explain why it had lost its drive.*

The Mike persona became very still as the Beast approached.

"This is your last shot to get out." McKay recaptured Mike's attention. The persona was slipping: she could feel it in the way its focus jumped from McKay to the Beast to the 'bots to nothing at all. There was a sense of hesitation as the puzzle pieces clicked and spun before it responded.

"Not finished yet."

"Yes you are. Miranda Bosch is out of the Swim. She chose to dump everything rather than undergo an extraction. She and Christopher are cleaning house, getting rid of everyone in their organization with outside ties and that includes the guys who were working with Rose. If you don't knock this shit off, get your ass out of the Swim, and start acting like a grownup, someone out there, someone in the real world, is going to get killed." McKay took a chance. All the evidence, everything she'd found to that point, suggested some kind of emotional entanglement between Miranda and Mike. That was the key, the first piece. Falling in love, really in love, in the Swim was exactly the kind of state change that would stop an outwrite cold. What that meant was that the facts, the information that Brighton so desperately wanted to save, had been tangled up in that emotion and held hostage unless McKay could write Mike back to his own body.

More clicking and spinning gears as the persona parsed this new information. Outside the bounds of the bubble McKay had created, the Beast code meandered past. Undirected as it was, McKay wasn't sure if it would retarget Mike as soon as she dropped the camouflage, but she did not want to take the risk.

"I'll write you out the best I can, but this is the only chance we have to make the jump. If this fails, we are waking you up." McKay pulled the cloak of information closer, made it just a little bit more opaque. "Brighton is fixated on getting you out. Rose is fixated on getting you to dump whatever it is you don't want to dump. I don't know what the hell Bosch is up to, but she intervened on my behalf when Christopher's guys ambushed me, and Christopher seems to think the whole lot of you are more a pain in the ass than anything else. If you're so determined to keep whatever it is, then so be it, but get your happy ass in gear so we can fix this shit."

McKay didn't know if the long pauses before Mike's responses were caused by glitches in the persona's disintegrating code, or if the guy was truly this thoughtful. Either way, she could only hold the eddy in place so long. They were going to have to reach an agreement quickly.

"Brighton is in trouble?"

McKay jumped on that point. *That point, ANY point I can use to get this guy on board with the plan.* McKay didn't want to talk about Rose, didn't want to go into depth on the train wreck that Brighton's investigation had turned into. To a livemind like McKay's, the Swim was an ultra-real experience. Even a mild emotional hit could be burned into the mind like a life-altering trauma. To a persona it was less so, but still significant. Trying to shoehorn the persona back into the real Mike Miyamoto's mind was going to be hard enough without having to factor in that extra level of emotion.

"Brighton says they are working unofficially on getting you back out. If that's not trouble in your line of work, I don't know what is."

Mike smirked, an arrangement of puzzle pieces and gears. "She is good at trouble."

Hah. So it's not just me, then. McKay increased her focus, shifting the code around them to open a tiny, pinhole window. Outside the protective eddy, the Beast was settling into the muck like a stingray in sand. A few brief flutters around the edges and its cobbled-together outer skin became invisible amongst the lost data.

"That there is problem number two," McKay pointed out.

The persona sprouted teeth in a snarl. "Christopher."

"No. Well, that's complicated, but I'm pretty sure some of that code is Christopher's, but someone else has hacked it and is keeping it hot on your tail."

"Who?"

McKay dodged the subject of Rose. "I have a couple theories, but whomever is running it is pretty determined. I need to get you out before they get back on the ball.

"Can you unravel it?" The wear of time on the persona was showing in the clipped phrases, the shortened responses. McKay got the sense that it was tired, nearing the end of its rope.

"That won't solve the problem of someone trying to end your program. I don't know what it is that you know, but Brighton has been going to a massive amount of trouble to get you extracted. This is our chance. If I can pull you out, then I can have your body moved to a closed-off system and do the extraction offline where nobody can interrupt. Then I can come back and worry about this bad boy at my leisure."

Again McKay found herself waiting on the turning of gears and the assembly of puzzle pieces.

"You understand, Mike, you're way past your expiry," she continued urgently. "I'm guessing you have a day, maybe two before your code is just too far gone to save."

"Understood," Mike finally replied. "I'm ready."

Relief flooded McKay, sharp and keen as water. *Almost all the pieces now. Brighton's on board, Trevor's got the splat drive coming, now to get Mike out and someplace safe. If Brighton keeps her word, Rose will be kept offline until I can get this done. If Rose is running the Beast code, that will be a huge help.*

"Stay with Spike. It will get you to the outwrite location."

Mike shifted to a more streamlined form and coiled up, waiting as McKay released the eddy. At her signal, the 'bots bunched up, ready to dart and peck at the Beast if it emerged. The eddy collapsed onto itself as McKay released her control and the persona shot off, followed closely by Spike. McKay waited, but the Beast extended a single, inquisitive tentacle, feeling around briefly before concealing itself. Again she got the impression that whatever was driving it was absent, that left to its own devices it would simply hunker down and wait for the next command.

Count your blessings, she thought, and fled back to the safety of her own mind.

TWENTY-TWO

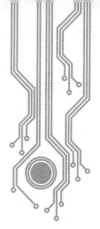

McKay barely made it back to her own head back at Katie's before the Overlay broke the connection to the headset and she simply failed to open her eyes, passing directly from the Swim into an exhausted unconsciousness. The two hours of sleep were probably the most restful she'd had since leaving Singapore.

When the Overlay prodded McKay awake, she found that Trevor had left behind a banged-up, two-foot-tall canister now converted to a makeshift splat drive and a note that called out an 85/15 percent split on the final patent filing. *Gonna have to argue that one later.*

"Finally! I thought you were going to be out all morning!" Spike's rattle-jawed icon winked in the corner.

"Yeah. Ran out of oomph." McKay hauled herself upright and removed the headset. The AI that ran Katie's servers had been kind enough to lock her out of the Swim once it detected the crash.

"Well, oomph up quickly. That Beast is back after Mike." The icon's jaw came unhinged and crashed to the bottom of her vision.

"What the hell? Rose is supposed to be sedated."

The Overlay reacted, reopening the links to Katie's servers, pulling in her security AI for backup. McKay tried to fumble the headset back into place and got the frantic impression of something fast and rough going on in the Swim around her. Katie's anti-malware kicked into high gear.

"What the hell was that?"

"Found *me*." Spike's icon winked out of existence. McKay saw eddies and ripples in the Swim that resolved around her. Something large and fast circled, unseen but felt, then moved off again like a shot.

"Shit!" She couldn't follow the sprite into the Swim but that didn't stop McKay from trying and failing and pulling herself up short, lest she push herself into another crash. Either Spike had escaped whatever it was, or it was a handful of bits and bytes of unraveled data bound for the metaphoric sludge at the bottom of the current. *Stay on target.*

McKay closed the Overlay's connections to the servers. She had to get Brighton and get to the access port to pull Mike out before the persona came undone. The heavy-throughput cable she needed was a specialty item; as impressive as Katie's server farm was, she didn't have what McKay needed. Brighton had found a location in the City that was unused, abandoned for the moment. Spike would get Mike to the right place in the Swim, McKay would pull him out and store the persona safely in the splat drive. She could worry about the rest once things were in motion.

The shock got her motor running, but she still stopped to grab a coffee and an energy bar on the way out. McKay headed for the elevator with barely a second word to the AI tending bar, then stopped short. A red warning light with Katie's distinctive logo blinked insistently in the corner of her vision a moment before Katie's voice sounded in her head.

"There's two guys here looking for you, both unwired, both carrying big, scary guns."

The Overlay analyzed the information as Katie spoke, scanning the area and feeding her details, far too late. They rounded the corner the same instant McKay turned to head for the terrace outside. One reached for his side, presumably to draw the gun Katie warned her about.

"I'm raising the phase array in thirty seconds." Katie's voice was harsh. She was angry, but at her or at them, McKay couldn't tell. "Save everything and spin down."

"What about everyone else in the club?" She pretended she didn't see them and kept on toward the French doors that led to the outside terrace.

"They've been warned. Nice thing about catering to the tech-head crowd, they listen when I'm about to fire up a microwave field. Twenty-five seconds."

McKay fired a communication off to Brighton, warning her she was on her way, spun the Overlay down and locked it tight. The two guys looked like a matched set, heavy Germanic features, suits picked out by someone else. A melted stretch of scar extended along one fellow's cheekbone, as if he'd been spattered with acid. The Overlay could have identified the source, but McKay's money was on one of the nastier biological weapons, particularly if they were native to Europe. *Definitely a "Thug with Upgrades" vibe.* A few hours' sleep and a clear path ahead gave McKay the kind of confidence she hadn't felt in days.

"McKay." One of them grabbed her good shoulder before she reached the doors, and spun her around.

"How can I help you gentlemen?" *Might as well start politely.* If they'd come to toss McKay over the edge, she'd heard the moat around the garden held some unpleasant surprises. The scarred man drew back his jacket threateningly, showing the holstered pistol butt. McKay kept her free hand carefully by her side and the one occupied with the coffee in clear view at all times. *Don't piss off the guys with guns, well, while they still have them.*

"You might want to take that off." She nodded at the sidearm. "Katie doesn't like people using firearms on her lawn. Screws up the nanograss."

"We're not here to make trouble, Ms. McKay. We've been asked to escort you to meet our employer."

McKay revised her estimate of the guy. He could speak in complete sentences.

"I'm not kidding. Katie really hates guns in her place." Her pulse crept upward, and the air began to feel a little warm as Katie's microwave array came online. *Good thing too.* She wasn't sure how long she could keep up the bravado. "You know your boss could have just sent me an e-vite."

McKay took a sip of the coffee through the hole in the plastic lid, mildly surprised when it didn't scald her tongue right off the bat. *Good omen, maybe?*

"He didn't feel you would accept." The two stepped closer, clearly intending to walk McKay between them back to the elevators. McKay regarded them both as steadily as possible and took another long sip of coffee, playing for time. *Figure out what they want and get the hell out of here.*

"You're probably right," she conceded, "but since he's the big fish in this pond, I probably should reconsider." She shrugged the thug's hand off her shoulder, settled the splat canister in the crook of her arm, and headed back to the elevators.

"Ow! Shit!"

McKay wasn't looking, but she could picture the look on Scar's face when he dropped his arm and the man's shoulder holster shifted, the motion pressing the freshly microwave-heated weapon against his armpit. There was a clattering sound as both men hastily got rid of their guns. The microwave phase array, targeted properly, could get the metal hot enough to blow their fuel cells if Katie was so inclined. McKay almost dared a smile, but not quite.

Guns make a good opener if you're trying to intimidate someone, but I doubt that's the end of their skillsets. She was willing to bet at least the scarred one was into chemical warfare, a nasty, sticky scene. As long as she didn't give them a reason to throw a punch, she might make it to see Christopher without freshening up her bruises. *Because of course it's going to be Christopher. Rose punches first, asks questions later, and Brighton likes to show up unannounced. That's pretty much the entire list of people who have it in for me this week.*

"We're coming back for those," Scar said. McKay risked a backward glance to see that the screen-faced bar AI had switched back to Lolly's smiling face.

"'Course you are, sweetie. You can pick 'em up right here at the bar once we know Eliza there makes it out of your meeting just fine." Two voomers, the ovoid floor-cleaning robots, zipped from under the bar and scooped the firearms safely into their bellies, chattering to each other excitedly.

"What're you, her mother?"

Definitely not bright. Carrying a concealed handgun into a private establishment wasn't illegal, but if Katie put the word out that they'd been taken down by something as simple as a phase array, their careers would be markedly shorter. That fact wasn't lost on Mr. Clean.

"Thank you, ma'am. We appreciate it, ma'am." He put a hand on Scar's shoulder to keep him from mouthing off anymore. Lolly gave them a smile much warmer than her plastic wave as the elevator doors shut behind them. Scar and Mr. Clean took up positions between McKay and the door, and she found herself facing a wall of pinstriped polywool. She spun the Overlay up and focused it on figuring out the two men without much luck. Their records were lost or destroyed or locked tighter than she had time to ferret out. The scar, which seemed like a promising lead, just wasn't enough for the Overlay's backup search program. *Dammit, Spike, you better be all right.*

The doors chimed and slid open. The Overlay informed her she was on a maintenance floor. No access except to authorized employees and management. Scar stepped out and a short, crisply dressed force of business stepped in. The line of pinlights along her temple indicated that Miranda Bosch's version of the Overlay was spun up and running. McKay's system reached out invitingly to make a connection, then recoiled as the other unit gave it a slap on the wrist.

"Ms. McKay," Bosch said as the elevator doors banged shut.

McKay retreated into her own headspace and kept a wary eye on the data that haloed her. Where most people tended to break up the flow of data, causing eddies and ripples with every transaction and interchange, Bosch was surprisingly quiet. She moved surrounded by her own, seemingly impenetrable, bubble of code. No ripples, no eddies, no dangling linkages. *Nothing. Beautiful. Cold.*

"Nice to officially meet you, Ms. McKay." Bosch's smile was genuine, but cautious.

"And you, Ms. Bosch."

Her presence in the Swim was chilling. She was pretty sure a man with Christopher's reputation had programming in place to reduce her Overlay to chunky byte soup if it came down to a head-to-head match. Bosch was different, minimal. McKay couldn't get a bead on her.

She gestured shortly at Mr. Clean's back. "It's nice to see there are no false pretenses this time around." *Let her talk first. Don't give anything away.*

"Hm. While Mr. David values initiative in his employees, Tanh was operating out of line. He's been . . . reprimanded for the part he played." The smile was genuinely pleased. "Rest assured, next time I will make sure your abduction is handled much more professionally."

"As long as you throw in a puppy as bait. I'm a sucker for puppies." McKay gave the Overlay some leeway, allowed it to probe around the edges of Bosch's halo of data.

"I'll make a note. I don't really anticipate direct conflict in the future. In fact, I'm hoping we will be able resolve this entire matter amicably."

"Which matter in particular?"

"Housekeeping." Bosch turned to face her, deliberately making eye contact despite the strange eyelight effect of McKay's Overlay spinning. "Your business is concluded. Every employee found in direct contact with Ina Brighton's freshly minted xWire, Rose, has had their employ terminated, their access revoked. There is nothing left for you, or them, to discover. You can tell Mike his operation was a success and write him back out to where he belongs."

Operation? Based on Brighton's file, that could be as many as twenty employees given the ax. She made a mental note to have Spike recheck the list, see who was actually found out and who got booted on suspicion. *If you ever see Spike again.*

"Then you should have nothing to worry about, and I'll be on my way." McKay acquiesced perhaps a little too quickly. She saw the glimmer of suspicion on Bosch's face, but logic seemed to win out after a few seconds and whatever she was about to say never made it to her lips.

Her business wasn't *with* Bosch or Christopher or any of that end of the equation. It was getting Mike Miyamoto's persona written back out. The rest of the pieces were secondary, troublesome layers stacked on top of that singular issue, but they all had an effect. Every piece she understood meant it would be easier to write Mike back into his body.

An answer materialized out of the blur of the past few days. *There is something else here. Bosch might have been using Mike to get a bead on their own traitors so she could clean house, fine. But then why does she want him written out? If we just yank the plug, his side of the operation loses everything, so why isn't she pushing for that?*

The silence between them won out in the end. "You are running out of time, Ms. McKay. There are enough bad actors chasing Mike as it is, actors *we* don't have control over."

This is about the wrong person running that malignant Beast program. Rose took over the Beast code and used it to do her dirty work.

Two and three came together to make five.

Fuck. Christopher hadn't known who'd stolen his software. Bosch used Mike to find out that Rose had been using her leverage with Vector7 to hire his guys on the side and figured it out.

Bosch had already turned to open the elevator doors when the pieces of the puzzle clicked together in McKay's head so suddenly she was afraid the sound was audible to the rest of the room.

"Miranda, one last thing." McKay kept it short, used her first name to draw her attention. "I need the unravel code." Almost every piece of complex software had one. Even Spike had one, a back door that could allow a savvy programmer to pull it apart from the inside.

She blinked. "I beg your pardon?"

"The unravel code for that nasty piece of search-and-destroy software that Rose took from Christopher." McKay met her calculating gaze steadily. No bravado this time. She knew that if she could get the unravel code from Bosch, then dealing with the Beast would be infinitely simpler. "Rose is using it to hunt down Mike. If it trashes something like a major bank or a security firm, hell, even your pet law firm, someone is going to get ahold of it and track it straight back to you."

Bosch appeared to consider her seriously for a moment, then cracked that genuine smile that seemed less so every time she saw it. "No, I think not, Ms. McKay." She tapped Mr. Clean's shoulder, and the wall of muscle obligingly keyed the door open.

Fuck, that's right. The Beast code started out as a copy of Spike. It's my *fingerprints that are all over the source.*

McKay went on the offensive. "I can eliminate your problem in one shot." She continued to press the point, refusing to let go. "Once Mike is out of the Swim, Rose running that thing is going to continue to be a problem."

"Who says it's *my* problem?" Bosch's smirk made it clear she had the upper hand. "Either you're good enough to handle it or not. Either way it's out of my hands. Your job is to write Mike back out of the Swim; I suggest you focus on that." Miranda Bosch left the elevator, and Mr. Clean moved smoothly to block McKay following.

"Piece of work," the programmer muttered, not bothering to use her inside voice.

Mr. Clean grunted, but whether assent or warning, McKay couldn't tell.

TWENTY-THREE

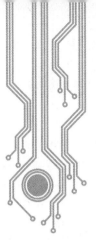

THE MIST THAT CAME IN the night before failed to give way before the onslaught of morning sunlight, and McKay hesitated a fraction of a second before stepping out of Katie's building. The gray fog lurked in the alleyways and trickled over the rooftops in a constantly moving mass.

"You've turned out to be a very popular person."

When Brighton's voice sounded in her ear she jumped, ducking sideways to put her back to the wall. The Overlay had put the voice call through without alerting her beforehand. Probably the work of Brighton's other hacker. She was going to have to fix that. A couple of dirty looks passed her way as she cut diagonally through the flow of foot traffic, but she was paying more attention to the conversation inside her head.

"If you're actually following me it would be helpful if you showed up *before* someone tried to strong-arm me, you know." The Overlay traced the sound patterns of her voice across the bottom of her vision and confirmed her identity at 100 percent. McKay was done trusting anyone.

"Well, you've made it clear that your privacy is important to you," Brighton dismissed her irritation. "We're good to go on our end. I had to get a warrant to get us access to the hardline you needed, but there's a time limit. They're going to have to shut down security to get us in there."

"Lovely. When does the clock start ticking? I'm on my way." She rejoined the flow, sending the request for a car over the public lines. The ripples of people in the Swim surrounded McKay. She could even catch echoes of the goings-on thirteen stories up at Katie's, but Bosch didn't even leave a glimmer. *I'm going to have to figure out how she does that.*

"As soon as we hit the front door. We can meet you and pick up the drive. You don't need to be here for this part."

Originally, McKay planned to hand the splat drive off to Brighton and let her people handle it, get it over and done with. *Now, not so much.*

"We had to change the design on the drive. I have to babysit the transfer. I can't just hand it off to you."

A long pause stretched out on the sound curve across the bottom of her vision. The car she'd called showed up at the curb, human-driven and, from the smell inside, probably used as a living space while off duty. It was, however, relatively hack-proof. The AutoPod crash hadn't yet faded in her memory and it took an effort of will to slide into the back seat.

"Shouldn't be a problem. I'll make sure you're cleared for the op." Finally Brighton was back.

"If I can't be there, we can't pull this off." She had to push herself to ask the question she didn't want an answer to. "How's Rose?"

"No improvement, but they've got her stateside now."

"Has she woken up at all?"

The soundwave on the bottom of her vision flattened out in a long arc of silence.

"They brought her out for a few hours yesterday, no improvement." Clipped, terse, whatever was going on with her investigation into Rose had Brighton on edge, but at least she'd loosened up, she was sharing. It was a marked improvement.

"That explains it."

"Explains what?" A stress spike in the soundwave imagery topped, then tapered back. She wasn't thrilled to think she might have to make her day worse.

"That nasty piece of software that's chasing Mike's persona woke up again last night." McKay sighed, suddenly tired at the thought of dealing with the Beast again. "I thought you were going to ask them to keep her under until we were done?"

"They can't, or rather, they won't. Too risky. I did ask them to move her to a secure room, completely isolated from the Swim, but I don't know if they've done it yet."

Shit. Okay, adding that problem back into the equation.

"Anything else you all want me to bring? Coffee? Danish? Armor-piercing rounds?" McKay's fatalistic sense of humor kicked back in, steering the conversation around and out of the dark.

"Jesus, I can just *see you* with a gun. No, bring the drive. We've got the rest covered. This ought to be easy and above board, no shooting, no running. Look for the yellow van out front."

"Yellow? Aren't government types supposed to drive black vans with tinted windows?"

"That's Homeland. We're on a budget." She cut the connection.

When the car dropped McKay outside the Kellerhammer Transit Building, she found the agent wasn't kidding. The mustard yellow van had seen better days and sported a tattered black-and-white "I brake for unicorns" bumper sticker. McKay opened up the Overlay as soon as she exited the car, giving it free rein to find and make every connection it could.

Security was tight enough. She caught whispers of voomers armed for security, cameras muttering to one another and passing data and images along shielded miteline cables to the central servers. It was a new-tech, completely automated hub of commerce. Vehicles pulled up and disgorged crates of every description under the all-too-human dock supervisor's watchful eye. The AI controlled loaders took them inside and sorted them by eventual destination, weight, longevity. A few companies stored their merchandise for months or years before moving it on. Security was tight, and required by law, since rumor had it that AI-run warehouses were easy pickings. Rumor was wrong: more than a few would-be criminals had gotten crushed by an AI forklift that didn't expect them to be there. *No wonder Brighton had to get a warrant.*

"Wow, could you be any more obvious?" The agent in question appeared out of the fog. The Overlay had picked up her approach, saving McKay the embarrassment of being startled again. Either Brighton was dramatically overdressed, or McKay was far too casual. The Overlay pointed out the defesive advantage of Brighton's poly-wool kinetoballistic armor. Even the agent's hair was something close to black, although better light might have shown some remaining red.

McKay glanced down at her two-day-old rumpled button-down shirt and slacks.

"Sorry, my bulletproof khakis are at the cleaners. You said something about no shooting?" She shifted the headset case on her shoulder and set the splat drive down with an unintentional clang. It was possible the thing was getting heavier over time.

"Better safe." She didn't bother to finish the adage. "Lyman's our offsite programmer on this one, he's on loan from Homeland. He wants you to button it up, stay out of the Swim as much as possible. He's going to handle monitoring everything. We *just* need you to run the drive, okay."

"Not a chance, but you can tell him I'll stay out of his way. So how do we do this?" McKay closed any direct links to the building but stayed connected to the larger City hub below. *No point in being totally blind if I can help it.*

Brighton held a wafer between thumb and forefinger. "Legally. The nice thing about being on our home turf is we can get stuff like this done without a laundry list of bribes and favors." She walked to the yellow van and rapped on the back door, which swung upward in one piece, revealing Rice wearing much the same thing as she, just a bit heavier and somehow far more imposing.

"Let's go. We have four hours before the access code expires." She jerked her head at the warehouse across the street. Rice eyeballed McKay with more menace than usual as she hiked the splat canister back up onto her hip.

"Tell me you didn't give this gal a weapon."

"I gave her a pair of Elite 28s. Happy?" Brighton's response was no-nonsense.

"Elite doesn't make a 28. . . ." Rice stopped himself mid-sentence, realizing she was yanking her chain. "Fine." He clambered out of the truck and gave McKay the once-over. "Is that it?" He jerked a thumb at the battered cylinder under McKay's arm. McKay supposed the thin drift of escaping nitrogen that trickled from the valves was not comforting.

"Yeah, sorry. Next time I'll be sure to stamp it with the company logo." It was an ugly, *ugly* piece of hardware. Ninety-five percent of it was batteries and cooling; the drive itself was only the size of three fingers.

Rice grunted and reached back into the van for an empty red, leather-bottomed school backpack. He shoved it into McKay's chest unceremoniously and stalked past her toward the front of the warehouse.

McKay fumbled the canister into the backpack and slung it across her shoulders. The headset case was already on its crossbody strap and she tugged it around to even out the weight. Brighton joined Rice, the two exchanging words she couldn't quite make out. She felt more like a third wheel than a working professional.

McKay caught up with them just as Brighton shoved the wafer into the access panel. A smaller, person-size access door slid open and Rice went through first. McKay followed into the well-lit space beyond and spun the Overlay up to full, keeping it from linking and interfering with anything Brighton's coder, Lyman, might be doing but still pulling information from every other available source.

The foyer was only twenty years out of date, clashing discount store patterns on the floor, and furnishings muted by a layer of dust.

With the AIs doing most of the work, a live human passed through once a year at best. The photophoric lighting came on resentfully. The entire place operated in the dark unless there were humans on the premises. The bulbs probably hadn't been changed in a decade.

"Oh, hey. I think my grandma still has that couch." Rice's booted toe nudged the forlorn furnishing.

"Stop it." Brighton's voice was sharper than it needed to be. "We don't need to manhandle anything. We're professionals, not pizza delivery guys." A low hum in the room got slowly louder as they crossed to the far side.

"Main warehouse through there?" asked McKay.

"Yeah." Brighton keyed her access code into the panel and the door opened on a wall of sound that made McKay wince and clap her hands over her ears. Rice followed suit, but Brighton stepped aside, a smooth, controlled motion that put her back to the wall by the doorframe. A packet in her chest pocket turned out to contain silicone earplugs, which she distributed to McKay and Rice with a rueful grin.

"Sorry, I forgot we would need these."

"You were saying something about being professionals?" Rice's acid edge was gone; the tension between him and Brighton fled for the moment.

"That must have been my evil twin," she countered. "The access port you're looking for is at the back of the warehouse, McKay. Let's get going."

The room was industrial standard, dimly lit even with the photophores powered up. Stacks of floor-to-ceiling shelves filled with containers disappeared into the dark unlit space above, but McKay could see the bright, winking points of light from AI-driven robots swarming over everything. The Overlay sang, literally sang, reaching out to the thousands of AIs in the room simultaneously. McKay had to pull it, had to pull *herself*, back under control before the sound in her own head deafened her.

Light touches—AIs requesting orders, identification, queries, connections—bombarded the Overlay continuously, drumming on her mind like rain, but the Overlay obeyed and turned them all down. McKay had not taken the general gregariousness of programmed intelligences into account, and thousands of them packed together in a single building made for a lot of chop in the Swim. She would have to compensate when she wrote the persona over.

"Shit." Rice said ahead of her. A voomer shot out and under his feet. "Aren't those things supposed to avoid tripping people?"

McKay shrugged. "AIs evolve to do a better job. They've probably been working in here alone long enough to forget that little bit of their rule system."

Rice turned to rebut, then paused and produced an Elite from under his jacket. "Oh, yeah? What about the bunch behind you?"

They had failed to show up on the Overlay. That idea alone made McKay uncomfortable. Twenty or thirty voomers were piled up behind them, tightly packed into the space outlined for human traffic.

"What the hell are they doing?" Rice asked. "We've got a four-hour clearance window."

Brighton gave them a nervous backward glance. "I'll have Lyman look into it." She put a hand to her ear and McKay felt the muffled buzz of a secondary conversation. She stopped, and the voomers stopped as well. She flicked her gaze over them, pausing on each in turn, letting the Overlay collect serial numbers, manufacturer data, time in service. Rice was right. They should have had some sort of internal safety code in place, if not to keep them from getting tripped on, then at least to keep them from bunching up like that. *Maybe they're just curious? Yeah. Keep telling yourself that.*

"Something's wrong, guys," McKay voiced the opinion out loud and quickened her pace after Brighton. She felt a presence in the Swim, a pressure on the Overlay, and felt the eddy pass over her toward the voomers. The tight-knit group abruptly came apart, each shooting off on its own pre-programmed errand.

"Lyman fixed it." Brighton stopped at the far wall to wait, her voice filtering through the earplugs. "Apparently we have only mostly total access. The voomers are supposed to keep us on-camera all the time."

"*All* of them?" Rice grunted incredulously. He returned his weapon to its holster, but didn't take his eyes off the zippy little 'bots as they flocked together again.

"Clumsy code, he says. They *all* got the order as a priority-one listing, rather than just the security 'bots." Brighton snapped her glasses into place and compared the map to the numbered doors. "Here we are." The door swung open at her touch.

"Well, shit." Rice's expletive followed the discovery that the room was being used as storage, packed with containers. "This is going to take a minute." McKay looked past them into what was once office space, and the Overlay mapped it, showing her the wiring in the walls, the access ports along the baseboard.

"Hang on." McKay allowed the Overlay to touch one of the spiderlike 'bots swarming over the shelves in the main room. It responded quickly, collecting one of the larger forklift 'bots and a couple of smaller lifters.

"Yeah, Lyman, she's got it." Brighton scowled, then turned the look on McKay. She stepped out of the way of the 'bots emptying the room without a second look. "McKay, please. Lyman's supposed to be handling the code on his end. Your job is the outwrite, nothing else."

"Yeah, got it." Sitting back while another coder handled things left a sour taste in her mouth. *Perhaps I've just been working by myself a little too much.*

The containers inside were shoved aside or removed, revealing a sheet of battle-scarred and neglected drywall. The Overlay picked up on the trickle of signal, showing her the wiring that lay underneath. It had been lazily patched over. A couple jabs with her finger punched through the thin drywall paste to reveal the tangled wires and the access port. She yanked it out into the room and blew the dust off. Still live.

"We burned too much time shifting the boxes," Brighton observed.

McKay didn't respond. With as much bandwidth as this connection had, she would be able to cut the transfer time down to half. It meant one hour running the headset and Overlay fully open, managing the transfer of the persona to the splat drive and burning neurotransmitters faster than her body could make them. She settled the headset into place and laid out the vials of neurotransmitter precursors on the top of the nearest crate. The two hours of unintended sleep had given her a boost, but she held no illusions. She was going to have to keep on top of her own brain chemistry if she was going to avoid crashing before she was finished.

"They're gathering again," Rice pointed out, just loud enough for Brighton and McKay to hear.

"You think this is going to go bad?" Brighton's voice was pitched to match, but conversational.

"Doesn't it always?" Rice again, but no edge there, no sign of stress.

"Let's move a few of these crates around just in case."

Every attempt Brighton had made to pull Mike's persona out of the stream, every attempt to write him out, had gone wrong somehow. There was no reason to think this might be different. McKay didn't blame them for being careful.

She took the canister from the backpack, careful of the cold surface on her fingertips. The coolant wisped from the top and dribbled down the sides as it transitioned to gas and took the splat drive's heat with it.

First things first. She chewed a caffeine tablet and washed it down with two bottles of precursor mix. The headset connected with prickling sensation as the pins punched through skin to the contacts the overzealous repair mites had covered over. McKay sat cross-legged on the concrete floor and set herself between the splat drive cylinder and the wall. She resisted the Overlay's urge to drop into her headspace prematurely, carefully connecting the thick rope of miteline cable from the wall to the jack in the back of the headset, then to the splat drive. Writing Mike out was going to literally have to go through McKay's head.

McKay hadn't counted on the drag. The canister's empty drive space was like a gravity well in the Swim. She dropped into the Swim and the concrete dome of the headset's bunker solidified around her immediately. *Holy shit.* It was like having an anchor line attached to her ankle. She righted herself in her own head and opened the connection to the splat drive all the way. Spike and Mike should be hiding in the Swim nearby. She just had to make contact.

The space in her head reflected the past few days' disarray. Filing stacks protruded from the floor and walls, some half opened, contents spilled out. The floor was sticky, like the stuff on theater floors or under the fridge. In the corner of her mind, the splat drive began to resolve, resembling a gaping black hole, cracking and chewing through the concrete floor. She felt it dragging at her, the drive's vast, empty space waiting to draw in and compress anything within reach. The headset kept it in check, a tenuous lead on the collar of a surly mastiff. *That is not at all what I expected.*

"McKay? Did you find him?" Brighton's tinny voice, too close inside her head, and the farthest wall of the dome flickered to life, showing her the view from outside her own head. Brighton's face came into view as she hunkered down and looked, deliberately, into McKay's eyes.

"The drive is online," she said with a little effort, pushing the words out. The splat drive's drag affected everything. She would have to stuff something into it soon or risk losing more than just the imaginary concrete.

"The voomers are getting antsy again. Lyman thinks they might try to jump the security override."

As if this wasn't hard enough. Now I've got to rush it.

"Understood. I'll be as quick as I can, but right now we're looking at about two hours." She checked the headset's security. Something rapped the steel airlock in the top of the imaginary dome. Once. Twice. Then stopped. *Someone on the other side, waiting for recognition. Spike and Mike.*

"It's go-time," she said aloud to Brighton.

In the space inside her head, she raised her hands and released the airlock in the ceiling.

The Swim came in.

A deluge of data roared down and puddled on the bunker floor. The flow from the ceiling resolved into a long, silvered form, like a snake coiling onto itself. One end lifted, grew teeth, luminous eyes.

"Ready?" McKay asked it. The Mike persona, roiling on the floor, sprouted scales and spines and shed gear teeth and puzzle pieces. The strain was almost too much for the headset. The readouts flickered and twisted in her vision, transfer rates stuttering. McKay shifted, adjusting the processing threads, making the Overlay take on the overflow.

"Ready." The voice was little more than a growl now.

McKay indicated the void in the concrete floor.

The persona paused, sniffing at the black hole as it chewed at the edges of the virtual concrete floor. "Unfortunate metaphor," it snorted and dove in, head and forelimbs vanishing as the splat sucked the data in eagerly, filling the drive bit by bit.

McKay had to fight to keep from giggling. *Damn, I'm already tired.* The Overlay ran up visual warnings on fatigue poisons and the quantity and speed of neurotransmitter uptake. *Dammit.* She peeked out from the Swim just long enough to fumble one of the vials off the crate in front of her and drink it down.

She turned back to the walls of code that erupted upward from the floor around her. The sheets showed her the programs running in tandem, overlaid one on another, the code that controlled the compression, the source code for the persona, the smaller programs she set to clipping out the bits of AI, leaving only the original copied-over human personality bits to be compressed and crushed into the splat.

It was like doing a half-extraction. A persona usually replicated the core elements of a person's mind, the personality, the way the mind made decisions, the logic. The framework was a single, standardized AI, used almost universally. When she wrote a person back to their body, she stripped the AI out, comparing the different quantum bits to determine where the fit went wrong and finessing it to slot everything back into its proper place. She was doing just the first part, stripping the personality clean, removing AI remnants or other garbage so it would fit into the splat drive. *You hope.* The filters she was running would catch obvious corruptions, viruses or other Swim detritus. The information went by fast, almost too fast. Around her, the bunker in her mind dimmed, the displays winking out one by one as she cranked her focus ever tighter. Only the sheets of data were left as the metaphor started to fail. Even McKay's virtual "self" stuttered and flashed as she slipped the transition from conscious mind into biological machine.

Spike screamed into existence in the empty space. "Eliza! She's here!"

Spike's warning came only a microsecond before malware from an outside source swamped the warehouse's computer system, a brute-force attack, slamming in and shutting down a handful of subsystems before it coalesced on a single target. Had she not been so highly focused already, McKay could never have reacted as quickly as she did.

Rose went straight for the security routines, hard and fast, no finesse. Poisonous code twined in like barbed wire, cutting as it went, leaving gaping, bleeding glitches in the information flow. McKay could see the changes, the voomer OSs overridden, their primitive AIs wiped. It pissed her off. Really, really pissed her off.

"*Rose!*"

Rose laughed.

Disturbing. The chill down McKay's spine came up against her righteous anger as the rogue hacker murdered the voomer AIs one by one and put her own code in control. More anger, sharp vicious edges, as McKay stepped to engage, prying subroutines free of her control and shunting them aside.

"*I owe you!*" Rose snarled.

Barbed tendrils of toxic code shot at McKay, seeking, looking for a hold on her, but the drag of the splat drive slowed everything down. McKay stirred up the dataflow defensively, slewing Rose's attack into the eddies, blunting the edges, feeding it back on itself.

Rose did not slow down, she just reabsorbed the attack, sprouted more spines, punched through layers of encryption. She was digging for something. The voomers were small fry, something to keep Brighton and Rice occupied. With an effort, McKay corralled her anger. *Focus, idiot.* She could not let her get near the download.

"Rose, you've got to stop." She was strong, really strong, but she was inconsistent, one moment spinning attacks at McKay, the next digging into the system, fractured and disordered as her focus shifted, shattered, then came together again. McKay was reminded again that she wasn't up against the clear, rational Rose. This Rose was all emotion, all those parts of the mind that keep motoring on even when a person was asleep or unconscious. Uncensored fear and insecurity and misconception all tied into a bleeding-edge Swim-capable computer and an Overlay AI that ran it with an eye toward what the user wanted.

"I had everything under control, do you understand? Everything would have been under control!" she screamed. McKay braced herself against the pressure wave that followed. "This was *my* place. These were *my* friends."

"So what happened, Rose? You couldn't keep up? Couldn't deliver on what you promised? You had to start stealing resources to handle the demand?" McKay tried to keep her unbalanced, keep her from getting deeper into her head until Mike was out. Rose's story, now that she understood it, was a familiar one. A professional at the limit of their capacity, dangerously close to burnout. A team that assumed everything was okay until they heard otherwise, and an agency that measured success in short-term results rather than longevity.

"They *needed* me." The voice was softer. McKay stayed well back as Rose focused on her, abandoning the security systems, but the voomers she'd corrupted were already at work. She hoped Brighton and Rice could handle whatever the security 'bots were about to throw at them.

"Yes, they did. So you cheated. You hired outside help, you broke the rules to deliver. You fed it all back on Christopher because you were investigating him already. You hired his people, you stole his code. His hands aren't exactly clean, after all, and you thought he was burning out Miranda Bosch the same way ANT was burning you out."

She was exposed. McKay could see the living code that made up Rose's mind, written into the Swim on the fly, just like she was. Whatever she did to the other hacker would hurt, transmitted directly to the mind and burned in as surely as any traumatic event in the physical world. PTSD without the T being visible on the outside. Talking her down would be the absolute best option.

"I *had* to. This was *my place*. This was *my home*," Rose snarled.

Rose was good, but not good enough to handle the demands of being on Brighton's team. Going X was her last-ditch attempt to transcend her limitations. *Jesus, Rose, they wouldn't have thought twice about keeping you on.* Her brief conversations with Brighton had made that clear.

"It must have killed you when they brought me on to extract Mike. They didn't know you botched the outwrite on purpose." She sharpened the words before she spoke them, willing them to keep Rose's attention on her rather than the outwrite in progress.

"Mike *knew*. He was investigating Christopher, he *found out* about my taking his search-and-destroy code, he FOUND OUT I was paying Tanh on the side. Then Christopher got involved and everything just came apart, but I was FIXING IT, DAMMIT."

The last piece clicked, and McKay almost lost her grip at the magnitude of it. She could see the paradigm shift that had affected Mike, clear as day.

All of this, *all of it,* had been compounded by a string of bad work habits, miscommunications, and arrogance. All the threats, the hits, the hours spent writing and rewriting code, the risks to her life and limb were all because the situation could not have come out any other way. *Miyamoto saw the bigger picture. He finally got his head around everything that was wrong with the way they were doing business, starting with falling in love with Miranda Bosch and ending with Rose's desperate attempt to stay on top of her game.*

The Overlay flashed warnings about her transmitter levels, the buildup of reactionary acids in her bloodstream. She felt sick.

"This was never *about just you*, Rose! It's about Mike. He stopped the outwrite in the first place, remember?"

McKay lost Rose's attention as she went back to excavating the security protocols and finally revealed what she was after, another level of warehouse security robot riddled with military-grade encryptions. Whatever bodies those AIs were controlling, they packed a harder wallop than those stacks of voomers that had followed them in. McKay dove for the strings of code, got to only one before Rose did, decided to shield the AI from attack rather than take it over. Her teeth ground as she attacked the encryption, shifting and redirecting as fast as she could throw up defenses.

Rose had processing power to spare. Rather than design an xWire system to complement her skills, she had simply gone for as much power as she could jam into her skull. McKay was outclassed, hampered by the limits of her own system plus the weight of the splat drive. She was losing it.

McKay sent one request to the AI she'd saved before backing off to recover.

It agreed.

TWENTY-FOUR

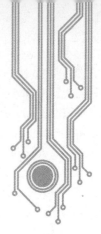

McKAY RISKED A LOOK into the real world, conscripting one of the warehouse security cameras to get a wider view. There was only one possible reason for Rose to go after the drone AIs. She hadn't been able to stop McKay in the Swim, so she was coming after them in the real world, either looking to cut the hardline that McKay was using to pull Mike out, or possibly just looking to kill everyone outright. She'd try to avoid Brighton and Rice if she could, but things were already messy and McKay was no longer sure that being Rose's friends gave them any kind of immunity.

Brighton and Rice had barricaded the doorway and were clearly gearing up to defend against something coming in.

"I thought they weren't cleared for live ammunition," Rice snapped.

"They're not." Brighton cracked her stunner open, pulled the blue-backed capacitor and swapped it for a heavier red-backed one. The weapon powered back up with an ominous crackle.

"So not only are we going to get shot at, these things are probably loaded with redhots or some other anti-personnel ordinance that looks awesome in a catalog," Rice griped as he copied Brighton and bumped his stunner to lethal range.

"Yep. Get ready." Brighton held her hand-scanner up and showed him the readout.

McKay got carefully to her feet. She'd managed to save one AI from Rose's attack. Hopefully it could intervene, give them an advantage.

The first weaponized drone rounded the corner, stepping over the carpet of voomers. These crowd-control drones were quadrupedal, each knobby-kneed leg ending in a rubberized, three-toed "foot" that let them walk right over the tops of tightly packed little voomers. The first one reached the barricade and reared up, its sensor dome searching for targets. Brighton and Rice stayed down behind the crates. Sweat began to bead on McKay's face, running down to leave its imprint on her shirt. The drone ran its facial recognition routines, McKay could feel it through the Overlay, then cycled its weapon until it settled on a choice of rounds.

"Jesus." Brighton noticed, moved to get McKay out of the line of fire, but the coder held up a hand.

"Stay down. That one's mine." McKay managed to get the words out. Splitting her attention like this was expensive: the drag of the spin drive slowed her down. In the corner of her mind, she kept an eye on Mike's transfer to the splat drive. *Nearly there. As long as Rose is trying to kill us in the real world, she won't be able to stop the transfer in the Swim.*

"Yours?"

"Rose has all the others." Her eyes were completely white, any semblance of humanity in them washed out by the volume of the data she was processing. Her fingertips twitched, a gesture she couldn't control.

"Rose is out of it, McKay. This has got to be the in-house security." Brighton glanced at Rice. "Or maybe we have a new player."

McKay smiled, an absent gesture that was more rote reaction than genuine pleasure.

"Same players. Rose is trying to change the rules," she said. "Get down. If it goes through with this, it's going to be messy." *If it doesn't, it's still going to be messy, but we might not be alive to care.* Rice took the hint, put one arm over his head to deflect flying debris. Brighton balled up, next to him, keeping her head below the top of the crate. McKay's drone turned to face the hallway, ratcheted through its magazines again, then opened fire.

It wasn't the noise that surprised her. McKay already knew that emptying the magazine in a confined space would be hellishly loud. It was the pressure she'd forgotten, the flat, merciless *thump thump thump* of vibration that shook the air, reaching into her skull and upsetting her concentration, shaking her heart inside her ribcage.

McKay lost her grip on the real world before she got the chance to witness the outcome. She dropped back into the space inside her own head in time to see the last strings of Mike's persona get sucked into the splat drive. It shut with a sharp *snick*, like a cigar cutter.

That *snap* freed her. McKay was whole again, standing in the vault of her own mind. She cut the connection to the splat drive and started shutting down every unnecessary program, feeling the quick surges as more and more processing power returned to her control. She opened her eyes and turned her attention back to the carnage in the real-world.

The room outside was now filled with shattered plastic and toxic smoke from the destruction McKay's volunteer drone had unleashed on its own zombie counterparts before Rose had finally gotten a grip and burned out its operating system.

The Overlay reached out and connected with the last standing enemy drone, recoiling as it encountered Rose's toxic code, then pushing past and opening a path of attack. McKay managed to force-start its maintenance cycle, peeling its armor open and exposing its innards, but it got off a dozen rounds before Rice's stunner fried the now unprotected circuitry. Brighton had put herself between McKay and the drone. The rounds took her in the back and slammed the both of them to the ground. The Overlay calculated the force of impact and gave her the readouts for Brighton's body armor. It must have hurt—the armor could only disperse so much of the force—but she struggled to her feet anyway. Clumsily, she reached out and caught the agent's arm.

"Mike's out," she shouted.

Rose was still there, prowling around the Swim, looking for something else to throw at them as her options vanished one by one. The headset was still open. If Rose came after her directly, she could kill her just as surely from within the Swim as from without. McKay dropped back into her own head again and started bringing all her defenses online, abandoning her body to Brighton to steer.

"Rice." Brighton yanked McKay to her feet, the cables to the splat canister jerking loose from the headset. She felt it, even barricaded within her own mind.

Rose found her as she finished sealing up the firewalls, furiously pounding on the outside of the bunker in her mind. McKay didn't have time to prep for it; the constant back-and-forth into and out of the Swim was starting to make her sick. She yanked the headset off defensively, the unconscious drive to save herself kicking into gear.

"McKay, what's wrong?" Brighton's voice again.

Great, I must have started drooling. "She's just really fucking angry."

She had to stall Rose, find out what she was going to try next. The fact that she'd resorted to the drones, that she was now actively trying the kill them in the real world, that was Brighton and Rice's territory. McKay could ask the warehouse AIs for help, but Rose was taking them over as fast as she could crack their security.

Oops. She calmed down. She felt the pressure of Rose's presence, one step removed now that she wasn't fully online, and jerked her body sideways, physically dodging a blow that slid by in virtual space.

"McKay, what the hell?" Brighton reacted to her motion, looking about for an enemy that wasn't there, not in the real world, at any rate. Even without the headset, Rose could still get at McKay through the Swim, she just couldn't kill her outright. It was getting harder for McKay to tell what was real and what was virtual.

The Overlay flashed a warning just too late to deflect a tentacle of code that erupted from the floor in front of her. Rose had brought the Beast into the system with her, and it was running full tilt. McKay found herself caught in the nasty piece of software's grip, and she had to focus, writing code on the fly to pry it loose.

"Time to go." Rice kicked a crate into the hall and cleared a path through the smoking voomer corpses. Brighton jammed the splat canister into the red backpack and shoved it at McKay. She stayed on her feet, but barely, still trying to pry her mind loose from the Beast that now hammered on the Overlay, trying to crash it completely. It took almost all of her focus to keep the malware from simply crushing the Overlay's AI out of hand.

"Eliza."

McKay turned glassy eyes on Rice, who held a finger in front of her face. McKay frowned and focused, the fingertip sliding back and forth across her vision, stuttering, hard to follow.

"Nystatic," Rice said, and slung McKay's arm across his shoulders. "Serotonin took a dive, right? You gotta disconnect."

Neither Brighton nor Rice could see the horror that had McKay in hand. They grabbed her and dragged her, unresisting, into the hallway.

The lights in the warehouse went out with a bang.

"What the fuck was that?"

"Rose is still trying to kill us," McKay managed to get the words out. Another effort, this time a desperate scramble to dig a never-used line of code from her memory. It was a longshot; if Christopher had done a proper rewrite of Spike's code, it wouldn't even work. Every piece of complex AI software had a back door, a shutdown code. *The Beast code's just a copy of Spike, corrupted, repurposed, but still just a copy. Let's hope Christopher was as lazy as the rest of us.* McKay launched her counterattack from the relative safety of the Overlay, waiting as the string of code she sent, *Spike's* unravel code, struck the Beast where it lay in wait.

The camouflage came undone, sloughing off and flinging outward as the Beast rampaged. This time McKay did not react, watching dispassionately as it thrashed about in the Swim at her feet. The unravel had it now, the unique code strings that let any programmer waltz right through its defenses to disassemble it from the inside. McKay got a glimpse of its true nature an instant after the camouflage stripped away and the thing unraveled into random strings of numbers and snippets of code, a lean, efficient, negative shape in the luminous, ever-moving Swim. Then it was gone.

The fire doors thudded shut all through the warehouse. Orange and red warning lights split the dark. Abruptly, all of the robots fell silent, went into lockdown mode, tucking in gripper arms and bumpers to keep them safe.

"Fire alarm?" Brighton asked.

They passed beyond the broken remains of the combat drones and voomers, headed out onto the warehouse floor.

"AI facility," McKay said. "Halon gas for the fire systems." While the AI-driven robots' physical bodies were silent, their programmed minds slipping into the Swim, filling the empty conduits. The Overlay stirred as the invisible space around them filled with AIs, making linkages here and there, nothing strenuous, just chatting, making connections. McKay smiled as AIs' sleek, otterlike forms swam around her, slipping and darting through the Swim. It was like a snow day for them, freed of their mechanical bodies until the lockdown was over. Rose had focused all her attention on the security AIs; the run-of-the-mill service units had all come through unscathed. There was no sign of Rose now. She'd vanished when the lockdown started, kicked out when the warehouse security systems came back online.

McKay was vaguely conscious of an interchange between Brighton and Rice. "Rebreathers," one of them said, probably Rice, "halon's inert. We'll suffocate in here if we stick around."

"Fine. I'll share."

She asked the Overlay a question, and it fired off a communication to a quicksilver AI passing in the Swim. McKay was conscious of a dull ache, pressure on her skull, and a red-tinged warning flashing in her vision. She ignored it, entranced by the rippling data flowing around her. She thought, if she could time it right, she could touch the Swim and join it. No Overlay, no headset, just one more push would do it.

"McKay, are you paying attention?" Brighton stared at her, frowning.

The Overlay said the AI had agreed to their request.

"They're going to get us out of here." McKay gestured toward a set of glowing red lights in the dark.

"Shit, she's too fried. She's not thinking straight." Rice again, irritated.

Perpetually irritated.

One of the small, cataloging drones unlimbered its legs and came to life. McKay pulled herself free as it approached. It shined its headlamp directly into her face and warbled a question. She stared unblinking into the light while the Overlay translated the drone's instructions.

"This way." McKay gestured stiffly and followed the spiderbot into the dark without a backward look.

"Jesus. She's good," Rice said around a mouthful of rebreather. Brighton said nothing, just shouldered the red and leather backpack and followed the coder out.

McKay's delirious composure lasted just long enough to get her back to the battered yellow van. She leaned against it, wondering why the designers bothered with different colored paint under the yellow, then remembered that she was still supposed to be in the real world somewhere.

"Get in, McKay." Brighton's voice again, but she didn't see her. She must have been on the other side of the van. She had to remind her of something, something important.

"Brighton." *What else, dammit.*

"Get in the damn van." The door slid open with that heavy, gravity-laden sound native to all vans since the dawn of automotive history. She lost her balance and slid to the pavement. There was something in her pocket. The drop to the ground pinched it against her hip, and she wiggled it out, a plastic bottle just larger than a shot glass. She popped the lid and drank it off. It tasted good. *Really good.* Probably the best thing she'd ever tasted, in fact.

"Brighton," she said her name again, trying to remember.

"Shit, I think she's out, Boss." That was Rice, not the person she needed to talk to.

Out. That's it.

"Mike's in the can." McKay was fairly sure she used her outside voice. "We have to get him written back out." The Overlay's warning lights came up one last time, and she convulsed, the plastic cylinder falling from limp fingers and clattering to the ground.

TWENTY-FIVE

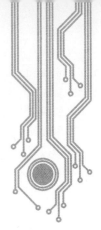

"Ow!" McKay wasn't entirely sure which voice she used, inside or outside, but it felt as if someone had pried an eyelid open and shoved in an ice pick. *Fucking hell that hurts.*

"McKay?"

She screwed her eyes shut and put a hand up to defend herself. The rattle of the van's dubious engine came to the fore, and she realized someone had seat-belted her in.

Wait, van? When did we get back to the van? She felt for her sunshades and sealed them over her eyes before opening them again. *Christ, that's not helping.* The daylight was too strong, even with the shades. She pressed both thumbs into the space between her eyebrows to relieve the pressure in her skull.

"Welcome back." Someone's voice—no, *Brighton's* voice—from the front seat of the van. She sounded . . . concerned?

"Ow." She felt compelled to repeat herself. Sound hurt almost as much as light. Total neurotransmitter crash. *Shit. Stupid, stupid, stupid.* Whoever was driving made a long, swoopy turn and she nearly lost her lunch. If she'd had any. She couldn't remember.

"Here."

She heard a noise, a horrific buckling sound that could have been movement had the volume not been cranked up so high. She dared to open an eye and saw a hand waggling a plastic vial in her face. *Ah, yes!* She took it and popped the cap off with her teeth, downing the contents in one shot. She knew it would take at least five minutes to feel the effect. *Christ, why can't those five minutes have started five minutes ago?* She closed her eyes again and leaned against the juncture of the seat and the blessedly cold window.

When she opened her eyes again, the pain in her head had gone from a shriek to a low grumble. The light was different. Brighton and Rice were deep in consultation about something, and the van had leveled off. When she'd crashed, the Overlay had spun into sleep mode. It flickered, quiescent, but didn't attempt to come online. It would wait until her neurotransmitter levels rebalanced before she could re-engage the system again. She turned to look out the window at the fog, where the vague forms of AutoPods slid in and out of the grey like ghosts on wheels. They had to be on the coast by now, maybe just south of the City. She couldn't have been out more than maybe twenty minutes. Even with the recovery shot Brighton had given her, the pressure was still there.

McKay fished a crash-pak out of the headset case. The emergency tabs went under the tongue, quicker than drinking the cocktails, but not without risk. She repressed a shudder as they dissolved into sandy, acrid goo in her mouth. She pressed the heel of her palm against her forehead, willing the last of the headache to submit. She'd expected Rose to try to stop her from pulling Mike out, but she hadn't anticipated her being quite so strong. *Or so angry.*

"You okay back there?" Brighton leaned over the seat, looked her in the eyes. "What the hell happened to you in the Swim? I thought this was supposed to be a simple in-and-out for you."

"How long until we get to Mike?" she asked, speaking quietly to avoid aggravating the headache. *Christ, I've still gotta do the out-write.*

"Half an hour. We need to swing by the safehouse first. Lyman was supposed to have our back at the warehouse: I want to make sure he's okay." She was still staring.

McKay'd seen that look on other faces before, like Brighton was trying to figure out if she was broken or not. She tried to ignore it. A total crash was about as much fun for other people to witness as it was for her to experience. She adjusted the subject.

"You have a safehouse?"

"We always have a safehouse. It's cheaper than anyplace with room service."

"Rose tried to stop me from pulling Mike out. She brought her big nasty piece of code with her. She took over the security AIs and triggered the fire safety systems."

"Shit."

"Shit is right. I think she was trying to kill us all." McKay's composure cracked with a visible, physical shudder. Rose had gone gunning for her own friends. Every time she dropped into the Swim, she would come after them again. McKay fought the urge to scream in frustration. There was no good end to this.

"McKay. . . ." Brighton began, then stopped as the van pulled up and expired with a rattle outside one of a thousand cloned houses along the Pacific Coast Highway.

"We're here," Rice said. "Stay here while we check it out." He glanced over his shoulder at McKay with a look that meant more than he said, then unlimbered his sidearm and checked the power-core. Brighton sighed and did the same.

"We'll be right back. Then we can get you to Mike before the spin in that canister starts to degrade."

Rice punched a few buttons on the dash and smooth jazz began to trickle from the van's speakers. "We'll leave the radio on so you don't feel lonely, maybe crack a window."

"Oh, *thanks*."

McKay pulled the headset case into her lap and unzipped it, gazing at the chaos within. *Total friggin' mess.* She must have shoveled everything in haphazardly. The last twenty minutes in the warehouse were decidedly fuzzy. She remembered the snap when the download completed, remembered struggling to beat Rose to the security software, but everything after that was fits and starts. *Probably for the best.* Experiences in the Swim, good ones and bad ones, would burn themselves into a mind. They would fade eventually, but they took time and therapy to get over.

The strange not-sound of stunner fire caught her attention. Through the window, she saw flashes in the windows of the house Brighton and Rice had gone into.

Oh no.

The two agents kicked the front door open and bolted down the stairs, bright blue zips of plasma right behind them, scarring the pavement and setting a hedge ablaze. Brighton was clipped, her shirt smoldering as she went down. Rice helped her up, getting his still-functioning KBA between her and the incoming fire. He returned the favor with carefully measured blasts from his Elite. The van's engine sputtered and rattled to life as they approached.

Shit! What do I do? She had no weapon, no access to the Overlay. McKay's mind went through the engage sequence three times before she realized she was trying to force the system to spin up. She dropped down as a plasma bolt struck the van and dissipated with a smell of burning paint. Rice never flinched. He shoved Brighton into the passenger seat and ducked around to the driver's side. The smell of burned fabric and flesh filled the van as Brighton struggled with the seatbelt.

"McKay, get the medpack. It's under the seat." Rice punched the accelerator, momentarily throwing McKay against the back seat.

"What the hell happened?" McKay unbuckled and scrabbled under the driver's seat for a bright red case with the medical trinity on it.

"They were waiting for us. Lyman's already dead. Get the burn patch, the big one on the bottom."

"Who the hell are they?" McKay pulled out a large paper packet.

"Give it here." Brighton straightened up as Rice rocketed up the hill toward the freeway. She unbuttoned her blouse and eased it off her shoulder, hissing slightly as it pulled away from the burned skin. McKay stripped the protective paper off the patch, exposing the glistening, 'mite-laden burn gel. Brighton grabbed the palm-size patch and slapped it into place.

"Here, let me." McKay reached to help adjust the dressing, but Brighton hissed.

"Fine, just be careful." She ground out the words against the pain. "We don't know who these guys were, but it's a safe bet that Rose sent them after Lyman to keep him from helping us out at the warehouse."

"They just winged you." Rice risked a look at the injury as they merged smoothly into the freeway traffic.

McKay tugged the patch on Brighton's shoulder, smoothing it out to cover red spots, and couldn't help noticing her skin was pale and lightly freckled. She saw the tension subside as the opiates in the patch took effect.

"That should do it," McKay said. "If I can ask, what are you colonized with? MetTech 25s, or something military grade?"

Brighton buttoned her shirt, the red bandage showing through the hole in the black linen. "What a question. Jeep42s, military grade, version six." A flush crept into her cheeks as the drugs in the patch worked through her system.

"Good units."

"Glad you approve," she said dryly. "Rice, get us to Saint Dymphna's."

"On it." The van's console spun up, painted in the air by the windshield, and Rice punched in the commands that engaged the vehicle's AI driver.

They couldn't have found a better place for her to finish the extraction. The idea of walking through the doors, however, felt strangely prescient. Sooner or later, almost every xWire passed through a facility just like that one. Not all of them came back out again.

"Rose doesn't know where Mike's body is. It was transferred here after she went under the knife, and we didn't put the information into the system." The redhead slid a palm-size tablet out of her pocket and punched something in on the screen. "Lyman...." Her cheek twitched, like she was gritting her teeth. "This explains why we got hung out to dry at the warehouse. She must have sent these guys after Lyman."

"What I don't get is why," Rice interjected. "What good is killing Lyman, killing *us*, going to do her? I mean, I get why she wanted to stop us getting Mike out in the first place, but the jig is up. She's been found out. There's no win for her at this point."

"It's not Rose," Brighton said quietly. "Not our Rose, anyway."

Smooth jazz and the hum of the van's wheels on asphalt filled the awkward silence.

"She's right, you know." Spike's voice tricked in from the van's sound system. Both Brighton and Rice startled. "That's not actually Rose you're up against, not all of Rose."

"What the hell, Spike?" In a strange aside, McKay realized she'd never actually heard the sprite's "voice" before, not outside the confines of her own head.

"I grabbed her medical records. She's never actually been conscious, even when they bring her up out of the coma. You're up against Rose without any of the things that *make* her Rose. They've got her conscious mind in a coma, but her unconscious is what's running rampant. Whoever installed her new xWire cocked it up good."

"McKay, who the hell is that?"

"That"—McKay stared disbelievingly at the van's dashboard—"is the best damn piece of software I ever wrote. And if it's talking to all of us, then it's probably worth listening to." She turned her attention from Brighton back to the lights on the dash. "All right, Spike, what do you have for us?"

"Those medical records are *medical records*, as in private. You can't *have* those," Brighton snapped.

"Look, Rose is coming after us." McKay finally turned on her. "Not just in the Swim any longer, she is actively coming after you guys here, out in reality. You can actually, *literally*, die from this. Your guy Lyman has *already* died from this."

Brighton looked angrily from McKay, to the dashboard, to Rice, who shrugged. "I'm with McKay on this one, Boss."

"Look, I get that she's your teammate," McKay appealed. "I get that I'm crossing a line here. But if you want to have a chance at saving your friend, we have to figure out how to stop her without making anything worse." *Or without getting anyone else killed in the process.* "In order to do that, we have to know just what state she's in, and at least whether there's something the medical team can do to keep her off our case."

"Fine." Brighton didn't like it, but she acquiesced.

"Is she in transit still?" McKay asked plainly. It would explain why Rose, the subconscious Rose, was still able to access the Swim. Transport meant open access through vehicle Wi-Fi signals, connections with city and state communications networks. If she was in a coma, they'd have sent along a nurse to keep her under, to keep an eye on her vitals, but they'd have no idea of what Rose's unconscious mind was getting up to.

"In the air as we speak," Rice said.

"Not one WORD about this gets out anywhere," Brighton growled. "Getting Rose help is the first priority after we get Mike back out. She's our teammate; she needs us." She stabbed a finger at the blinking lights on the dash to emphasize each word.

Rose needed help before all this. Now it's just a patch up. McKay squashed the idea, didn't let the thought pass her lips. There was no good reason to point out the flaw now.

"Of course not." Spike sounded positively insulted. "Just what kind of low-rent search engine do you think I am?"

"Enough." McKay stepped in. "Spike, give us what you got. We need a new plan."

TWENTY-SIX

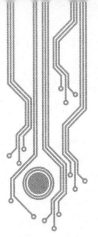

LIKE ALL HOSPITALS, every surface of Dyna's radiated cold. Nearly an hour south of the City, the weather was twenty degrees warmer, the inevitable fog held miles away beyond the low-lying hills and still, McKay suppressed a shiver when they passed through the main doors. McKay had spent the travel time threading her way through a sequence of recovery steps to mitigate the side effects of dragging Mike out of the Swim. The emergency tabs had been a start, but they were rough and fast and caused the kinds of neurotransmitter spikes that could kick her out of the Swim if she wasn't careful. She still had to finish the second part of the job before Mike's persona was too far gone.

"You really ought to consider buying a room here if you're going to keep doing stupid stuff like getting involved with Brighton and her crew," Spike observed. After delivering its information dump on Rose, the sprite hid out in McKay's head, reemerging when the Overlay finally spun back up.

"Do I *need* to change the security codes in my head?" McKay asked acidly with her inside voice. She didn't think Dyna's people would jump her with a straitjacket for talking to herself, but she didn't want to take chances when she was this close to her goal. It was making her antsy. Rose's unconscious body was due to arrive in a couple of hours: Dyna's was the best place for her to be, after all. Rice was inside the door, just in case there were any more real-world surprises left for Rose to spring. The nurse on duty, after a careful assessment of McKay that ended at her eyes, showed her to Mike Miyamoto's private room.

Over time, McKay had seen dozens of people trapped in the Swim for various reasons. Some in public "persona cafés" but more often in research labs or private rooms. They usually looked like they were sleeping, sometimes curled up awkwardly on the angled couches. Ninety percent of the time, you dropped into the Swim for an hour, maybe two, woke up, went on your way. Here in the austerity of Dyna's, the results of too much time in virtual space were laid out in full view.

The living body of Mike Miyamoto was older than McKay expected, more lines in the face, more grey in the hair. The version of Mike in the files Brighton had given her, the version she'd been chasing for what seemed like forever, had seemed younger, more vital. Some of that could be attributed to the IV lines, to the coverlet pulled up over the chest to ward against the creeping cold. Some of it was simply the result of the fact that, for all intents and purposes, there was nobody home.

She wondered if Rose had the same empty look, or if her subconscious running loose made a difference.

The Swim-space inside Dyna's was almost non-existent. Faraday cages in the walls kept any stray signals on the outside, kept access to the unrestricted Swim at bay. Dyna's was intended to be a refuge, a place of recovery and rehabilitation for anyone who had pushed too hard, who had overrun the limit of what their own mind could handle. This was where Duck had come to recover from her disastrous attempt to go xWire all those years ago. It was the perfect place for McKay to attempt to write a well-past-expiry, repeatedly re-extracted, probably not-quite-all-there persona back to its original body. If anything went wrong, they'd be able to support Mike until the effects of a bad outwrite faded away.

Even with the Overlay spun up, McKay felt like a girl in a bubble, the experimental wiring in her head just a little better than a glorified calculator stapled to the back of her skull. The Overlay informed her that the network had too much capacity for the job it actually did. The communications- and information-sharing between the various medical devices crawled, weighted down by encryption, along the bottom of a space designed to hold a much larger volume of information. She would certainly have room to move, if she needed it.

"His vitals have remained stable. The brain has registered no activity above the required levels since he arrived." The duty nurse was young, freshly scrubbed, and moved with the confidence born of modern medical training. McKay, on the other hand, was sure she looked one step closer to a private room herself. She gave the nurse a smile, which was returned timidly, well out of arm's reach.

Can hardly blame her. She set the backpack with the canister on the floor at the head of the hospital bed. All the chemicals in her system made her hands tremble. *You really need about twenty-four hours of shut-eye before you try this.* But the splat drive wouldn't be able to hold on to Mike's persona for that long. This was her one shot at making this work. *No pressure.* Wisps of vapor seeped from the steel cylinder as the coolant evaporated, leaving white crystals in their wake. The hospital had topped it off with liquid nitrogen, but it was a Band-Aid, a stopgap. The clock had started ticking the minute she'd finished pulling Mike out back in the Kellerhammer warehouse.

"How long until we know if this worked?" Rice was still in his warehouse-raiding attire, armed to the teeth. *At least he's talking to me now. Not sure if that's a good thing or a bad thing.*

"The extraction's going to take about an hour, maybe more," McKay said absently, lost in consideration of the problem at hand. "I cut the persona's AI substructure loose when I wrote him into the canister. It was the only way I could make him fit, so half the job's done already. It's going to take some time for him to recover from the fact that you've kept him in a coma for a couple of weeks, but that's all medical stuff, out of my hands." McKay pulled the bedside tray table over and locked the wheels. "If this were a garden-variety extraction, you'd know as soon as he woke up. Stacked on top of a couple weeks of brain inactivity. . . ." She glanced at the nurse, who regarded her preparations with distaste. "You've got a hospital full of experts here, no better place to be." The nurse met her gaze this time, surprised at the vote of confidence.

"We have people standing by," Rice confirmed.

McKay cracked the headset case open, cringing at the disarray inside. She'd tried to reorganize it, but her thoughts were just as scrambled. She began lining up components in the familiar half-circle in front of her.

"Leave the monitoring equipment hooked up to him, just in case."

The nurse regarded her archly. "Standard procedure for extractions is to remove all unnecessary equipment. . . ."

Oh, one of those. "This isn't a standard extraction." McKay checked the rig that embraced Miyamoto's skull for access ports, found a standard set just below the left ear. Nothing custom in the setup, which was a bonus. Ironically, the brand was Bellicode.

Unimaginative, but working with off-the-rack hardware is a hell of a lot simpler.

"I'm not sure I can let you work outside the official parameters. . . ." The nurse glanced agitatedly from the unconscious form of Mike to Rice, who peeled himself off the wall and came over to take her by the elbow.

"You know how tech-heads are," he said in a low voice and shot McKay a look that warned her against further explanation. "Always trying to make it *sound* like they're doing something really cutting-edge." Rice drew the nurse away from the bedside so McKay could get to work. *Quick thinking there.* She hooked a foot around a chair and dragged it over. *No time for showboating. If you crash in this place, they might never let you out.*

"Are you ready?" she asked the unmoving form of Mike Miyamoto. The lights and sensors continued their slow steady pulse. *I'll take that for a yes.*

McKay closed her eyes and turned her focus inward, letting the strain and apprehension resolve into a little knot, which she tucked away in the corner of her mind. Denial was something she was well versed in.

The concrete dome in her head, somewhat worse for wear, swam into existence and the Overlay voiced its concerns, peppering the walls with lines and graphics painted in colors of warning and mayhem. McKay took a long, slow breath in and let it out. She wasn't in as bad a shape as she'd thought. The chemicals and precursors had brought her mind up to full functionality, but it was a tenuous peak, without the reserves she was accustomed to working with. As the newest set of precursors crossed into her bloodstream, the colors cooled and the warning lights dimmed. McKay opened the wheeled door in the center of her mind, turning the heavy steel lock by hand rather than allowing the Overlay to do it for her. It helped her to slow down, to reorient herself to the reality of the Swim.

There was resistance, almost like the Overlay was stalling.

She emerged into Dyna's network space, conscious of how still it was, how tightly contained. The goal wasn't so much to keep people out of Dyna's, rather it was to keep people in. The difference was mostly semantic, but it still prickled at her mind, the feeling of being locked in, caged up.

McKay slipped out, flattening and twisting into a form better suited for the thinner, lighter flow of information. *Something efficient, something quick.* She slithered the short distance to the inner workings of the persona software that kept Mike's mind in stasis. This was the program that wrote minds into the Swim as personas, then translated them back out again into their own living bodies. McKay stifled a snort. This version was an old workhorse, the moving parts grinding through a well-oiled synchronous metaphor.

Focus. She asked the Overlay to fiddle the neurotransmitter uptake, to optimize for clarity. A few quick touches and the connection between the headset and the persona software was locked in tight. Next she had to connect to the splat drive. Much like she had back in the warehouse, McKay's own mind would serve as the bridge. The persona software would handle most of the tedium, but McKay would have to step in and hand-code around any place where the experiences of the persona no longer fit the space in the original mind. After the hatchet job she'd had to do back in the warehouse, she was anticipating a lot of those.

Paranoid, she double- and triple-checked the server around her, but it was devoid of even the lost 'bots and bottom-feeding AIs that were present in any viable space. It was like standing in a trickle of alkali water in the middle of a desert. Nothing around for miles, nothing to interrupt or impede the transfer as she wrote Mike back out into his own body.

Nothing yet, at any rate.

McKay opened her eyes and connected the splat drive's fat, black cable to the headset. The persona software spun up in response. She imagined she could *feel* it, the clicking vibration in her skull as it slowly reeled in the data. This was a different process than her frantic download back at the warehouse; this was a tightly controlled mechanical tension.

The harsh, flat error tone as the software encountered the first discrepancy was almost lost in the ever-increasing vibration and virtual noise of the process.

That was quick.

McKay opened her eyes to the source code, the perception of the vault fading as she slipped below the metaphor and began to write Mike Miyamoto out of the Swim.

TWENTY-SEVEN

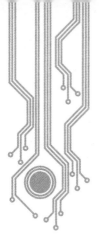

"Eliza." Spike swam across her vision, spun out into sharp-edged snippets and too many tails. "Eliza, take a break before you go cross-eyed." The sprite swam through again, pausing to break McKay's line of perception. The persona software emitted its harsh, grating tone for perhaps the five-hundredth time. McKay had lost count. She pushed again, making a change here, editing out a line there, until the experience fit and the software kicked back into gear again.

"Spike?"

McKay felt the connection between the splat drive and the persona software shiver, a vibration like a plucked guy-wire. She'd acclimated to the noise and motion and now the change in the tension sounded clear, like a chime on a windless afternoon. *That's not right, either.*

She reached out along the line, feeling more plucking and trembling. The inside of the network had become thick and oily, making the line slippery to the touch. McKay spared a moment's attention checking and adjusting as the Overlay began painting up readouts. She was holding her own, but the balance between ingesting the supplements and turning them into neurotransmitters was a fractious one.

"Spike, are you seeing this?" She figured it out even as the words were formed. "Rose found us, didn't she?"

"She's *here*. The plane caught a tailwind." Spike shifted to something more defensive-looking with leather and knobbly armor. It took McKay a moment too long to register the warnings inside her head. "She's two floors up. They just rolled her in."

"And Brighton didn't know she was coming *EARLY*?"

"She's working on it, but you know doctors. They want to do things the right way, protect the patient, yadda, yadda. They just brought her out of the coma."

So if I can just keep her distracted long enough for Brighton to get her put back under again, we might get through this.

McKay popped back into the real world just long enough to shoot another one of the preprepared neurotransmitter cocktails, releasing yet another round of the chemicals into her bloodstream. *At this rate, I'm going to bleed caffeine.*

She dropped back in to find Rose calmly circling the connection between the splat and the persona software, stretching it, plucking at it. The software geared down, adjusting its speed to keep the tension steady as it continued to copy Mike's tattered soul back into the mind it belonged with. She tugged again and the persona software errored, bleating in distress.

This was a different Rose, more thoughtful, less angry, less ready to kick the shit out of everything in the space. Maybe, just maybe, the things she'd said back at the warehouse had had time to sink in, were unconsciously understood. McKay hoped it would buy her the time she needed to finish.

McKay moved slowly and carefully to fix the error as Rose prowled around, watching her, keeping an eye on Spike who, uncharacteristically, hadn't fled the scene yet. Now that McKay knew they were dealing with Rose's subconscious, she could take a different tack.

Here inside Dyna's server, Rose appeared low-slung, striped with an ever-changing pattern that mimicked ripples in the Swim. A virtual tigress. As a metaphor for pure power she was beautiful, amazing even. McKay forced the Overlay to steady her heart rate, ignoring the warnings about fiddling with the chemical mix. The hairs on the back of her neck prickled as she imagined being torn apart by the not-so-tender ministrations of those claws and teeth. As long as Rose stayed back, McKay could keep working. As long as Rose just continued to watch, not interfere, she could get through this. As long as she didn't inadvertently do anything to piss her off.

McKay stepped up and pushed the persona software, guiding it through the next error and the next, ignoring the dimming of her vision around the edges. Each stoppage in the code was almost a physical impact by now, a jarring of synapses already battered and abused, but Rose didn't make a move, she just kept circling, watching as the last silver strings of Mike's persona slipped through her fingers and into the persona software.

"Spike, keep an eye on her. Don't piss her off. We need to keep her off the persona software so it can finish. . . ." McKay's instructions to the sprite were interrupted when Rose hit her from the side. The shock she felt was as much from the impact as from the direction of the attack itself. *I thought tigers always attacked from behind.* The errant thought slipped out like a stream of bubbles and she popped back out to the real world for just a moment.

"Rice, it's Rose. Get Brighton." McKay wasn't even sure Rice was still in the room. She managed to get the words out, then dropped back to defend herself.

Her job was over; the persona software had to handle the last of the work now. It meant she could focus on Rose, on keeping her distracted.

She paced in the network, well out of McKay's reach, great flat paws stirring up the data where it puddled on the floor. Her gaze rested squarely on the persona software as it clicked and ground through the final stages of its process.

It PING-ed again, hung up for a moment on some minutiae that McKay had missed, and the sound made Rose jump, a low snarl building in her throat.

No, no, no.

Without thinking, McKay lashed out, an action designed to catch her attention, to get Rose focused back on HER. It worked.

McKay was unprepared for the fight that followed. The whirling, snarling mass snapped, teeth bared, claws extended. She ducked and scrambled away, not nearly fast enough. Rose had hooked a claw into her, like a cat with a fish.

I've got to get her out of the network, away from Mike.

But in a place like Dyna's there was no place to go. No access to the Swim, no unencrypted computers.

McKay scrambled to escape and dove for the only available exit. Rose stayed hooked tight and used her own momentum to gain access to the concrete bunker in her head.

In.

Her.

Head.

Oh shit.

The concrete bunker shook, cracks appearing as the mental construct bore the unfocused brunt of Rose's attacks. Claws rent the concrete like cheap cotton, exposing the glittering numbers underneath.

Great plan. Mike's safe, but now what?

McKay shielded herself, pulling code out of the floor and walls even as Rose vented her frustration on them. Here inside the safety of her own head, she had a full arsenal at her disposal. There had to be something she could use to bring Rose back to herself.

The Overlay leaned into the effort, drawing every bit of spin the headset had to give into the fight to keep McKay's own mind intact. The complex mesh of 'mite and mind started shutting down any unnecessary processes to bolster her defenses.

McKay started laughing.

The sound was hollow and empty in the concrete bunker. Rose had torn her way in, data rushing through the hole from Dyna's network and pooling around her knees. A maelstrom in the teacup of McKay's mind, Rose's horrible thrashing, coupled with the ever-present drag of the now-empty splat drive, threw everything into confusion.

The splat drive.

McKay gathered her wits and charged. It was a move Rose hadn't been expecting. The other programmer stepped sideways, just a fraction too close to the drive's influence. She sank a great, crippled paw into the ferroconcrete floor tiles, getting a grip against the pull. She saw the danger now, moments too late.

The splat drive has her.

The sucking black vortex that Mike had dived so eagerly into back at the warehouse had caught Rose and was pulling her mind, what there was left of it, into cold storage.

A livemind written out. McKay eyed her coldly as she managed to maintain her grip on the floor by sheer force of will. She had no idea what that would do to Rose, the living person, but it was a fair bet that it would solve her immediate problem. She hesitated while the other programmer hung there. Rose turned with snarl, trying for a bite, but McKay's processors were still faster than hers by an eyeblink, and she missed.

Spike peered in through the hole in the bunker to regard Rose as she struggled against the inexorable drag of the splat.

"Damn, that's a brilliant idea! Do you think you can fit a program that pissed off into a space that small?"

"Let's find out."

New cracks opened in the concrete and data continued to slosh in. McKay closed her eyes. She took a deep breath, followed by another. She wasn't sure how long she could hold out. The bunker was collapsing. Mike had already been written out, her job was supposed to be done. McKay turned to Rose where she lay, panting with the effort of staying out of the splat. "You just don't quit, do you?"

Her black lips curled back in a smile, showing yellowed teeth, sharp, angular, cutting surfaces. "No," she said before making another lunge at her.

McKay bypassed her defenses, slicing cleanly through the Swim-patterned fur and bone, into the core of Rose's own, incomplete code. She snarled and screamed, but McKay worked fast, slicing through layers of experience, memories, finding the little black knots of secrets and collecting them. They were tight-knit and toxic and she found them all before releasing her. Rose slipped into the embrace of the splat drive, still fighting, shattered claws scrabbling for purchase on the bunker floor.

She was gone.

"Um, Boss?" The sprite looked shaken.

"Get out, Spike, I'm crashing." The lights stuttered and went out. Spike winked out like a spent match, fleeing for the relative safety of Dyna's network.

McKay opened her eyes into the real world and shut the headset and Overlay down, taking the pain and noise with it.

The room swam in front of her eyes, the solid forms and lackluster paint contrasting with the fire in her head. She blinked and managed to lay a hand on one of the vials that littered the tabletop in front of her. *Stay standing just a bit longer or they'll never let you out again.* Her motions in the Swim must have bled through somewhat. The little plastic bottles were scattered, out of reach.

She shakily pushed the chair away from the bed, taking the splat canister with her into the corner of the room as the nursing staff descended on Mike Miyamoto's sleeping form.

With the monitoring equipment still in place, Mike's EKG registered increased brain activity even before McKay got the headset back in its case. She knelt over it, placing each component neatly in its socket, every vial, packet, wire, and chip in its home. It helped her cover the shaking, the fits and starts in her vision, until the drugs from the final vial took hold and dimmed the pain in her head. She felt oddly balanced, like she could keep going if she just didn't lean too far to one side or another.

That's not going to last, she thought ruefully. *Pass out here, worry about the rest later? Can't do that.*

She let her body run on autopilot, drawing a finger along the edge of the headset case to lock the seam, getting to her feet. The flurry of activity surrounding Mike continued and McKay was escorted out of the room. She noted that Brighton had reappeared somewhere along the line, the activity in the hall suggesting an emergency somewhere else.

Rose, she's got them checking on Rose.

McKay didn't want to be there any longer, didn't want to see what happened to a livemind when you yanked a big chunk of it out of the Swim, sane or not. She headed out into the hallway, dodging scurrying forms in blue and green scrubs, finding a space along the wall that seemed out of the way and propping herself up against it.

McKay's conscience caught up with her as the shock of the conflict started to wear off. She tried to remember Rose when they'd first met, in the repurposed office on the fringes of Orchard Road, but that mental image was gone, overwritten by yellow eyes and a glut of power. She cast a glance back into the room where the still-unconscious Mike continued to be examined. She held her breath against the decision she had to make, willing it to the back of her mind. She fingered the canister that held the splat drive, the cool vapor bathing the backs of her hands. She could throw the switch, shut it down, and the version of Rose contained within would vanish, lost when the q-bits scrambled in the rising heat.

Brighton appeared in the hallway, some doors down from where McKay was attempting to prop up the wall. Someone in a blue coat and an ID badge was talking urgently to her and the expression on her face made the decision all that much simpler. Her hair had gone from auburn to black. Midnight black. Even the red in the highlights was gone.

If anyone can fix Rose, Dyna's can. The better part of herself prevaricated against the icy logic of her decision to let the splat drive have Rose.

Maybe. But are you willing to keep looking over your shoulder until they do, and even after? Are you going to be able to look in the mirror again if you shut down the spin drive?

"Brighton." Her voice sounded odd in the air, like she hadn't used it for far too long. McKay cleared her throat and tried again. "Brighton."

Brighton tore her attention away from the conversation at the end of the hall, eyes reflecting a concern McKay hadn't expected.

The programmer nodded in the direction of Mike's room. "In there. Keep the canister cold or her data's going to degrade."

Puzzlement flickered across Brighton's face as she put two and two together, coming up with a number greater than five. Puzzlement crossed into horror.

"You didn't. . . ."

"I had to. Rose came after me again during the outwrite. I had to put her somewhere."

Horror changed to betrayal and for one brief second McKay thought Brighton might actually pull her weapon and shoot her where she stood.

Fair enough.

Brighton restrained herself with a visible effort and jogged down the hall to collect the neurologist. McKay didn't wait to see the end result. She leaned her head back against the wall and waited for judgment.

TWENTY-EIGHT

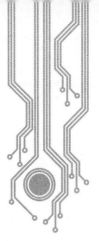

"WELL, I CAN SEE why they blacklisted you. You don't leave a lot standing when you're all done." Mike Miyamoto's voice was not nearly as impressive in the real world as it was in the Swim. McKay had been handcuffed, marched in, and dropped into the seat across from the hospital bed. These were generic government thugs, there was no sign of Brighton or Rice. *Not that you expected any different, right?*

McKay was, for the moment, as average as any other unconnected human. When Brighton had sent Rice to confront her in the hallway, she'd been hard pressed to make it to her feet. She'd been zip-tied and locked in an empty storage room while Brighton took the canister to Rose's doctor, trying to explain exactly what had happened.

The nursing staff had been kind enough to give her another round of precursors to keep her conscious, but mixed in with that amino acid soup had been something that disrupted her 'mite pathways, effectively keeping the Overlay, from any of her systems on down to the medical repair 'mites, from coming back online. *The xWire version of muscle relaxants.* She'd given up trying to get the door open and spent the next hour crowded up in the corner against a mop and a hard place, trying to sleep it off.

"I didn't really have much of a choice," McKay replied carefully. She was on thin ice. Technically, legally, she'd done nothing wrong, but that was only because the law hadn't yet caught up to what an xWire was capable of in the Swim. Morally? Looking in the mirror was going to be hard. *But at least you can still look in the mirror,* she reminded herself. Instead of the feel-good flush that came from success, guilt whispered in her ear. It sapped any joy from the victory, from her survival.

"The jury's still out on that." Miyamoto folded his hands in his lap. "Before we go any further down that road, however, I wanted to say thank you. You helped me save something very important to me."

"It wasn't just falling in love with Bosch, was it? It was something bigger. Your case against Christopher, all those revelations, all in a row," McKay prodded, needing to know that Mike understood the reasons.

"Bosch was the start. Feelings like those don't come along very often for someone in my line of work." The older man drew his lips into a line and stared down at his hands. The color had returned to his skin; the EKG beeped softly next to his bed. "Then, when I understood what Rose had been up to and why, how she'd been breaking the rules just to try and stay relevant. . . ." He scrubbed his hands up and down his face. "Brighton's willingness to sacrifice so much to close this case against Christopher. . . ."

Standard procedure meant the nurses at Dyna's would keep Mike awake for the next twenty-four hours, checking on him constantly to be sure his mind remained clear, but it was clear the extended stay in the Swim had taken a toll.

He sighed. "The truth is, when you've been as many people as I have, both inside and outside the Swim, an understanding like that doesn't come along very often. If I'd given it up, forgotten it for the sake of escaping, we'd all be right back where we started. Our process, our team dynamic, is broken. It's going to have to be fixed. And fixing it is going to hurt us all a little bit."

"Was it worth burning the house down for?"

McKay had to ask. The cost of bringing Mike back out of the Swim had been high, not just to her personally, but to Brighton's entire team. Lyman was dead. Rose was incapacitated. Christopher's organization had cleaned house and plugged all their leaks, so that investigation was likely over. McKay wasn't sure if Mike was preternaturally calm by nature, or if they were keeping him drugged to speed up his recovery.

"What happened with Rose"—Mike paused, swallowed—"was inevitable. Given the asks of the job, given the way we operate, she wasn't the first operative to burn out trying to keep up. But crossing the line, trading immunity from Vector7 in order to get her dirty work done, even if it was our dirty work? I don't know if she can come back from that."

"So what now?"

"Now. Now I have a very large mess to clean up, Ms. McKay." Mike gestured to one of the men in suits to come and remove the handcuffs. "But you've made sure I came out with the tools to do just that. Now, I believe that besides paying you an obscene amount of money, I heard that Brighton made a deal with you regarding getting your 'mite licenses back."

McKay rubbed her wrists, scrubbed her hands through her hair to check the contact points. There were a few new loose ones. She'd have to keep the headset off until the repair 'mites were back online and could rebuild. She hadn't forgotten about her deal with Brighton, but right now, in light of cold circumstance, she didn't see a way clear to collect without burning bridges.

"That was a side deal, call it hazard pay, but yes, she did." McKay closed her eyes, bracing herself for the NO. *All that work, the expense, the cost in blood and psyche and you blew it at the end. Rose didn't deserve that and now the bill is due.* Guilt returned, whispering that she deserved everything they threw at her.

"If I still have a job after all of this gets sorted out, I'll make sure that process is begun. I have some work to do, if I'm going to make sure that what happened to Rose is the exception, rather than the rule."

McKay's hands started shaking, just a slight tremor, *a side effect of the 'mite dampeners wearing off.* She tried to convince herself of the lie. The truth was, it felt like the entire world had just opened back up, like she could suddenly, finally, breathe again. The guilt was subsumed, rolled under the tide of emotion and drowned in that moment.

"Can I ask you a question?" Hope had quickened McKay's pulse . . . maybe made her a little too bold.

"No, I don't know how long it will take to get your licenses back. In fact, I don't even know if I will be in a position to get it done once word of this travels to my superiors."

"I understand that. What I want to ask about is the list."

"The list?"

"When Brighton brought me on, she said I was on your list."

Mike steepled his fingertips, tapping his index fingers together. The EKG continued its soft beeping, filling the silence. "We eat people, Miss McKay. Not in the literal sense, of course, but we have a very limited set of tolerances. Agencies like ours bring in personnel, use their talents unwisely, and spit them out again. Some eventually rise above." He gestured in McKay's direction. "Some, not so much. All of those people still have much-needed skills, and I believe in second chances." He raised an eyebrow, lips pursed in a frown. "Sometimes I'm wrong."

"Wrong about me?"

"Bringing you on was Brighton's decision, not mine."

"That's a decision I'm pretty sure she regrets." Guilt again, less strong than before, but it was fighting tides of other emotions that McKay had to struggle to keep in check.

"That's a fair assessment. The truth is, I don't believe she will ever forgive you, even if Rose makes a full recovery. But like I said, Miss McKay, I do believe in second chances."

McKay took a deep breath and allowed herself the win. "I do believe in taking them."

AFTERWORD

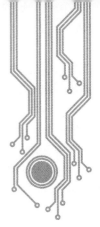

IN ALMOST EVERY pop-culture science-fictional universe out there is a story about someone getting stuck in some kind of reality simulation. It happens quite a lot. And as anybody who has been a freelancer understands, business is all about finding a niche. If people regularly get trapped in virtual reality, then it must follow that there is somebody out there whose job is getting them back out.

What a job that would be!

Enter Eliza Nurey Wynona McKay, or rather, an earlier version of that character with a less-lyrical name. Go ahead, say it out loud, you'll see what I mean.

While the very first draft of *The Extractionist* was written before Oculus popped up as a bright idea on Kickstarter, the world had already taken a few runs at developing virtual reality in the past. And in all those early iterations, one thing was clear: virtual reality, much like reading a book or watching a movie, requires buy-in on the part of the user. It is a choice to put on the headset; it is a choice when to take it off. Like all "choices," it might be heavily influenced by outside factors like the need to pee or the fact that you have to get out of bed at 6 a.m. to get to work, but it is still an active choice you make.

And if there is choice, there is agency.

Brains are weird. Minds are even weirder, but they almost all still follow some very fundamental rules. Ways of processing information and making decisions serve as points of commonality across ages, across cultures, across geographic boundaries. It is these similarities that allow us to relate to one another no matter the time or the place or the language or the culture barrier. Advertising works because human minds are similar. Romance works because human minds are similar. Diplomacy works, society works, parenting works because in almost every human brain on almost every continent there are basic points of hard-wired commonality that can be be used to build a foundation to work together.

It is this very universal kind of "same" that allows the technology in *The Extractionist* to do what it does.

Now, for Eliza McKay, extractions are a fallback gig. Her one true passion is the design of nanomachines and the systems that control them. But to do that, she needed the kind of unrestricted instantaneous access to the Swim that only building an Overlay into her skull could give her. She had to start with a deep understanding of how to build the interface and she had to design it herself to really get it right. And it worked very well, up to a point. When she was banned from working with nanotech for . . . reasons, conducting extractions became her new normal.

In their best form, extractions require a little of Column A (agency on the part of the trapped), a little of Column B (an understanding of the things we all have in common), and a bit of Column C (a ground-up sense of how the whole process works). It's an imprecise skillset: it's not the kind of thing you could take a college class to be able to execute.

In retrospect, an extraction is almost a mirror image of what a designer of virtual-reality experiences does. When you build a game (any kind of game, really) you have to take into account player agency, you have to understand the kinds of common impulses that will encourage almost any player to stay and play, and you have to understand how the whole art/code/sound/player interaction works together in order to build something that engages. But whereas a designer is convincing a real person to come and join their digital reality, McKay is using those same pools of knowledge to convince a digital persona to allow themselves to be written back out to the real world.

Talk about an empty niche!

And, like so many freelancers out there, McKay finds herself successful not because she is a mastermind at countering a compelling virtual simulation, but rather because she has mastered one singular skill on top of the rest.

Figuring out what the other guy really wants.

KIMBERLY UNGER made her first videogame back when the 80-column card was the new hot thing and followed that up with degrees in English/Writing from UC Davis and Illustration from the ArtCenter College of Design. Nowadays she works with bleeding-edge VR; lectures on the intersection of art, narrative, and code; and writes science fiction about how all these app-driven superpowers are going to change the human race.

tl;dr: She writes about fast robots, big explosions, and space things.